To
'D.' and ROLAND PERTWEE
Who see the Jest in most things
this Book is Affectionately Dedicated

LOVE WAS A JEST

LOVE WAS A JEST

Denise Robins

CHIVERS
THORNDIKE

This Large Print book is published by BBC Audiobooks Ltd, Bath, England and by Thorndike Press®, Waterville, Maine, USA.

Published in 2004 in the U.K. by arrangement with the author's estate.

Published in 2004 in the U.S. by arrangement with Claire Lorrimer.

U.K. Hardcover ISBN 0–7540–9663–7 (Chivers Large Print)
U.K. Softcover ISBN 0–7540–9664–5 (Camden Large Print)
U.S. Softcover ISBN 0–7862–6488–8 (General)

The text of this Large Print edition is unabridged.
Other aspects of the book may vary from the original edition.

Set in 16 pt. New Times Roman.

Printed in Great Britain on acid-free paper.

British Library Cataloguing in Publication Data available

Library of Congress Control Number: 2004101994

BOOK ONE

CHAPTER ONE

'Scharlie, are you going to dress for dinner now?'

Scharlie—Mrs. Alec Mason—with one hand on the banister and one small foot on the first step of the oaken staircase, turned and looked at the man who spoke to her.

'Yes, I am. Aren't you?'

'Yes. But, Scharlie, it's early; none of the others has gone up yet. By the time we're dressed, they'll be just going up. Will you hurry and meet me down in the drawing-room?'

'I oughtn't to,' she said.

'You must,' said Hugh Ellerby in a slow voice. His hand closed over hers. 'I haven't said a word to you alone for days. It's driving me mad.'

'Oh, Hugh!' said Scharlie, and caught her lower lip between her teeth, which she only did when she was very stirred and excited. It was a very exciting and stirring thing to be looked at the way Hugh Ellerby was looking at her; talked to, the way he talked. A very dangerous thing, because, if he was in love, she was more so.

'My dear,' he said. His fingers pressed hers down on the banisters so tightly that they hurt.

1

'I wonder if you know how adorable you look!'

'Oh, Hugh, don't be so silly.' Scharlie laughed. 'I'm all hot and flustered after my tennis.'

'You look adorable,' he persisted.

'You're rather a nice person to look at yourself, Hugh Ellerby.'

'Rot!' he said.

But they looked at each other after the manner of a man and a woman who are desperately in love and were satisfied in their taste. They made a very attractive couple. The man, tall, lithe, with a fair boyish head, very blue eyes and a fresh complexion tanned by the sun and wind. Weakness lay in the rather spoiled, sulky curve of his well-shaped mouth, but on the whole Hugh Ellerby was an extremely good-looking man with the charming, facile manner, which women like. Scharlie Mason, whose curly brown head barely reached his shoulder, was as slender as a girl in her teens, and looked nowhere near her twenty-two years and not at all like a married woman.

An exquisite skin of the transparent quality that flushes easily; a small, tip-tilted nose and large, grey eyes, which seemed to alter rapidly to green when she was in one of her excitable moods, fringed by ridiculously long lashes, gave Scharlie that air of extreme youth which women from all generations have coveted. The youthfulness was intensified in Scharlie's case by the modern dress. Hugh Ellerby, looking at her with the hungry eyes of a would-be lover, thought how fascinating she was; like a child in her short straight tennis-frock of white linen; with long slim legs and really lovely ankles; cheeks burnt red, half from the exertion of her match, half from the thrill of his flattery. He loved the way her hair curled, short, brushed boyishly back from her forehead. He was never tired of looking at her narrow, pretty hands with their glistening nails. She had an almost foreign trick of gesticulating with them when she spoke. She was wide-awake, vital; a creature of fire. Yes, Scharlie looked like a slender child of fifteen, but Hugh, not without experience of women, saw passion in the curve of her lips and he was intrigued. The amorous, rather disillusioned young mouth of Scharlie challenged him.

'Say you'll come down and talk to me,' he begged.

'Very well,' she said.

'You darling!' he whispered.

She ran up the stairs very quickly. He turned and strolled back to the drawing-room, where his hostess and three other members of the house-party at Gateways were finishing a game of bridge. He opened his cigarette-case and tapped a cigarette upon it thoughtfully. He wondered if he was a fool to let Scharlie Mason intrigue him to this extent. Certainly he was a knave. He admitted that. She was a married woman and he was engaged to be married. His fiancée, Eleanor Gorring, was also a member of the Wilberforce house-party. It was rather low and beastly of him to make love to Scharlie behind her husband's back—not that he had ever met the husband or cared a damn about him, for, from what people said, he was a swine. But he was her husband. And there was Eleanor. The whole situation was trying.

Nevertheless, the game was exciting, and perhaps all the more so because it was perilous. From the beginning of time, man has wanted what he cannot have. From the moment Hugh had arrived at Gateways and been introduced to Scharlie Mason he had been attracted—found her most disturbing. She was disillusioned in marriage and unhappy, but at the same time she was rather brave and gay and insouciant, which Hugh found praiseworthy. He hated women who whined.

He had never heard Scharlie whine. Only from time to time he caught a tragic look of discontent in those wide, grey-green eyes of hers; and caught a smile that plainly said: 'I am so bored; come and be nice to me.'

Hugh, weakest of men with pretty women, couldn't have helped responding to that. And, anyhow, most men wanted to be nice to Scharlie Mason.

'It's the devil,' said Hugh, and leaned over

the chair of a middle-aged widow at the bridge-table, who called 'Two hearts' in a luscious voice, then looked coquettishly up at Hugh and added: 'Beating as one. What do you say, dear Mr. Ellerby?'

'Oh, lord!' he thought, smiled at the widow, and moved quickly away. He stood by the tall windows looking out at the sunlit garden and smoked gloomily. 'It's the devil,' he said again, and thought of the curve of Scharlie's upper lip and the way, sometimes, she broke from a solemn speech into a sudden ripple of laughter.

Scharlie ran upstairs to change for dinner and walked straight into a tall girl who was on the landing. She was about two years older than Scharlie and looked twice Scharlie's age. A good-looking girl; typically English; eyes gravely blue; fair hair parted in the middle, plaited, and worn in coils over both ears. She had a charming sympathetic expression. She was Eleanor Gorring—Hugh's fiancée. She laughed at Scharlie.

'You're in a hurry, Mrs. Mason,' she said.

'I'm so awfully sorry—did I hurt you?' stammered Scharlie.

'Not a bit. You've been playing tennis?'

'Yes. Major Croker and I have just whacked Mrs. Austin and young Pole Hays six to four.'

'Good work,' said Eleanor. 'You play rather a nice game. I've been watching you. I don't know how you get that smashing service of yours over the net—you're such a slip of a thing.'

'Oh, I'm very strong,' said Scharlie. 'See you at dinner,' she added, lowering her lashes, and hurried on.

Eleanor Gorring was a nice, amiable creature—so generous in her praise. She made Scharlie feel guilty and unhappy.

Scharlie's face was gloomy—all the radiance wiped from it—when she entered her bedroom. It was a big, sunny primrose room in the west wing, with oak beams and diamond-paned casements like most of the rooms in Gateways which was one of the loveliest old Tudor houses in Sussex.

Scharlie threw her racquet on the bed; stripped off the tennis-dress and slipped on a green satin wrapper. She was hot and tired. She had been playing tennis the whole afternoon. She wanted a bath.

She lingered a moment to light a cigarette and stood by the open casement. She stared over the beautiful, formal gardens with their magnificent clipped yew hedges which were hundreds of years old, and famous; beyond to the dark shadow of Ashdown Forest.

While she smoked and stared, some of the hot colour faded from her cheeks. She looked suddenly pale and even pinched. She was worried. She realised that she was very much in love with Hugh Ellerby and that her passion for him was rapidly getting out of her control.

And his passion for her appeared also to be too much for him.

She knew that if she dressed quickly and went downstairs and found him alone, he would kiss her. He had not kissed her yet. They had contented themselves with a look; a look as significant, if less satisfying, than a kiss. A flash of the eye; a pressure of the hand. In other words, a flirtation.

But the thing which had begun as a flirtation had developed into something more harmful; much more dangerous.

Scharlie had fallen in love. And she was married; had been married for four years. And Hugh was going to marry Eleanor Gorring.

'What a rotten mess,' Scharlie thought as she smoked, and a wave of profound melancholy engulfed her and grew deeper as she reviewed the situation.

It *was* a rotten mess . . . yes, that was slang, but it described it. Life was rotten. Unfair. And love—if one loved without hope, without promise—was crueller than the grave—a sort of death in life.

So far, she had had little happiness in her life. At seventeen, she had left school to take up a difficult existence with a widowed mother who was very pretty and youthful and absurdly jealous of Scharlie. A stupid, vain woman who was the complete egotist, taken up with her own ideas and pleasures and annoyed that she had a young daughter to launch; a daughter with so much beauty and vitality and charm. Men pursued Scharlie at once. Scharlie, straight from a modern school with modern views, could take care of herself, but she was too pretty to be safe, in her mother's estimation. She had been brought up in a post-war hysterical atmosphere. She had seen her pretty, widowed mother indulge in half a dozen flirtations. She had nobody to give her advice or start her on a normal, sensible course of existence. Only the mother who bickered with her and who deplored and tried to alter the shape which she herself had moulded.

Scharlie threatened to be a nuisance. On her eighteenth birthday, Mrs. Croft gave a party and introduced to Scharlie Alec Mason, a stockbroker twice her age, a bachelor of somewhat set habits and old-fashioned views. Mrs. Croft hinted that Scharlie, married, would soon 'tone down' and make an excellent little wife. Also Mason was more interested in finance than women. He did not understand them. But he found himself as wax in the hands of a clever woman. He proposed to pretty Scharlie within a month.

Scharlie refused him four times, and was bullied and cajoled and hustled into accepting him the fifth. It was pointed out to her that Alec, if not the romantic hero of her dreams, was a sound, dependable person: making money, and able to give her a good home.

Scharlie, not having met the man she wanted to marry and only a child of eighteen, succumbed to the elder woman's influence. Besides which, by then Alec Mason was physically, if not mentally, very much in love with the gay, insouciant girl. He spent a lot of money on presents for her; flattered her, and gave her, erroneously, the impression that she could do much as she liked once she was married.

Scharlie was married to Alec Mason with due pomp and ceremony, after which her mother gasped with relief and departed for South Africa with every intention herself of getting married again out there.

Poor little Scharlie, really very ignorant when Alec Mason met her, woke up, suddenly, after her marriage, and discovered that she loathed her husband. She was violently miserable and disappointed in life.

As soon as the honeymoon ended, Alec returned to the normal; a selfish, self-centred, narrow-minded man, who lacked generosity and kindliness. Unfit to be any woman's husband, still less the husband of a sensitive and excitable young girl, he killed what affection she had for him long before that honeymoon ended. He was hurt and annoyed by her lack of response to his passion. He failed to understand why she should dislike him for lecturing her about expenditure, or upbraiding her for wanting amusement, in one

9

breath; and, in the next, saying in his pompous manner: 'And now, my dear, come and kiss me.'

Oh! how she hated Alec's pomposity; Alec's meanness—his spiritual rather than his mercenary meanness, because generosity of spirit meant so much more to Scharlie than an allowance. How she hated him when he was in his hectoring, lecturing moods! And how much more did she hate him when he was amorous; when he came towards her with that self-satisfied smile and said, 'Now, my dear, come and kiss me.' One day, she thought, she would hit him when he said that.

Four years of Alec and such a marriage had been a strain for her almost beyond her endurance. And now, at twenty-two, she was still pathetically young; still enthusiastic about life; yearning to wring the beauty, the passion out of it. She was like a starved thing; hungry for romance.

Alec was, of course, jealous. He was forty, now, and old for his age, bald-headed and aware that he cut rather a sorry figure beside his wife, with her youthful loveliness, which was like a flame; her natural gaiety, which even her association with him had not entirely quenched. In consequence he rarely allowed her to leave his side, and could not tolerate any young men among her friends.

When Scharlie, a week ago, had received an invitation from Dorothy Wilberforce, who had been at school with her, to join their house-party, Alec had at first refused to let her go. He was busy in the City. He could not get away. He did not see why he should be left alone in their London house 'at the mercy of servants,' as he put it, though in Scharlie's estimation it would be the other way round—leaving the servants at the mercy of Alec. However, for the first time, she openly rebelled.

'Dorothy and I were pals at school. I haven't seen anything of her since she married Tim, and I don't see why I shouldn't go and stay with her for a week,' she had said.

They had had a row about it. Then Alec caught a cold. When Alec had a cold everybody in the house suffered. He was a tyrant and a nuisance. Nothing was right. Alec retired to bed with aspirin and hot-water bottles and ranted at the household. Scharlie left the house.

'I won't catch your beastly cold,' she had said. 'I'm going down to Gateways.'

She went. And Alec, pained and resentful that she should disregard his wishes, remained in bed and sniffed to himself.

The week had developed into a fortnight. Mrs. Wilberforce, very fond of Scharlie, prevailed upon her to stay on. Scharlie felt deliciously wicked away from Alec, and stayed. She was like a bird out of its cage. She had never looked so lovely or been so amusing. She played excellent tennis and she was popular with the men, even if some of the less attractive women had catty remarks to make about her.

It was inevitable when she came in contact with Hugh Ellerby, who was so handsome, so young, so charming, she should fall head over heels in love with him. And at first Eleanor had not been there. She had only joined the house-party yesterday. Without her it had not seemed so 'rotten' to flirt with Hugh. And now, when the whole thing seemed thoroughly rotten, and futile into the bargain, Scharlie could not pull in the reins.

She was frantically in love. After the misery, the repression of her life with Alec, she was greatly in need of Hugh: of his sympathy, his charming *tendresse*: all that Alec Mason lacked.

She stared at the woods which were sombre and lovely against a sunset sky, and the tears came into her eyes.

'How can I go back to Alec?' she thought. 'Oh, Hughie . . . how can I . . . loving you so much!'

She bit fiercely at her lower lip, but the tears would well over and trickle down her cheeks. She picked up her towel, a sponge, and some bath-salts, and marched to the door; her slender, childish figure erect; head flung back as though in defiance of fate.

CHAPTER TWO

When Scharlie went downstairs, Hugh was waiting for her, alone in the drawing-room; a lovely long room with many windows; bookcases let into the walls; old rugs on an oak floor, old prints against a wheaten-coloured wall. On a June evening like this it was full of the slanting red and amber shadows of the sun, which shed a last blaze of glory before it sank behind the dark rim of the forest.

Scharlie hated wearing evening dress on these summer evenings. It 'showed up her war-paint,' as she called it. But there was really very little paint to show up on Scharlie's face—the merest touch of vermilion on the lovely mouth that challenged Hugh so irresistibly. She was fresh; charmingly slim in a green and white dress of flowered georgette; long at the back and short in the front; sleeveless, showing the white beauty of slender arms and throat and sloping shoulders.

She came across the long room conscious that she had a high, nervous colour and that her heart beat with an excitement, a thrill to which she had no right. The man—as fresh, as attractive in his dinner-jacket as only a fair-haired Englishman can look—watched her come. His own pulses were thrilling. Without a word, he held out his arms.

Scharlie walked straight into them. But she hung back in his embrace.

'Hugh, we're being mad.'

'I can't help it. I must kiss you, Scharlie, or I shall go crazy.'

If you do kiss me, I might go crazy.'

'I don't care. I love you.'

'Oh, Hugh!' She shut her eyes, tilted her head backwards. He looked at her hungrily. She was a bewitching creature; a flame a torment, in his arms. The sun caught the close-cut ripple of her hair. It was the colour of chestnuts. And there was a provocative tinge of red in the tips of her lashes. He had never seen such lashes as Scharlie's. They curled straight back, and looked almost too stiff, too thick to be real.

'What a lovely thing you are, Scharlie,' he said.

She felt him shaking. She opened her eyes. She put up a hand and touched the smooth, warm bronze of his cheek. If he found her lovely, his physical appeal was equally fascinating to her.

She thought of Alec; his short, pompous figure and high, bald forehead; and she loathed the memory of him. It wasn't fair of her mother to have pushed her into marriage with Alec when there were men like Hugh in the world. A yearning to know even one moment of happiness with Hugh overwhelmed her. She curved an arm about his neck.

14

'Kiss me,' she whispered.

He tightened his arms about her. They were lost in the ecstasy of that kiss. Scharlie, with a rapt, white face and closed eyelids, under the fierce pressure of his lips felt that she was blinded by the sudden vivid beauty of love; of life. This was living—feeling—as a woman was meant to live, to feel. This was revelation. The beginning and the end.

Being a woman and very young she was just a little more lost than the man who—half drunk with the sheer intoxication of Scharlie's whole-hearted surrender—soon grew sober and knew he must regain control or court disaster. At any moment one of the guests or the servants might enter the room.

He raised his head; looked quickly over Scharlie's at the closed door. He framed her face with his hands, kissed her swiftly, on the eyes and cheeks and lips, and under her chin.

'Dear, adorable little thing,' he said.

'Hugh, what are we going to do?'

'Do you really love me, Scharlie?'

'Would I have kissed you like that if I hadn't?'

'I suppose not.' He laughed and reddened slightly. 'Well, I can only tell you that it will be wise if you don't kiss me like that again, darling.'

'Hugh—' She was flushed and distressed now. 'Am I frightfully bad? Do you think I am?'

15

' "Frightfully bad" is putting it a bit strong, sweetheart. One kiss—' He shrugged his shoulders. Then he dropped a swift kiss on her hair, and let his arms fall away from her. 'I must have a cigarette,' he added.

She stood very still while he lit his cigarette. His hands were not steady. He had very nice, long, brown fingers.

Oh, the difference between those fingers and Alec's white, podgy hands!

'I'm so sorry, my dear.' Hugh offered his case. 'Have one.'

'No, thanks.'

He took one or two breaths of his cigarette, then smiled down at her.

'Don't look so tragic, darling.'

'But, Hugh—' She stared. The grey of her eyes had changed to green, and the pupils were very large. 'It *is* a tragedy. You men are so funny—you take things so coolly. A moment ago, when you were kissing me . . . we were both crazy. I am still. But you're absolutely different.'

'I assure you I'm not. I'm feeling right off my rocker, Scharlie. Your lips, my dear—' He laughed self-consciously. His fresh complexion was bright pink to the roots of the fair hair. 'You'd send any fellow crazy. But we must keep our heads.'

Now there was not a vestige of colour in Scharlie's cheeks. She clasped her hands tightly together. She was trying to find her

16

control, and it was not as easy for her as for the man. To him it was all 'damned awkward and maddening.' He was engaged to one woman of whom he was extremely fond and he was for the moment infatuated with Scharlie. He had been infatuated in his life before. But to Scharlie it was all new; a terrific upheaval; a kind of mental and physical explosion. Life could never be quite the same again. Hugh was the first man about whom she had ever really felt like this. If it was, also, infatuation on her part, it seemed real enough tonight.

'Hugh, what are we going to do?' she asked again.

'What can we do? You're married. I'm engaged.'

Scharlie put a hand to her forehead.

'I don't feel I can possibly go back to Alec now.'

'Oh, my dear—you must,' he said hastily. 'Good lord, we must behave sensibly. We can't muck up the whole show just because we—we care for each other.'

'No,' said Scharlie in a very low voice, 'I suppose we can't.'

'You see, there are so many of us involved. You—your husband—me—Eleanor. Eleanor's such a dear—' He bit his lip and stared gloomily out of one of the windows. 'I'm tremendously fond of her.'

'I know. I like her too. She's a dear.'

'She—she's damn' fond of me, you see,

17

Scharlie.' Hugh's colour was a hotter red now. 'I couldn't let her down, could I? We've fixed our wedding for August.'

Scharlie nodded. She made no effort to touch him, to deviate him from his line of argument. She just looked at him with a white, set young face. The man felt suddenly ashamed of himself. He picked up her right hand and put his lips to the palm.

'Scharlie, this is all my fault.'

'It isn't—it's just as much mine,' she said miserably.

'No, I've been pursuing you. I know it. I made you come down here like this and—kiss me. I ought to be shot.'

She shivered as she felt his lips on her hand, but she shook her head at him.

'No—please! It's my fault, too. I've been—fooling round with you. I—I just couldn't help falling in love with you.'

'I couldn't help it either, darling,' he said huskily. He kept her hand, and kissed every finger with returning passion. 'It's the most damnable thing, for both of us to be so tied up. But we aren't in a position to do anything. I mean, even if I let Nell down there's your husband to consider. You couldn't leave him—have a beastly divorce.'

'A divorce couldn't be as beastly as my marriage with Alec has become to me,' said Scharlie.

'Why you ever married the fellow—'

'You know. I've told you. I was coerced—made to.'

'A mere kid—your mother ought to have been shot!'

'I know. But it's too late to worry about that now. Only, Hugh, I can hardly bear to go back to him.'

'You'll have to try to, darling. It's impossible to think about a divorce, for you anyhow. We'd never be happy feeling we'd given everyone a dig in the back. Mason doesn't sound a very attractive fellow and he ought never to have married a child of eighteen, but I suppose he's fond of you?'

'Yes . . .' she shivered.

'Probably damned jealous,' added Hugh gloomily.

'Yes, and possessive; he would refuse to divorce me.'

'There you are. Well, you aren't the sort of girl, darling, to stick the sort of life we'd have to lead if we ran off and he refused to set you free.'

'I suppose not. But I don't think I can be very good or religious, Hugh,' she said wretchedly. 'I just feel I wouldn't mind what I went through—so long as I could be with you.'

'Oh, Scharlie . . . dear . . .' He closed his eyes and put his cheek against her hand. 'Why should you care so much for me?'

'I just do.'

He felt unhappy and very troubled. He

didn't really want little Scharlie to become too serious about him. It would make life so complicated. He was quite crazily in love with her. He didn't want to lose her altogether. But what could he do? There was Eleanor. The thought of marriage with Eleanor seemed a little flat—after this. She was a darling but quiet and reticent. A man couldn't always tell what was going on in her mind behind those grave blue eyes of hers. When they had first met, six months ago, Eleanor's reserve had intrigued him. He admired her character—she was rather a fine person—dependable and sweet. Physically attractive, too, with her tall, straight figure and blonde hair. She rode well, danced well; and she was an excellent hostess. Since the death of her mother she had made a success of entertaining for her father, Walter Gorring, who was one of England's leading book-publishers.

Hugh, who had lately entered the firm as advertising manager, stood a very good chance of being taken into partnership with Gorring and his son, Henry, after his marriage with Eleanor.

To give up Eleanor, therefore, meant giving up any prospects of that kind. They were brilliant prospects, too. Walter Gorring would probably be knighted next year and would retire. But Henry Gorring was a clever young man with ideas, and would no doubt modernise and improve an already flourishing business.

Hugh was ambitious. He had a private income of £250 a year and a Public School education behind him, but no prospects of inheriting more than another £500 a year from his own father, who was a retired doctor. Therefore the rosy prospects to be counted on once he was Eleanor's husband and a member of the Gorring family were not to be lightly thrown aside.

If he eloped with Scharlie Mason, he would be throwing everything else on one side. Being a selfish male being—and Hugh Ellerby—he was not so much in love that he was prepared to do that.

It was different for Scharlie. Life for her held nothing but the dull monotony—and at moments the sheer purgatory—of sharing a home with Alec.

Big tears welled into her eyes as she looked at Hugh.

'Oh, Hugh, darling,' she said under her breath, 'I suppose it's all got to—end. I mean—*this*.'

'It's damnable, but I'm afraid so, dear.'

'Then the sooner I . . . go home . . . get away from you . . . the better.'

Her underlip quivered like a child's. She was so like a pretty, hurt child. Hugh knew that he had helped to hurt her. He hadn't meant to. Life was like that. One couldn't always control one's feelings. Poor little Scharlie! He was a bit sorry for himself tonight, too. He would like to have been free and had a lot of money. Then, of course, he could have taken Scharlie away, and—divorce or no divorce—nothing would have mattered. They might have had a wonderful time travelling. Scharlie in the South of France—wearing wonderful clothes and dancing with him—laughing with him. She was made for fun, for dancing, for laughter. Poor pretty Scharlie!

'I say, don't cry, darling,' he said. 'I can't bear that. Someone may come in, too.'

'I'll go up to my room for a bit,' she said. 'I—oh, if you *knew* what I'm feeling!'

'I do know. I'm feeling it, too.'

'All those people coming down—the whole evening to sit through—to look at you—see Eleanor take your hand—I can't endure it!'

'Oh, Scharlie—sweetheart!'

The man was flattered and touched, and, for the moment, in love. He flung away his cigarette, and swept her into his arms again and kissed her hungrily. She kissed him back with all her soul on her lips. And the man saw, plainly, how unsafe, how disastrous it would be to carry on an intrigue with Scharlie. She wasn't a creature one could love lightly. This slender, ardent witch of a child—she didn't love lightly, either.

When he let her go, he was miserable and unnerved. He was glad that she made no effort to plead with him or make any impossible

22

demands. She was really rather gallant and adorable.

She broke from his arms, ran straight out of the room, and shut the door behind her.

Hugh stared moodily at that closed door. He felt depressed and bad-tempered. One was always having to do without things one wanted, and vice-versa. Why was life so difficult, so tantalising?

He saw a gossamer green chiffon handkerchief on the rug at his feet. Scharlie's handkerchief. He picked it up, held it to his lips. It had Scharlie's lovely smell . . . that scent she used . . . she had told him what it was yesterday . . . *Numéro Cinq* or something . . . of Molyneux.

'Oh, damn!' said Hugh. He put the wisp of green chiffon into his pocket, and lit another cigarette.

CHAPTER THREE

Scharlie was particularly gay and amusing that night. Hugh, who did not get another chance of speaking to her alone, watched her from time to time. He saw her—flushed, sparkling, feverish—trying to teach old Major Croker to dance; flirting a little with young Derek Pole-Hays, who obviously adored her; chatting, laughing with Dorothy Wilberforce.

Again and again Hugh heard that infectious laugh of hers ripple out. But when he turned his head and caught her eye, he saw that she was tragically unhappy. Yes, she was gallant. He admired her.

Mrs. Wilberforce—known since her schooldays as 'Little Dee'—knew Scharlie as well as anybody and was the least deceived by her hectic gaiety.

'What's wrong with you, Scharl?' she asked once during the evening when she came in contact with the girl.

Scharlie smiled at her. She was fond of Little Dee, who was a small, pretty woman with brisk, bird-like movements, a shrewd, level brain, and the general character and outlook of a rather decent boy. She was five years older than Scharlie, but she had only been married a year, and Scharlie envied her her happiness. She adored the big, blue-eyed, genial man whom she called Tim. Timothy Wilberforce was one of the best. She adored him and bullied him, and he returned her adoration and assured their mutual friends that without Little Dee and her tyranny he would never be the man he was.

Scharlie looked at Little Dee Wilberforce tonight and envied her more than usual. She had the man with whom she was in love. What more could a woman want?

'Oh, Dee,' she said, 'I feel suicidal.'

'Good heavens, my dear, why?'

24

'I don't want to go back to Alec.'

'I'm furious with you for marrying Alec. Why did you let your annoying mother mess up your life, Scharlie?'

'I was so young, Dee, and I wanted to see life and get away from Mums.'

'You backed the wrong horse, my love.'

'I know, Dee.'

'Poor old Scharlie.' Mrs. Wilberforce put an arm about the girl. 'But what can we do about it? Alec is very much alive. I can't get Tim to kill him off, can I?'

'No,' said Scharlie, and laughed miserably.

Dee's bright eyes searched the girl. She saw her gaze wander across the room to the fair-haired, good-looking man who was doing a cross-word puzzle with Eleanor Gorring— Eleanor, who looked rather lovely tonight in a black lace gown which showed off her superb shoulders and arms.

Mrs. Wilberforce turned back to Scharlie.

'My dear,' she said, 'you haven't been silly enough to fall in love with Hugh Ellerby, have you?'

Scharlie blushed bright pink.

'Good gracious, no! You *are* stupid, Little Dee,' she exclaimed.

Whereupon Little Dee knew perfectly well that she was not at all stupid and that Scharlie *had* fallen in love with Hugh Ellerby.

She was sorry. She was also a little afraid for Scharlie. But she thought it wiser to say no

25

more about it.

When she was in bed that night, she spoke a few words on the subject to her husband.

'Tim, what's going to happen? Poor Scharlie has lost her heart to Hugh, and Hugh belongs to Eleanor, and Eleanor is the nicest girl I know. It *is* a pity.'

Wilberforce, fresh and glowing from his bath, looking like a very large boy in his striped pyjamas with his curly head and dimpled chin, planted his fifteen stone down upon the bed beside his diminutive wife and played with her wedding-ring in silence a moment. Then he said:

'Are you fond of Scharlie Mason—really fond, Little Dee?'

'Yes, really fond. She's an absolute darling, and I'm sorrier for her than for anyone I know. She's had a rotten time with that rotten, selfish mother of hers, and she was pushed into marriage with Alec. I've only met him once and I loathed him. Pompous ass!'

'Tut, tut!' said Tim.

'Well, I did, Tim. But why do you ask if I'm fond of Scharlie?'

'Because I like the child. And I see disaster ahead.'

'You do, Tim?'

'Yep. She's unhappy and too devilish pretty and appealing to get through without a mess-up with some lad.'

'But it mustn't be Hugh, Tim.'

26

'I hope not. He'd be a swine to make love to Scharlie. Nell Gorring's a damn' nice girl. Matter of fact, I think she's too good for him. I'm not sure I like Ellerby.'

'Oh, he's all right, Tim.'

'Bit of a bounder. All you women fall for Ellerby's type. It beats me.'

'That, my dear Tim, is rank jealousy on your part.'

Wilberforce gave his wife a look of disdain. He stood up, and, with a downward swoop of two great arms, lifted her out of the bed and suspended her in the air.

'I shall drop you into the bath and turn the shower on you, you little beast,' he said.

'Tim, put me down.'

She laughed helplessly, and raved at him. She was as thin and straight as a boy in her silk pyjama suit; smooth hair cut in a straight fringe across a straight, candid brow. Her head was that of a mediaeval page.

'*Tim*, don't be such a great mutt. We're trying to talk about poor Scharlie.'

'Scharlie must work out her own salvation,' said Tim Wilberforce. 'I like her, and we'll do what we can for her, but take it from me, my Little Dee, folks are better left to their own follies. It doesn't pay to interfere. Now I shall throw you out of the window.'

'Kiss me, Tim, and shut up.'

He set her on her feet. Her page's head only just reached his shoulder. He wrapped her in a bear's hug. They adored each other. And their marriage was a very perfect one.

In a room not very far away, Scharlie sobbed herself to sleep.

In his bedroom, Hugh Ellerby continued to smoke far too many cigarettes and enjoyed none of them. He could not sleep. He could not stop thinking about Scharlie, and wanting her. He was much too much in love with her for his peace of mind. And downstairs, after the others had gone up, he had had five very uncomfortable minutes with Eleanor. When he kissed her good night in the usual way and said:

'Well, darling, sleep the sleep of the just. Bless you' (which was what he usually said), Eleanor detained him, which was most unusual with her. They were standing at the foot of the staircase leading up from the lounge, and it had struck Hugh, guiltily, that this was where he had held Scharlie's hand earlier this evening and made love to her with his voice and his eyes.

'Hugo,' said Eleanor, and put her hands on his shoulders and looked at him rather gravely, 'anything wrong?'

'What should be, my dear?' he said.

'Look at me, Hugo.'

He looked, but very quickly turned his gaze away. Eleanor, being a woman in love, noticed that, of course.

'You're not like your ordinary self, my dear,'

she said in a worried way. 'You seem nervy and distrait. Is anything troubling you?'

'Not a thing,' Hugh lied.

'You'd tell me if there was?'

'Of course, old thing.'

Then she rubbed her head against his shoulder; that fair, charming head with the satin plaits coiled over both ears.

'My darling!' she said, with unaccustomed warmth and demonstration. She was by nature a reticent woman who found it difficult to express her feelings.

Hugh, disturbed, wishing she would not choose tonight of all nights to be emotional, put his arms round her and kissed her head.

'Darling!' he said. It seemed the best and easiest thing to say. He was so awfully fond of her and he was going to marry her, and six months ago it had thrilled him to kiss her. Well, her kisses still thrilled him. But not quite in the same way that Scharlie's did.

'Love me, Hugo?' she asked. He had felt sure that was coming.

'Of course,' he answered.

'You're everything to me now, Hugo,' she said.

'Of course, I couldn't possibly let her down,' he thought, and kissed the palm of her left hand—a fine-shaped strong hand, slightly tanned by the sun; Eleanor played a lot of golf. Not in the least like Scharlie's narrow hand, with its white, tapering fingers and exquisite

29

nails. Damn! Why must he keep thinking about Scharlie? He gritted his teeth and held Eleanor closer; kissed her on the lips with almost desperate passion.

'Good night, Nell. You're simply marvellous to me, always,' he said huskily.

She laughed, and looked pleased and happy.

'Dear old Hugo! I'm terribly lucky to have you—to know I'm going to marry you.'

He felt a beast because she was a loyal, straight creature, whom any man would like to think of as the mother of his sons. And he was crazy for Scharlie . . . mad for her. He knew he would have left Eleanor and taken Scharlie away if he had enough money. How beastly it was! He hated himself.

Eleanor said:

'I've always thought Dee and Tim the happiest married couple I know, but I do believe you and I are going to run them close, Hugo.'

'You bet we will,' he said with forced cheer.

'I'm so terribly sorry for women who aren't happy. Like that poor little Mason girl.'

Hugh's heart jerked a bit.

'Mrs. Mason?'

'Yes. Dee and I were talking about her this afternoon. Dee says she's an awfully nice child and has a wretched sort of husband.'

'Oh!' said Hugh shortly.

'She's so pretty, don't you think so?'

'Yes,' he said, and wished Eleanor wouldn't

choose to discuss Scharlie.

'She plays very good tennis. What a funny name Scharlie is, isn't it? Dee says her father was called Charlie and wanted a boy, and when she was born insisted in putting the "s" in front of his name. It's awfully quaint and attractive—Schar-lee.'

The name seemed to fill Hugh's ears. He could bear no more. He kissed his fiancée and drew away from her.

'Good night, Nell, old thing.'

'Good night, my dear. By the way, Henry is driving down from town tomorrow to fetch me.'

'I'd better go too,' said Hugh hastily.

'Well, you've got another week's holiday from the firm, haven't you?'

'Yes. But I must go up to Cromer and see the pater.'

'Yes, of course. And I've got to get home to fix this dinner Daddy and Henry are giving for Snaffer, the New York publisher man.'

They were half way up the stairs. Eleanor stifled a little yawn. But Hugh was looking straight ahead, across the landing at the door which he knew had just closed on Scharlie.

That was the end of a very difficult day.

CHAPTER FOUR

Hugh Ellerby and his fiancée left Gateways at midday that following day. Scharlie was supposed to go home that morning too. But, following so closely upon the one passionate, all-revealing scene with Hugh, she felt it intolerable to return to Alec, so she wired that she was staying on at Gateways another day.

She, who never rouged, borrowed a little 'tangee' from Dee that morning because she thought she looked so pale when she woke up, after a broken and miserable night.

She saw the man with whom she was now violently in love alone for a few minutes just before he departed. He had finished packing and wandered into the garden to find Eleanor, whom the butler said was in the rosary with Mrs. Wilberforce. Scharlie had escaped from the unfailing attentions of young Derek Pole-Hays and was on the tennis-court, pretending to interest herself in the state of the grass. It had rained during the night. She had been asked to make up a foursome before lunch.

Hugh caught sight of her. She was slim as a schoolgirl in her white tennis-frock; a sleeveless green cardigan; a green silk handkerchief tied round her head. He could not resist snatching a moment with her.

She saw him walking towards her and hated the sight of the dark lounge suit which meant town—meant he was leaving the house-party. She felt a fierce ache of the heart when he joined her on the court, but the sunlight made her screw up her eyes, so he did not see the tears in them. He said, in a hurried undertone:

'You know I'm going in a moment, Scharlie. Henry Gorring is coming for Nell, and I'm driving up with them and then going on to Cromer to my own home.'

'Yes,' she said.

'I just want to say good-bye, my dear.'

'Don't,' she said. 'I'd rather you didn't.'

'Scharlie, I had a damnable night.'

'I can't say I slept much.'

'I'm terribly in love with you, my dear,' he said with genuine feeling. 'But I had a talk with Eleanor last night, and—oh, well, it showed me what a cad I'd be to let her down.'

'We decided that before, didn't we?' she said in a tired little voice. 'It's all right, Hugh. I understand.'

'But don't think I don't care.'

She looked up at him, and she felt nothing but that fierce ache and pain in her heart; the intolerable need of him.

'I'll remember you do . . . I'd like to remember that. Hugh, darling, darling, I love you so much.'

'Little Scharlie!'

He wanted to take her in his arms, but the

33

tennis-court was much too public.

'I daren't kiss you,' he added.

'I know.'

She was so little and slim and lovely. He liked to think of her as he had seen her yesterday on this court; swift and graceful, head tilted backwards, arm flung high, racquet poised waiting for her ball. It was a pretty sight to watch Scharlie playing tennis.

'Look here, my dear,' he said on a sudden impulse. 'We've got to give this thing a chance—I mean try to forget each other, for everybody's sake—mostly for Nell's and your husband's. But if things get too strong for us— well, we'll have to let each other know.'

'Yes, Hugh—' She wondered if he could guess what it meant to her to lose him—to go back to Alec. Did he understand? Perhaps— perhaps not. Men didn't seem to love with the same concentration that women did—didn't even find it hard to love one or two people simultaneously. But she had no room for any other man on earth except Hugh. Certainly no room for Alec, who didn't know how to be friendly or kind or anything but a pompous and possessive husband.

Hugh pulled a card from his pocket-book. He thrust it into her hand.

'That's my address, my telephone number— if any time you want me. I'll always do anything for you. Count me as a pal, please, Scharlie dearest.'

'Thank you,' she said, and took the card and found it comforting. *Mr. Hugh Brian Ellerby, 19 Conder Mansions, Conder Street, Piccadilly, W.*

'That's the address of my service flat,' he told her. 'The 'phone number is in the book under Conder Mansions. Let me know one day—how you are.'

'If I dare,' she whispered. 'If I dare speak to you, darling Hugh. And, if you want me, my number is in the directory, under Alexander Mason. Yes, my husband's name—he's called Alec, but his real name's Alexander. Frightfully pompous—just like him.' She tried to laugh; '21 Arlingham Place, South Kensington.'

'I won't forget. I must go. That's Nell's brother coming now. I recognise the horn of his car. Good-bye, darling child.'

He held out a hand. She put hers into it, and for an instant he wrung it so tightly that she winced with the pain. But there was no longer any need for rouge in her cheeks. That passionate pressure brought the fiery colour to her face, her throat.

'Good-bye, darling,' she said in a choked little voice.

He left her standing there on the tennis-court, shading her eyes from the sun with one slim, shaking hand, while the other furtively wiped away her tears.

Scharlie wanted to sit down there on the grass like a child and cry.

A few moments later, when with powder-puff and mirror she had removed the traces of tears, she walked back to the house. She found most of the members of Dee's party gathering in an admiring circle round a huge Isotta which had just been driven up to the front door and was standing under the ivy-covered portico. The engine was still throbbing, almost noiselessly. A wonderful, long, slim car with an aluminium body. A young man wearing horn-rimmed glasses was at the wheel. He was showing Derek Pole-Hays the gears.

Eleanor Gorring saw Scharlie's lone figure and thought, suddenly, that the girl looked forlorn.

'Come and be introduced to my nice brother, Mrs. Mason,' she called gaily.

Scharlie could not escape. She was seized by Eleanor and taken to the side of the Isotta.

'Behold the "Silver Streak" and the driver thereof,' said Eleanor. 'My brother Henry. Henry, this is Mrs. Mason. She is the young Suzanne of our party, and has whacked us all.'

Henry Gorring removed his hat and said:

'Oh, really? How do you do,' and turned to the gears and the enthusiastic Derek again.

Scharlie was conscious of being snubbed. Henry Gorring was a rude young man, she thought. He had a very abrupt manner and none of his sister's charm. Scharlie was surprised and a little piqued. She was not used to being ignored by men. Besides, she had heard Henry Gorring's name mentioned so often during the last week or so, and always to his credit. He was so clever, so industrious, so interesting. He might be all three, but Scharlie did not find him attractive.

She did not even admire his looks. He was tall; of Eleanor's fine build; and as dark as she was fair. He had a square face with rather blunt, strong features and broad nostrils. The eyes behind the horn-rimmed glasses were light grey—unlike his sister's and as hard as hers were tender. In that one brief glance he had flashed her, Scharlie had sensed something approaching hostility. She asked Dee about Henry Gorring after, and Dee explained things by saying that young Gorring was reputed to be a woman-hater.

'Curly eyelashes and a dream of a figure have no effect on him,' Mrs. Wilberforce announced. 'I know him . . . I mean I meet him now and again in town. He always treats women as though they don't exist. He adores his sister, and I believe she's equally devoted. He's mad about his work. They say the whole show at Gorrings rests on his shoulders, now. But for girls he has no time. Such a pity, because he's got money and brains and I rather admire his looks myself. He has tremendous strength in his face.'

'I suppose so. He isn't my type,' said Scharlie, thinking of Hugh.

'I daresay he'll fall for some girl one day,'

added Dee optimistically. 'His sort always does, and falls with a wollop.'

Scharlie thought no more about the blunt and rude young man with the horn-rims and the Isotta car. She proceeded to indulge in melancholy retrospection about Hugh and her hopeless love-affair—and the last look he had given her as he drove away.

CHAPTER FIVE

Dinner in the Masons' house was always a stiff and formal affair. Alec Mason liked his food. It must be well cooked and well served to meet with his approval, and under no conditions must an excellent dish be spoiled by aimless chatter, which would remove his concentration on food.

Scharlie, to whom meals were merely necessary and quite uninteresting, hated this enthusiasm which her husband displayed over his meals. Tonight, the first night back from the Wilberforces' house-party, she was, however, glad of the silence which reigned while Alec enjoyed his *sole bonne femme.*

She wanted to be quiet. She wanted to think about Hugh. She wanted to forget Alec. But with all her will-power she could not remove her fascinated gaze from the man who gloated over his dish opposite her.

38

A dinner-jacket did not suit Alec. He was too square and solid. His shirt-front bulged. His bull neck seemed red and even more unattractive than usual in the stiff white collar. He had been, in his first youth, tolerably good-looking. Once, he had a good, fresh complexion, bright blue eyes, and curly hair. Indeed, Scharlie had been shown photographs of the little Alec with a mass of curls stiffly brushed up, the pride and joy of his mother. But now, at forty, there were only a few scanty curls at the back and at the sides. Alec was very bald. Scharlie thought he looked rather absurd with that bald head which gave him such a high domed forehead. Too much rich food, heavy wines, this gluttonous indulgence, had altered the good complexion to a distinctly florid one. His eyes seemed to have grown smaller as his face grew grosser. They had pouches underneath. His cheeks were flabby.

No sensitive beauty-loving girl could have found Alec Mason prepossessing, these days. Scharlie found him even repellent. And when she thought of Hugh—oh, the lithe, clean lines, the fair handsomeness of Hugh! It was intolerable.

Dinner over, they moved into the drawing-room for coffee and liqueurs. Alec must have his Turkish coffee, his brandy or benedictine; his cigar; the final rites of the feast over which he presided like a fat and pompous priest. He sat in a low arm-chair with his podgy legs up on a Queen Anne stool. Scharlie, who often had what she called funny thoughts, thought how the lovely little Queen Anne stool must hate the burden of Alec's unlovely legs.

She took her usual, favourite seat on a hassock beside the open window. During the summer, the hot languorous days which seemed so wasted in London, she spent a lot of her time by the open windows. Yet it was only to see the hard unfriendly pavements and the tall blocks of flats opposite their house in Arlingham Place. Such a limited vision. Scharlie felt, in London, like a bird in a cage. But then she always had this caged sensation, living with Alec.

She was essentially a creature of the open country, the sunshine, made for a beautiful environment. She had loved Gateways, Little Dee's home. But she told herself that if Alec had been there everything would have been spoilt. And if Hugh were here in this rather depressing, ornate drawing-room of the mid-Victorian period—it had been the late Mrs. Mason's home—Arlingham Place would have become heaven.

Alec Mason finished enjoying his food. He now stirred his coffee, sniffed the bouquet of his brandy, and turned his attention to his young wife. It struck him, suddenly, that she had been unusually quiet tonight. It had also struck him, lately, that Scharlie had become more silent with every passing year. When he had married her she had been full of bright chatter. This he had listened to, tolerantly, on their honeymoon. Later he had been testy, short with her; accused her of asking stupid questions, and suggested that she left him in peace. Now, Scharlie no longer bothered to question him about stocks and shares or show any intelligent interest in his business.

Alec Mason was so entirely self-centred and conceited that it never for an instant struck him that she had long since lost all interest in him as a personality. He took it for granted that this pretty child whom he had married—rather against his better judgment—silently respected and admired him and looked up to him as her lord and master. He had had his moments of jealousy. Last summer, for instance, down in Devonshire, at the Torquay Palace Hotel, when she had flirted with that fool of a boy—he had even forgotten the fellow's name—who played tennis with her. He had shown her, then, quite plainly, that Mrs. Alec Mason could not behave in that outrageous fashion and get away with it. He did not think she would ever try to flirt again.

'Well, my dear,' he said, taking the cigar from his mouth and looking at the ash, 'you've come back from your little holiday without much to say for yourself. You haven't told me anything about it.'

'Haven't I?' said Scharlie.

'No. What did you do? Who was there?'

'Oh, a Major Croker, a Mrs. Turner—several people.'

'And what did you do all day? You stayed away from me long enough. I may say, my dear, I was extremely hurt and surprised that you should have left me in bed, ill, in that heartless fashion.'

Scharlie turned her head and gave him an almost ironic little smile.

'You had a bad cold, Alec. I didn't think you were very ill.'

'Well—er—I don't say I was seriously ill, but I was indisposed, and a loving little wife—'

'I don't think I am a loving little wife.' That slipped out before Scharlie could restrain it.

Alec raised his eyebrows.

'My dear Scharlie, come, come, that's not a very nice way to talk to me.'

Scharlie closed her eyes very wearily, then opened them again and looked at Alec. She felt very tired. There was a tired feeling in her heart, her mind, as well as her body. She wondered desperately how long this would go on, this sort of thing. Long years with Alec, trying to attune herself to Alec—and loving Hugh—wanting Hugh.

'Come, my dear,' said Alec, 'let us have a pleasant evening. I can't think why you've taken to sulking. You used not to sulk when I first married you.'

'When one marries,' said Scharlie slowly, 'I don't think one suspects what strange habits

42

one's husband or wife might develop. It's all rather frightening.'

Alec gave her one of his tolerant smiles. A most curious girl, Scharlie! Always had been a little abnormal—over-excitable, in his estimation. But she had toned down. Yes, he considered he had had a very good influence upon Scharlie. She was much more dignified and reticent these days. He was sorry they had no children. A child would have greatly improved her; toned her down a bit more. And he would have liked a son in his own image and likeness.

Once, Scharlie had had her dreams of being a mother. She had liked the idea of having a baby of her own. But all that had died soon after the honeymoon, when her affection for Alec had died too. And now nobody but Scharlie knew how glad she was that she had not been fated to produce a son in the image and likeness of Alec!

'Any young men at Gateways running after you, my dear?' asked Alec.

Scharlie realised that he was trying to be amiable; that this was an attempt on his part at humour. Oh, the pomposity, the self-satisfaction of Alec! Never would he tolerate the thought that she might become seriously involved with any young man!

'Scharlie, what's the matter with you? You haven't answered my question. My dear, you really are preoccupied. Aren't you well? I shan't let you go away by yourself any more. It doesn't seem to do you any good. I think it was very unselfish of me to let you stay on at Gateways so long.'

'Was it?' said Scharlie.

She hunched her knees, put her elbows on them, dug her chin into the palms of her hands. Her eyes stared beyond Alec. They were seeing the long, delicious drawing-room of Little Dee's house, and herself clasped in Hugh's hungry, fierce embrace. She wondered that her heart did not break in two.

'You haven't answered my question yet, Scharlie,' said Alec. 'Who were the young men at the Wilberforce party?'

'A boy of nineteen, named Derek Pole-Hays. A man named Hugh Ellerby—' Scharlie forced herself to speak that name. 'And his fiancée,' she added bitterly.

'Ah well, my dear,' said Alec, 'you don't seem to have enjoyed yourself very much. I daresay you are glad to be home.'

Scharlie laughed. She really could not help it. She laughed, slim shoulders shaking with a kind of helpless, miserable mirth.

Alec Mason laid the stump of his cigar on an ash-tray. He held out his right hand to Scharlie.

'My dear child, what are you laughing at?' he said. 'Come here.'

Two little red spots appeared on Scharlie's cheeks.

'Oh, don't worry me, Alec.'

'Worry you! That's a nice thing to say! 'Pon my soul, you're a most peculiar girl. Come here. I haven't seen you for over a week. Let's have a look at you, Scharlie.'

She shivered.

'There's nothing to look at. I'm all right—just the same as ever.'

Alec began to lose his good humour. He became irritable.

'Scharlie, I don't like this sort of attitude. It's very lacking in—er—wifeliness.'

'Don't start lecturing me, for God's sake, Alec.'

A shocked look crossed Alec's flabby face.

'Really, Scharlie!'

She got up and moved restlessly across the room. The heavy Victorian furniture; tall china-cabinet with the Crown Derby tea-set in it; the walnut grand piano that hadn't been played upon for years; the florid carpet and heavy satin-damask curtains, all chosen by the late Mrs. Mason, offended Scharlie's sight. Her home was oppressive, gloomy. It never pleased her. It had disappointed her four years ago when Alec had brought her to this expensive but so ugly home and told her he could not afford to dispose of his possessions and let her re-decorate and re-furnish the place.

With her modern tastes, her love of the artistic and beautiful, the environment of the house in Arlingham Place increased her unhappiness. Tonight she found it all intolerable, and, because she was in love with Hugh, she found her husband the most intolerable thing of all.

She wanted to escape from his questioning, his prying.

She hoped to get away to her bedroom and pretend to be asleep when Alec joined her. For two years now she had hinted broadly that she disliked sharing a room with him; wanted to sleep by herself. But he had refused to tolerate the thought of separate rooms.

'I consider this separate-bedroom business for husband and wife most improper and ultra-modern,' he had said on several occasions when she had broached the subject. 'My mother and father shared this bedroom for thirty years—from the day they bought the house. It was good enough for them. It should be good enough for us. Your mother did not bring you up with a proper outlook on matrimony, Scharlie.'

Scharlie found it too tiring and too futile to argue with Alec on such subjects as these. But she would have liked to have pointed out that in her estimation it was improper for two people to share a room when one started to hate the other as much as she hated him. That wasn't true marriage. It was a sacrifice of all one's deepest feelings, one's privacy, one's ideals. It was hideously improper.

46

She told herself, tonight, that perhaps it would have been better for her if she had never met and cared for Hugh. Before she went away, it had been difficult to live with Alec. Now, when she loved another man with all the fervour and ardour of her being, it was worse than death.

As she passed her husband's chair, he put out a hand and caught her wrist.

'Where are you going?'

'To bed. I'm tired.'

'Why should you be so tired? You've done nothing, except take a short train journey from Sussex. It's your first night at home after being away from me. The least you can do is stay and talk to me.'

'There's nothing to talk about, Alec.'

'Scharlie, you're being difficult. I do so dislike this sort of mood.'

'I know you don't approve of me, Alec. Let me go.'

For a moment he stared at her. She looked very white and unhappy. Her pallor was accentuated, perhaps, because she was wearing a black lace dinner-gown. She wore a huge artificial flower—scarlet silk—on one shoulder. Her cheek close to the flower looked all the whiter for the contrast.

'My dear girl, I think you must be ill,' said Alec.

'Perhaps I—I am going to have a cold,' she said with an hysterical little laugh.

He pulled her down on to his knee.

'Come and kiss me, my dear,' he said, and touched her cheek with a podgy forefinger in a playful caress.

She wanted to scream. She wanted to hit him. She would have enjoyed hitting that self-satisfied face of his. But instead, she lay against him, mute and stiff.

'This is what hell must be like,' she told herself.

'It's quite a long time since I've had a kiss, my dear,' said Alec. 'Now you're blushing. That's better. You wanted me to put a little colour in those cheeks. Your husband and home are better for you than late nights and cocktails and parties, away.'

For a moment Scharlie bore with him patiently. He kissed her on the lips, twice. Alec's kisses were hearty, smacking things. There was no subtlety in them. As a lover he was obnoxious, and always had been. She knew she could not bear much more of it, and after a moment, she dragged herself out of his arms and sprang on to her feet.

'I don't want to be kissed. I don't want to be touched. Leave me alone, Alec, or I shall go mad!' she said violently.

Alec stared up at her. His face reddened. There was an almost comical expression of surprise in his eyes. Then he rose grandly to his feet. He was very little taller than she was. He said, in a voice that bristled with suspicion:

'Scharlie, what does this mean?'

She put her hand to her head. It ached and throbbed.

She knew that she had gone too far; that she could offer no plausible explanation of her attitude. She had never before shown him, openly, that she loathed his kisses. She had considered it her duty to submit to them. But now that she cared for Hugh so absolutely, her emotions were stronger than her sense of duty. Yes, they were too strong. And they made her stronger than she had ever been in her dealings with her husband. Hitherto he had seemed so much older; he had made her feel like an obedient child.

Tonight the child had grown up—she had become a woman in Hugh Ellerby's arms two days ago. She was not going to obey Alec blindly; suffer Alec's tyranny with patience any more.

'What does this mean?' he repeated.

'It means that I don't want to be kissed and I don't want to be touched,' she said through her teeth. 'Isn't that plain?'

'You're mad, Scharlie.'

'I'm not. I'm just going to be myself in future instead of your slave,' she said. She was trembling; breathless. 'For four years I've answered your beck and call, Alec. Kissed you every time you said: "Come and kiss me." But now I'm through. I'm going to call my soul my own. My body my own too.' She laughed

49

wildly.

The man looked round the room as though seeking for help in the presence of a lunatic. Such laughter, such behaviour, such ideas in this dignified room which reeked of the Victorian submissiveness of his mother, was profane and unseemly.

'Scharlie,' he said, 'I think you must be out of your mind.'

'Because I don't want to kiss you?'

'But—but—l-look here, it isn't right that you shouldn't want to kiss me. I'm your husband.'

'Modern people,' said Scharlie, with another laugh, 'declare that wives never do want to kiss their own husbands.'

Alec gaped.

'Of course you are out of your mind,' he said.

'Very well, Alec. Leave it at that.'

'I don't intend to leave it at that, Scharlie. You've behaved most strangely, and you've insulted me.'

'I'm sorry, Alec. I'll continue to do my level best to run your house in a satisfactory manner, and entertain your guests, and be a companion to you—not that you've ever wanted me to be a real companion. But I will not fall into your arms and kiss you every time you say, "Now you may come and kiss me."'

Silence. Scharlie's eyes were very dark and green. There was a curious light of victory in

50

them. She felt that she had scored a victory, at last, over this bully who had made life a torment for her ever since she married him. He—shocked; amazed; bitterly affronted—stared at her, lips working. He was on the point of losing his temper. But something checked him. It was as though Scharlie's expression conveyed to him the fact that she was no longer a child over whom he could tyrannise; a reed that he could bend to his will. He was a little scared of this new Scharlie; scared of what she might say or do next.

At length he cleared his throat and said huskily:

'You are shocking me—distressing me very greatly. Am I to understand that you dislike kissing me?'

'Yes,' said Scharlie.

Alec swallowed hard. 'And how long have you felt like this?'

'Must we go into details, Alec?'

'Answer my question. How long have you felt like this?'

'For a long time, Alec. If you want the truth, I've never really liked kissing you. I was only eighteen when I married you, and it was all wrong! You and my mother knew so much more about life and everything than I did. It wasn't fair.'

'But what wasn't fair? I've been a good husband to you—faithful—generous. You've had everything you wanted, within reason.'

'Yes, but we weren't—I mean we aren't suited—'

She made a gesture of despair with her slender hands. 'Oh, you must understand in your heart, Alec.'

'I don't understand at all. Only one thing is clear to me. You are sorry that we are married.'

'Yes,' she said in a low voice, 'I am.'

His nostrils dilated. He thrust out his jaw in an aggressive way.

'I see. Well, this state of mind can only have been brought about by some other man. Oh, yes, don't deny it. There is another man in this, somewhere.'

Scharlie lowered her lashes. She did not know what to say. After all, Alec was right about this and she felt a little guilty. Alec's eyes became suffused. With every minute his suspicions of his young wife increased. His temper blazed out.

'What the devil have you been doing while you were away from me? What man do you imagine yourself in love with, eh? Answer me! Don't try to tell me there isn't anybody. You little—!'

'Alec!' she broke in. It was amazing how calm she felt; how able to deal with Alec tonight. Love was making her strong. Yes, whatever else happened, even if she never saw Hugh again, at least her love for him had enabled her to break loose from bonds that

52

had been so hateful all these years. 'It's no good losing your temper and shouting at me. It won't help matters. If you think I'm in love with someone else—go on thinking it. I haven't said so.'

'But I know that you are!' he shouted. 'And I won't have it! I won't have my wife fooling round with any other man. I won't have the name of Alexander Mason dragged in the dust by you.'

Very white, very straight, she stood there before him. She was not even sorry for him. He cut such a poor figure in the role of outraged husband.

'There's no need for you to worry about your name or my morals, Alec,' she said. 'I'm not contemplating an elopement, I assure you.'

'But there is another man—tell me, admit it!' he blustered.

'I shall do nothing of the kind,' she said quietly. 'You are merely being absurd. All this has arisen from the fact that I don't want to kiss you. Well, I'm not going to. And I'm not going to share a room with you any more, either.'

His jaw dropped. He looked ludicrously amazed. He was so angry that he was speechless. Then Scharlie delivered her final ultimatum.

'And I warn you, Alec, that I've come to the end of my tether. If you worry me, nag at me, bully me like you've been doing so long, I shall go away by myself and stay away. Now I am going to tell Edith to move my things into the spare room. Good night.'

She turned and walked quietly out of the room.

Alec Mason sank heavily back into his chair; seized his brandy and gulped it. He needed the stimulant. He had never been so shocked, so outraged before.

He wanted to follow Scharlie. To forbid her to move into the spare room. To force his rights upon her. He felt primitive fury against her for defying him. But that last threat of hers held him back. The sweat broke out over his forehead at the thought of his wife going away. His reputation—his good name in the City— what his friends and relations would think? Good God! it would be a catastrophe if Scharlie ran away.

He had been a fool to marry such a young temperamental girl. He admitted it. But he had done it, and now he must make the best of it. He wasn't going to agree to any kind of separation—let alone divorce. He wasn't going to submit to this separate rooms business either. He'd leave her alone tonight. She was nervy and upset about something. But tomorrow he'd see to things—and make her see them from his aspect too.

He re-lit his cigar. He half closed his eyes. They became slits in the reddish folds of fat. And he thought:

54

'Who's the man? *Who the devil is the man?*'

CHAPTER SIX

One sweltering day towards the end of July, Scharlie enjoyed the rare privilege of shopping in the West End without Alec's car and Alec's chauffeur, who seemed to watch her movements.

Ever since the outburst of a month ago Alec had appeared intensely suspicious of her. He was certain that she had a lover. He had not openly accused her again, but she knew from his attitude that the suspicions were there. She felt, also, that he bribed the servants to spy on her. She had never liked the chauffeur, Benton. He had a mean, ferrety face. Lately Alec insisted upon Benton driving her, here, there, and everywhere, in their Armstrong-Siddeley saloon. It was difficult for her to say she preferred to walk, when only a little time back she had complained of exhaustion; begged Alec for the use of the car.

Then there were the maidservants in the house. The cook was all right; in fact, it was never the same cook for long. And the minor servants did not worry her. But the parlour-maid, Edith, was a spy. Scharlie knew it. She was in Alec's pay. She was a woman of fifty. A gaunt unattractive female with black-rimmed spectacles and a starchy manner. In her young days she had been servant to old Mrs. Mason. Obviously she lamented the marriage of Mr. Alec to this young modern girl who had none of Mrs. Mason's aptitude for marking and counting the linen; for inspecting the table silver; running a staff as Edith considered it should be run. Why, old Mrs. Mason had taken the silver basket up to her bedroom and put it under her bed every night of her life. Edith was quite certain young Mrs. Alec wouldn't care if an army of burglars broke in and looted all the precious silver with the precious Alexander Mason crest.

Oh, undoubtedly Edith was a spy, and would tell Mr. Alec if she heard her mistress telephoning some young man; or report to Mr. Alec that she had been out of the house so many hours and state at what time. Alec wanted to catch her out. Scharlie knew it. That was why he was lying quiet; why he was making no fuss; why he was not venting his rage upon her for refusing him her kisses.

When they were alone, these evenings, she was quieter than ever and he was sulky; surly; seemed to watch her with his suspicious little eyes; to wait for a chance to spring upon her and make her pay for her insubordination.

Scharlie had had no communication with Hugh. She had neither seen him nor heard of him since their good-bye on the tennis-court at Gateways at the end of June. A whole month.

And every day the ache, the need of him, had grown fiercer. She had hoped it would grow less. She had never been in love before, but she had always heard that passion diminished with time and the pain of loving grew less acute. But in her case it had increased. It seemed to thrive, rather than to die of hunger.

She had lost much of her vivacity. She was much too thin. There were always shadows under her eyes, as though she was tired and did not sleep.

She was a little sorry for Alec these days. He was so very disgruntled. His vanity was hurt. He could not understand, even now, why she should dislike his love-making. She supposed that he could not help being unattractive and selfish and pompous. In his way he was to be pitied. But he was forty. He had known what he was about when he had married her.

She was only twenty-two, with all her life before her. She wanted happiness and love and laughter. She could not bear to think that all these things were to fade before her eyes and finish before she had ever really found them. That, spiritually, she was to die before she lived.

In this new, acute state of suspicion Alec seemed to take a delight in keeping Scharlie to himself—in forcing her to submit to solitude with him. This month they had not done any of the things they usually did. Scharlie did not care for his friends and still less for his relations. All the Masons were pompous and had no conversation except food and finance, but occasionally Scharlie enjoyed a game of bridge when she and Alec dined out or somebody dined with them. Occasionally she went to private dances or they gave a little party to some of his business friends. Now and then she came across a kindred spirit; a girl of her own age or a young man who knew how to laugh and make life worth living; make a jest of the things that Alec found so grim, so deadly serious.

But all this month they had spent night after night alone in Arlingham Place. Scharlie had her bedroom to herself. Her nights were her own. Alec could not destroy those moments when she lay alone in the darkness thinking about Hugh.

But she was intensely bored and immensely lonely. Time after time she had been tempted to go to the telephone and ring up Conder Mansions—Hugh's number—speak to him— get into touch with him again.

What a tantalising thing the telephone could be! To know that the one person one wanted beyond anything in the world was at the other end of a line; and in a flash one could be speaking—in touch. Yet one daren't, mustn't! It was cruel.

This afternoon a certain sense of freedom came upon Scharlie. Thank goodness, the car had to be de-carbonised and had gone into dock, and Benton was not there to watch her go into a shop and come out again.

Alec was trying to win her back again by what means he possessed. He had increased her allowance. Last night he had reminded her that it was her birthday on Friday; told her to buy herself a new frock; suggested that they might drive down to the river—to Maidenhead or Henley. The river would be cool and beautiful at this time of year. Scharlie would have loved the river if she could have gone there with anybody in the world but Alec. But she was not even allowed to go away with a woman friend. Alec had been so persistently rude to the girl friends she had possessed before her marriage, none of them was left to her now except Little Dee. They had been young, gay people still in their teens, like Scharlie, and had found Alec a bore. So Scharlie was very much alone, now.

She walked down Bond Street and stood for a moment looking into a hat shop without much real interest in the hats. Then somebody called her name.

She swung round, tingling from head to foot at the sound of a voice that had such power to stir her to the depths of her being.

'Hugh!'

Ellerby stood before her holding his hat in his hand for a moment as he looked at her.

'Little Scharlie!' he said.

'Oh, Hugh!'

59

She couldn't say anything else. Her heart beat violently. To meet him again, see him again, was such ecstasy. In her excitement she dropped a parcel she had been carrying. Simultaneously they stooped to pick it up. Her face almost touched his. She tingled from head to foot. He said:

'My dear, it's good to see you again.'

'It's marvellous to see you, Hugh.'

'Were you just going to buy a hat? If so, I shall insist upon coming in to choose it for you.'

She laughed—the first real joyous laugh for weeks. The ripple of it fascinated the man just as it had fascinated him down at Gateways. He had been working hard since then. Walter Gorring had practically told him that he was to be made a partner next month, immediately after his marriage with Eleanor. There was a great deal to be done on the advertising side of the firm and Hugh was anxious to give his best work. It was an interesting job and he liked his share of admiration as much as anybody else. It pleased him when old Gorring or Henry congratulated him on what he did for the firm.

So hard had he worked, indeed, and so engrossed had he been in his spare time with Eleanor, that he had not really thought much about little Scharlie Mason. Now and then, of course, he had remembered, regretfully, the thrill of her lips and her fervent, youthful passion. He had remembered her with some

60

pity for her unhappiness and some irritation because he was not permitted to console her.

This afternoon, when he was face to face with her again, the old seduction was there; that unconscious appeal which she made to Hugh's senses. She was prettier than ever, he thought. She had grown thinner, but it suited her. Very slim women attracted Hugh. Eleanor was a little on the heavy side. And, lord, he told himself, she looked young! An absolute kid in her grey silk jumper suit; grey straw hat with a wide drooping brim; pearls, and some carnations pinned to her shoulder. She was a poem in grey, with just that touch of red in the flowers and in her lips. She was a little too pale, perhaps. She had an almost delicate look about her with those lilac shadows under her eyes. He wondered if she had been ill.

'Scharlie, you don't look well,' he said.

'Oh, I'm all right. This hot weather in town tires me.'

'Is that all?'

She looked downwards at the pavement. The stiff curly lashes that had intrigued him so a month ago were asking for his kisses now. Yes, the flame was still there. And it burnt up in Hugh's heart as hotly as ever. He knew it. He knew that there was something about Scharlie that was irresistible to him. Dangerous, too!

'Scharlie, have you forgotten—?'

The lashes lifted. The eyes, so green today,

so wistful, glowed at him.

'You know I haven't, Hugh.'

'Neither have I.'

'I'm glad,' she whispered.

'Scharlie, have you—been fretting—I mean, you look rotten—lovely, adorable, but not well!'

He hadn't meant to say any of those things. It was damn' stupid—damn' risky to start this sort of thing all over again. But he was weak. Away from her, under Eleanor's grave, fine influence, he could be a very fine fellow. But it was difficult to be anything but a lover in love when he came in contact with Scharlie.

'I've had a month of absolute hell,' she was telling him.

'Your husband—is he making life unbearable for you?'

'Yes. In a way. I wanted to see you—oh, Hugh, it's been rotten.'

'Poor baby!'

'Don't, Hugh. If you talk to me like that I shall burst into tears.'

His eyes caressed her. How blue they were she thought. How fit and brown, and good to look at, he was!

'Don't let's stand here,' he said. 'Come and have some tea with me.'

'Very well,' said Scharlie recklessly. 'I will.'

She found herself sitting beside him at a little corner table in a tea-shop somewhere off Bond Street. One of these modern mushroom places that spring up in a night. All crude colour; blues and yellows and greens; artistic china; reproduction antique furniture; a blatantly new atmosphere that begs to be advertised as old-world charm.

This particular shop to which Hugh took Scharlie was called 'Elizabeth's Tudor Tea Rooms.' He had not seen it before in his life. Neither had she. Probably neither of them would ever see it again. But today it provided peace and quiet; an hour's solitude. Down below the windows the traffic roared and rolled along. Humanity pursued its course. But Hugh and Scharlie stared into each other's eyes and were lovers again, oblivious of the fact that love was forbidden to them both.

'Scharlie—how lovely you are!' said the man.

She, forgetting to pour out the tea, could only look at him and say:

'You're rather good to look at yourself.'

'I've heard you say that before—on the stairs at Gateways.'

'Yes, I remember. Fancy you remembering.'

'I've forgotten nothing, Scharlie.'

'Sometimes,' she said, 'I wished I could forget. It's terrible to be married and to feel as I have felt about you. Hugh, if you care for me as much as I do for you, I don't know how you're going to be happy with Eleanor.'

He lit a cigarette. Neither of them touched the cakes set before them. The red crept up under his tan as he thought over her last remark. He didn't care for Scharlie quite so much as she cared for him. He loved Eleanor in his way. They had moments together when he was really very much in love with her. He would not find marriage with her at all distasteful. Was he a cur? Was he capable of loving two women at the same time in different ways? He certainly didn't love with the concentration that Scharlie displayed. Poor little girl! She must have fallen very much in love with him down in Sussex. She had made herself quite ill over him. It would be sweet to take Scharlie in his arms and comfort her.

'What has been happening, Scharlie?' he said after a pause. 'You haven't told your husband, I suppose?'

'No—heavens, no! But he thinks I am in love with some man. That's because I've refused to share a bedroom with him any more.'

Her cheeks burnt for an instant, but when the colour died away she looked all the paler. Hugh smoked fiercely for a moment.

'That must have made him suspicious. Why did you—'

'Hugh!' she protested. 'Surely, if you love me, you must understand—you couldn't want me—'

She broke off. The man floundered, a little out of his depth. Women were so intense and selective. Of course, he preferred not to contemplate Scharlie in the arms of her husband—but they had agreed to give the thing a chance. It wouldn't do any good to make Mason suspicious.

'Darling, of course I loathe to think of you living with a man you dislike,' he said.

'You'd dislike him too, Hugh. And it's positive torture to go on living under his roof. We've nothing in common. And now it's worse than it ever was because I care so much for you.'

'Little Scharlie—' Moved, flattered, he leaned near her and covered her hand with his. Her slim fingers clung to his hand frantically.

'Hugh, I don't know how to bear it.'

'It's ghastly for you, my dear,' he said, 'but I don't know what the devil we can do.'

'Nothing, I suppose. I've got to grin and bear it.'

She tried to laugh. She had never whined. She didn't want to whine now.

'Tell me about yourself, Hugh. Don't talk about me.'

'I've been frightfully busy at the firm. And Eleanor and I have been looking for a house. I think we've found one in St. John's Wood.'

'Of course,' said Scharlie in a dull little voice, 'you're going to be married in August.'

'Yes,' he said. He looked at Scharlie with a quick frown. When he was with Scharlie he found it difficult to think squarely about his marriage with Eleanor. A pity one couldn't eat one's cake and have it. He wanted Scharlie; her beauty; her fervour; her passion for himself, which so intrigued and flattered him.

He did not stop to consider that it would be kinder to her in the long run, and wiser from every point of view, to leave her alone. They had decided that they must lead their separate lives. Why not leave it at that? Scharlie could not go on being in love with a man who refused to let her love him.

But Hugh, having had a month of hard work and a virtuous engagement, wanted a little excitement. Wanted to renew the thrill that he had known down at Gateways with Scharlie. He crushed her fingers with his.

'I must see something of you before I am tied up for good and all, Scharlie.'

Her heart missed a beat. That didn't sound quite right somehow. It was a little mean. But she was sincerely in love with this man, and the king could do no wrong.

'Oh, Hugh, Hugh, if you knew how much I'd like to see you—'

'Well, surely we can sometimes.'

'How—how?'

'I must think of a way. Can you ever get away from your husband?'

'Hardly ever. He never leaves me, and I think even the servants spy on me.'

'Oh, hell!' said Hugh. 'That makes it all damn' difficult.'

'I know,' said Scharlie miserably.

'What are you doing on Saturday? Eleanor's got to go to Reigate to an old aunt who is very ill. I offered to go with her, but she thought she'd better let Henry take her.'

'I see,' said Scharlie. 'Henry is the rude young man with horn-rimmed glasses and the Isotta car, isn't he? I mean Eleanor's brother.'

'Yes, is he rude?' asked Hugh vaguely.

'I thought he was, down at Gateways.'

Well, I'm not very fond of brother Henry,' said Hugh moodily. 'He thinks of nothing but work—never seems to me to get an ounce of fun out of life. But the Gorring family rave about him and Nell worships him. I have a shrewd idea brother Henry doesn't care for me either. I'm not sure he isn't suspicious of me—I'm certain he doesn't think me good enough for Eleanor.'

'It seems to me,' said Scharlie with a faint smile, 'we're both under suspicion. Anyhow, you asked me what I was doing on Saturday. Alec wants me to go to Maidenhead for the week-end. It's my birthday on Friday.'

'Is it, Scharlie?' Hugh gave her a long look. 'Poor little baby! How old will she be?'

'Twenty-three.'

'An absolute kid. I'm five years older than you are. I must give you a present. I've never given you one, and this may be the first and last.'

'Oh, Hugh!'

'May I?'

'You know I'd love to have something from you—to keep. I'd like your photograph more than anything.'

'That's impossible, my dear,' he said hastily, and added: 'I wish I had one of you.'

'Why did you ask me about Saturday?' she persisted.

'I was only thinking—as Eleanor was going away—if you and I could have gone out somewhere.'

'Hugh—if only we could! Oh, my dear!'

'I suppose it's impossible?' he said gloomily.

Her face puckered like a child about to weep.

'Oh, it's—it's—damnable! It would be so heavenly, and yet I don't see how I can get out of going away with Alec.'

'No, it's no good losing our heads and upsetting the whole show. But it is a pity.'

'I shall be cross-questioned tonight till I scream,' she said, looking at her wrist-watch. 'I ought to be home now. Alec generally gets home at five.'

'Well, my dear, don't let's make things any worse than they are. I'll take you back.'

He sent the waitress for his bill. In silence they walked out of Elizabeth's Tudor Tea Rooms. They had only been there twenty minutes.

'I'll get you a birthday present and send it to you anonymously,' he said, as they stepped out into the sunlight.

'Thank you,' she said.

She felt sick with misery at the idea of separating from him again—perhaps not seeing him again for weeks. And when she did see him again he would be a married man. She felt as though she were choking.

Hugh signalled a taxi. 'I shall drive some of the way back to your place with you, Scharlie,' he said tersely. 'I must kiss you once again.'

She caught her breath. The look he gave her shivered through her as though it were already a kiss.

In the taxi he drew her into his arms.

She took off her hat and let it drop on to the floor. She didn't care whether it was trampled on or not. She clung to Hugh for a moment in speechless grief; arms about his throat.

'Scharlie!' he said.

He bent his head and put his lips to her mouth. He knew when that kiss ended that he wanted her more madly than ever. And she knew that the fight on her side was too strong. The contest was too fierce, too bitter. She was lost.

'Hugh,' she said, 'I can't bear it. I can't go back to Alec. Hugh, be kind to me—help me—take me away—anything, only don't make me go back to that man.'

CHAPTER SEVEN

The taxi pulled up with a jolt. They were in a traffic jam at a busy corner. Inquisitive eyes from buses, from the other vehicles around them, disturbed their privacy. Hugh let his arms fall away from Scharlie and sat back in his corner.

'Oh, damn!' he growled.

'I can't bear it, Hugh,' she said.

He looked at her gloomily.

'Oh, my dear, it's rotten, but what on earth can I do? You ask me to take you away—but you know how impossible that is.'

She sat still and upright on the edge of the seat; a clenched hand pressed to either cheek.

'I'm sorry. I must apologise—for giving way like that.'

'Oh, my dear—darling little Scharlie—don't apologise, for the love of heaven.'

She looked at him and shivered.

'But I must. I—oughtn't to have asked you to take me away. I felt so desperate for a moment, that's all. I'm all right now. The traffic jam has been quite useful.' She tried to laugh, and, stooping, picked up her hat and crushed it down on her head. 'I can't cling furiously to you and howl for help with various bus-conductors and old ladies peering at us.'

She was the gay and gallant Scharlie again.

70

He was relieved. He could deal with this Scharlie more easily than with Scharlie uncontrolled.

'Darling child,' he said, taking her hand. 'I wish you wouldn't think I don't *want* you to cling onto me and howl for help, as you call it. I do. I'd like to take you and never let you go. Scharlie, believe me, kissing you again just now has decided me I can't go another month without seeing you or holding you in my arms.'

Her fingers wound about his. Her eyes flashed a swift, warm look at him.

'Do you mean that?'

'Yes.'

'You do love me a little?'

'Good heavens, my dear, too much.'

'Then what are we going to do?'

'Meet somehow, somewhere.'

'I see.'

She nodded and bit her lip. He wanted her in his way; a funny way. Not her way. She would have gone with him gladly; faced a divorce; lived in a cottage; and, being a very young woman in love, would be content to live on love. He looked at things more practically. He did not want to take her away and figure as a co-respondent in a divorce case. It would ruin his prospects at Gorrings. And there was always the unfortunate Eleanor. Scharlie was ashamed when she remembered Eleanor.

'I really am sorry, Hugh, for being so hysterical just now,' she said in a low voice. 'Of

71

course—there's too much against it—you can't take me. I'll have to go back to Alec and stick things.'

'I wish to God it could have been otherwise,' the man said, with a flash of genuine feeling. And his passion was genuine enough when he put his lips against the slender white hand he held. 'We might have been awfully happy, darling. We're made for each other.'

The taxi moved on. They rolled smoothly through Hyde Park towards Knightsbridge. He pulled her into his arms again.

'Kiss me again, Scharlie.'

'No—I'd better not.'

'Yes, do.'

'I—I can't think straight when you kiss me, Hugh.'

'Never mind, poor baby.' The selfish sensual male was uppermost in Hugh again. 'Scharlie—yes, dear, yes, yes, kiss me.'

She gave way. She wanted to. The hat came off again, and she clung close to him, shutting her eyes.

They came quickly to Kensington. Scharlie sat up straight and combed her hair, two red spots burning her cheeks. The man lit a cigarette and blew a cloud of smoke through his nostrils.

'Look here, my dear, I'll try and fix a way— a day—when we can meet, and you must see if you can manage it. It's all wrong, of course. You're married and I'm a disloyal brute to

Nell, but I'm not trying to excuse myself, only to tell you that I do love you and want you, sweetheart.'

'Yes, Hugh.' She was almost inarticulate. Every second was bringing her nearer Arlingham Place.

'Well, shall we take what we can get out of life? I mean—if we can do a dance or a show together, somewhere—will you come?'

'Yes,' she whispered.

'You want to?'

'You know that.'

'Yes, I think I know, darling. I hate you to be miserable. I'll try and make up for it all somehow. If it can't be managed on Saturday—I'll work out a scheme for next week.'

'It would be lovely.'

'I'll 'phone, shall I?'

'Yes,' she said recklessly. 'Alec is always out, in the City, in the mornings, and if Edith spies and listens, she'll have to. I won't say anything on my side that she can understand, anyhow.'

'Right-oh. We must be discreet, mustn't we?'

'Oh, yes,' said Scharlie dully.

'Where shall I drop you, darling?'

'Here—this corner. I'll walk the rest of the way.'

'Sure?'

'Yes. I daren't drive up to my house.'

'Then I'll go on in the taxi to my digs.

Good-bye, sweetheart. Till we meet again. We must. I'll 'phone.'

He leaned out of the window and spoke to the driver. The taxi pulled up. Hugh opened the door for Scharlie. She stepped out and slammed the door after her. She stood on the pavement an instant, screwing up her eyes in the bright sunshine. Her lips quivered piteously.

'Good-bye, Hugh.'

'Buck up, darling,' he said, and smiled at her.

She smiled back and waved a hand. The taxi moved on.

She walked round the corner to Arlingham Place. She felt unutterably depressed. She had wanted, terribly to see Hugh again; to feel his arms about her and his kisses on her mouth. She had gained her wish quite unexpectedly. But what happiness had it brought? Only the fleeting thrill and passion of a moment. And now reaction, misery. A flat sense of loneliness; of intolerable depression because the Moment was gone. Hugh was gone.

Was it worth it? Was love for a man worth all this aching unhappiness? Perhaps not. Scharlie could not reason it out nor find any sensible solution to a problem which has tormented the mind and heart of woman from time immemorial. She only knew that Hugh was in her blood and that she could not give him up. She was weak and could not stop

74

wanting him. She could not stop even for the sake of Eleanor Gorring.

'I suppose it's rather beastly of me,' she thought. 'And sinful. And that's why I'm getting no happiness out of it.'

But if Hugh telephoned to her, arranged a meeting, she couldn't refuse to go.

When she reached home she went up to her bedroom; took off her things; put on a dressing-gown, and lay down on her bed for half an hour's rest before she changed for dinner. She put her arms behind her head and closed her eyes. She relived the last hour; the last, long kiss that Hugh had given her. A shudder went through her. She bit fiercely at her lip, but the tears would roll down her cheeks.

'Hugh—Hugh—' She whispered his name to herself repeatedly.

The more she thought about him, the more convinced was she that she couldn't endure life without him; that it wouldn't be possible for him to marry Eleanor Gorring in August. He was trying to do the right thing. But was it the right thing—for a man to marry a girl he did not love in every way? Wouldn't it be right for him to break with Eleanor and take her, Scharlie, away?

'Of course he would if he was as much in love with me as I am with him,' Scharlie reflected. And winced at that thought. Hugh was not so much in love as she was. No—she must admit that. It hurt dreadfully. And she deserved to be hurt, because she was married and he was engaged. This was her punishment.

And now she must face a ghastly week-end with Alec; a wretched birthday—with Alec.

She was in torment.

And the man for whom she was tormented drove to his flat in Conder Mansions in a restless irritable state of mind and decided that women play the devil with a man's nerves.

Little Scharlie was altogether too attractive, he considered. He had very nearly lost all sense of proportion and propriety when he had held her, kissed her, in that damned taxi. No man could resist her—she was so appealing, so unhappy, poor little girl. But take her away— face a divorce—lose all that he had worked for in Gorrings—no, that was not to be contemplated.

He had a couple of short drinks and felt better. Bathed, changed into a dinner-jacket, and went round to his fiancée's home, where he was dining tonight. There were few nights that he did not dine with the Gorrings nowadays.

He tried to put Scharlie out of his mind. It was a good deal easier to Hugh Ellerby to be a practical, level-headed fellow when he was removed from a woman's physical presence, her allure. He could think of Scharlie with passion; with longing; but it was all quite under control now. It was astonishing, really, how rapidly even the thought of her faded once he was away from her. He wanted to see her again, but he was not at all sure he would fix that meeting. After all, it was not giving Eleanor a square deal. He must think carefully over things before he acted, anyhow. He would go to Aspreys and buy a little birthday present for Scharlie tomorrow. Poor, pretty Scharlie!

He was still thinking of her regretfully—and with some uneasiness—when he reached the Gorrings' house in St. John's Wood.

Eleanor was not yet down. She was still dressing. When Hugh was shown into the library, he found Walter Gorring there, alone with his son.

The two men were in evening dress. The head of Gorrings, one of the biggest book publishing firms in England, sat in a deep saddlebag chair, reading a paper. Henry Gorring stood with his back to the mantelpiece, a cigarette between his lips. He was making pencil-notes in the margin of a manuscript.

Hugh regarded the younger Gorring with a slightly scornful look. Was there ever a moment that Henry did not have a pen or pencil and paper of some kind in his hand? He seemed to live only for his work. It was highly commendable, of course, but he seemed to Hugh an intolerable prig; a cold fish-like individual with none of the natural foibles or follies of youth. What was he? Barely twenty-nine, and concentrating on business—almost ferociously concentrating upon it. Why? Why did he deny himself any of the pleasures he might have at his age with his money, his position?

Why didn't he care for women? Had he had an unfortunate affair with some girl which had embittered him? Hugh did not know. Henry was the member of the family about whom Hugh knew least and liked least. He was certain, as he had once told Scharlie, that Henry did not like or approve of him. Henry would not understand about Scharlie, for instance; or the hot blood that runs swiftly through a man's veins and makes him crazy for a woman's lips; disloyal against his better judgment.

Hugh pictured Henry discovering that the man engaged to his sister was having an intrigue with another girl. Heavens! What a row there'd be—what a rupture! Henry adored Eleanor. She seemed the one person on earth, the one thing except his work, for which he had any real affection.

The two Gorrings looked up and greeted Hugh as he strolled into the library.

'Hello, Hugh,' heartily from the old man who liked and believed in his daughter's good-looking fiancé. Hugh had charming manners, and was always at his best with the old man, and Walter Gorring liked that. He deplored the fact that the majority of young folk in these

78

days failed in courtesy.

'Evening,' from Henry Gorring. He then became absorbed in his manuscript again.

Hugh pulled out his cigarette-case.

'Well, my boy, and how goes it?' asked Walter Gorring.

'Oh, all right, sir.'

'Nell will be down in a moment. She got hung up at Lady Winthorpe's party and she's late dressing. Have a drink. Henry, my boy, give Hugh a drink.'

'Not for me, thank you, sir,' said Hugh.

Henry glanced at him briefly—a look which said: 'Good job too'—and continued to make notes on the margin of the paper he was holding.

The Gorrings, father and son, were of similar build. Tall, sparse, erect. Both had the same stubborn chins and broad, sensitive nostrils. But there the similarity ended. Walter Gorring with his grey, curling hair, blue, kindly eyes, so like Eleanor's, and courtly manner, was a man who had taken life easily, although he had worked hard enough. His character in business had always been unimpeachable. His word was his bond. He was the father of struggling journalists, almost a patriarchal figure in his world of publishers. He had no enemies and innumerable friends.

But Henry, his son, was strangely different; a reticent, difficult man, with more cynicism than kindliness in the clever grey eyes behind

79

the horn-rimmed glasses. Thin-lipped, even austere, he made few friends, although his character in business was as integral as his father's. He was respected. He was also admired. There was no doubt he had twice the brains Walter Gorring had—and used them.

Among the staff in the office where Hugh had worked in constant touch with Henry Gorring for some considerable time there were men who literally adored Henry. Those, perhaps, to whom he had shown a softer side than Hugh had ever seen. A little clerk, for instance, with a wife dying of some incurable disease. Henry Gorring had taken the trouble to investigate the matter, and had himself seen that the woman was put into a convalescent home and the little clerk's salary was raised. And there were other things, probably that nobody knew about. Henry was like that. He made little show about what he did.

It struck Hugh that quite possibly Henry Gorring had never opened up to him in any way, not only because they were poles apart in temperament, but because Henry was jealous. Yes, jealous of his sister's love for her promised husband. Eleanor was one of the few people on earth about whom Henry really cared. There was no gainsaying that fact. He did not want to see her married; have her taken away from him. He resented Hugh.

On many occasions Hugh would discuss Henry with Eleanor.

'He's such a queer chap—so unlike the rest of you. What is it, Nell? And why doesn't he like me?'

And Eleanor laughed and answered:

'Silly old boy! Of course Henry likes you. But he is an undemonstrative person. Perhaps he is unlike the rest of us. Dad and I are alike but I think Henry is most like my mother. She was a wonderful woman. People found her most magnetic. But she was hard to know. Henry has inherited that reserve of hers. But when you get through it there's nobody in the world like him. You've no idea what a fine person Henry is.'

Hugh told himself, rather sarcastically, that he certainly had no idea what a fine person Henry was. Henry was a prig.

'I'm sure he's been disappointed in love, Nell,' on another occasion he had said to his fiancée.

Eleanor, with one of her moments of strange reticence which she rarely produced for her lover, had answered guardedly:

'Perhaps there was a woman—a couple of years ago—somebody Henry cared for terribly. She let him down. And that sort of thing isn't good for a nature like his. But we never talk about it. And I'm under oath never to tell anybody—even you, darling.'

Hugh investigated no further. He wasn't really interested. Henry Gorring must be a fool. Why let one unhappy love-affair embitter his whole life? There were as good fish in the sea as came out of it. Women like Eleanor—like Scharlie Mason—and a good many others too.

Tonight, Walter Gorring was, as usual, charming to his future son-in-law.

'Henry and I were just talking about you, my boy,' he said with a smile. 'You've done very well this last month, Hugh. You're a worker, and I must say very few young men are these days. In fact, there are one or two things Henry and I want to discuss with you later on this evening.'

Hugh's handsome face flushed a little. His pulses quickened.

'Oh, indeed, sir?' he said.

Henry looked up from his paper.

'My father thinks it would be a good plan, Hugh, if we get out a contract and make you a partner the beginning of next month,' he said. He had a clear, precise way of speaking which irritated Hugh.

But Hugh, with a vision of a very considerable rise in his fortunes—a partnership in one of the biggest publishing firms in England—forgot to be irritated by Henry tonight. Hands in his pockets, eyes bright, he looked at Henry with unaccustomed friendliness.

'I say, this is very decent of you both,' he said. And he was in that moment what he looked—an attractive eager boy who had his

82

weaknesses but was without any real vice.

Henry had no use for him. He was quite certain that Hugh Ellerby was not good enough for Eleanor. He wished Eleanor had never fallen so deeply in love with the fellow. Without having any definite proof, he was positive that Hugh Ellerby was not made of loyal stuff—would not be above an intrigue with a woman behind Eleanor's back. It was sheer guesswork on Henry's part. But he had, occasionally, rare flashes of insight into the characters of those he met. However, Eleanor loved the chap, and there it was. For Eleanor's sake Henry strove to put aside his prejudices and to accept Hugh as one of the family.

'I thought we weren't going to alter the present situation at the office until I—until Eleanor and I—er—'

Hugh broke off with some embarrassment. Old Gorring said:

'We did propose waiting for your marriage, my boy. But there have been unexpected developments. Haynes, whom you know has been my general manager for years, is retiring next week. He's too old for the job. Like I am,' he laughed. 'And it is much better for the old to give place to the young. Fresh brains, fresh vigour—that's what sets a business on fire. Well, Haynes is going, and Henry and I, having talked things over, propose that you take over the general management next week—under Henry's directorship, of course. And that will start you off as a junior partner. Isn't that the idea, Henry?' He turned to his son.

Henry took the cigarette from his mouth and regarded it reflectively.

'That's it,' he said.

'This is tremendously good of you both,' said Hugh.

'It's only a month earlier than we anticipated,' added old Gorring. 'After all, you're as good as in the family now, my boy. You and Nelly are being married next month. We take it for granted you're not going to split before the date fixed, eh? Ha! ha!'

His eyes twinkled at Hugh, who became very red, and bit hard at his lip.

'Good God, no!' he said.

The thought of Scharlie faded into the background. Her beauty, her youth, her physical allure, became frail, shadowy things, without substance. This was the substance— this splendid chance the Gorrings were giving him. And Eleanor loved and believed in him. What a swine he'd be to let her down! What a fool he'd be to chuck away his own chances, because of a temporary infatuation.

He was going to prove himself worthy of the trust this family was putting in him. Poor little Scharlie! He'd send her that birthday present, and there the thing must end.

Eleanor came into the room. She looked her best in a cream lace dress, with a little lace coat to match and her favourite pink carnations pinned to her shoulder. Her cheeks were glowing, fresh from her bath. Her grave blue eyes looked at her lover with great tenderness.

'Sorry I'm so late,' she said. 'How are you, Hugo, my dear?'

'We've just been telling your young man, Nelly, my dear, that we're taking him into partnership next week,' said Walter Gorring.

Eleanor reached her lover's side. She put both her hands in his.

'Hugo! But how lovely!'

He looked at her with very real gratitude for her beautiful affection and devotion to him.

'I don't deserve it, Nell—I'm simply overwhelmed!'

'Of course you deserve it, darling.' She pressed his hands tightly and turned round to her father and brother. 'Doesn't he, Daddy? Doesn't he, Henry?'

'Of course,' said Mr. Gorring. 'He's done very good work for us.'

'Of course,' echoed Henry.

Hugh caught the younger Gorring's gaze for an instant. And his enthusiasm was temporarily checked by the undeniable hostility that lay in the eyes of Eleanor's brother.

'I swear he doesn't believe in me,' he thought moodily. 'Well, I'll show him that he's wrong—damn his priggishness!'

CHAPTER EIGHT

Hugh's birthday present to Scharlie reached her by post after Alec Mason had gone to the Stock Exchange. Scharlie was still in bed. She never had breakfast; only coffee and rolls, French fashion, in her room, at 9 o'clock.

She was twenty-three today. She might have been seventeen, sitting up in bed in a short satin jacket, red brown hair ruffled over her head. She hated shingle-nets and never wore them. Her hair curled naturally. She had no need to think about waves that must be set and preserved.

So far it had not been a very joyous birthday. A letter from her mother who was still in South Africa, wishing her many happy returns of the day and saying that a small gift would follow. Most of the letter was a rhapsody on a middle-aged Colonial about whom Mrs. Croft was spreading her toils.

'Mother seems to enjoy life much more than I do,' Scharlie told herself with some cynicism.

Little Dee had written. She always remembered Scharlie's birthday. And Alec had come pompously into her bedroom before he left; kissed her, which Scharlie had very much disliked, and presented her with a new diamond and onyx ring—a beautiful costly jewel. He had put it on her finger and Scharlie had not troubled to take it off. It looked very nice there. Rings showed to advantage on Scharlie's pretty slender fingers. But it brought her cold comfort. It meant nothing.

Her birthday meant nothing. Everything was flat and depressing. Hugh had not written. Had not sent that present he had promised. She didn't want diamonds from him. A bunch of roses would have satisfied her. It was just the absurd, sentimental craving for *something* from him.

He had forgotten her. And he had not 'phoned her as he had promised. Every day since she had seen him she had waited for that telephone call. Every time the telephone bell had rung, her heart had jumped. But it had never been Hugh.

She rose, bathed, and put on a new silk jumper suit, warm coppery brown like her hair; beautifully cut. But she dressed mechanically. It didn't seem to matter what she put on. Tomorrow Alec meant to drive her down to Maidenhead for the weekend. She didn't want to go. She was aching, breaking for a word, a sign from Hugh.

Then by the later post came a packet. She unwrapped it eagerly. This, surely, was from Hugh. A little box marked Aspreys. A tortoiseshell cigarette-case. A fragile pretty thing. And no name with it. No card. It was from Hugh. He had said he would send her the present anonymously.

The world changed. Scharlie's spirits mounted. She swung, in her excitable childish fashion from misery to delight. She filled the tortoiseshell case with cigarettes and put it in her bag. She smoked many more cigarettes than usual just for the joy of lifting her new case from the bag and using it.

She felt sure that Hugh would 'phone to her today. Yes, surely he would not let her birthday pass by without speaking a word to her. She yearned to hear that husky voice of his say: 'Scharlie, little Scharlie, I love you!'

She did not leave the house that day. It was absurd. She felt she was being ridiculous and could not help herself. She did not want to miss that call when it came. But it never came. She wandered about the big, gloomy house in an agony of impatience, fingers clutching at the cigarette-case as though it were a mascot. But Hugh did not 'phone.

By the time Alec came home she was as flat and depressed as she had been earlier in the morning. Alec wanted to take her out to dine; to celebrate her birthday by a little dinner at the Carlton. He had been very affable first thing this morning. As though attempting to show her that he wanted peace between them—wanted to renew their old intimacy. She shuddered at the thought.

She was half-dressed sitting in her bedroom when he came home, disconsolately staring at her nails, which she had been polishing.

Well, my dear,' said Alec, advancing upon her, 'and how's the little birthday girl?'

'I feel rotten,' she said, without looking at him. 'Don't worry me, Alec.'

He frowned at her.

'What the devil's wrong now?'

She shrugged her shoulders.

'Well, get dressed, and let's have a little dinner,' he said.

'I'd rather not, Alec.'

'But don't be so stupid. You've complained that I've stuck in the house for nights this last month. You told me last night that I was horrible and suspicious and that you resented my attitude. Well, here I am trying to show you that I—I'd like to be friends with you again. You might at least meet me half way. I have acted very generously considering your treatment of me.'

She lifted her long lashes and looked at him an instant. Poor Alec! He was to be pitied. In his own estimation he had been very ill-treated and after his own lights he was acting generously. Yet she could not meet him half way. This tremendous passion for another man which had come into her life made it for ever impossible for her to hold out a hand to Alec Mason again.

'I am really sorry, Alec, but I don't want to celebrate my birthday. I don't want to do anything—don't want to go away tomorrow— Oh, I wish I could go away by myself—!' She suddenly lost control and burst out crying; the noisy, pitiful crying of an unhappy child.

Alec stared at her for a moment in silence. He alternated between bewilderment and suspicion. He could not believe that Scharlie would behave like this—become so hysterical and nervy—unless there was another man in her life. Her crying irritated him. What did the girl want? That diamond ring had cost him a pretty penny, and here she was howling, instead of wearing the jewel with delight, anxious to go to a smart hotel and show it off.

'Damn it, Scharlie,' he said testily. 'I don't see what you've got to cry about. And I'm hanged if I'm going to let you go away by yourself. The last time you went away without me you came back in a most disgraceful mood. It shan't be allowed to happen again.'

She covered her face with her hands and went on sobbing desperately.

Alec moved to her dressing-table, picked up one of her ivory-backed hairbrushes, and tapped it in an angry way on the palm of his hand. Then his gaze lighted on a tortoiseshell cigarette-case which lay on a glass tray holding a few small toilet requisites. He put down the brush and picked up the case. He regarded it perplexedly.

'Where did this tortoiseshell cigarette thing come from?' he asked.

Immediately Scharlie's hands fell away from her face. Her eyes were swollen with weeping;

90

her mouth was quivering. In an ungovernable moment she snatched the case from his hand.

'Don't touch that. It's mine,' she said.

Alec became very red.

'Really, Scharlie!' he protested.

She breathed fast, clasping the case between nervous fingers; cheeks hot and wet with tears.

'Where did that case come from?' Alec demanded.

'It was sent to me for my birthday.'

'By whom?'

'A friend of mine.'

'Man or woman?'

'I won't be cross-questioned by you, Alec!' said Scharlie breathlessly.

His eyes were slits now; the muscles of his face working. All the old suspicions were awake; bristling.

'If you can't tell me the name of the person who sent you this case, then obviously it's a man and you are ashamed to own up to it,' he said.

'Oh, if you want the truth, have it!' she flashed back. 'It was sent to me by a man. A birthday present. And why shouldn't I have a birthday present from a friend of mine?'

'A lover, perhaps,' said Alec Mason through his teeth.

'No!' she gave a miserable laugh, 'he isn't my lover.'

'But you'd like him to be—eh? You little liar! The fellow *is* your lover I daresay. And I daresay this is the cause of your treatment of me lately. You've been meeting this man behind my back. Who is he? Tell me his name!'

Scharlie sprang to her feet.

'I tell you I won't be cross-questioned!' she said.

'And I won't have my wife receiving presents from other men!'

He suddenly snatched the tortoiseshell case from her hand. She gave a little choked cry and caught his arm.

'Give it back to me! How dare you take away my present!'

'So much in love, are you?' he sneered.

'Alec, you've no right—'

'It's you who have no right to accept presents from other men.'

'A cigarette-case! Good heavens! You're mid-Victorian, Alec; like everything else in this—this horrible house!' Her control was snapping again. The tears poured down her cheeks. 'You can't bully me—tyrannise over me—like this! Hundreds of married women these days receive presents from other men— innocently!'

'Innocently, indeed!' he sneered again. 'Men are not likely to carry on an innocent friendship with a girl as pretty as you are, Scharlie. You're my wife, and you're going to remember it!'

Before she could prevent him he dropped

the tortoiseshell case on the floor and stamped upon it with the heel of his boot. The delicate, brittle thing powdered under that grinding heel.

Scharlie stared at the fragments for an instant in silence; stupefied. Then, when she realised that Hugh's beloved present—that one and only pitiful thing which she had to comfort her—had been smashed; that she had been robbed of it by this tyrant of a husband whom she hated with all her soul, her fury knew no bonds.

In blind rage and misery she struck out at Alec with her clenched hands.

'You beast! You utter beast! To smash it—break it like that! I'll never forgive you—never!'

He was startled by her outburst, by the violence of her grief over the loss of the case which he was certain had been given to her by another man—a man whom she loved. He, too, lost control. He hit her suddenly—a sharp blow across her face with the flat of his hand. She lost her balance, swayed, and crumpled up on the rug at his feet.

'Perhaps that will teach you not to fool round with other men,' Alec Mason said. He gave her an uneasy look, but added; 'And my last words to you, Scharlie, are these—any more of this behaviour and you can get out. Yes—get out of my place and go to your lover, and be damned to the pair of you!'

CHAPTER NINE

At a quarter-past seven that same evening, Hugh Ellerby was standing before his dressing-chest, tying a black tie. He was fully dressed except for his jacket. He looked handsome and happy and he was humming a little tune. This afternoon he had gone over the new contract with the Gorrings. It was going to be a fine thing to be a junior partner in the firm. He was very pleased with life at the moment; pleased with everything.

He had felt a qualm about little Scharlie when he had sent off that cigarette-case from Aspreys. He hoped she wasn't too unhappy. It would have been very pleasant if he could have become her consoler—tasted a little more of the honey that lay on her lips. But things were moving too rapidly with the Gorrings. He couldn't afford to fool round with Scharlie now.

Eleanor was a darling, too. Yesterday afternoon they had chosen some furniture for their house. They had been very happy. In the car, driving back to St. John's Wood, she had emerged a little from her habitual reticence. He had never known her to be more responsive; more passionate. He had been touched and stirred. He was going to make a good husband to Eleanor and never look at another woman, once she was his wife.

Grafton, the butler-valet of his service flat, came into his room. Hugh finished tying his tie and turned to him.

'Everything ready, Grafton?'

Hugh was giving a little dinner in his flat tonight. For Eleanor and brother Henry. Brother Henry as chaperon, of course. Even in these days, it was not quite the thing for a girl to dine alone with her fiancé in a bachelor-flat.

'Please, sir,' said Grafton, 'there's a lady wanting to speak to you.'

'A lady,' said Hugh. 'Miss Gorring, you mean?'

'No, sir,' said the man, 'not Miss Gorring. A young lady I haven't seen before.'

Hugh frowned and slipped into his dinner-jacket. Who the devil could it be, he wondered. One of the typists from Gorrings, perhaps. But surely not at this time. Then the thought leapt into his mind: Scharlie! Was it possible she had come round? With a thrill of trepidation, Hugh walked into his sitting-room.

The curtains had not been drawn. The summer sun was still streaming brilliantly through the window. At one end of the room a gate-legged oak table had been laid for three. Grafton had done good work with the carnations that Hugh had purchased in Eleanor's honour. Everything looked very nice, A champagne bottle on the sideboard in its ice-pail, all ready. Hugh liked to do people well when he dined them.

Leaning with her back to the mantelpiece stood Scharlie.

Hugh shut the door behind him and looked at her. So it was Scharlie. And she was in some distress, too, so it appeared. She wore no hat. A fur-trimmed grey velvet evening-coat over a grey georgette evening-gown. Very pretty; Scharlie could not fail to look otherwise; but not quite as pretty as usual. Her lovely colour was gone. She was pale. Her eyelids were rimmed with pink. She looked as though she had been crying violently.

She put her bag on the mantelpiece and held out both her hands to him.

'Hugh!' she said, with a break in her voice.

He walked towards her slowly. The gesture with which he took her outstretched hands was mechanical rather than impulsive.

'Scharlie! My dear—you—I mean, what's happened?'

'I had to come. I can't stand it any longer. I'm half off my head. Hugh! Save me—save me from that man!'

'Scharlie! my dear, what has happened?'

'He hit me,' she said through clenched teeth. 'He hit me, Hugh.'

'Hit you?' Hugh stared at her aghast. 'You mean your husband—Mason hit you?'

'Yes'—she pointed to her left cheek—'hit me there.'

96

'But why?'

She made an effort to control herself. An effort not to break down and cry again as she had cried at Arlingham Place. She told Hugh, rather incoherently, what had taken place between Alec and herself half an hour ago.

'When he smashed my case—the case you'd given me, Hugh—I went mad. I lost my temper completely. I know it. And he hit me! If he'd done anything but that—I'd have forgiven it.'

In shocked silence Hugh looked down at her. He said, quickly: 'It was a damnable thing to do. Damnable for a man to hit a woman. It's incredible. But I suppose he was jealous. I oughtn't to have sent you a present.'

'Why should I be tyrannised over like that?'

'No reason, but why did you let him know it was a man who gave it to you?'

'I don't know. It just came out somehow.'

'But you didn't tell him my name?'

'No,' said Scharlie slowly.

Her lashes flickered a little. She stared up at him; a frown between her brows. He puzzled her. His voice, his manner puzzled her. This was not quite the lover who had driven her home in a taxi a week ago. Not quite the ardent consoler she had expected to find. Her heart jerked unevenly. The colour came to her cheeks and went again.

'Hugh,' she said, 'are you angry with me for coming to you? You gave me this address—said if ever I wanted you—'

'Yes, of course,' he broke in. His own face reddened slightly. He squeezed her hands. 'But it's rather unexpected—I mean—I don't quite know what to say or do.'

She looked up at him miserably.

'You don't know what it's been like living with Alec lately. I tried to tell you a bit when we met the other day. But tonight he was worse than he's ever been.'

'And you just cleared out?'

'Yes. He meant to take me out to dinner to celebrate my birthday—what a birthday!' She gave a wretched laugh. 'But when I was dressed I made up my mind I couldn't bear it—after that blow in the face. I just took a taxi and came round here to you. I had to come to you. You mean everything—everything, Hugh.'

He dropped her hands. He turned from her and stared at the table that was laid for three.

'My God!' he thought. 'Here's the dickens of a mess. Eleanor, Henry coming—and if they find her here—!'

Scharlie's spirits had been low enough when she came. And now they sank to zero. Hysteria gave place to dull misery.

'Hugh,' she said, 'you don't want me here. You are angry with me for coming. I can see it. Oh, Hugh!'

He turned back to her quickly. The poor, pretty little face was so tragic, it roused some tenderness which broke through the crust of the man's selfishness.

98

'Scharlie, darling child, I'm not angry, only—'

He broke off. She had thrown her coat on the sofa and was in his arms. Slender, fragrant, seductive in the delicate chiffon dress, with the remembered perfume of her hair against his lips. He should have been firm, and dealt kindly but wisely with her now. But he was weak, and the sensual side of him could not resist Scharlie's allure. He held her tightly. Her arms went round his throat. She clung to him with passion.

'Hugh, Hugh, I've been frantic with misery. Be kind to me. Help me—tell me what to do—I love you so!'

'Little Scharlie—poor little thing!'

He kissed her wet lashes and then her lips in hungry passion. It was not passion that she needed, really, now. It was his tenderness, his sympathy, and his protection. But because she was in love with him she let him hold and caress her as he wished. His kisses eased some of the aching misery in her heart.

But after a few minutes the man drew away from her. He caught a handful of her curly hair in his hand almost roughly.

'Scharlie, this won't do. Look here! There'll be the hell of a mess up in a moment if we don't take care. My fiancée—Eleanor—and her brother are coming here to dine. They're due at seven-thirty. It's twenty five past now.'

Scharlie leaned back in his encircling arm.

'Hugh, don't send me away—'

'But you can't stay here, my dear old thing. It will be a frightful mess if you do. You can't be found here in my flat by the Gorrings. Think what *they'd* think.'

Scharlie bit her under-lip. Her face was glowing from his kisses. Her eyes were brilliant and beautiful.

'Hugh, I love you so frightfully that I can't do without you. And you love me. You've said so. Don't make me go back to Alec now.'

'I don't want to make you go back to him, but I've got no choice.'

'Then you don't really love me?'

Passion had cooled in Hugh. He was master of himself and his senses again. Scharlie was charming, and he had every wish to keep her here. But he also had a very clear vision of what might happen if she stayed. The row there'd be. The misunderstandings—the suspicions. There was that contract he had gone over with the Gorrings this afternoon. Damn it, he'd be a fool to let any feeling for Scharlie ruin his career. He became entirely selfish and a little brutal.

'I do love you, Scharlie, but not in the way you want me to,' he said.

She stared at him dumbfounded.

'What do you mean?'

He shifted uneasily from one foot to another, his hands in his pockets.

'I mean you want me to love you to the

exclusion of everything else, and I can't. I've got Eleanor and my job.'

Silence a moment. Scharlie felt that something in her died. Her heart hurt so badly, it was a sheer physical pain.

'You see, my dear old thing,' added Hugh, 'you're like most women—you're swayed by sentiment and you forget the practical side of things. We agreed, anyhow—didn't we—that we wouldn't muck up our lives over this affair. And, after all, it hasn't been a very serious affair. There's still time for us to break with each other and do the right thing by those we belong to. And we must.'

Again silence. She was speechless. He wished she wouldn't look at him with those stricken eyes. His forehead felt wet. He fumbled in his pocket for a cigarette. It was very trying. He didn't want to be a brute to Scharlie. She was an absolute darling and greatly to be pitied. But she was landing him in the dickens of a hole. This was altogether too perilous. And now that the crucial moment was come when he must definitely choose between Eleanor—his job; and philandering with Scharlie; the former won.

He lit the cigarette and puffed at it. He frowned through the smoke at Scharlie.

'You do understand, don't you? I'm tremendously fond of you, dear. If we'd been free I daresay we'd have fixed things up and been very happy together. But there is your husband. And there is my future wife.'

Scharlie found her voice. It was husky and sounded a long way away, strange to her. She put one hand against her throat.

'So you—don't love me?' she said.

'I suppose I don't in the way that you want,' he muttered.

'And you've never really cared for me at all.'

'I have—I still do, Scharlie.'

'No. Not as I love you.'

'Oh, my dear!' He frowned harder. Her obvious agony worried him. He was not altogether a brute. And this was like hurting an unfortunate child. He realised that he had been wrong in the first place to pursue her, run after her as he had done down at Gateways, until he had caught her and made her care for him. He realised that what to him had been a momentary infatuation, to her had been something much more real and serious. What a damn' fool he had been not to see the danger, or, if he had not seen it, not to be warned! It was only to be expected that a young, impressionable, unhappily married girl would end up like this.

'I would have died for you,' he heard Scharlie's husky little voice, 'gone through anything with you—for you!'

'Don't!' he said.

'You sound bored—' She was trying to laugh. 'And I seem to have made myself altogether ridiculous. Perhaps you think you'll alter my opinion of you if you behave like a brute, and that I'll stop loving you.'

'Don't!' he said again. 'Look here, Scharlie old thing, why don't you chuck me? I only make you unhappy.'

'Haven't *you* chucked *me*, Hugh?' She was laughing again.

He loathed himself when he saw how he had hurt her. But he was not prepared to be hurt for her sake. And Eleanor and Henry were coming. He pulled at his collar.

'Scharlie, don't let's part bad friends. I care much more for you than you think, but I'm not *free*—'

'No,' she broke in. 'Neither am I. And we weren't free at Gateways. Only fools. I suppose I was the biggest fool. I believed you really loved me. I came to you for protection tonight because I believed that. Never mind. Good-bye.'

He saw the tears gathering in her eyes; trembling on the stiff black lashes that had never failed to move, to excite him. He felt that he had been a cad. Her husband was a beast who had struck her, and she had come to him, and this was how he had received her. It was damn' difficult and disturbing.

She moved towards the door. She did not look at him. But he followed her and put his arms about her, weak to the finale of their little drama.

'Don't be angry with me, Scharlie. Darling

child, I'm absolutely tied. It's the devil—but what can we do—?'

He broke off and kissed the top of her head in a helpless fashion.

Scharlie, who had been like one dead, came to life again in his embrace and put her arms about his waist. Leaning her cheek against his shoulder, she held on to him in a moment of sheer anguish.

'Oh, Hugh, I can't bear it—I can't bear it, Hugh—'

The tears began to pelt down her distorted young face.

The man held her and caressed her. But his ears were strained for the sound of a car driving up to Conder Mansions, and he heard one.

'Scharlie, for lord's sake pull yourself together, darling, do. This may be my fiancée—her brother—they simply must not find you here.'

But she was crying passionately. She scarcely heard what he said.

'I can't chuck you, Hugh—I can't—don't make me—'

Hugh felt positively sick with worry and nerves. The hum of the lift ascending to the third floor—*his* floor—filled his hearing now. It was Eleanor and Henry. The worst had happened. They had come, and Scharlie was still here. How could they put anything but the worst construction on the situation? A young pretty married woman, dishevelled and in tears, in his flat.

He put his hands on Scharlie's shoulders and shook her a little.

'For God's sake—they're coming, I tell you.'

She drew in her breath and stopped crying.

'I'm sorry—what can I do?'

He did not answer. With a sullen, furious face he stood rigid, listening. Scharlie listened too. She heard a woman's light cheerful laugh. Eleanor Gorring's voice:

'What a mutt I am, Henry. I've left my shawl in the car.'

Henry Gorring's clear, direct voice:

'I'll fetch it, Nell.'

'No,' from Eleanor. 'I'm in the lift now. The porter can take me down. You go on in and have a cocktail with Hugo.'

The clang of gates. The hum of the lift again, descending to the ground-floor. Hugh's face was scarlet.

'Nell's gone down . . . but Henry's coming in . . .'

Scharlie had no time to answer. Grafton had let Henry Gorring into the flat. Scharlie put up a shaking hand in a futile effort to tidy her rumpled hair and wipe the tears from her cheeks. Hugh flung out his hands with a gesture of despair.

'Blast it!' he said savagely.

Scharlie seemed to die again; to wither under this display of indifference from the man with whom she had fallen so violently in love. His real indifference to her. Why, if he cared so much for Eleanor and his engagement, had he ever said he loved her, Scharlie; kissed her as he had kissed her a few moments ago?

Henry Gorring walked into the room.

'You there, Hugh—' he began.

He stopped short. He looked blankly at the slender girl in the grey chiffon evening-gown. Through the horn-rimmed glasses his keen, quick eyes surveyed her and at once noticed the disorder of her hair; her distraught, tear-stained face. She looked back at him speechlessly. Hugh was equally dumb.

Henry Gorring's brows met. In a lightning flash he recalled this young woman. Yes, he had seen her before. At the Wilberforces' house; he had been in the Isotta; his sister had called the girl up and introduced her. Henry never forgot faces or names. He remembered Scharlie's name. Mrs. Mason. And Nell had called her a champion tennis-player. He had never thought of her since.

But now—what the devil was she doing in Hugh's flat? She had been crying. Why? Suspicions of a somewhat unpleasant kind came into Henry's mind. His lips tightened.

Then Hugh broke the awkward silence:

'Evening, Henry. Scharlie . . . you must go . . .'

'I'll get my coat,' she said. She turned

blindly to the sofa. Under the suspicious gaze of Eleanor's brother, her cheeks were fiery red. The hum of the lift started again. Henry, very straight and grim, stood blocking the doorway. He said:

'Just one moment. Hugh, do you realise that Nell is coming up—in fact, she's here—'

The hum ceased. A gate clanged. Eleanor's voice was heard in the tiny hall saying, 'Good evening, Grafton.'

Beads of moisture gathered on Hugh's forehead. He looked panic-stricken. Henry recognised the fact. And Mrs. Mason was struggling into her coat.

'You must be crazy, man,' Henry said to Hugh in a low, terse voice. 'What's this girl doing here? You knew we were coming, surely?'

'Yes, but I—oh, hell—' Hugh kicked his heel on the ground.

Scharlie wrapped her velvet coat around her; she moved towards the door.

'I'd better go,' she whispered.

'What'll I say to Nell—' began Hugh.

Henry saw plainly that this was an intrigue between Hugh and Mrs. Mason. The swine—the utter swine—engaged to Nell—Nell who was the best and dearest thing on earth!

Henry, who knew his sister so well, realised in the midst of a savage resentment against Hugh that Nell would break her heart if she came into the room and saw the whole situation as he, Henry, saw it.

It would never do. Nell adored Hugh; trusted him. She was to be married to him in a few weeks' time. And on Monday he was to be a partner in the firm. Henry knew he must act; and act promptly if he was to avert a catastrophe.

He had ever been a man of prompt action and cool brain. He used all his resources now. Not for Hugh's sake, but for Nell's. He wasn't going to see all the radiance wiped from her face on account of a rotten intrigue between her lover and this Mason girl.

He marched to Scharlie's side.

'Mrs. Mason,' he said in a rapid undertone, 'I don't know why you are here, and I wouldn't much care if it wasn't for my sister. But she's coming in now. Will you please leave things entirely to me.'

Scharlie was much too miserable to do anything but acquiesce. She nodded. Henry glanced at the other man.

'Not a word, Hugh. This is my show. Understand?'

Hugh nodded, ashamed and furious.

The door opened. Then Scharlie felt Henry Gorring take her hand in a light yet firm grip.

Eleanor fresh, charming in a white lace gown, walked into the room. A cream silk Spanish shawl, embroidered with scarlet roses, trailed over one arm. She was smiling; she brought with her an atmosphere of buoyant happiness and assurance.

'Hugo, dear, I'm so sorry. I was a mutt to leave my shawl—'

She broke off. Her gaze travelled swiftly from her fiancé to the girl in grey who was holding Henry's hand.

'Why, it's Mrs. Mason!' she exclaimed in a voice of amazement.

Silence for the fraction of a moment. Hugh tugged at his collar and swallowed hard. Scharlie looked dumbly at Eleanor. Henry spoke.

'Yes, you remember Mrs. Mason, at Gateways, don't you, Nell?'

'But of course!' Eleanor stared. She was startled to say the least of it, and perplexed. 'But why—how—'

'I asked her to come along and meet us here,' said Henry.

It was probably the first real good lie he had told since his childhood. He was not a liar. He did not approve of lying, more from the point of view that lies invariably produced difficult complications than from a passion for truth.

Eleanor's thick, fair brows knitted. She was frankly nonplussed. Henry, and little Mrs. Mason. *Henry!* But it was extraordinary. She didn't think he knew her well. He had only met her casually that once down at Gateways.

Her natural good manners came to her aid. She held out a hand to Scharlie.

'But how delightful to see you again, Mrs.

Mason! Is the tennis still going strong?'

Scharlie limply put out a hand.

'Yes, thanks. How are you, Miss Gorring?' she managed to say.

She felt Eleanor's firm clasp and hated herself. What a nice creature Eleanor Gorring was! Scharlie felt unspeakably mean—about Hugh.

Henry was forced to enlarge a little on his lie.

'I expect you're astonished, Nell. I haven't said anything about it, but I—er—Mrs. Mason and I have met once or twice since that day you introduced us down in Sussex.'

'Oh, indeed!' murmured Eleanor. But she thought: 'How perfectly extraordinary. When I asked Henry what he thought of Scharlie Mason, that day, he said he didn't think anything at all—didn't even notice how pretty she was!'

'Come and take off your coat, Nell,' put in Hugh. The *contretemps* was so awful, he was past worrying. Henry had taken it upon himself to save the position, so let him save it. He dared not look at Scharlie. He seized his fiancée's arm and drew her towards the sofa.

Eleanor hung back a moment. Her grave blue eyes stared at Scharlie curiously. The girl looked distraught. She had been crying. What *was* it all about? Surely Henry—Henry who maintained women played no part in his life—had not—Her thoughts broke off, abruptly.

She had caught her brother's gaze. Behind the glasses his eyes were almost appealing; as though beseeching her to understand.

She adored him, and she came, so she thought, to his aid—at once.

'But how nice to think you and Mrs. Mason are friends, Henry.'

'Yes, isn't it,' he said in a grim voice. 'I—er—hoped this was going to be a foursome. I spoke to Hugh about it earlier in the day. Mrs. Mason came along, but, unfortunately, she's got to leave us right away.'

'Oh, but why?' said Eleanor.

Scharlie swallowed hard. She felt hysterical—as though she would burst out laughing at any moment. It was all so funny and so tragic. To have this strange young man, Henry Gorring, with his cold, superior face and suspicious eyes, holding her hand and claiming an intimate friendship with her.

Henry could lie no more. He turned to Scharlie. And now his eyes appealed to her in an angry fashion.

She blurted out the first explanation that came into her head. She was quite willing to support Henry Gorring, since she had made up her mind that Eleanor must not associate her with Hugh. After all, Hugh didn't love her any more. He had made that plain tonight. What was the use of messing up all their lives?

'I—my husband is rather seedy—I don't want to leave him. I came round to explain to—to your brother and Mr. Ellerby, who so kindly invited me here. I—wanted to see you again, Miss Gorring.'

'But how charming of you,' Eleanor smiled. And she thought: 'I can't believe that. There's something most peculiar about this. I'm afraid Henry's been a naughty boy. And how quiet he's kept about it all, too!'

Henry drew Scharlie's hand firmly through his arm.

'I'll just see you down to a taxi,' he said. 'Come along.'

Scharlie nodded. For an instant her eyes met Hugh's. He reddened and averted his instantly.

'Good night, Mr. Ellerby,' she said in a low voice.

'Good night, Mrs. Mason,' he said.

She knew that it was their last good-bye. She felt crushed by a devastating sense of loss; of misery. She exchanged 'good nights' with Eleanor Gorring. Henry Gorring led her from the flat.

CHAPTER TEN

They descended in the lift in stony silence. At the front door Henry said:

'I'll ask the porter to fetch you a taxi.'

'Thank you,' said Scharlie.

Henry gave the man an order. When he was alone with Scharlie, he dug his hands in his pockets and stared at her—glared at her, so Scharlie thought. She put a hand to her head. It ached and hurt. She felt sick; empty—a dizzy sensation, as though she were going to faint. Henry caught a glimpse of her white, unhappy young face half buried in the big fur collar of the velvet coat.

He had an awkward feeling that she was crying. Nothing could have caused him greater embarrassment. But he was much too angry to pity her. He said in a low voice:

'Mrs. Mason—I very much dislike interfering in other folks' affairs, and if this—er—didn't concern my sister, I wouldn't interfere now. But as it does—I am bound to say—'

'What are you thinking?' she interrupted. Her head shot up. He found himself looking into two defiant eyes. Eyes more green than grey, with large black pupils and the longest, thickest lashes he had ever seen. Not made up, either. Naturally beautiful. She was altogether very attractive, physically. Yes, he was forced to admit that. But not his type. Just the silly, pretty babyish kind of girl to make fools of men like Hugh.

'What are you thinking?' she repeated.

'I don't quite know,' he said.

'But you imagine because I was in Hugh's flat—'

'I'd really rather not discuss that side of it.'

'But you've jumped to conclusions?'

'Possibly. One is inclined to be suspicious when the happiness of someone very dear to one is threatened.'

The concise, clear voice maddened Scharlie.

'I see,' she said, breathing hard. 'So you are suspicious—about me.'

'Mrs. Mason—please—!'

'Why shouldn't I talk? You've interfered—taken it upon yourself to claim friendship with me because you thought your sister would mind me being in Hugh's flat.'

'Quite so. And she would, very naturally, have minded.'

'We aren't living in Victoria's day.'

'Mrs. Mason—it doesn't matter how modern you are or my sister is—you can't pretend she wouldn't have every right to feel annoyed, if not very distressed, if she thought you had gone to Ellerby's flat for the purpose of seeing him. Besides, your whole attitude—I mean—' He broke off with a gesture of impatience. 'You know exactly what I mean.'

Scharlie's little bubble of defiance, of resentment against Henry Gorring burst. She felt nothing but fatigue and that frightening, faint sensation. She tried not to break down and cry.

'Oh, all right,' she said. 'Think what you want. You've saved things, haven't you—quite wonderfully!' She gave an hysterical little

114

laugh.

Henry frowned.

'For the moment, yes. Look here—this is most abhorrent to me—but I've got to say it. I want your word that you won't do anything silly like this again. I mean—I—er I, oh, you must understand,' he stammered. 'My sister is going to be married very shortly to Mr. Ellerby.'

'I know that.'

'Then please leave him alone. It's only fair.'

'Fair!' Scharlie echoed the word bitterly. She laughed again. 'You are jumping to conclusions, aren't you? And being rather insulting.'

'I am sorry.'

'You aren't. You meant to insult me.'

'Mrs. Mason—please!' said Henry, reddening.

'You did. How do you know my friendship with Hugh isn't an entirely innocent one?'

'It may be, for all I know. But it isn't the thing for you to visit his flat alone at night. People finding you there, in tears, are liable to misunderstand.'

Scharlie subsided again. Oh, this hateful, superior young man. So correct; so cold. And he was right, too. She knew he was right; that he had every reason for reproaching her and for championing his sister.

'I assure you it wouldn't matter to me in the least if I didn't know how devoted my sister is to Mr. Ellerby,' Henry added stiffly.

Scharlie thought:

'What am I going to do? How can I go back to Alec now? I can't. I've got nobody—nobody in the world who cares. I wish I were dead . . .'

The big gloomy hall of Conder Mansions, with its tesselated stone floor, red strip of carpet, and large glass doors, began to revolve slowly round her. She had not eaten anything all day. And she had worked herself up to a state of acute emotion and nerves. Now she came to the end of her strength. She looked up at Henry Gorring and saw him as through a haze. She cried out piteously.

'Oh—I'm so sorry—I'm going to faint.'

Henry uttered an exclamation and sprang to her side. She swayed forwards, rested her full weight for an instant against him. He supported her with both arms. He looked at her with dismay. Of all the aggravating things to happen . . . for the girl to go and faint in his arms, like this. He wanted to get rid of her—get back to Eleanor. Heaven alone knew what Nell was thinking by this time. What a position! Confound Hugh and his liaison!

'Mrs. Mason—oh, I say—Mrs. Mason!' Henry said sharply, and shook her slightly.

She was extraordinarily light to hold, and so soft, so helpless. She looked a pathetic child, with her half-opened, pitiful mouth and closed eyes; the stiff black lashes curving against the pallor of her cheeks. How small and slim she was! Her head only reached his shoulder. There were rich tawny lights in her hair. The light weight of the supple young body and fragrance of her revived sharp, painful memories in Henry.

It was two years since he had held a woman in his arms. And then he had held one particular woman with passion. He had been tormented; crazy with love; obsessed by it. *She* had used some scent like this that came from Scharlie Mason's hair. Henry Gorring didn't want to be reminded of the past—of that most intolerable period of his existence. He shook Scharlie again.

'Mrs. Mason—please—try and pull yourself together.'

Scharlie heard his voice as from a long way off. She opened her eyes.

'I—I'm so sorry,' she whispered. She tried to move away from him. 'But I feel so—sick!'

'Oh, lord!' Henry Gorring said, and felt more frightened than he would have been facing a hungry tiger. He looked round as though for help. There was something so comic in his obvious terror that even Scharlie, plunged in gloom though she was, saw the humour of the situation.

She gave half a sob, half a laugh.

'I—oh, I am sorry. But don't worry. I am better—only faint—'

'Will you sit down for a moment?'

'No—I can't stay here,' she whispered.

She drew away from him. She seemed unsteady on her feet, so he was forced to hold her arm. The porter came back.

'Taxi's here, sir.'

'Come along,' said Henry firmly, and drew Scharlie towards the doors.

'It's—my head,' she said. 'I feel—all giddy. Had no food—that may be it.'

Henry's lips tightened. The little fool. No food and tears and hysteria. No balance, that's what it was. Yet how could he continue to feel angry with such a very young and helpless creature? She wasn't at all an experienced vamp with whom he could deal definitely; treat as harshly as she deserved. She was an absolute kid. Who would believe she was married? And what sort of fellow could the husband be, to let her go gadding about with other men; getting into hot water like this?

He helped her down the steps on to the pavement.

'Will you be all right, now?'

Scharlie put a hand to her temples.

'I suppose so. But—things keep going round and round.'

'Damn!' said Henry under his breath. But he saw the path of duty before him and faced it. 'Then I'd better come with you and see you home.'

'Please don't trouble—'

'Jump in,' he said, in a peremptory voice.

She felt so dizzy that she neither argued nor

protested now. She sank into a corner of the taxi; leaned back, and shut her eyes.

'What address shall I say?' she heard Henry's voice.

'I don't know,' she said.

'Your home.'

'No—no—I can't go there.'

Henry put a head in the taxi.

'My dear Mrs. Mason—for goodness' sake—'

'No, I can't go there,' she repeated, and opened her eyes and gave him a beseeching look. 'Please!'

'But, look here—you must—I mean—what did you intend to do? You knew you couldn't stay at Hugh's flat.'

'Yes, but I thought he—'

'Well, what?'

'Would help me—tell me what to do . . .' She whispered the words, conscious of humiliation; of defeat. This was an admission to Henry Gorring of her intimacy with Hugh. She saw Henry's eyes sparkle angrily behind their glasses.

'Well,' he said sharply. 'What did he suggest? For heaven's sake, give me some address. We can't stay here arguing. What my sister imagines now, I daren't think.'

His sister—always his sister. And with Hugh it had been always 'my fiancée.' Nobody thought of *her*. Scharlie began to feel desperate. She could not, would not be bullied into returning to Alec . . . after what he had done, earlier this evening. She said wildly:

'Oh, I'll go to an hotel—any hotel.'

'But you have no luggage.'

'I'll send for some. Yes, an hotel—please.'

Henry Gorring had faced many difficult situations, but this one seemed to him the most impossible and trying in which he could have found himself.

'Which hotel, Mrs. Mason?' he snapped.

Scharlie racked her brains. Then she said:

'The Atlantic . . .'

The Atlantic, in Knightsbridge, was quite new. A small, select place just opened by a man who had been on the Stock Exchange with Alec and had become a hotel proprietor instead of a jobber. He found it more lucrative. Scharlie knew him slightly. He would take her in without luggage, if need be. She would have to give some plausible explanation; and, after all, it was only eight o'clock.

Henry climbed into the taxi and seated himself beside Scharlie. They moved off. Scharlie stole a glance at him. How stern he was! He seemed to have none of Eleanor's charm or affability. His arms were crossed on his chest, and he scowled out of the window. By this time, no doubt, he was in a raging temper. Scharlie was roused from a stupor of misery to the feeling that she really owed Henry Gorring an apology. Yet why should she make it? She hadn't asked him to interfere.

They preserved silence for a few moments. When they were driving down Maida Vale towards Marble Arch, Scharlie had a sudden fit of coughing. Henry glanced at her.

'You all right? Not still feeling sick?' he asked awkwardly.

'No, I'm all right,' she said.

'You'd best have something to eat as soon as you get to your hotel.'

'I don't want anything.'

'It's lack of food that's making you faint.'

'I don't care,' she said miserably. 'I really don't care if I die tonight.'

'That,' said Henry, 'is stupid and childish.'

'I daresay. I may be childish. I know I've been stupid—horribly stupid!' She choked and hid her face in her hands again.

Then for the first time Henry softened towards her.

'Look here, Mrs. Mason,' he said, 'if it's going to help to clear up matters—for heaven's sake tell me all about it—I mean, if there's anything to tell. It worries me considerably. My sister is the dearest thing on earth to me, and I—well, I don't want her to suffer.'

'No—I know,' whispered Scharlie. The hot tears trickled through her slender fingers. 'I'm dreadfully ashamed . . . whenever I meet her. She *is* so nice!'

Henry softened still further.

'Then, look here—if this has been a foolish sort of affair and not a very serious one—you must chuck it—both you and Hugh.'

'It's quite all right,' said Scharlie. 'He—he's already chucked me.'

Henry pulled at the lobe of his left ear, which he always did when he was troubled.

There was something damned pathetic in the way the girl said that, he thought: *'He's already chucked me.'*

'There wasn't anything serious between you, was there?' he asked.

'I—suppose not.'

'Well, that's all right,' said Henry, much relieved.

Scharlie looked up, her eyes glittering with tears, her face hot, miserable.

'It isn't all right. I loved him—adored him. You don't know how much—'

Henry frowned.

'But, after all, look here . . . Hugh is engaged to my sister.'

'I know. Don't keep rubbing that in.'

'And you—you're a married woman, anyhow.'

'Well, and what do you know of my married life? Of the hell it's been—the absolute hell!'

Henry pulled at his ear. It tingled.

'I'm—er—very sorry, if that's so. But even if it's true—you can't expect to get out of your hell by creating one for someone else. Or by trespassing on other folks' property. If your married life is a failure and you wish to get out of it, do so, but leave engaged men alone.'

'Oh!' gasped Scharlie. 'Why should you think it's all my fault—all on my side?'

'I don't doubt Hugh is just as much to blame,' said Henry coldly.

'Nobody's to blame. You can't control love.'

'That,' said Henry, still more coldly, 'is rot.'

'You can't!' exclaimed Scharlie. 'I tried to—he tried, down at Gateways.'

'A foolish infatuation which began at a house-party—the sort of show where everyone's bored and has nothing better to do than flirt with other people's husbands or wives as the case may be.'

'It wasn't infatuation,' Scharlie said hotly. 'Not on my part. I loved him. I still do.'

'And might I ask if you intended to go away with him?'

'Yes, if he'd have taken me.'

'And an innocent trusting woman like my sister is left to suffer. I call it damnable.'

'It may be. It probably is. I'm not trying to defend myself.' Scharlie gave a miserable sob. 'Only to tell you that I did love Hugh with all my heart. But it's ended now. He ended it.'

'He's to be commended for that.'

'It's easy for you to sit there so calmly and judge and condemn. I don't suppose you know what it is to care for anybody!' Scharlie said in a choked voice.

Henry's face was grim and expressionless. But behind the glasses the clever, cynical eyes suddenly narrowed. He flinched as though something had hit him. He said:

'That may or may not be the case. Anyhow, I have no wish to judge or condemn. I only want to ensure my sister's future happiness.'

'You needn't worry,' said Scharlie bitterly. 'I shan't see Hugh again.'

'You mean that?'

'Yes.' She shivered and bit fiercely at her lips. The tears were running down her cheeks again. 'He doesn't care for me now—like he did in the beginning. He wants to marry your sister and live happily ever afterwards, and I daresay he will. I don't matter—I don't matter to—to anyone!'

The concentrated misery in her voice broke through a layer of reticence, of cold censoriousness in Henry Gorring. The girl was so obviously unhappy. Her frank passion; her despair troubled him. Hadn't he once cared, this way, about a woman who let him down? And it had hurt—like the devil. This child had had no right to fool round with Hugh. But it was Hugh's fault, and, no doubt, her husband's. She wasn't entirely to blame.

'Mrs. Mason,' he said more gently, 'don't cry. Try and get a grip on things. Listen—you must realise that it would have been impossible for you to run off with Hugh—it would have ruined so many lives.'

'Yes,' she whispered.

'He had no right to make love to you at all. It was caddish of him.'

124

'No—please!'

'Well, you must forget it—put him right out of your life.'

'Yes.'

'And go back to your husband,' Henry added.

'No—never!' Her head went up again. Her fingers clenched in her lap. 'Never! I loathe him.'

'But why?'

'He's—intolerable. You don't know Alec. Nobody who hasn't lived with him could know what Alec is like. He's much older than I am. I married him when I first left school. I hate him now. And tonight he—he hit me.'

'Hit you?'

'Yes . . . across my face. A blow that knocked me down. When I got up I swore I'd never go back to him, and I won't.'

Henry was speechless. He believed the girl was speaking the truth, and it was a beastly unpardonable thing for a man to have done— to hit his wife—knock her down. The act of a bullying navvy; not of a gentleman.

The light from street-lamps, as they flashed by, lit up Scharlie's white, tear-wet face; revealed the slim, lovely lines of the young figure in the chiffon gown. What sort of man, Henry Gorring wondered, could be brutal enough to hit this pretty child?

'I won't ever go back to him,' Scharlie said again.

'Then what will you do?'

'I don't know. Work for my living, I expect.'

'Have you—money of your own?'

'No, nothing. I'm absolutely at his mercy, financially.'

Henry stared out of the taxi-window broodingly.

'You'd better go back to your mother, then.'

'She's in South Africa, and she wouldn't have me, anyhow.'

'H'm,' said Henry. 'Then I don't know what to suggest.'

'You needn't suggest anything,' said Scharlie, with a miserable laugh. 'I shan't ask for *your* help, Mr. Gorring.'

Then she thought:

'That was unnecessarily rude and silly, but I can't help it. He's so hard and critical, and he thinks I'm a rotter. He's hateful!'

Henry was not feeling particularly hard or critical of Scharlie in this moment—only vastly sorry for her. But he kept his peace. He had certainly interfered in her affairs—for Nell's sake. One was never thanked for interfering, in this world. He couldn't expect Scharlie to be pleased about it or grateful to him. However, he felt a strange sense of responsibility, which he didn't in the least want to feel. But Henry was built that way. He never shirked facing problems or troubles that he bought. And he had bought this one, by removing Scharlie Mason from Hugh's path tonight.

What could he do about it?

The taxi drew up at the Atlantic Hotel. Scharlie gathered her coat about her. Henry opened the door, stepped forth, and helped her out. They faced one another on the pavement a moment. The night-breeze blew a strand of chestnut hair across her face. How pale and tired she looked!

Henry Gorring had only developed what Hugh called a 'cold, fish-like temperament' during the last two years. Years of rigid repression; reaction following a stormy and ill-fated love-affair. In former days he had been far from cold towards women in general. He was by nature passionate rather than austere. Circumstances had changed him, and to a certain extent remoulded his character. But the old Henry was still in existence, and it was the old Henry who understood a little of the pain this girl was suffering; who feared a little for her safety. She was so very young and helpless; a lovely, provocative creature whom men would desire and pursue. He felt, almost, that he had no right to leave her alone in an hotel tonight. Yet she was married—damn it—and there was her husband. He must be a swine, too—

'Good-bye, Mr. Gorring, and thank you for bringing me here. I feel quite well again . . .' Scharlie's voice interrupted his train of thought. She held herself proudly.

Henry pulled the lobe of his ear and

hesitated. There was the question of money.

'Mrs. Mason—you have your bag with you. I mean—'

'I have enough money, thanks,' she interrupted, but looked up at him coldly.

He was a tall, rather fine figure, standing there, bare-headed, in the starlight. Scharlie suddenly saw and recognised the quality of power in him; of reserve strength. Dee Wilberforce had called him handsome. Well, perhaps, in a way, he was, with those strongly marked features. Scharlie regarded the slightly hooked nose; curved nostrils; square, jutting chin and clever forehead. He had very thick dark hair; hair that was almost black; brushed to one side; dead straight; not a wave or kink in it. The horn-rimmed glasses gave him a slightly American appearance.

In no way did he appeal to Scharlie. His very strength, his cold, commanding personality frightened rather than attracted her. She felt, too, that they were enemies. That they could never be friends. He, on his side, would never forgive her for her intrigue with the man who was engaged to his sister.

'Good-bye,' she said again, and moved away from him and walked into the hotel.

Henry Gorring stared after her with an irresolution foreign to him. He was frankly worried—not at all happy about leaving Scharlie Mason alone tonight. There was no knowing what she might do; the silly, emotional child. She was unfit to take care of herself.

While he stood there, reflecting, cursing Hugh for landing him in this position, a man came up to him and touched his arm. A middle-aged man of stocky build, wearing a grey coat over evening-dress; and a light grey Homburg.

'I want a few words with you, my friend,' he said.

There was nothing Henry objected to more than being addressed as 'my friend' by a total stranger. He gave the man a frozen look.

'I beg your pardon, but what—who—'

'My name is Alec Mason,' said the man shortly. 'That was my wife whom you have just installed in the Atlantic Hotel. I have known, mark you, for some weeks, that she has a lover. She refused to give me his name. When she ran away from me this evening I took it for granted she would go to him. She did not think I would follow her, but I did. I saw her enter Conder Mansions. I saw you enter it, later, and later come down again with her. Through the doors I saw her in your arms. I presume you had an assignation there in the flat of a mutual friend. I asked the porter your name. He told it me. My solicitors will communicate with you in the morning.'

CHAPTER ELEVEN

Scharlie was trying to explain to Mr. Summers, the manager of the Atlantic, why she wanted a room at the hotel at this curious time of night, and why she had no luggage. She had no really good explanation to make. She floundered hopelessly. Mr. Summers, therefore, came to the inevitable conclusion that pretty little Mrs. Mason had run away from her husband. And although she was pretty and appealing, Mr. Archibald Summers was Alec Mason's friend; had known him well on the Stock Exchange, and was as pompous and righteous as Alec himself. He was courteous to Mrs. Mason, but regretted that he had not one single bedroom vacant; while making a mental decision to 'phone through to Mason and inform him that his wife was here.

Scharlie was a little frightened when Mr. Summers refused to take her in. She knew that no respectable hotel in town would admit a woman in evening dress without luggage. She had been a fool not to pack a suit-case when she left home. But she had been so agitated, so certain Hugh would help her.

'Are you sure you can't find me a room, Mr. Summers?' she asked in distress.

'I regret, my dear Mrs. Mason—not one.' He spread out his hands.

Scharlie stood still. Her shoulders drooped. Her under-lip trembled.

The plate-glass doors of the hotel revolved and Henry Gorring walked in.

Scharlie glanced up and saw him come. She was very surprised. Why had he come back? What further had he to say to her? He looked rather strange too. He was white with anger. There were two sinister lines on either side of his mouth.

He came straight up to her. Mr. Summers moved away.

'Mrs. Mason,' said Henry, 'your husband has just introduced himself to me out there in the street. I think he's mad.'

Scharlie gasped.

'My husband! Alec!'

'Yes.'

'Good heavens, but how did he know—I mean—'

'He has been following you the whole evening.'

'But good heavens—!'

It is "good heavens,"' said Henry grimly. 'It may amuse you to know that he has accused me of being—your lover.'

Scharlie went scarlet. She stared at him. Then she laughed.

'But of course—he *is* mad!'

'On the other hand, he saw me come out of Conder Mansions with you. He suspects us of having met there by appointment. He also saw me bring you here. He has been jealous of you for weeks—he poured out a violent story of his suspicions. He has now fastened them upon me.'

Scharlie, bewildered, stared up at him. Her heart beat very fast. She felt hot, then cold.

'But Mr. Gorring—I—it's absurd.'

'It is absurd. I've never heard anything more absurd. But your husband appears to be an aggressive and obstinate fellow, and, having got this idea into his head, it'll be hard to remove it.'

'It's got to be removed.'

'I quite agree.'

'I shall tell Alec at once that he's wrong.'

'I have already told him that. I informed him a few seconds ago that he was totally wrong. He then said he preferred to make his own deductions and act upon them.'

'Oh, Alec has always been an absolute mule.'

Henry twisted his lips. He had his own private opinions of Alec Mason, and 'mule' was a kinder word than he would have used. He thought Scharlie's husband one of the most objectionable fellows he had ever met. How could he blame a woman—any woman—for running away from him? On the other hand, that did not excuse this girl for fastening upon Eleanor's fiancé as her means of escape. For the moment he had no room in his heart for pity. He was too furious. Tonight's little episode had landed him in a *contretemps* which he found extremely distasteful.

'What did you say to him—what did he say?' Scharlie questioned him.

'He said what I have just told you—that he suspected me of being your lover. When I repudiated it, he merely told me he'd had enough of you, and that as you'd come to me I could keep you.'

Scharlie's cheeks burned.

'Oh, but it's outrageous! He can't mean that.'

'I am telling you what he said.'

'But what did you say then?'

'I started to argue with the gentleman, and he turned his back on me and walked away.'

Scharlie could picture Alec making a dignified retreat after flinging his ultimatum at Henry. At *Henry*, of all men in the world. It would have been funny if it hadn't been so serious. Eleanor's cold, censorious brother. Her lover . . . ye gods!

There was a spark of humour in Scharlie which had not been totally eradicated by the tragedies and disappointments of her young life. She had to laugh. She put the back of one slim hand to her lips and tried to suppress the laugh, but it would come. The low ripple of laughter that Hugh had once found so enchanting.

'Oh, I *say*, how absurd of Alec!' she gasped.

Through the horn-rimmed glasses Henry's

clear grey eyes regarded the spectacle of Scharlie, laughing, with stony amazement. She had a pretty good nerve, he thought, to find a joke in this. There was no joke that he could see. It was a damned bad show, in his opinion. A tangle from which he wished to extricate himself at once. The sooner the better.

'I'm glad you find the situation amusing,' he said stiffly.

Scharlie's spark of humour flickered out. She grew grave.

'Mr. Gorring, I'm sorry—I don't find it amusing, really. Only—the idea that my husband should think that *you*—'

'Quite so,' broke in Henry. 'But you must understand that there are no limits to the suspicions of a jealous husband. This thing must be dealt with at once.'

'He just walked away, declaring that you . . . that you could keep me?'

'Yes.'

'He's always said he would never divorce me.'

'He may have said so to you, but my belief is that your husband would lose no time in divorcing you if he had sufficient evidence. He's probably sick and tired of the situation as it is, and I can't blame him for that. After all, you and Hugh—'

'Hugh and I have scarcely met at all,' broke in Scharlie, with a gesture of her hand. 'Only once—we had tea together—it was all absolutely innocent.'

'You can't expect a husband to believe that, when you have been showing yourself thoroughly unhappy at home and sick of him.'

'But it's true. Hugh was never—my lover—in that way.'

She broke off, scarlet. Henry frowned. His own face was hot and red. Scharlie added:

'I only—just loved him. That's all. And until tonight I thought he loved me.'

She said it very simply. Henry could not accuse her of lying in order to gain an effect. He thought she spoke the truth. But even if she was guiltless, except for an indiscretion, the fact remained that she had chosen Nell's fiancé for her consoler. He couldn't excuse that. There was still less excuse for Hugh. He'd have something to say to that young fellow, tomorrow, about this show. It would be a long while before he'd forgive him for his disloyalty to Nell.

'It was all innocent,' repeated Scharlie.

'The fact remains that your husband suspects you of having a lover. But as he has no proof that you've been unfaithful to him, you can go back to him. He can't refuse to take you in. If he does, you can get the law on to him.'

'I shall never go back to him.'

'But my dear girl,' said Henry impatiently, 'you must; otherwise you see what will happen.'

'What?'

'He'll have you watched.'

'He can. He won't find me with a lover. You know I've said good-bye to Hugh.' Scharlie's face was pale, miserable again.

'You'd much better go back to your husband.'

'You'd advise that—after dealing with him yourself? And seeing what he's like?'

'I can't pretend I like him. But you married him.'

'I've made my bed and must lie on it. Is that what you want to tell me?' she asked bitterly.

Henry scowled. She made him feel uncomfortable.

'Well, you can't break a contract once you've signed it . . . no matter how unpleasant it becomes.'

'I see. Having married Alec when I was a child in my teens—harried into it by my mother—having spent four years of misery— I'm to go back to him and put up with it for the rest of my life, am I?'

'It's nothing to do with me, is it?'

'No. You don't care,' she suddenly flashed out. 'You know he hit me tonight—I told you he did—and you advise me to go back and be hit again—be humiliated and bullied—just because it's the right thing to do. You're an intolerable prig. You haven't an ounce of kindly, human feeling. Not an ounce. You don't think of anybody but your precious sister

136

and her happiness. Oh, go away! Leave me alone. Go away, Mr. Gorring—do. And don't be afraid that your good name will be injured. I'll make it very plain to Alec that *you're* not the man I care for!'

She broke off, breathless, crimson. Her eyes were brilliant with resentment. Her under-lip was quivering again.

Henry Gorring remained silent for an instant. Her outburst disturbed him. His self-confidence was slightly shaken. An intolerable prig, she called him. Good lord, he didn't want to be that. The last thing he wished to be was a prig. What did this girl expect him to do? Did she expect him to be in sympathy with her when she would have snatched dear old Nell's happiness from her if she could? Yet she looked such an unhappy child; a child whom life hadn't treated very kindly either; standing there, glaring up at him with her big, angry eyes. Such a lot of passion and fire in her, too. And with the under-lip trembling, in that hurt way as though she were about to cry, she appealed to a man's protective instinct. Henry invariably protected weaklings—had a mania for helping the under-dog.

'Go away—leave me alone!' she repeated.

He said:

'Mrs. Mason, I'm not really an intolerable prig.'

'You are.'

'I'm not, really.' Scharlie saw just the

137

suggestion of a smile playing about his hard lips. 'And I don't want you to think I'm inhuman or unkind. Believe me, I'm neither.'

'You've been beastly to me, anyhow.'

'But look here, my dear child—'

'I'm not your dear child.'

The smile lifted the corners of Henry's mouth now, and made him look years younger and unexpectedly attractive.

'You are being a silly kid,' he said quite kindly. 'Look here. What *do* you expect? You've played the idiot with the man who's going to marry my sister and—'

'Oh, I know,' she broke in wearily. Her temper subsided. 'I daresay you have every right to despise me.'

'I don't despise you.'

'Yes, you do, and you want me to go back to a life of purgatory with my husband in order that your sister's happiness should be ensured. Well, I promise you it *is* ensured. Hugh wants nothing now but to marry her and settle down.'

Henry bit his lip.

'It's a damn' shame,' he thought. 'Hugh's been a swine. I believe she's rather a sportsman, after all.'

'But I won't go back to Alec,' added Scharlie.

'How are you going to live?'

'Somehow. I'll earn my own living.'

'What can you do?'

'Nothing,' said Scharlie, with a crooked

138

smile. 'I've learned no trade. But I can dance rather well. I expect I could get a job as a dancing-partner somewhere.'

'My dear child, you don't know what you're talking about. Dancing-partner, indeed. You don't know what a rotten life those girls lead. It must be poisonous.'

'P'raps it's all I'm fit for,' said Scharlie.

'Now you *are* being silly,' said Henry. Really, he thought crossly, she was ridiculous. He felt almost paternal about her. 'Look here, what are you going to do tonight, anyhow?'

'I don't know. Mr. Summers won't take me in here—says he hasn't a room.'

'And you've no luggage—nothing. It's most difficult,' said Henry. He tugged at the lobe of his ear. He had never felt more worried. Against his will he was actually being made to feel responsible for Scharlie.

He looked at his wrist-watch. Half-past eight. Hugh and Eleanor would have finished dinner. He felt past worrying what Nell thought of him. She would, of course, take it for granted he was acting the fool with Scharlie Mason. She would also think it extremely rude of him to stay out like this when he had been invited to dine with Hugh. Damn Hugh! All this was his fault. But if he'd spared Nell a heart-ache, it was all that Henry wanted. He'd been through all that agony, two years ago. He knew what it meant to one to lose all that one had believed in, cared for

139

most. He wasn't going to let dear old Nell go through it if he could avoid it.

'Look here,' he said, with a troubled glance at Scharlie. 'Whatever you decide to do—will you swear to me that you won't let your husband get hold of Hugh Ellerby's name?'

'Yes,' said Scharlie. 'I swear that. I don't want Miss Gorring to suffer. Haven't I said so, but you won't believe me.'

'All right. I will believe you, and thank you. But look here, honestly, Mrs. Mason, I'm not blind to the fact that Hugh's more to blame than you are. And, I daresay, now things have come to this pitch, Hugh should be the one to protect you. But he's made up his mind to stick to my sister, so, for God's sake, don't let's deter him from that.'

'I'm not going to,' said Scharlie in a tired voice.

'I've taken it upon myself to interfere, so I must accept the consequences,' added Henry. 'Anything I can do to help you I will.'

Scharlie drew the fur collar of her coat close about her neck.

'Thanks—I shan't want your help.'

'Now you're being—unreasonable.'

'All right. Leave it at that, but I'll take care of myself.'

He was struck for the second time that night, by the sporting quality in Scharlie. She was really game—the child. He liked her pride, her spirit. She began to walk towards the revolving doors. He followed her.

'Where are you going?'

'Home, to pack my things and tell my husband you are not my lover,' she said, chin in the air.

She swept out into the warm dusk of the summer's night. Henry put on his hat and followed.

'Mrs. Mason, look here—'

Scharlie turned and faced him.

'Well—what?'

'Your husband won't receive you kindly. I don't want—I shouldn't like to think—' He broke off, floundering.

Scharlie didn't help him. She felt she had nothing to thank Eleanor's brother for. In her opinion he had been hard, beastly.

'I mean—if he is the type of swine to hit a woman—' Henry continued to stammer and broke off again.

Scharlie gave him a set smile.

'Oh, I see. You're afraid Alec might hit me again. Thanks for the consideration. But don't worry. If he does, he does. But I'm going to get my things and quit, and after that he won't have another chance of hitting me.'

Hitting her. This slim, pretty child. The mere thought brought the red to Henry Gorring's cheeks. It was intolerable. He remembered the softness, the fragrance of her when she had fainted, in Conder Mansions, and he had held her in his arms. And that stout, pompous, hateful fellow who had accosted him in the street tonight was her husband, a cad who had hit her and might hit her again. Henry began to feel very worried, indeed.

'Mrs. Mason, if you need help—' he began.

'I shall not come to you or your family for it, Mr. Gorring,' she cut in. 'Good-bye, and tell Hugh he won't hear from me any more, either.'

'But, look here,' he stammered. 'Money— you said you hadn't any. You've no idea how it distresses me to think you might find yourself stranded. I—'

'Oh, do go away!' she said, and stamped a small, satin-shod foot angrily. 'Go back to your sister and forget I've ever existed.' She turned to the hall-porter, who was standing on the steps of the hotel. 'Taxi, please.'

Henry said no more. He watched her drive away. He shrugged his shoulders, hailed a taxi for himself, and drove back to Conder Mansions. He had saved the situation for his sister. But he felt far from victorious. He was haunted by the memory of Scharlie's unhappy pretty face.

'Damn it all, it's a bad show,' thought Henry.

He found Hugh, bare-headed, hands in his pockets, standing outside the doors of Conder Mansions. He looked pale and anxious. He greeted Henry with a mixture of sheepishness and relief.

'I say, Henry, where on earth did you get to? I've been half off my head—and Nell's amazed. I came down to see if there were any signs of you—'

Henry advanced grimly up the steps into the building. He gave Hugh an expressive look.

'You've made a damned fool of yourself, Hugh.'

'I know that. But what's happened?'

'You're a swine, too. The girl's only a kid.'

'But good heavens, I haven't seduced her or anything.'

'I should think it was only lack of opportunity if you haven't.'

Hugh tugged at his collar. His brow was damp.

'I resent that, Henry, even from you—'

'Resent what you like and be damned. You made love to her.'

'Yes, I suppose I did.'

'You know you did.'

'Yes, and I regret it.'

'And what about her side of it?'

'It hadn't gone very far—she'll forget it.'

'Meanwhile, she's a married woman, and her husband is a rotten little cur who knocks her about and is now seeking evidence for divorce.'

Hugh went scarlet. A frightened look came into his handsome eyes.

'Ye gods! A divorce. But—he has no

143

evidence—he can't bring my name—I mean, surely Scharlie hasn't—'

'She hasn't told him a damn' thing. She's more of a sportsman than you are,' snapped Henry.

'Then it's all right.'

'No. All wrong. He followed her tonight and saw her here in my arms.'

'Your arms!'

'She fainted. I had to hold on to her. Mason saw it. I didn't know he was spying. I took her to an hotel. He followed us. He found out my name from the porter, here. Now he's fastened on me as Scharlie's lover.'

Hugh stared at Henry with an expression of almost ludicrous dismay.

'Oh, good God, what a mess.'

'Yes, and it's your mess, too, my dear Hugh, and, like most fools who get themselves into one, you leave someone else to clear it up.'

'But Mason can't prove anything—'

'No. Only make things damned unpleasant. He's the sort to write stinking letters to Dad and accuse me of seducing his wife.'

'You don't think he'll do that!'

'He might.'

'What the devil's to be done?'

'I don't know. We shall have to see.'

'Where's Scharlie?'

'Gone home to face an infuriated husband and pack her clothes,' said Henry. And added: 'Poor kid.'

'I am damned sorry, Henry. Honestly I am.'

Henry, with one of his unexpected moods of understanding, suddenly put a hand on Hugh's shoulder.

'My dear chap, don't apologise to me. It isn't me you've offended. It's Nell, and you've hurt that unfortunate girl. She seemed to care about you.'

'I know. I was a swine.'

'It isn't as though she was an experienced woman. She's such a kid.'

'I know,' Hugh bit savagely at his lip. 'I was bowled over, Henry. I was so sorry for her—she seemed so unhappy.'

'My dear chap,' said Henry again, 'we all make ruddy fools of ourselves over women at times. But when you're engaged to a girl like Nell, it's up to you to control your longing to comfort unhappily married women.'

'Yes, I know.'

'Anyhow, for God's sake, don't let a word of this get to Nell's ears. I'd do anything rather than upset her.'

'So would I, honestly, Henry. You may find it hard to believe, but I'm heart and soul devoted to Nell.'

Henry's hand fell away from Hugh's shoulder.

'Stick to her—stand by her, then, till all's blue. She's one of the best.'

Hugh moistened his lips with the tip of his tongue.

'I wonder you want to see her married to me.'

'I don't particularly,' said Henry bluntly. 'But she loves you, and I know Nell's nature. She'd crumple right up if she found herself playing second fiddle to another woman. She has a very exaggerated idea of your virtue and charm, my dear old chap.'

Hugh, reddening, followed his future brother-in-law into the lift. He felt strangely humble.

'It was a flash in the pan, Henry. It won't happen again—I swear it. I'll devote the rest of my life to Nell and my work. Don't think too badly of me.'

'Oh, all right,' said Henry shortly. 'Shut up about it now.'

'But just one thing, old man—' Hugh's blue eyes were apologetic. 'I mean, Nell thinks you're having an affair with Scharlie, and if there are any consequences of this business with Mason—it isn't fair that you—'

'Leave that to me,' cut in Henry. 'I'll deal with it. All you need to do is to stick to Nell.'

Silence then. They ascended to Hugh's flat in the lift. Henry took off his glasses and wiped them with a white silk handkerchief. He blinked short-sightedly as he did it. His lips were a straight, hard line. He was much more worried than he was going to let Hugh know. And worried, not so much about Nell now as about Scharlie, herself.

CHAPTER TWELVE

Scharlie had her latch-key in her bag.

She let herself into the house in Arlingham Place. There was a light burning in the library. She knew that Alec was there. He was reading, or writing letters. She tried to slip upstairs before he heard her, but his sharp ears had caught the sound of the front door closing. He emerged from the library. He advanced upon her, his lips twisted.

'So, my dear, loving wife, you have changed your mind and come home.'

Scharlie stood with her back to the banisters.

'No, Alec. I haven't changed my mind. I've merely come home to pack my things.'

He raised one eyebrow.

'Indeed! Pack your things! Staying the night with Mr. Henry Gorring, are you?'

She actually laughed.

'Don't be too absurd, Alec.'

His face went crimson and his smile vanished. He marched up and caught her wrist.

'Absurd, am I? It's you who'll look absurd, my girl, when you find yourself disgraced—divorced. You don't imagine I am going to stand much more of this, do you?'

She snatched her wrist from his fingers.

If she felt weak and nervous, she was not

147

going to let Alec see it.

'I don't ask you to stand any more. And I don't intend to stand you any more. As for divorce—you won't be given an opportunity to divorce me. I have no lover, and never have had one.'

'Be damned to that for a tale.'

'It's no good swearing at me, Alec.'

'Swearing at you! I'd like to put you across my knee and give you a good spanking, which is what you deserve.'

She set her teeth.

'Why not hit me in the face like you did earlier this evening, you beast—you bully!'

He swallowed his rage. But he shook with violent temper.

'You made me hit you—you drove me to it with your insolence—defying me—refusing to go out with me—crying for another man. Yes, and I know the man now. I've had a few words with him. I've told him he can take you and keep you.'

'If you think Mr. Gorring is the man—'

'I don't think. I know.'

'Just because he very kindly saw me to an hotel—?'

'You little fool! D'you suppose I believe a man takes a girl like you to an hotel, at night, just for the purpose of "seeing her there?"'

'You have a mind like a sink, Alec. You always have had.'

He swore again.

148

'It's something new, this taking the high hand with me, Scharlie.'

'Perhaps,' she said. 'I've only just woken up. I realise I've been crazy to let you tyrannise over me. When I married you I vowed to love, honour, and obey you. I was quite fervent and idealistic—I meant to keep my vows. But you didn't know how to treat a woman—you made love ugly—you killed every illusion I had—you made me loathe you—kept me chained to you and expected me to be happy. I've been miserably unhappy for four years. It's only because I'm young and naturally full of life, that I've managed to see a joke in anything. You're an animal—you only think of your food and comforts—you want a woman who'll be a meek sort of slave. You don't want a real wife—a companion. You go out and buy a diamond ring and think that makes up for days and nights of bullying. You're nothing but a selfish, sensual tyrant. I'd rather *die* than live with you again!'

Hotly, excitedly, the words poured from her. She stopped for breath, her face white with concentrated feeling. And Alec Mason, like one dumbfounded, stared and listened, his mouth agape. She turned and began to run up the stairs. Then he gulped and called to her.

'Scharlie—'

She turned and looked down at him.

'Well?'

'You—you've insulted me grossly.'

149

'I'm sorry. I've only said what I feel. It's better you should know.'

'But you're crazy!' he stuttered, the muscles of his cheeks working. 'Out of your mind—to say such things to me.'

She saw how she had hurt his dignity. He would resent that even more than the fact that she was leaving him. She felt, after her outburst, that she was curiously free. It gave her a sensation of strength. She said:

'It's no good talking, Alec. I'm going to quit.'

'You're trying to put the blame on me,' he said furiously. 'Trying to make out that I've ill-treated you.'

'What about this evening?'

'I know I hit you. I lost my temper.'

'I preferred the blow to some of the times when you've hurt my mind.'

'Hurt your mind be—'

'Don't shout at me, Alec. Your precious servants will hear you and think badly of you.'

He choked and tugged at his collar. The perspiration ran down his cheeks.

'You can't put the onus on me like this. You're running away from me because you want to go to your lover.'

A little tremor went through her; a tremor of pain. She thought of Hugh. He had never really been her lover. And now he was nothing to her; forever lost.

'I have no lover, Alec.'

'Henry Gorring—'

'Is a friend.'

'The first time I've heard of it. Perhaps he was the fellow who interested you at the Wilberforces' house-party and sent you back to me so damn' discontented. Perhaps he gave you that cigarette case.'

She winced.

'No, Alec.'

'Then who is the man? You went to Conder Mansions—the porter told me there you'd gone up to a Mr. Ellerby's flat.'

Her heart missed a beat. She had promised Henry she would not let Alec connect Hugh's name with this affair, and she must keep her word. Hastily she lied:

'I didn't go to see Mr. Ellerby, I assure you. He's engaged to Miss Gorring. It isn't likely I'd have an affair with an engaged man.'

'Very well. Young Gorring's the man. He met you there—took you away.'

'You're all wrong.'

'Well, I fancy I'm right!' shouted Alec. 'And I shall take action.'

Scharlie's fingers twined nervously about the banisters.

'What sort of action?'

'I shall communicate with Mr. Walter Gorring and tell him that his son has seduced my wife.'

'But, good heavens, he hasn't. It wouldn't be just or true.'

151

'I prefer to believe it.'

'You couldn't prove it. You couldn't begin to get a divorce. You know I've never stayed away a night from you except when I was down in Sussex, and Mrs. Wilberforce will testify to the fact that Mr. Gorring was not a member of that house-party.'

'You've met him in town, since, though.'

'You're all wrong, I tell you.'

'Naturally you defend him.'

'No. If he were my lover, I'd go to him. Believe me, I'd go to the man I loved!' said Scharlie passionately. 'But I'm going to nobody. I shall be alone.'

'I won't believe that. I shall watch you.'

'You can.'

'And I shall have a few blistering words with old Gorring. He's a stickler for honour and righteousness in the publishing trade. We'll see how he likes the idea of his son and heir carrying on an affair with my wife.'

'Alec, you'll drive me mad in a moment if I have to tell you much more often that Henry Gorring is only an acquaintance —a friend.'

'I don't believe a word you say.'

'Very well. Leave it at that. Now I'm going.'

'And I won't give you a penny. You can come back to me, respectably, decently, as my wife and do as I tell you—or starve.'

'I've starved mentally, for years—living respectably and decently as your wife, Alec,' she said. 'Now I shall begin to live, I hope. I shall earn my own living.'

'You can't get away with that high-minded stuff. Walter Gorring shall hear from me in the morning.'

Scharlie made a gesture of despair. Alec was quite adamant on that subject. Obsessed by the notion that Henry was her lover. It would be truly awful if he put all kinds of wrong ideas into the head of Henry's father. It would cause no end of trouble.

But she had not lived four years with Alec without knowing the mulish obstinacy of the man. It was waste of breath to try and convince him that Henry was not her lover.

'You must do what you wish, Alec,' she said, turning from him wearily. 'I can only assure you there is no foundation whatever for what you think about Mr. Gorring and myself.'

'My last words to you, Scharlie, are that you'll live to regret this.'

'Never.'

'And that you're an ungrateful little baggage.' He pulled a handkerchief from his pocket and passed it across his lips and forehead. 'God alone knows what your mother will think—and my relations—my friends—' he added.

'Your relations will say I'm an ungrateful baggage and pity you deeply, Alec,' said Scharlie, with a set smile. 'And my mother won't care. She never has cared about me. She's too busy husband hunting in South

Africa.'

She reached the top of the stairs. Alec stared up at her. There was an almost comic expression on his face. He was thwarted; defeated by this slip of a girl. It maddened him.

On the landing she leaned over the banisters and spoke to him:

'If you don't object, I'll ask Edith to bring me some soup or something. I've had nothing to eat since lunch. I'm going to pack my things now. I'll leave all my jewellery on the dressing-table, and anything of value that you've given me.'

'Scharlie, look here—' he began.

She shook her head and vanished. He heard her bedroom door close. He walked back to the study, defeated.

A few minutes later Scharlie's bedroom was in chaos. Trunks open; clothes strewn over the bed, the chairs, the floor. Drawers open; a general atmosphere of confusion. Scharlie sat before her dressing-table, going through her jewel-case; carefully placing the valuables which Alec had given her on one side. She had little of her own except a diamond ring left to her by her father, and which had belonged to her grandmother on his side; and a few trinkets; relics of her childhood.

She was very tired and she felt a little frightened. She was making a bold move in leaving Alec and facing life quite alone. She didn't know quite what she would do or what would happen to her. And she could not stop thinking about Hugh. A horrid, sick sort of feeling came over her at the thought of Hugh. She felt so cheated; so cheapened. She had loved him and gone to him, and he had finished with her. She wondered if she would ever get over the humiliation of that last meeting with him—the subsequent scene with Henry Gorring.

What a little fool she had been to take Hugh's love-making so seriously. It was a bitter lesson. A rotten thing to happen to one. It made it so difficult for one to believe anything that anybody said to one ever again.

Where was she going, tonight? It was growing late. What could she do? If the Wilberforces had been in town she might have fled to little Dee for protection; for a night's shelter, anyhow. But Dee was in Sussex. And Scharlie knew nobody else in town except Alec's old aunts and married sister, and she wasn't, obviously, going to any of them. They would condemn her, unseen and unheard, for leaving their precious, worthy Alec.

Edith came in with a meal on a tray. She looked grim and disapproving. Scharlie felt glad she wasn't going to see much more of this estimable spy.

Edith laid the tray on the dressing-table.

'The master has asked me to give you this,' she said haughtily; handed Scharlie a sealed envelope, and swept out of the room, her nose in the air.

'Cat,' thought Scharlie. Then, with a sigh, opened the square white envelope.

She wondered what he could have to say. The contents of the letter rather surprised her.

DEAR SCHARLIE,—I see you are determined to ruin yourself and bring a great deal of unnecessary trouble and annoyance into my life, so there is no more to be said on the point other than I have already said. But I suggest you remain in the house tonight. It is too late for a girl of your age to start looking for rooms. And I do not wish it said that I turned my wife into the streets at night. So kindly oblige me by remaining until morning. There is no necessity for us to meet and have another painful scene. I can only say I am extremely shocked by your attitude.

'A. M.'

Scharlie finished this note, then sat back in her chair and gazed round the disordered room. Her lips twisted into a wry smile. That letter was so typical of Alec; the colossal egoism of the man. He did not ask her to stay tonight for her sake, but for his. He was, as usual, afraid of public opinion.

Well, why not stay? She was so terribly tired. And he said they need not meet. That meant

156

he would not intrude himself upon her, and tomorrow she could go, early, before he was up.

Scharlie went to the little walnut writing-bureau which stood in a corner of her room. She scribbled a few words on a sheet of paper.

'DEAR ALEC,—Thank you. I will stay tonight.
                                    'SCHARLIE.'

She rang the bell for Edith.

'Give this to the master, please.'

Then, when she was alone, she locked her door and continued her packing. When she had finished she undressed wearily, and slipped into bed. She was so exhausted in body and mind, she could not sleep for a long while. Her nerves were jumping. She lay awake, staring at the shadows on the blind; re-living every moment of the disastrous scene in Hugh's flat.

'*So you don't love me?*' . . . she had asked him.

'*I suppose I don't in the way you want,*' he had answered.

The thing had bitten deeply into Scharlie's sensitive mind. She had been so certain that he really cared. And now he would marry Eleanor and be quite happy, and she, Scharlie, would be very much alone.

She wondered if anybody on earth was as unhappy as she was tonight. She turned her face to the pillow; a face with all the youth, the eagerness wiped from it. She began to cry.

CHAPTER THIRTEEN

Scharlie wakened suddenly, with a violent jerk of the heart, and that feeling of disaster which attacks one when one is very suddenly roused.

The sensation of disaster became acute when she became aware that Edith was bending over her, shaking her by the arm.

'Wake up, wake up, please, madam . . .' she was saying.

Scharlie sat up straight. Her eyelids felt weighted. Her temples ached. She had cried herself to sleep long after midnight, and she was thoroughly exhausted. She rubbed her eyes and stared in a bewildered way at the maid.

'Edith, what on earth's wrong—'

'It's the master, madam . . .'

The woman looked strangely unlike her stiff, starchy self. Her lips trembled. Her eyes behind the black-rimmed spectacles were round and scared.

Scharlie threw off the bedclothes and sat on the edge of the bed.

'What's the matter with the master, Edith?'

'Something terrible . . . I don't know . . . but please come.'

Scharlie's lips felt dry. She turned and picked up her wrapper.

'Good heavens, what do you mean, Edith?'

'I went in with his tea as usual at eight o'clock. He was lying in bed, looking something terrible . . .'

Scharlie began to breathe fast.

'Edith, explain yourself . . . what do you mean . . . "looking something terrible?"'

The woman began to sob. She was hysterical. Scharlie had never imagined Edith could be so changed; so altered from the robot-creature that she was, ordinarily.

'I think he's dead,' she said in a hoarse, frightened voice. 'Oh, madam, I think he's dead.'

'Don't be absurd, Edith,' said Scharlie, 'I'll go and see him . . .'

But her cheeks went white as she rushed into Alec's bedroom. She was remembering something that the family doctor had told Alec many months ago. Something about his heart. He had had an attack of pain . . . when was it? . . . last Christmas, following a huge dinner. He had been warned that he ate too much and too frequently and was much too fat . . . yes, the doctor had mentioned fatty degeneration. Alec had rejected the verdict as being ridiculous; had assured himself and everyone else that he had indigestion. Nothing would induce him to give up his food. Then . . . another attack of pain . . . another warning. A strict injunction from the doctor, to go easy . . . to control his temper. He was so excitable; so volcanic; his heart would not stand the strain.

Had last night's scene with Henry, outside the Atlantic Hotel, followed by the one with her, proved too much for him? Scharlie wondered. She felt suddenly afraid as she remembered his rage. He had been shaking, almost purple in the face, with it.

The moment the entered Alec's bedroom she knew that the worst had happened. Death had visited here. The room was dark, grim, and quiet; the curtains still drawn; the atmosphere sickly with the odour of eucalyptus, which Alec had been using for his cold. The body of the man lay unnaturally bent, across the bed; head and shoulders half out of it, hanging down. The position suggested that he had been seized with a violent pain, had been about to get out of the bed; when a fatal spasm had gripped him and he had died.

Yes, he was dead. Scharlie had no doubt about that at all. His mouth was open; his eyes open and staring dreadfully.

Edith, peering over Scharlie's shoulder, gave a sob.

'He is gone, isn't he, madam? . . . Oh, you don't know what a shock I've had . . . I shall never get over it . . .'

Scharlie felt very sick. She began to shiver. She turned from the sight of that still and awful body on the bed. She could scarcely believe that life had gone from it . . . that the end had come with such terrible suddenness for Alec. She pulled Edith out of the room. Her teeth were chattering.

'We must 'phone for Dr. Heslop—at once—quickly—'

'Oh, oh, oh!' Edith broke down completely and went into violent hysterics. This was accompanied by a sudden spasm of hatred directed against her young mistress. She screamed at Scharlie: 'It's all your fault. You killed him—you killed him—with your goings on . . . I heard you last night . . . threatening to leave him for some other gentleman . . . Oh, you've murdered my master . . . oh, oh!'

'Stop! Be quiet, Edith! . . .' Scharlie, shocked and unnerved by the attack, caught the woman's arm and shook her. 'Be quiet, I say. How *dare* you, Edith! . . .'

'You murdered him!' Edith shrieked, pointing at her. 'You gave him his death-blow, and if my dear mistress had been alive in this house today, she'd have said so, too . . . yes, she would, so help me, God.'

'I think it's so help *me*, God,' thought Scharlie, and found it difficult not to break down and go into hysterics herself. Some-how or other she managed to take command of the situation. She pushed Edith into a chair on the landing outside Alec's bedroom. She rang the bell, and a scared-looking housemaid appeared. Scharlie said:

'Nora, take Edith to her room. She's had a dreadful shock . . .'

Then she telephoned for Heslop, who had been the Masons' physician for years and had attended old Mrs. Mason during her lifetime.

While she waited for him to come, she hurried into some clothes. Her thoughts were chaotic. She could not stop shivering. She was haunted by the ghastly picture of that fat, rigid body; half in the bed; half out of it. And by the violent denunciation of the hysterical Edith.

'You murdered him . . . with your goings-on . . .' the woman had said.

Was it true? Was she responsible for Alec's sudden and fatal heart-attack? Had he gone to bed in a state of dangerous excitement, brought on by her refusal to remain with him and his belief that she had a lover, and died, miserably, before he could ring for help?

It was an unpleasant thought. But even though she might believe that a certain responsibility rested on her shoulders, and regret that fact, Scharlie could not genuinely mourn for this man who had made her so unhappy.

'I'd be a hypocrite if I shed one tear, for myself,' she thought. 'But it was terrible for him . . . poor, poor Alec. I'm sorry for him . . .'

That was the feeling that remained with her during the rest of that day. A hectic, unforgettable day without one peaceful or

pleasant moment in it. From the time that
Dr. Heslop arrived, examined Alec Mason and
pronounced life extinct, Scharlie was plunged
into veritable chaos.

'Heart failure,' Heslop told Alec Mason's
youthful widow. 'Yes, I warned him . . . His
heart was weak as a boy. He ate to excess, poor
fellow . . . much too fat for his age, and took
no exercise . . . I warned him . . .'

'Dr. Heslop, I'll be quite frank,' Scharlie
said. 'My husband and I had a row last night
and we were on the point of separation. Had
that . . . anything to do with his death?'

'You mean he was upset . . . angry?'

'Yes.'

'Over-excitement following a very large
meal . . . yes . . . no doubt that contributed
towards the—er—final and fatal attack,'
Heslop said gravely. 'But I shouldn't let that
worry you or prey on your mind,' he added,
with some kindness. 'Your husband might have
died at any moment, after any kind of physical
excess. You mustn't blame yourself.'

'Thank you,' said Scharlie. 'I don't want to
feel that it's my fault. Alec and I . . . parted
enemies . . . We hadn't been good friends for
weeks . . . I'm dreadfully sorry. But we weren't
suited . . . I . . . I'm sorry . . .'

She broke off, suddenly in tears. The doctor
patted her shoulder and comforted her. She
was such a child, he thought. A poor, pretty
child. Of course, the marriage had been most

163

unsuitable. Alexander Mason, God rest his soul, may have been an estimable fellow, but he had been a glutton and a bit of a bully. Heslop, having known him from his boyhood, knew all about that. He felt, secretly, that little Mrs. Alec was to be congratulated rather than pitied. But, of course, one couldn't help being sorry about Mason, poor chap.

With these reflections and an added word of consolation to the widow, Heslop signed the certificate, and went his way.

After that, for Scharlie, a series of telephone-calls; and callers. A constant stream of people arriving at and departing from the house of death in Arlingham Place. Nobody that she wanted to see. She had to force herself to see them. Alec's solicitor, Philip Lawton; his married sister, Frances, Mrs. Lee-Jones, and her husband. One after the other Scharlie interviewed them.

They seemed to her hard, unfriendly people who regarded her gloomily; almost with hostility, as though they took it for granted her recent conduct had hastened Alec to the grave.

Frances, her sister-in-law, was particularly hostile. She was a much older woman than Scharlie. She had two passions in life; bridge and conversation of a libellous kind. She was of her brother's build, short and stout; and always meticulously dressed. She had never approved of Alec's marriage to little Scharlie

Croft, and it was obvious to Scharlie now that Alec had told Frances of his recent 'difficulties' with his wife.

'I am sure you will be haunted to the end of your days by the knowledge that you made poor darling Alec very unhappy in the last weeks of his life,' Mrs. Lee-Jones informed Scharlie this morning.

'I'm sorry, Frances, if that is what you think. But there were faults on both sides, perhaps,' Scharlie answered, hardening under the woman's venomous attack.

'Nonsense,' said Mrs. Lee-Jones. 'Alec gave you everything you wanted. You never appreciated him—did she, Edward?' . . . She turned to her husband for support.

Edward Lee-Jones, having lived in constant friction with his wife for fifteen years, had learned to take the line of least resistance and agree with her on all occasions.

'No, dear,' he said.

But he looked over the neatly and permanently waved head of his wife at Scharlie's slender, drooping figure and thought how pretty she was, in spite of pale cheeks and heavy eyes. And he wondered if she had endured a similar sort of purgatory with Alec to his own with Alec's sister. Scharlie looked back at him. She had always been sorry for the thin, bald-headed Edward, with his patient, submissive eyes and general attitude of melancholy. Their gaze met in a glance that might have been mutual understanding. His, at any rate, was tinged with compassion. It was the sole look of kindness that Scharlie received from any of the family that day, and she appreciated it. She was to put up with worse insults than those Frances directed at her, from Alec's old aunts, who came round to the house later in the day and flayed her.

Even Philip Lawton, Alec's solicitor, was hostile towards Scharlie. There was also a curious smile playing round his lips; secret satisfaction in it which suggested to Scharlie that he knew something unpleasant which was in store for her.

'Your husband paid me a visit only the day before he died, and wrote to me last night,' he told her. 'He must have had some premonition that he was dying.'

'Perhaps,' said Scharlie. And she thought: 'Alec's altered his will—cut me out of it—I'm positive. But I don't care a bit.'

She was exhausted, mentally and bodily, long before the end of that black day. She was given no time to rest or think. She had barely a moment in which to sit down and review the fact that her husband was dead; that never again would she hear his voice or have to fight against his tyranny, or run away from him. He was dead and she was a widow—free.

Once during that morning, when she was not answering the telephone or interviewing somebody, she found time to think of Hugh.

The thought was no comfort to her. It only brought a revival of an old pain; the hurt and bitter sensation that her freedom would mean nothing to him. There was Eleanor . . . he had not loved her, Scharlie, anyhow.

Then, soon after lunch that day, like a bolt from the blue, Henry Gorring turned up at Arlingham Place.

CHAPTER FOURTEEN

Scharlie was sitting at the bureau in the library, writing out a cable for her mother, when Nora, the housemaid, showed Henry in. Edith had retired to her bed and refused to leave it, having horrified the entire staff with the information that Mrs. Mason had murdered her husband.

Nora's voice, still scared, announced:

'Mr. Gorring, please, madam.'

Scharlie dropped her pen and swung round. 'Mr. Gorring! I didn't expect you,' she said.

Henry walked across the room, which had, he thought, an oppressive, opulent atmosphere. He greeted Scharlie with a formal little bow.

'I came to see your husband, Mrs. Mason,' he said. 'I was very amazed, horrified, to hear from the maid that he has died, very suddenly.'

Scharlie stood up. For a moment she was

167

silent. She leaned a hand on the arm of the chair in which she had been sitting. Henry Gorring was struck, at once, by her extreme pallor and the pinched, exhausted look about her mouth. She looked ill, he thought. Suffering, no doubt, from shock.

'Yes, Alec died from heart failure during the early hours of the morning,' she said. Her voice was quite cold and composed.

'But you didn't expect—I mean—'

'I didn't dream his heart was in such a rocky condition, no,' she finished. 'The doctor had warned him, but he took no notice.'

'I see.'

Henry pulled the lobe of his ear. He glanced uneasily round the room again.

Scharlie could not control a sensation of resentment at the mere sight of the tall, stiff figure and the glacial eyes behind the horn-rimmed glasses. Somehow she could not eradicate the feeling that Henry Gorring was responsible for her loss of Hugh. He had interfered; he had acted quite ruthlessly; caring nothing for her misery; anxious only to ensure his sister's happiness.

'Why have you come?' she asked.

'To see Mason about this . . .'

Henry pulled a letter from his pocket. He handed it to Scharlie, with a grim smile.

'This must have been written and posted last night before your husband was taken ill.'

Slowly Scharlie took the letter. She looked

at it, and recognised Alec's small, crabby handwriting. The envelope was addressed to Walter Gorring, Esq.

'My father received this by the first post this morning,' said Henry. 'It's an outrageous accusation against me, concerning you. But my father knows me very well, and is not in the habit of having to account for my conduct. He asked no questions. He merely advised me to deal with it as I thought best.'

Scharlie's hands trembled as they unfolded the sheet of notepaper with her address at the top of it. Her cheeks burnt while she read what Alec had written and posted in the heat of the moment, last night.

It was, as Henry Gorring said, an outrageous accusation. Her nerves, already jumping, and now ten times worse after this fresh disaster, were keyed up to breaking-point. One or two paragraphs of Alec's hateful and unjustifiable letter stood out in particular:

'. . . may be as horrified and upset as I am to know of the disgraceful liaison between your son and my wife . . . no room for doubt because I saw her in his arms . . . conveyed her to an hotel late this evening . . . must have been going on for weeks . . . sent her expensive presents . . . secret meetings . . .'

Each poisonous sentence danced up and down in front of Scharlie. She was hot and quivering when she finished the letter. She handed it back to Henry.

'That's a pretty rotten thing to have done,' she said. Her voice was no longer cool or composed. 'He must have been mad . . . to send such a letter to your father.'

'My father did not believe a word of it,' said Henry. 'He was, naturally, very sick at having such a disgusting epistle sent to him. But even if he had believed it, he wouldn't have reproached me or criticised my morals, which is what your husband wished him to do. I'm not a callow youth to be lectured on my behaviour. As I said before, my father asked me to deal with the thing as I saw fit. But unfortunately your husband also took it upon himself to write to my sister.'

Scharlie's face was one scorching flush again.

'To—Miss Gorring?'

'Yes. He appeared to imagine that my family would plead with me to clear off and leave you alone,' Henry's voice was ironic. 'He informed Eleanor that I had been meeting you in Hugh's flat. He suggested she might keep an eye on me.'

'Oh!' said Scharlie. She flung herself into the chair before the bureau and covered her face with her hands. 'It's intolerable!'

'In my sister's case it is more serious,' continued Henry. 'Because, as you know, she found you in Hugh's flat and I accepted the onus of the whole thing. She now has it well in her head—and who can blame her?—that I am having an intrigue with you. She tore up the letter, but not before she had shown it to me. She, like my father, would not dream of criticising anything I choose to do. But she was extremely upset and worried, and begged me to be careful. Of course, she imagined I might find myself before the limelight in a divorce case.'

The cold voice ceased. Scharlie did not look up. She felt unutterably ashamed and humiliated. Then Henry added:

'I came round to have this thing out with your husband and ask him to see reason. The last thing I expected was to hear of his death.'

Scharlie raised her head.

'You're not going to offer me condolences, are you?' Her voice was almost as hard, as sarcastic as his. And Henry Gorring saw plainly that between last night and this morning this girl had aged. Something soft and childish about her had vanished for good and all. And it seemed a little tragic. He stared at the old Persian rug in front of the fireplace. A shaft of the hot summer sunlight, escaping round a corner of the lace-edged blinds, which were drawn, touched up the faded blues and reds of the rug. For no reason at all Henry Gorring's gaze became riveted on that circle of light, and he thought what a particularly good rug it was.

'No, I won't offer you any condolences,' at length he said. 'Obviously you wouldn't want them.'

'No. I'd be a hypocrite to suggest I did. I was leaving Alec today for good and all, and, now that he's dead, I'm not going to start saying I cared for him. I didn't in the least bit . . . not the *least* bit . . .' Scharlie's voice became suddenly passionate. 'Oh, you may blame me for falling in love with Hugh. But I was unhappy . . . you know what Alec was like . . . you must know what he was like . . . after meeting him last night . . . No girl could respect or care for a man who could write rotten, beastly letters like those to your father and sister. I'm sorry he sent them—I'll apologise for him—if that's what you want.'

Henry's grey eyes suddenly thawed. Last night he had had a sleepless night, worrying over things in general, and he had felt particularly worried about Scharlie Mason. The letters to his father, and to Eleanor, had enraged him. He had come round here without feeling much sympathy for anybody; thoroughly disgusted about the whole affair.

But now he was definitely sorry for Alex Mason's young widow. She was right. No girl could have respected that swine. He could not blame or reproach her for wishing to leave Mason. He might never have despised her at all had she chosen any man but Nell's fiancé to comfort her. He saw that she was at the end of

172

her tether now, and he was very gentle with her; more gentle than Scharlie had dreamed Henry Gorring could be.

'Please, Mrs. Mason,' he said, 'don't apologise. I don't want you to, I assure you. You didn't write the rotten letters, and I'm quite sure you'd have kept your word to me and spared my sister any anxiety. But look here—Mason's dead. There's nothing more to be said or done, now. The thing's over.'

She felt tears sting her eyes. She tried not to cry. In the same gentle voice, Henry added:

'I wouldn't have come, naturally, and bothered you about this if I'd known about Mason. It's a pretty ghastly business. Sudden death in any shape or form is unnerving.'

'Yes,' she whispered, and hid her eyes with one hand.

'I'm only in the way. I'll be getting along,' said Henry, moving away from the mantelpiece. 'There's nothing I can do for you, is there?'

'No, thank you.'

'I mean—' He hesitated, and looked uncertainly at the drooping young figure in the chair. Why was it that he worried over this girl, who was, after all, an entire stranger, and one whom he had at once condemned in his heart as a 'little rotter' who threatened Eleanor's peace of mind? He didn't quite know. But he realised that he had been wrong about her in the first instance. She was not a rotter. She was

173

only a thoughtless child who had been married to a swine, and Hugh had made love to her. At Hugh's door lay the real blame. Yes, somehow he did worry over Scharlie. He felt almost angry with himself. He was a fool. She hated the sight of him and didn't want his solicitude. Why give her a second thought?

Scharlie drew the back of her hand across her wet eyes and stood up; her face turned from Henry.

'There's nothing you can do, thank you . . .' Her tone was not encouraging. 'Except assure your father and sister that my—my unfortunate husband was not in his right mind when he wrote to them, and that his statements were entirely untrue.'

'I doubt if my sister will accept that—after last night.'

'What does it matter? She's got Hugh . . . she doesn't suspect him.'

The bitterness in Scharlie's voice disturbed Henry. He frowned and ran a hand in a nervous way over his straight black hair.

'No—thank God she doesn't.'

'Then it can all subside . . . be washed right out.'

'Yes, I hope and believe it will.'

'Then what is there to worry about?' she said.

Henry felt himself dismissed. Yet he lingered. She gave him a look of surprise.

'What *are* you worrying about?' she asked

wearily.

'Strange to relate—about you.'

'Me?' She stared, then laughed hardly. 'Good heavens, why? I'm not going to commit suicide and write to Hugh or Miss Gorring before I take the plunge into the river, or anything dramatic of that sort.'

'No—that hasn't struck me.'

'Then do you suppose that because I'm free now I shall attempt to get Hugh back? Because I shan't. I've finished with love for good and all—believe me.'

Henry looked at her ruminatively. She looked desperately tired and white, and those great eyes, under the absurdly long lashes, were hard; hurt. She had been badly hurt. It awoke a chord of sympathy in Henry Gorring. He remembered a bitter day in his past when he had said:

'I've finished with love . . .'

'I'm not worried about that, either,' he said. 'I know you won't try and get Hugh back.'

'I never want to see Hugh again,' she said.

'I give Hugh no marks over this business,' said Henry. 'You've borne the brunt of it.'

'Oh, it's an accepted fact—the woman pays.' Scharlie became flippant because there was such a nagging, desperate little pain in her heart; such a lonely, hopeless feeling. And she couldn't bear Henry to see it. 'But I don't care—believe me. I had my congé last night and it's cured me.'

'Don't let it hurt too much,' said Henry.

The kindliness in his voice, in his eyes, amazed her. She was irritated by it, angry that this strange, blunt young man should be able to see that she was hurt when she tried to hide it.

'It may help,' he added, 'when I tell you that Hugh has honestly made up his mind to be loyal to Eleanor and settle down to work. They've fixed their wedding for a fortnight ahead. I'm telling you that so that you may be quite certain in your mind that Hugh is going to do the right thing, that he wants to.'

'Thanks,' said Scharlie. 'It all leaves me quite free to settle down in my turn to my own life, and I shall live it, I hope, without interference from anyone.'

That was frightfully rude, she thought miserably. She knew it. She couldn't help being rude to Henry Gorring. She expected him to turn on his heel and march out of the room. She was immensely surprised when he came right up to her and held out his hand.

'I *have* interfered, I know,' he said in a gruff voice. 'And you're having a pretty thin time. I'm sorry. Good-bye. Will you shake hands? I think you've taken the whole thing rather splendidly. Let me know if I can ever do anything. Good-bye.'

She stared up at him. Instinctively she put a hot little hand into his. Cool, strong fingers closed around hers. It was a curiously protective, encouraging clasp. She heard her own voice, as from a distance, say:

'Good-bye.'

Then Henry Gorring was gone, and the library door closed quietly behind him.

It seemed to Scharlie, after he had gone, that, although she had thought of him as her enemy, he had been more her friend today than any of these other people who had come here to judge and condemn her, and it seemed, too, that Henry Gorring had taken with him the last remnant of her intimacy with Hugh. Hugh was going to settle down and be happy with Eleanor . . . he was going to marry her in a fortnight's time. So that was all very definitely ended . . . all that feverish excitement and all the passion and heart-break and despair.

Scharlie was left with a feeling of profound depression and loneliness. There was nothing to look forward to in the future. Nothing at all.

She sat down at the bureau and stared at the cable, which she had been writing when Henry called. She had got no further than her mother's name and address.

She added the words:

'Alec died last night.—SCHARLIE.'

She wondered if her mother would rush across to England from South Africa on receipt of this news. She didn't want her mother here. There was nothing—never had been anything—between them but misunderstanding and unpleasantness.

She stared at the pen in her hand, then at the drawn blinds. In a room over this lay all that was human of Alexander Mason. A still, mute body that would never move or speak again. It was really very horrible to think of him dying like that in the night. Poor, wretched Alec! How quiet the house was. The servants moved about on tiptoe. It was Nora who had drawn all the blinds; with the domestic servant's fervent belief in flaunting one's grief. Scharlie wouldn't have drawn those blinds. She hated the hot, oppressive gloom of the house. She liked the sunshine.

She had told Henry Gorring that she had finished with love. Yesterday, when Hugh had failed her, she had felt that love was dead within her. Yet now she was agonisingly conscious of the need for him. She did not realise just then that it was a craving for love, for sympathy, rather than a desire for Hugh, personally. But she was afraid of herself.

She suddenly reached for the telephone which stood on the desk. She must 'phone for Dee. Yes, little Dee Wilberforce would come to her and was just the person she needed. A practical, sensible, little thing, and her real friend.

Dee Wilberforce arrived, soon after four o'clock, to find a white-faced, distraught

Scharlie anxiously awaiting her. Dee neither kissed her nor sympathised with her, which she knew would reduce her to tears. She just tucked an arm through hers and walked with her up to her bedroom.

'Come and help me wash my face. It's dusty. Parkins was electrified because I drove the Bentley at seventy-five along the London Road. I was out, and I didn't get your 'phone message until I got home a couple of hours ago. I was throwing a fly down at the Sloop Pool with Tim. But I came as soon as I heard what had happened. My poor dear, you look all in.'

'I am,' said Scharlie in a stifled voice, and was infinitely glad of the sane, and at the same time, intensely sympathetic presence of her old school friend. 'Dee, isn't it frightful?'

'What—the decease of Alec? I suppose it is for him, but, my dear old thing—he's at peace and so are you. That's what I said to Tim.'

For the first time that gloomy day, Scharlie smiled. 'Dee—you are absurd!'

'That's better,' said Dee. 'Now come and tell me all about it.'

'It's marvellous of you to have come.'

'Not a bit.'

'Didn't Tim hate me for sending for you?'

'Of course not. He was much too busy trying to land a minute trout, about the size of a sprat, which he declared nearly pulled him into the water. I left him to it. He'll probably come

179

up to town later on, and we'll all retire to an hotel for the night and drown our sorrows in drink.'

'Oh, Dee, will you stay with me, then, for a bit?'

'For as long as you need me, old thing. You can come down to Gateways with us after the funeral. When is it to be?'

'Day after tomorrow. Mr. Lawton, the solicitor, is arranging everything. All Alec's relations blame me for his death. They've been frightful.'

'Blame you—why?'

'They say I drove him to it . . . because I had a lover.' Scharlie blurted out the words.

Mrs. Wilberforce closed the bedroom door behind her and gave Scharlie a searching glance from eyes which were as bright, as kindly inquisitive as a robin's.

'Have you, Scharl?' she asked.

Scharlie sat down on the edge of her bed and put her face in her hands.

'Not . . . really. My love-affair didn't get very far. It wasn't a success.'

'I see, my dear. Well, that's all right. Don't let it worry you.'

'It wouldn't. Only Alec wrote abominable letters to various people about it. I'll tell you later . . . and, among others, he wrote to Lawton, the lawyer. But I fancy Alec has cut me out of his will . . . I'm positive I shan't have a bean. Not that I care. I'll earn my own living.'

180

'That's the spirit. My God, but if Alexander Mason wasn't lying dead in this house, I'd say a few blistering words to him. My poor dear, you've had a pretty thin time.'

Scharlie was mute. But in Dee's words she heard an echo of Henry Gorring. 'A pretty thin time . . .' he had said that. He had been strangely kind . . . the man she thought such a prig, such a brute.

Mrs. Wilberforce came up to the bed and patted the girl's bowed head.

'You're not to cry, Scharlie. This is the best thing that could have happened, my dear. You're free now, and you've all your life before you.'

But Scharlie's lonely and wounded heart cried:

'What . . . what have I got before me. Only existence. Nothing that means anything.'

'After all, Scharlie,' said Dee, 'life's an absolute jest, and, if you look at it with a sense of humour, so is death . . . the biggest jest of all, with the laugh waiting for us on the other side. And love is a jest, too. Nothing should be taken seriously.'

Scharlie looked up at her with eyes full of tears.

'You may be right about life—about death. But if love is a jest, Dee, then at times it's a pretty poor one. I can't see the joke . . . I can't . . .'

'But it's there, my dear. This year you weep

181

over it. Next year you'll laugh. That's the joke. Aren't we being subtle? Come and find a pot of Velva cream and let's do up my dusty face.'

CHAPTER FIFTEEN

For the two days preceding Alec Mason's funeral there was comparative peace for Scharlie. Dee Wilberforce bore her off to an hotel in Knightsbridge. Tim joined them; somewhat chastened in spirit, having lost his fish, which, he insisted, had weighed four pounds, while his wife declared it was no bigger than a sardine.

They bickered and argued persistently and affectionately. Scharlie loved being with them. They were both charming to her, and they made her laugh and forget the gloom of Arlingham Place.

But all the unpleasantness broke out for Scharlie with renewed vigour on the day that Alexander Mason was conveyed to his last resting-place. Scharlie hated every morbid minute of the funeral. She knew the disapproving eye of the family rested on her continually. She was expected to appear in widow's weeds; to lean upon somebody's arm, cover her eyes and sob. She could do nothing like that. She wore a black georgette dress and a big black straw hat which made her look very thin and very pale. But she leaned upon nobody, and she was too sincere to simulate a grief which she did not feel. She just stood beside Frances, who sniffed audibly all the time; and stared not in the yawning grave, but at the clear blue of the sky and the bright green of the grass. It was such a perfect summer's day. She felt that death and all the conventional aftermath of it; the dismal black; the awful ugliness of a newly made polished coffin; the ugly brown hole into which it was placed—were all wrong, on such a day as this.

She supposed Alec, poor man, would have liked it this way. He had been conventional; meticulous about sending wreaths to the funerals of his relatives or friends. He would have enjoyed seeing that quite a number of wreaths and crosses had decorated his own hearse.

But Scharlie hated it. She, who loved flowers, could not bear these formal wreaths of white, waxen-looking blooms; or even the coloured ones, which were so stiff and unnatural wired to their frames. As Alec's widow she had been forced to add to the so-called 'floral tributes.' But the old aunts had mentioned that they disliked her choice; a sheaf of scarlet roses, which they thought flaunting and not suitable.

'When I die,' thought Scharlie, 'I hope my funeral won't be like this. I can't bear it . . .'

She looked round the family; the aunts; the

Lee-Joneses; two first cousins; an uncle; one or two friends from the Stock Exchange. Alec's near relatives were closing round the grave now that the service was finished. Scharlie did not move. They eyed her resentfully. They objected strongly to her composure and reticence, which they mistook for disgraceful lack of feeling. They had always suspected that poor Alec had married a silly frivolous child, and now they knew it.

To Scharlie they were like a lot of black crows, flapping round Alec's remains . . . They were only waiting . . . hoping to benefit under his will. They did not really mourn for him. During his lifetime they had rarely troubled to come and see him.

'It's a farce,' Scharlie reflected.

She pictured the right sort of funeral. No coffin, no hearse, no tombstone. Just a laying down of a tired body under the trees in some dim and mighty forest; just a covering of leaves and wood-violets, with only the birds and the stars to mourn. There would seem nothing dreadful or frightening about death, then. But this funeral of Alec's—the first she had ever attended—seemed to her a ghastly thing.

When it was over, the family gathered in the library and waited for Mr. Lawton to read Alexander Mason's last will and testament. Scharlie crouched like a child in a big saddle-bag chair. She felt limp; exhausted. She longed to get back to her hotel and the Wilberforces.

It was so hot and oppressive in this room. Frances Lee-Jones would keep sniffing and wiping her eyes. The old aunts, Agatha and Cissie, whispered to each other, as though they thought it indecent to talk aloud.

Scharlie wished that Dee were here. But Dee had said:

'I shall stay away, my dear. I can't bear funerals, and I shouldn't be a success in the family circle, anyhow.'

Scharlie felt that she, herself, was far from a success. Only Edward Lee-Jones, who was not of the Masons, cast her an occasional glance of sympathy from his large, melancholy eyes. Scharlie could hear his meek voice, constantly answering his wife with the habitual: 'Yes, dear.' She was sorry for him.

The uncle, the old Alexander Mason, who was nearing seventy-five, and wore a white beard and gold-rimmed glasses, was full of rheumatism and asthma. He was deaf. He heard little and said less. He peered with small menacing, red eyes round the circle, and barked and wheezed at regular intervals. The cousins, one married, one single, were representatives of Alec's mother's side. They were younger than Frances and more modern. But they were dull girls; badly dressed and plain, with lank bobbed hair and the thick, short necks of the family. One of them, the unmarried one, sucked lozenges without ceasing, and had but one topic of conversation.

Should tonsils be removed or should they not?

She asked Scharlie about this, but beyond that made no further conversation and eyed her with gloom. Scharlie felt that none of these women approved of her attire. The georgette dress, with its transparent sleeves and rather long, flowing skirt, was well cut; and gave Scharlie that *chic* appearance which the others lacked. The Masons would consider it wrong to look *chic* at a funeral.

In any case, Scharlie was certain that Frances had broadcasted her belief that it was the conduct of Alec's wife which had given him his death-blow. The atmosphere in general was so hostile.

Scharlie did her best to remember the nice things about Alec; the Alec of four years ago who had been quite kind and amiable and crazy to marry her. She had liked him then. He had been the first man to propose to her. She had been flattered by his passion for her; influenced by her mother. And she had been much too young; too thoughtless and inexperienced to look far ahead and see that such a marriage must necessarily end in disaster. The disparity in their ages had not seemed to her very great at the time of their union. He had done his best to amuse and please her, to pander to her wishes. She had met none of the family, then, except his sister Frances. It was only later, when she, herself, had matured and gained experience, that she saw how utterly Alec was unsuited to her; and then it was too late.

When she sought to remember the first, happier days, she was conscious of failure. She could think of nothing but the Alec of this last year; the Alec who had grown fat, gross in mind as well as body; who had bullied and harried her; who had finally insulted her; struck her across the face.

She shivered and closed her eyes.

'Alec,' she whispered, 'I'm sorry . . . if you can hear me the other side, I'm sorry. But I am glad you are gone . . . yes, I'm terribly glad I'm free.'

'What was that . . . what was that you said?' The thin high voice of old Uncle Alexander suddenly disturbed Scharlie's thoughts and made her open her eyes.

'I said, Uncle Alex, that poor, darling Alec had very little real happiness in his life. He worked much too hard,' repeated Mrs. Lee-Jones, and cast a bitter look at Alec's young widow.

'I agree—I agree,' barked old Mr. Mason. 'Much too close in here . . .'

'He's deafer than ever—it is trying,' Frances complained to her husband.

'Yes, dear,' he said.

A faint smile hovered on Scharlie's lips. It was really very funny. They were all so serious and comical.

Winnie Emmott was talking in a lachrymose

voice to old Aunt Cissie.

'What do you think, Aunt? Some people say it's very silly to have your tonsils out, and others say it's absolutely necessary.'

Aunt Cissie—an enormous body in voluminous folds of very hot-looking black alpaca—wiped her forehead with a handkerchief which had, thought Scharlie, the dimensions of a pillow-case.

'You keep away from the surgeon's knife,' said Aunt Cissie. 'It's all stuff and nonsense, this modern craze for operating, my girl. I've never had a doctor in my life, have I, Agatha?'

Aunt Agatha, thin and small and dried-up, with the appearance of an old, squeezed lemon, replied:

'Certainly not, Cissie.'

'Nor a dentist,' added Aunt Cissie triumphantly. 'Have I, Agatha?'

'Certainly not, Cissie.'

Winnie Emmott, having received no satisfaction here, turned to old Uncle Alexander. She plaintively questioned him about throats. He peered at her and wheezed:

'Yes, yes, yes, you've grown a fine big girl . . .'

Winnie in disgust lapsed into silence.

Philip Lawton cleared his throat and began to read the will.

Then came Scharlie's bad hour. Before Mr. Lawton had finished reading the document, she was sitting up straight on the edge of the chair; her cheeks fiery red; her breath quickened; nervous fingers tearing her handkerchief to shreds. And the entire family focused a shocked censorious gaze upon her. If, before, they had disapproved secretly, they openly condemned her now.

Alec had taken his revenge. An incredibly mean one; so mean, so indelicate that Scharlie could scarcely believe her own hearing. She knew that Alec had been enraged by her determination to leave him. But she had not dreamed that, in his violent anger, he would make a public exhibition of her; even of his own failure; and, worst of all, bring into unpleasant publicity the man who was blameless of the whole affair.

With a sensation of deep humiliation and injustice, Scharlie heard the clear, staccato voice of the lawyer. He was reading the codicil which had been added by Alec Mason shortly before he died.

'Every penny of the money which I would have bequeathed to my wife, Scharlie, under normal circumstances, I now leave to be divided between my sister, Frances Lee-Jones, and my cousins Winifred Emmott and Ida Parker. My wife has shown me clearly that she dislikes me and that she is in love with another man, and I would like it known that this is the reason why I have altered my will. I wish my Executors to pay Edith Mitchell the sum of £100 in recognition of her faithful services to my mother and myself . . .'

The lawyer's voice ceased. There was a deadly silence. Then Uncle Alexander said querulously:

'What was that? What did Lawton say?'

Then Alec's sister, triumphant:

'Disgraceful! I'm horrified. Absolutely horrified!'

Scharlie looked at her. Mrs. Lee-Jones's face was radiant. Scharlie could have laughed if things had not been so serious. Frances was not at all horrified. Only delighted. This gave her food for scandal for the next few months.

From Aunt Cissie, in a fat breathless voice:

'Well, well, *well*—what a thing!'

'What a thing!' echoed Aunt Agatha.

Scharlie swallowed hard. She cast a swift look round the circle. She saw an expression more of envy than of horror in the eyes of Cousin Winnie. She wondered if the poor sickly spinster, tired of too much virtue, would have liked to have been accused of having a lover—and with reason.

Then Scharlie stood up.

'Alec was quite mistaken,' she said. She spoke calmly in spite of the heavy beating of her heart, and her scorched cheeks. 'I have no lover. It's most unfair—most unjust!'

A mixed chorus from the family:

'Alec would never have made such a

190

mistake . . .'

'My brother was *not* a liar . . .'

'My nephew would never have concocted such a tale . . .'

'Oh, Cousin Scharlie, well, I *never* did!'

And from Uncle Alexander:

'I haven't heard a word. To whom has Alec left his money?'

Lawton shouted to him:

'It is to be divided between his sister, Mrs. Lee-Jones, and his cousins, Miss Emmott and Mrs. Parker.'

'But what about Alec's wife?' wheezed Uncle Alec, peering at Scharlie.

'She's cut out, Uncle Alex,' screamed Mrs. Lee-Jones, with a fierce note of satisfaction. 'Cut out of it because my poor brother discovered that she had a lover.'

'A brother?' repeated Uncle Alex. 'I didn't know Scharlie had a brother.'

'No, a *lover*, Alex,' Aunt Cissie breathed into his ear.

'A lover! Dear me! Good gracious me! . . .' Uncle Alexander's rheumy eyes grew round and petrified behind their magnifying glasses. 'Good gracious, good gracious, what next, what next!'

Scharlie was really afraid she would laugh in a moment.

'You're all wrong, I assure you,' she said. 'Alec couldn't have been in his right mind. I've never had a lover.'

'Alec was much too just and truthful to have invented it,' declared Frances Lee-Jones. 'Wasn't he, Edward?'

Mr. Lee-Jones glanced at Scharlie; at the young slim lines of her body; at the beauty of her face, challenging them all in the gloomy, funereal room. And he thought of the gross form and mind of his late lamented brother-in-law, and pitied Scharlie. If she had taken a lover, good luck to her. But the habit of years was strong, and he answered his wife as she expected to be answered:

'Yes, dear . . .'

'None of you can prove it, anyhow. Alec couldn't prove it,' said Scharlie, and tilted her head backwards. 'Alec himself couldn't prove it. You can't prove a thing that doesn't exist.'

'One moment,' said Mr. Lawton. 'My late client wrote a letter to me the night before he died.'

'My lord!' thought Scharlie. 'Poor Alec seems to have spent his last hours on earth writing libellous letters. What has he said now?'

'What does he say, Mr. Lawton?' asked Mrs. Lee-Jones, with a black-edged handkerchief to her lips.

Mr. Lawton cleared his throat and cast an uneasy look at Mr. Mason's young widow.

'He—ah—appears to have had some presentiment of his death. At least—ah—he says in this note that he was writing to me because his wife was on the point of leaving him and he wished me to be in possession of—ah—certain facts.'

'But what right had he to do all this?' exclaimed Scharlie. 'What happened between Alec and myself was surely private.'

'You can scarcely run away from your husband *privately*,' said Mrs. Lee-Jones in an acid voice.

'Scarcely,' echoed Aunt Cissie.

'Scarcely,' re-echoed Aunt Agatha.

The cousins, with pursed lips, nodded to each other.

'Alec would have divorced you if he had lived, of course,' said Mrs. Lee-Jones.

'But he had no reason to divorce me. All this is without justification,' said Scharlie. She clenched her hands and turned to the lawyer. 'Mr. Lawton, really, since Alec chose to make our quarrels public, then I now declare in public that he had no cause to accuse me of infidelity; no grounds for divorce; and no right to place me in such a position as this. I don't care a bit about the money. I don't want it. But this attack on my character is outrageous!'

Edward Lee-Jones looked at her with his mournful eyes.

'What a pretty child,' he thought. 'The lover's a lucky fellow. Alec was a swine. The poor, pretty creature!'

Mr. Lawton glanced at the letter in his hand.

'I very much regret, Mrs. Mason, that I must proceed with this very painful business, but I must respect my late client's wishes.'

'Naturally,' said Frances Lee-Jones.

Mr. Lawton began to read the letter aloud.

DEAR LAWTON,—Tonight my wife announced her intention of leaving me. Nothing I can say or do will induce her to change her mind. This fact satisfies me that I was justified in altering my will a few days ago. And tonight's procedure has satisfied me that my wife has been unfaithful to me.

'One never knows when one's last hour will come. Should mine come before I can protect the honour of my name I would like you to use this letter with its information and make it known to my family that the name of my wife's lover is Henry Gorring, son of the well-known publisher, Walter Gorring. As soon as I have strong enough evidence for divorce I will write to you again . . .'

The lawyer looked up. Scharlie was trembling. It never entered her head that Alec would go so far as to drag Henry Gorring's name into the limelight in this way.

'Oh!' she gasped. 'It's outrageous—it's untrue—you see what he says—*when* he has the necessary evidence—and he would never have had it—never!'

'Don't be a fool, my good girl,' said Mrs. Lee-Jones. 'You know perfectly well you were on the very point of running away from Alec.'

'But not with anyone,' declared Scharlie.

Mrs. Lee-Jones began to sob.

'Alec wrote that letter only a few hours before he died. My poor unhappy brother—he must indeed have had a presentiment that the end was near at hand,' she said. 'It isn't the slightest bit of good this girl denying anything. Alec even knew the name of the man. Henry Gorring! The blackguard! I shall write to him and tell him he sent my brother to the grave.'

The aunts in loud whispers exchanged remarks.

'Young Gorring, the publisher . . .'

'Scandalous!'

Old Uncle Alexander barked:

'What's it now? What's it now? I can't hear a word!'

Aunt Agatha took it upon herself to scream at him.

'Poor Alec wished us to know the name of the villain who came between him and his wife. It's young Gorring, the publisher . . .'

Scharlie put her hands to her ears.

'Oh, stop, all of you! It's a wicked libel! It's most untrue!'

'I have every intention of writing to the young man and telling him what I think,' said Frances Lee-Jones.

'So shall I,' said Aunt Cissie, and wiped the

195

moisture from her downy lip. 'He'll have a piece of my mind. One of these wasp-waisted dancing men, I'll be bound!'

The thought of Henry as a wasp-waisted dancing man almost restored Scharlie's sense of humour. She didn't know whether to laugh or to cry. But she thought how petrified Henry would be when he knew about this. Heavens! But the attempt on his part to cover Hugh for Eleanor's sake had had dire results.

As futile for her to argue or reason with Alec's family as it had been to argue or reason with him in his lifetime. Alec had always been a queer creature with a streak of malice in him. Nobody but Alec would have written such bitter, libellous statements to Walter Gorring and to Mr. Lawton just because he had been enraged and defeated.

The harm was done now. Nothing she could say would undo it. It placed her in an impossible position, and Henry in an equally difficult one. For neither of them could explain what had really happened. Hugh, who had so nearly been her lover, was right out of it now. It was truly ironic. And if Frances and Aunt Cissie kept their words and wrote to Henry, what would he do? What could he do but suffer in silence? It was so absurd; the mere notion of the Mason family, *en masse*, descending in wrath upon Henry Gorring— Henry who was not her lover; scarcely her friend.

In a confused way Scharlie reflected that she would now be thrown upon her own resources, not only penniless, but disgraced. When her mother heard about this, she would remain discreetly abroad and be out of it. She would have no use for a daughter whose name had been touched by the finger of scandal. She had had very little use for her before.

It seemed curious to contemplate that all this chaos was the result of the passion that had awakened in her for Hugh. Such an empty, sterile passion, after all! She was beginning to feel very bitter about life. Nothing seemed worth while.

The family had risen with one accord to their feet. They were circling round Mr. Lawton. The library buzzed with voices. Scharlie stood apart, quite conscious that the accusing finger was pointed at her and that she was now an outcast. She even caught the tail end of a remark from Frances:

'. . . no right to stay in my brother's house . . . She'd better let this Mr. Gorring support her . . .'

Scharlie spun round and faced them, tears more of anger than of grief blinding her sight.

'Oh, you needn't worry, Frances. I'm going. I meant to go before Alec died. I've always hated it here. Hated it! And it's no good me telling you that Alec's made a dreadful mistake—that Mr. Gorring is not—never has been—my lover! You wouldn't believe it—

you've got such beastly, horrible minds! I don't want to see any of you again. I hope I never will!'

She walked past them and out of the library, and closed the door behind her.

'Most unpleasant, all this,' murmured Mr. Lawton, coughing.

'The young hussy,' sniffed Aunt Cissie.

'Fancy dear Alec remembering me in his will,' sighed Ida Parker.

'Now I shall most certainly,' said Cousin Winifred, 'have my tonsils removed by the *best* man in town!'

CHAPTER SIXTEEN

Scharlie returned to the hotel not as Dee Wilberforce expected to see her, which was depressed and quiet. She was flushed and furious, and the light of battle was still in her eyes when she marched into the lounge. Dee was sitting there, talking to Tim, who had just returned from his club. They looked at Scharlie and then at each other.

Dee said:

'Well, my dear, how goes it? You look all het-up.'

'Het-up!' repeated Scharlie. 'I am!'

'What, after a funeral,' said Dee and blinked at her. 'What's happened? Have the

Mason aunts been bullying you. You're very flushed, my child; not that it doesn't become you.'

'She has the complexion of a tangee lipstick,' said Tim, and grinned at Scharlie.

'Oh, Tim, don't be so stupid,' protested his wife. She patted the sofa beside her. 'Come and sit down and tell us all about it, Scharl.'

Scharlie sat down and removed her hat. She ran a hand through her curly hair.

'I'm so hot and so furious, I can hardly speak.'

'Order tea, Timmy,' said Dee.

'Tea for two and a whiskey-soda for one,' said Tim.

'Nothing of the kind,' said Dee, with severity. 'It's only five o'clock. You can't order whiskey till cocktail time.'

'You're a horrid little bully,' complained Tim.

Dee turned her back on him.

'I shall ignore you,' she said. Then, with a kindly look at Scharlie, whose colour was fast fading and who now had an air of deep dejection: 'What have they been doing to you, infant?'

'What they've done is only secondary to what Alec did before he died. Dee, it may be wicked to speak against the dead, but, *really*— Alec carried his spite too far. It's simply impossible.'

'What's he done?'

199

'Cut me out of the will and left his money to his various relations. Well, that doesn't matter so much. I shall earn my own living. But he did something meaner than that.'

'What? Cutting you out was pretty cheap of him.'

'Yes, but what about this?' Scharlie's colour was rising again. 'He added a codicil to the effect that he knew I was an unfaithful wife and'—she gulped—'wrote a letter to the lawyer, asking him to inform the family of this fact. He even went further: he told Mr. Lawton to tell the family the name of the man he imagined was my lover.'

'My dear Scharlie, he must have been mental.'

'Sheer spite—malice—jealousy—whatever you like to call it,' said Scharlie. 'You never knew what Alec was going to do when he lost his temper.'

'Anyhow, what harm can it do you, Scharlie?' said Dee.

'No real harm except that my name's mud in the Mason family—and I'm cut out of the will.'

'That's a damn' thing,' said Wilberforce. ' 'Pon my soul, it is. *De mortuis* and the rest . . . but I'd like a few words with Mason about this.'

'He had no right whatsoever to name the man. It's a bit awkward for everyone concerned,' said Dee.

'Specially awkward,' said Scharlie, 'as he has

200

named the wrong man.'

Little Dee's face suddenly creased into laughter.

'My dear Scharlie, do forgive me . . . but it sounds priceless. What on earth made Alec do that?'

'Oh, it's a most complicated story,' said Scharlie.

'So it seems,' remarked Wilberforce. He signalled to a waiter and ordered two teas in a loud voice, then, with a grimace at Dee, added, 'And two whiskey-sodas for me as soon as the clock strikes.'

'Fool,' said Dee, scowling at him. 'You'll die an alcoholic death, and I shan't mourn for you. Go on, Scharlie.'

'Are you taking me seriously?' asked Scharlie. 'I'm feeling frightfully worried.'

'My dear,' said Dee, 'of course I'm taking you seriously, but one can't listen to a great mutt like Tim and be serious, can one?'

Scharlie had to laugh.

'You're an absurd pair.'

'Carry on, Scharlie,' said Tim, his eyes twinkling. 'Only don't tell me that Mason named me as your lover, because Dee's that jealous!'

Dee withered him with a glance.

'Scharlie, continue. You say the lawyer told the family this man's name. And what else?'

'Well, it was the wrong name, but the aunts and Alec's sister, Frances, intend to write to this—this pseudo-lover and defend the honour of the family name.'

'Heavens, how funny,' said Dee.

'It would be funny,' said Scharlie, 'only the man is going to be pretty fed up. It puts him as well as me in a frightful position.'

'Who is it, Scharlie?'

Silence a moment. The colour swept Scharlie's cheeks again. Her lips tightened. Then she said in a low voice:

'Henry Gorring.'

Dee Wilberforce stared at her and sank back on the sofa, simulating complete collapse.

'That's more than I can bear. *Henry—Gorring?*'

'Yes.' Scharlie bit her lip. 'It is amusing, isn't it?'

'Gorring the publisher,' said Tim. 'Phew!'

'That estimable young man with horn-rimmed glasses who hates women and has eluded the marriage-bond for years . . . 'Dee went off into a fit of helpless laughter. 'Scharlie, what a *scream*! How on earth did Alec arrive at that?'

'I suppose I'd better tell you everything,' said Scharlie. 'But it's frightfully secret, Dee. Nobody must know the truth.'

'My dear, Tim and I are safe as houses.'

'Tell us, Scharlie. Perhaps we can help,' said Wilberforce kindly.

Scharlie told them the story from the beginning.

202

'I know it was rotten of me to ever start an affair with Hugh Ellerby,' she finished miserably. 'Because of Eleanor Gorring. But there it is . . . one can't always control love. And how could I have guessed, that fatal night, when I went round to Hugh, that he was expecting Miss Gorring to dinner? Oh, it's a complete mess, and the business of Alec's is the last straw. You can both see what a wretched position it is.'

The Wilberforces exchanged glances. They had listened gravely to Scharlie's story: without any flippancy. The affair certainly had its comical side; but they could see that it was without humour for Scharlie. She had thought herself wildly in love with Hugh Ellerby, and he had failed her. It was no good judging the affair from a conventional standard. No good saying she, a married woman, had no right to have a love-affair with an engaged man. For, as she said, one cannot always control love. And she had been so unhappy: so in need of a lover.

Behind all the ragging, Dee and Tim were warm-hearted understanding folk. They were intensely sorry for Scharlie.

'My dear,' said Dee, 'it's all most unfortunate. I'm not going to blame you for falling in love with Hugh. Don't think that, for a moment. As a matter of fact, when you were at Gateways, I guessed there was something up between you and Hugh. Remember?'

'Yes . . .' Scharlie's head sank.

'But I don't think he was worth a broken heart, old thing, and Tim and I have often said we don't think he is good enough for that nice Eleanor Gorring. He's very good-looking and charming, but frightfully weak with women.'

'But I did care for him, Dee . . .'

'I don't doubt you. But you couldn't have married him, Scharlie. Eleanor Gorring did rather complicate things . . .'

'Oh, yes, and I was married. I was a fool. I know.'

'Who isn't a fool about these things at times,' said Tim. 'Look what my own folly has brought me to . . .' He pointed at Dee, who grimaced at him.

Scharlie's sense of humour crept back. How could one be tragic for long, with these two dear and absurd friends?

'It would have been all right if it hadn't developed this way,' she sighed.

'Of course, for Henry Gorring to be so involved is terribly funny, but most awkward for you both,' declared Tim. 'He adores that sister of his, doesn't he?'

'Oh, yes,' said Scharlie. 'He has only one idea in life: to spare her unhappiness.'

'Well, she need never know about you and Hugh.'

'I don't want her to,' whispered Scharlie.

'You poor infant . . .' Dee's voice was warm and kind now. 'It's tough luck on you . . . all of it.'

'It certainly is,' said Tim.

Scharlie's eyes stung with tears.

'Don't pity me. I shall cry. I know I shall.'

'My dear, don't cry. Drink your tea and have a cucumber sandwich,' said Tim hastily. 'Or a sip of my whiskey.'

'No, thanks . . .' Scharlie smiled wanly at him.

'The present difficulty so far as I can see,' said Dee, 'is Mr. Henry. He'll doubtless receive infuriated letters from these frightful women.'

'Exactly,' said Scharlie. 'And, by the time this is all finished, he'll be imagining that I'm at the bottom of it—trying to compromise him.'

'He couldn't think that,' said Dee. 'He put himself into the position by interfering that night in Hugh Ellerby's flat.'

'But things have fairly hummed round his ears since then, Dee,' said Scharlie.

'He may behave like a perfect gentleman and come forward and propose to you,' suggested Dee.

'My God, that would be awful! I can't bear him, and he despises me.'

'First-rate reasons for marriage,' put in Tim. 'It ought to be a great success.'

'Shut up, Tim,' said his wife.

'There won't be any question of marriage between Mr. Gorring and myself,' said

Scharlie grimly. 'But I must say I hate the idea of all this scandal about us. A woman like Frances can spread it right round town.'

'H'm,' said Dee. 'Well, what can we do about it?'

'You've done quite enough for me, Dee,' said Scharlie, with a grateful look at her. 'And I don't know what I'd have done without you and Tim. There's nothing to be done about it, anyhow. But tomorrow I shall start looking for a job.'

'What kind?'

'I can't do anything well except play tennis and dance. You can't earn your living playing tennis, but you can get work as a dancer.'

'My dear child . . . what sort of dancer?' inquired Tim.

'Oh, a partner—an instructress in one of these dance-halls.'

'Scharlie, *not* a dancing-partner!' protested Dee.

Scharlie's lips were tight and her grey, wide eyes strangely hard.

'Why not? What's it matter? Nothing matters now.'

'Scharlie, you mustn't become bitter.'

'But I am . . . I feel it.'

Dee looked at her and was suddenly anxious. She hated to see how Scharlie, the child, had hardened. How the chaos of these last few weeks had altered her. And she was obviously miserable.

'Tim,' said Dee, turning to him, 'what can we do? We can't let the child become a dancing-partner. It's absurd; a most wretched life.'

'I mean to do it,' said Scharlie, 'I must do something.'

'We might find you a job with better prospects,' said Tim.

'But what?' Scharlie shook her head and smiled. 'I'm no earthly good at secretarial work, Tim. I can't even type. I'm not clever. But I can dance. I'm simply facing facts.'

They argued about Scharlie's job and Scharlie's future until it was time to dress for dinner. The Wilberforces wanted her to go down to Gateways with them on the morrow and stay there for the time being. But Scharlie refused.

'It's adorable of you both—but I'm not going to land myself on my friends. I'm going to work. I've removed all my possessions from Arlingham Place. I'm a widow; absolutely free, even if I'm penniless. My mother certainly won't want to be saddled with me, and the last thing I want to do is to go back to her. We never got on. So I shall fend for myself.'

That was her final word to Dee and Tim.

When they were alone the Wilberforces discussed the situation gravely.

'I can't bear the idea of the child living alone in town in some cheap digs and being a dancing-partner,' said Dee.

'I agree, my dear,' said Tim, 'but she refuses to do anything else, so we can but come up to see her and keep a friendly eye on her. You know, my little Dee, that kid has pluck.'

'I always knew Scharlie was game. But she's never had a chance in life. Her mother was impossible and her husband was worse.'

'I like her spirit. She's not going to sponge on anyone.'

'Oh, no—not Scharlie. Lord, if she was a gold-digger, she could get what she wanted out of young Gorring. He dreads women and marriage, and to stop a scandal he'd probably write a handsome cheque. But Scharlie'd tear it in half if he did.'

'I like her spirit,' repeated Tim. Then added: 'It's damn funny, you know, Dee . . . Gorring saves his sister from a broken heart in most dramatic style and finds himself completely tied up with the girl . . . If I weren't so sorry for the kid, I'd be tickled to death.'

'And if you only knew what Henry Gorring is like!' said Dee. 'I agree—it's *most* funny!'

In her own room, Scharlie dressed for dinner in a state of deep gloom. Once away from Dee and Tim, her sense of humour would keep vanishing behind a cloud of depression. She looked at herself in the mirror; a pale, shadowy-eyed Scharlie in a black lace dress that made her look very slender and rather lovely. Even she, herself, could not deny that gun-metal silk stockings and black satin shoes showed off her long slim legs and small, arched feet to perfection. They were essentially feet for dancing.

'Dancing is all you're fit for,' she said to her reflection, with some bitterness. 'You've no brains.'

She wished suddenly, passionately, that she had been very clever; that she could do great things with her life. She wished, too, that she had not wasted the last four years in that hateful existence with Alec. She was free now. But what was this freedom worth? There was nothing to look forward to. Nothing nice to look back upon. Nothing in particular to live her life for. It was all going to be so aimless.

If Hugh had really cared . . . ah! but it was futile to think of *that* . . . because he belonged to Eleanor and he hadn't really cared. She would never see Hugh again. It was only a pity she had ever loved or kissed him; even believed in him. She could not even believe in love now. So much the better, perhaps. It didn't pay to have a heart. She would be heartless in future. She would make a good dancing-partner. That's what they should be like, those girls . . . they should have good ankles . . . no heart . . .

In Hugh's arms, down at Gateways, how terribly sentimental she had been! Striving after an ideal love . . . developing a soul. From now onwards she mustn't have a soul. No soul. No heart. Only a body. How dreadful that

209

sounded. Dreadfully cynical. And lonely. It must be a very lonely state; to care for nobody; have no one to care. And Alec had cut her out of the will because she had a lover . . . because he thought Henry Gorring was her lover.

Scharlie stared at her reflection and began to laugh. But the laughter ended in tears.

CHAPTER SEVENTEEN

The Wilberforces had to return to their Sussex home that following morning. They were expecting friends from abroad. Much against her will, little Dee left Scharlie alone in town.

'It's very naughty and silly of you not to come down to Gateways with us,' she grumbled. 'You're a stubborn child.'

'I'm sorry, Dee, but I simply can't come. I must start to look for work and make something out of my life,' Scharlie said.

And as soon as Dee and Tim departed, she settled down to the readjustment of her life. And she found it all most trying and difficult. For whatever else she had endured as Alec's wife, she had been used to bodily comforts. Now she no longer had those. And Scharlie was soon to realise how greatly material comforts add to the pleasure of one's existence. It is easier to be unhappy in luxury than to be unhappy and inpecunious at the same time. She was utterly thankful that she need never again sit at a well-laid table opposite Alec's gross form and watch him gluttonously devour his food. Nor have to share a dignified and well-appointed bedroom with him. Nor have an Edith Mitchell to wait on her and spy on her, too. But she was to miss the luxuries of existence, and miss them badly, at first, because she was as fond as any other woman of a soft bed; linen sheets; a good bath; plenty of hot water and bath-salts and expensive soap; a maid to wait on her.

She would have nothing like that now. On the morning that Dee and Tim departed—they insisted upon settling up her hotel-bill there—Scharlie had to move from an expensive locality like Knightsbridge to cheap rooms in Bayswater. And when she had pawned the one or two pieces of jewellery which she possessed, and a few other things of value—wedding presents which belonged to her and which she had removed from Alec's house—she found she had less than a hundred pounds in the bank.

Ninety-odd pounds and all her life before her!

A long cable from Mrs. Croft in answer to hers reached Scharlie that morning.

'Deeply regret Alec's death was married yesterday to George Nye cannot come to you do you wish to come out here to me

211

very inconvenient cable me Mother.'

Scharlie read this with some amusement. It in no way added to her depression. It was only what she had expected. Her mother had gone to South Africa with every intention of finding a second husband. Being pretty, smart, and youthful for her forty-five years, she had found one. She had mentioned the name George Nye in a previous letter. He was, so far as Scharlie remembered, a diamond merchant from Kimberley, and ten years younger than Evelyn Croft.

Had there ever lived a more selfish woman than her mother? Scharlie wondered bitterly. Those words 'most inconvenient' spoke volumes. She had, for the sake of appearances, asked her daughter if she cared to join her. But she had known Scharlie would not accept. The last thing on earth Scharlie would want would be to become an unwanted third out in Kimberley. The newly married Mrs. George Nye would not appreciate the arrival of a widowed daughter. Scharlie pictured her with a husband, younger than herself, in a constant state of jealousy.

'No, thanks, mamma,' thought Scharlie, and cabled back a refusal.

Of course, Mrs. George Nye did not know of the debacle that had followed her son-in-law's death. It would never enter her head that Scharlie had been left without a penny—and why.

Scharlie did not hasten to write the evil news.

She was on the point of leaving the Knightsbridge Hotel to move into the Bayswater boarding-house, when Henry Gorring appeared on the scene.

Scharlie was not surprised to see Henry. She had half expected him. Knowing Frances Lee-Jones, and the old aunts, she thought it quite on the cards that they would lose no time in writing their indignation and scorn to 'the man who had betrayed poor Alec.'

Henry called soon after lunch. Scharlie was standing in the reception-bureau, waiting for her luggage to come down from her room.

When she saw Henry's tall, erect figure and the stern face, with the horn-rimmed glasses, which had become so familiar of late, she gave a somewhat twisted smile and walked forward to greet him.

'I expected you'd come,' she said.

Henry had removed his hat when she approached him. He gave her a penetrating look. There was nothing friendly in his demeanour this morning.

'Oh, you expected me,' he said shortly. 'I see. I presume, then, that you know . . .'

'That my late husband's relatives have sent you libellous letters? Oh, yes. They threatened to.'

'When, may I ask?'

'After the funeral, when the will was read.'

'And you encouraged it?'

A bright flush of sheer anger stained Scharlie's cheeks. She had had a trying morning, looking for a cheap room and telephoning to various acquaintances who might help her get into some dancing-establishment. She was hot, tired, cross, and generally out of countenance. She was not, in any way, in the mood to stand that sort of tone or insinuation from Henry.

'What do you mean?' she said in a furious undertone. 'What *do* you mean by that?'

'We can't talk here,' he said. 'Please let us go somewhere where we can be quiet.'

Scharlie, too angry to speak, turned and walked towards a door marked 'Writing-room.' This room was empty. She faced Henry Gorring, but she did not sit down.

'Well?' she said.

Henry's temper was equally short. He, too, had had a trying morning. He had received various commiserations from certain members of the Mason family which had made his hair stand on end. Disgusting, defamatory letters. He had been extremely busy in the City, and much too busy to come and see Scharlie Mason until now. But the memory of the letters had troubled him; interrupted his train of thought the whole morning. He found it difficult not to believe that Scharlie was at the bottom of this. In fact, he was not far off thinking that this girl was, after all, a little adventuress who first of all tried to take Hugh from Eleanor; and now was trying to drag him into her toils.

'Well?' Scharlie said again.

Henry drew three letters from his pocket. He flung them on a small round table beside them with a gesture of disgust.

'Read those . . .' he snapped.

Scharlie glanced at the envelopes. The large, loopy hand-writing of Frances; the spidery scrawl of Aunt Cissie; the neat and meagre printing of Aunt Agatha. Her lips twisted.

'I'd just as soon not read them. I know who they're from. I can guess what's in 'em.'

'You know what they contain? You mean you fully realise that every word in each of those letters is a disgraceful libel . . . that it is not a question of insinuation, but a direct attack; a plain accusation that I betrayed Mason and committed adultery with you?'

'You're a bit blunt this morning, aren't you?' said Scharlie, her cheeks fiery red. Her lips grew a trifle harder.

'Your husband's relatives have been pretty blunt with me. I am being blunt with you.'

'Very well. Go ahead.'

Henry tapped the letters with his hand.

'Read them.'

'No. I don't want to. I know the sort of thing they say. And you've just put it very delicately.

215

We are accused of having committed adultery.'

'Quite so . . .' Henry's eyes were glacial behind the glasses, but his own face was hot. 'Mr. Mason's sister, Mrs. Lee-Jones, not only makes this accusation, but says I was the cause of her brother's death; that heart failure was brought on by his discovery of our wickedness. A lady who signs herself Cissie Mason writes in the same strain, but adds that she trusts that when I am married to you and enjoying the fruits of this wickedness that I will remember that I killed her poor nephew. Miss Agatha Mason, slightly concerned for your youth, hopes that I do intend to marry you, and that I will not let her nephew's widow walk the streets of London, disgraced and deserted . . .'

Some of Scharlie's anger evaporated. Henry, himself, was so angry that the funny side of it struck her. She tried not to smile.

'Well, really!' she exclaimed. 'Have you ever heard any thing more ridiculous?'

'It may be ridiculous,' said Henry. 'But it's extremely distasteful to me.'

'Only to you? What about me? Or are you really of the opinion that I'm at the bottom of it?'

He eyed her mistrustfully.

She read the mistrust and flared up again.

'If you do really think I wanted those horrible women to write to you—to compromise you—you must be mad. It's the last thing I want. I'm sick of the whole

216

business.'

Henry averted his gaze from her. The way those big grey eyes of hers flashed at him made him uneasy. He fixed a sullen glance on the letters.

'Perhaps you'll be good enough to explain—I'm rather in the dark—I mean, naturally I didn't expect to be openly attacked by your—your late husband's relatives. I was quite aware that I'd placed myself in an awkward position with him, by covering Hugh's tracks. But how did these women find out—?'

'Alec told them,' Scharlie broke in. 'On the night he died he wrote to his lawyer. He was in one of his violent rages, and he wasn't responsible for anything he did. He told Mr. Lawton that you were the man who'd come between him and myself; he instructed Mr. Lawton to make that fact public to the family after his death. Sheer spite on his part.'

Henry looked at her incredulously.

'And you mean to tell me he acted on such instructions . . . ?

'He did—to the entire family circle in my presence. Mr. Lawton seemed only too delighted to give the information.'

'I see,' said Henry. 'Well, he's given it . . .' He tapped the letters. 'It's damnable . . . all these scandal-mongering old women, bandying my name about town in connection with facts which are quite erroneous.'

'Oh, I daresay my charming sister-in-law,

Frances Lee-Jones, will whisper it at every bridge-party in town. She knows everyone.'

'And everyone knows the name of Gorring,' said Henry bitterly.

'Well, libel is against the law in England, isn't it?'

Henry looked up at her with a quick upward jerk of the head.

'You know quite well it is impossible for me to start a libel case; to make the thing any more public than it is. Good God, the whole truth would have to come out if I started.'

Scharlie began to feel tired. She sat down on the arm of a chair and looked helplessly round the cheerless, unattractive writing-room of the hotel. She wanted a cigarette and hadn't got one. She felt disinclined to appeal to Henry.

'Yes,' she said wearily. 'I suppose you'd have to explain about Hugh and say you were quite guiltless of the whole affair.'

'Well, that's impossible. My sister is on the point of being married to Hugh.'

Scharlie winced. Henry picked up the incriminating letters and began to tear them to pieces.

'I shall just have to ignore these,' he added. 'And if any more come, I shall put 'em on the fire. But if these interfering women spread too much scandal round town about me, and my father and sister get wind of it, there'll be the devil to pay. Endless trouble. It's a foul position, because my tongue's tied and I can't say a word.'

'It doesn't pay to interfere, does it?' said Scharlie sarcastically.

'No,' said Henry grimly. 'It does not.' Hands in his pockets, he began to pace up and down the room.

She looked at him through half-closed lids. Her lids curled scornfully. She said:

'Do you know, Henry Gorring, you're the most abominable and selfish prig I've ever met in my life.'

Henry flushed to the roots of his hair. He stopped in front of her; blinked at her through his glasses.

'You've called me a prig a good many times. May I ask why I am a prig at this particular moment? Is it unreasonable that I should be annoyed about those letters?'

'No. You have every reason to be annoyed. But you only look at the whole affair from one standpoint. Your own. What about mine? Oh, you can tell me that it's all my fault, originally, for indulging in an affair with Hugh. I'll admit it. I was a little fool. And any woman's a fool for loving *any* man . . . not one of you is worth it . . . not one!'

Scharlie's voice, passionate, hotly resentful, broke off. She swallowed hard.

'I think men are a most despicable sex,' she added.

Henry was dumb for a moment. This

outburst against men, from Scharlie, was unexpected and a somewhat angular development of their discussion. He pulled the lobe of his ear. It was tingling. Then he said:

'But, look here, what's that got to do with me?'

'With you? Nothing, of course. My contempt for men cannot interest you. But I despise you.'

'I'm sorry,' said Henry stiffly.

'You're concerned about your sister and yourself, and I can be pitched on to a bonfire in the market-place and burnt, for all you mind,' added Scharlie.

It struck her, as soon as she had made this speech, that it was childish and lacking in dignity. In fact, the whole conversation with Henry was becoming a vulgar brawl. She was so annoyed with herself for losing her temper and so tired that she suddenly burst into tears. That was dreadful. To cry in front of this despised male creature. She had her face in her hands, vastly ashamed, and tried to check her sobs.

Henry stood still, staring at her. He felt hot and embarrassed. A woman in tears was a sight he could not stand. His anger died. His suspicion of Scharlie died, too. Hadn't she already proved herself game? He might have known she wouldn't have encouraged those evil women to write: wouldn't want to compromise him. No wonder she despised him. He had behaved in a despicable fashion. She was right. He was very selfish. It was natural that he should resent the possibility of his name being publicly connected with hers; but he need not bully the child about it.

She *was* only a child after all. She looked about seventeen, huddled there on the arm of the chair with her face in her hands weeping. She had taken off her hat. The bright, chestnut hair was attractive in its untidiness. She was wearing a black tailor-made and white satin jumper. The short skirt had rucked up and showed one charming, rounded knee in thinnest of grey silk stockings. Henry's eyes focused on the knee, then ascended to the bowed, curly head. He coughed and cleared his throat.

'Look here,' he said gruffly. 'I say—don't cry.'

'Go away,' said Scharlie in a muffled voice.

'No, look here . . . don't cry. I've been a cad. I'm damn' sorry. But I was so furious about the letters.'

'You had every right to be. But it wasn't my fault. It was the *last* thing I wanted.'

'I'm sure it was.' Henry frowned and drew in his lips. He drew out his cigarette-case.

'Look here, have a cigarette. It'll soothe you. I don't want you to sit there and cry like that, my dear child—really!'

Scharlie fumbled in her bag.

'Damn, I haven't got a handkerchief,' she

whispered.

Henry produced a large silk one; grey-blue, to tone with his suit. He pushed it into her hand.

'Here you are,' he said.

Scharlie wiped her eyes with it, then handed it back.

'Now I'm a sight,' she said. 'But I don't care.'

Henry regarded her. Her cheeks were flushed and her eyelids red; her small tip-tilted nose was pink and shining. Tears still glittered on the longest lashes he had ever seen. He stuffed the handkerchief back into his pocket.

'You look all right,' he said kindly. 'Now sit down and have a cigarette and let's discuss this calmly. We've both been losing our hair about it, and it's so futile. Being angry with each other or anyone else isn't going to help put things straight, is it?'

She shook her head. He lit her cigarette for her. She held it with slim fingers that shook slightly. She felt thoroughly unnerved and dejected. She hated Henry. But she could not resist the feminine inclination to pull a little round gilt case from her bag and powder her shining nose. When it was powdered she felt better. Henry began to walk up and down the writing-room again.

'I don't suppose this business of the Mason family connecting my name with yours is going to make any serious trouble,' he said, after a pause. 'The best thing to do, in my opinion, is to sit tight and say nothing—ignore these people. Don't you agree?'

'Yes.'

'Of course'—Henry spread out a hand—'if the story is circulated round London Society by Mrs. Lee-Jones and reaches Eleanor's ears, she'll believe what she hears. She already believes I've had an affair with you.'

'Yes,' said Scharlie in a low voice.

'And she, no doubt, will consider I ought to marry you.' Scharlie flushed.

'There's no need for you to do that, I assure you,' she said sarcastically.

Henry pulled his ear. He averted his gaze from her.

'It's a very delicate position. If I hadn't interfered and your husband had fastened on Hugh as the man, Hugh might have considered it his duty to break with my sister and marry you . . . under these circumstances.'

'The question won't arise,' said Scharlie.

'No. But I'm not as self-centred or priggish as you think, and I do look at it from your point of view, also. Your name is tied up with mine. We're supposed to have been lovers. There's your character . . .'

'Please don't worry about that. Even if you were quixotic enough to think it your duty to marry me, I wouldn't accept.'

Henry was silent an instant. He glanced

sideways at her. It struck him as being most amazing that he should ever find himself in such a situation with Scharlie Mason; that their names should ever have been linked. And since they had known one another they had done nothing but bicker and argue. So she wouldn't accept him if he were quixotic enough to propose to her? That interested him. He was quite definitely ashamed of himself for thinking that she was at the root of the trouble.

'Listen,' he said. 'Since this has happened and we are in for a certain amount of trouble, supposing we stop squabbling and become friends.'

Scharlie blew a cloud of smoke into the air. Through it she looked at Henry. What a powerful face he had; strong, curved nostrils; thin, bitter lips. A man of sensibility, may be, she thought. But a man without sensuousness; to whom a woman's pretty figure or ankles or sex-appeal would mean nothing. She wondered if he had ever felt the thrill of passion in his life. If he had, his woman would be of his sister's type; a gracious, rather splendid creature; a woman of reticence; of brains.

'I suppose,' thought Scharlie, 'he looks on me as a stupid sort of butterfly. He doesn't really want to be my friend. He only wants peace at any price.'

'You know,' Henry said, 'I feel a sense of

224

responsibility towards you after all this.'

'You needn't,' she said. 'I can take care of myself.'

'H'm,' said Henry in a disbelieving voice. He gave her a thoughtful look. 'And may I ask what you intend to do now?'

'Yes, if it interests you,' said Scharlie coldly. 'I'm going to try and get a job as a dancing-partner, in some dance-hall or night-club.'

'But surely you've no need to do any such thing. Hasn't Mason left you fairly well off?'

'My husband cut me out of the will. He has left me nothing.'

'Nothing?' repeated Henry. 'Good God, do you mean that?'

'I do. He stated in his charming way that, owing to the fact that I was in love with another man, he would not leave me his money. So it's gone to his family.'

Henry stubbed his cigarette on an ash-tray. His eyes were dark with anger.

'That's the most outrageous thing. He had no proof—'

'None,' she said. 'Only this furious jealousy about you.'

'Good God!' said Henry again.

'So I must earn my own living, you see,' she added.

'I doubt,' said Henry, 'if Hugh quite realises how much harm he has done by his little lapse with you.'

'What's it matter now?' said Scharlie.

'It matters quite a lot. You're in a rotten position all round. Good heavens!'—he waved an arm—'the Masons think you're cut out of the will because of *me.*'

'Yes.'

'It's intolerable. Hugh must be told.'

'To what purpose? He's marrying your sister in a few days. It might upset him'—her voice was cynical—'even though he didn't care about me very much, it might make him ashamed of himself. What's the use of that?'

'He ought to be ashamed of himself.'

'Oh, no, let it alone; let him be happy with Eleanor now,' said Scharlie. 'I don't care about the money, anyhow.'

'But I do. It's unthinkable that a child like you should be chucked on her own in the world like this . . . Good God! You've no family of your own, have you?'

'Only my mother in South Africa, and she has just married again. She's asked me to go out to her, but nothing will induce me to.'

'But why not—?'

'Because, to begin with, my life would be impossible out there as a third. And, to end with, when she hears that I've been left nothing by Alec, and why, she won't want me.'

'So the rumour of our fatal intrigue is likely to reach as far as South Africa?'

'I'm afraid so.'

'If you'll pardon me saying so, I consider the whole business b—y,' said Henry.

Scharlie gave a deep sigh.

'It can't be altered now. But it'll all die down, and you won't see or hear of me again after today, I hope.'

'That's absurd.'

'Not at all. We aren't likely to meet . . . the famous publisher and the sixpenny dancing-partner.'

'You're trying to quarrel with me again,' said Henry. 'But I won't rise. Look here—you can't go off on your own and take a rotten job like that.'

Scharlie stood up. She pulled her hat down over her rumpled hair.

'I can and will. In fact, I'm interviewing the manager of a night-club this evening . . . a place Alec used to take me to occasionally. He knows me. He may offer me a job.'

'But wait,' said Henry. 'Where are you living?'

'In "digs." I'm moving to them now.'

He stared at her, nonplussed. Somehow the idea of this girl, living alone in 'digs', earning her living at a night-club, worried him beyond belief. And all because Hugh had made love to her; then thrown her on one side. Surely he, who had taken Hugh's place in this show, ought to offer her some sort of protection? She asked for nothing. She was game to the end. And if she had wished, she could have ruined Eleanor's happiness and Hugh's career. She might also, if she wished, force his hand today. But she did nothing . . . made no demands.

'Look here, Scharlie,' he said . . . her Christian name slipped out unconsciously for the first time. 'You must let me help you. You really must.'

Then Scharlie turned round on him in a fury.

'Do you think?' she said, with blazing eyes and scarlet cheeks, 'that I'd accept help from you? Are you going to offer me money? If so, please don't waste your breath. You've got yourself to thank if our names are unpleasantly linked; you shouldn't have interfered with Hugh and me. But you've done what you wanted—your sister is quite blissfully unconscious of the truth and Hugh's happy, and what do I matter, anyhow? I only ask you to leave me alone and let me forget you and your whole family. Good-bye.'

'Wait—' said Henry.

But Scharlie walked straight past him and out of the room.

BOOK TWO

CHAPTER ONE

Scharlie Mason sat on the floor, cross-legged, bare-footed; clad only in a pair of white crêpe-de-Chine cami-knickers; beside a chest of drawers. She was examining a jumbled pile of silk stockings of varied colours.

'Damn!' the said. 'If there isn't a hole in the heel of one, there's a ladder in the leg of the other. I am fed up.'

'My dear, it's *too* tragic,' said a plaintive voice from the other side of the room. 'Why *can't* they make forty-four gauge stockings that can't ladder? It's too *terribly* expensive, constantly having to buy stockings at fifteen and nine a pair. I haven't got one to my name that I haven't mended.'

'Well, this lot is nah-poo,' said Scharlie. She pushed the despised heap of stockings away from her and stood up. 'I must go and buy some. Can you lend me a quid, Boo?'

The girl addressed as Boo raised herself on one elbow from the bed on which she had been lying. She, also, was attired only in cami-knickers, but of a pinker and lacier kind than Scharlie's. She had a novel in one hand and a cigarette in the other. There was ash over the bedspread and pillow and on the floor and on her chest. She was a very fair, pretty girl not more than twenty-two, with a plump, charming figure and that exquisitely white skin of the pure blonde. She had heavy-lidded blue eyes which were always half shut, and gave her a sleepy, indolent appearance. Her lips, day or night, were rouged to a bright vermilion.

She had a husky, drawling voice, which was not unattractive. Everything in life to her was either 'too tragic' or 'too delicious.' Scharlie's request for money was the former.

'My dear, how *too* tragic! I haven't a cent. It's payday today, thank goodness.'

'Mine, too,' said Scharlie cheerfully. 'Oh, well, I must go out and draw on my deposit account, which is against my principles.'

'You're lucky to have a deposit account,' said the girl called Boo. 'I wish I had one. It would be *too* delicious.'

'Well, my dear old thing, I've only got one because of my mamma's quite unexpected generosity this Christmas; to say nothing of the kindness of my friend, little Mrs. Wilberforce.'

'My dear, anyone'd be kind to you,' said Boo. 'If I had a fortune I'd give you half. Look how decent you've been to me.'

'Shut up, Boo,' said Scharlie. 'And it's time you got dressed. It's half-past five. I must go out and get those stockings before the shops close.'

Boo dropped some more ash on her book; swept it off and settled back on the pillow.

'I can't dress yet. I must finish this chapter. The hero is *too* delicious, Scharlie. He's just kissed the heroine so brutally that she's lost consciousness.'

'Oh, you sickening woman—shut up!' said Scharlie.

Boo giggled and continued to read in silence.

Scharlie walked to the window and glanced out. It was August. One of those hot, breathless London days when the sky is grey rather than blue and there is a dark, brooding atmosphere of heat; of storm. Unpleasant, sombre weather.

'Lord, it'll be hot at the club tonight, Boo,' said Scharlie, still staring down at the pavements which seemed to throw up a shimmering warmth. 'Who wants to dance in this heat?'

'I know, it's beastly,' said Boo. 'You get all hot and sticky, and the men's hands are hot and sticky and they spoil your frock. My pink georgette will be a rag. It's *too* tragic!'

'I'd like to find myself on the river or in a forest,' said Scharlie.

'I like the river, dear, and a nice punt,' said Boo. 'But there are too many insects in a forest. That's one thing about London—you do escape the gnats.'

'My dear, the human gnat in London is the worst of all insects. Poisonous. You can get badly stung.'

'Oh, Gawd, you're being smart, Scharlie, and I can't follow you when you're smart,' said Boo.

Scharlie laughed.

'I'm going to dress and go out,' she said.

'I must get up, I s'pose,' sighed Boo; laid her novel down and shook the ash from her chest. 'I wish I hadn't eaten that new bread for tea, Scharl. I feel blown out.'

'Don't be silly. You had practically no lunch.'

'My dear, I had heaps, and I'm putting on weight every day. You *know* I am! Dancing half the night doesn't reduce me. It's *too* tragic.'

'You've got a complex about fat, Boo. You aren't fat.'

'My *dear* . . .' Boo sprang from the bed and stood before Scharlie, arms stretched above her head. 'Look at me . . . there are *rolls* of fat everywhere. Dunlop tyres round my waist and hips. You can't deny it.'

'I do. You're a bit plump, but just right.'

'Plump!' groaned Boo. 'Oh, you beast, Scharlie! Just because you're deliciously thin . . .'

'I'm too thin. Look at the hollow in my throat and my shoulder-blades.'

'It's marvellous, Scharlie. I'd give anything to be as slim. Oh! I must bant and stick to it or I shall get *enormous*!'

They held this conversation regularly. And

232

regularly Boo 'banted' for a day, then ate chocolates, cream buns, and new bread the following day. Boo's passionate desire to get thin and the refusal of her naturally plump figure to oblige her was a standing joke with Scharlie. She, herself, had lost nearly a stone this summer. She really wanted to put on weight in spite of the fashionable slenderness.

She left her companion to do her 'slimming exercises'; walked down five flights of stairs to the dark, stuffy hall of the building known as 'Stone Mansions,' and into the street. There, the heat of the August afternoon struck her like a blast. In spite of the thin flowered chiffon dress and big shady straw hat which she wore, she felt hot and tired before she had walked five hundred yards.

She went to the nearest 'Etam's' for her stockings. Stone Mansions was in a turning off New Oxford Street. It was not a very aristocratic neighbourhood, but convenient for the shops and buses. The flat, right at the top of the building, consisted of three rooms, a tiny kitchen, and bathroom. The rent was moderate.

Exactly a year ago this August, Scharlie had taken the flat with the girl known as Boo— otherwise Barbara Octavia Orbutt. As Boo explained to her friends, she had been the eighth daughter, and her disappointed mother had insisted upon christening her Octavia. But her initials, B.O.O., settled the question at an early age. She had been known from her babyhood as Boo.

Scharlie had first met Boo at the Dominoe—a flourishing little night-club—during Alec's lifetime. Alec had never been a dancing man, but his partner in the firm was what Alec had termed 'a bit of a gay dog.' He was at one time a member of the Dominoe. One night, about six months before Scharlie's first open rupture with Alec, they had gone to the Dominoe in a party. They were a woman short, and he had secured one of the dancing-partners for the evening and attached her to the party.

'If you others don't mind,' he said in his jovial way. 'It's so aggravating to be a girl short, and this Barbara Orbutt is a good dancer and a nice kid into the bargain. Works damned hard, but she's straight as a die.'

Thus Scharlie came into contact with Boo. And had liked the plump fair-haired, sleepy-eyed woman with her amusing, drawling voice, quaint tricks of speech, and a *savoir faire* which Scharlie—then very young and ignorant—admired. She met Boo on several occasions after that at the Dominoe, and from thence onwards found her just as she had been described—a hard worker who was straight as a die. And, as Scharlie was afterwards to discover, sometimes it is not easy for a pretty dancing-partner in a night-club to keep body and soul together and remain straight.

Walking to Etam's this afternoon through the teeming thoroughfare, Scharlie looked back on her year of widowhood and thought what a curiously crowded yet empty year it had been. Crowded with petty incident. Empty of any real happiness.

A very few days after she had said good-bye to the Wilberforces and moved to Bayswater, she had paid a visit to the Dominoe Club and solicited the help of the kindly, and friendly Boo Orbutt. She wanted a job; a dancing job. She felt that Boo, who had been an instructress and partner in the Dominoe for a couple of years, might be able to help. And Boo was only too ready to help. She was not quite of Scharlie's class. She was from the North and self-educated. She had, herself, been brought up to earn her living, and before her dancing job had been a shop-girl in a big draper's in Lincoln. She had liked and admired Scharlie from the moment they had met that night at the club. Envied her her position in life; her good clothes; her air of *chic* and breeding; and cordially admired her youthful beauty.

She was flattered and touched when Scharlie, widowed and penniless, came to her for aid. She gave it generously. She had always been on good terms with André Lavelle, the Frenchman who so successfully ran the Dominoe. She introduced Scharlie to André and asked him to give Scharlie a job. Scharlie danced for André and with him. The job was secured within a few moments. Monsieur Lavelle knew beauty and good breeding when he saw it. He also knew that Scharlie, although an amateur, could dance exquisitely, and that men would like her.

So, for a whole year now, Scharlie had danced every night at the Dominoe. And that was the beginning of a new life and a new, firm friendship with the girl who had introduced her to it.

Boo was alone in the world. When Scharlie came along, she—like Scharlie—was existing somewhat drearily in a boarding-house. They discussed ways and means; decided they would like to share a little flat; make some kind of home. They found Stone Mansions and the vacant top floor and they moved into it.

Dee and Tim Wilberforce had insisted upon helping them furnish it when they heard of the venture. They considered it a good thing for Scharlie to share a home with another girl; much better for her than eking out a miserable, solitary existence in a boarding-house.

'The attics at Gateways are crammed with odd bits and pieces of furniture,' Dee had told Scharlie. 'Things from my old home when Mum died, and from Tim's grandmamma, which we don't ever use. I shall send you a cart-load.'

Which, she did, promptly. A very grateful

Scharlie and Boo found themselves the tenants of a modest but comfortable little flat, quite tastefully furnished. To Scharlie it was a haven after the storm. To Boo it was a paradise. For the last seven years she had been alone and homeless. Her parents were dead, and the sisters of her family who were alive had married; several had gone abroad. She had yearned for her own home and never been able to afford one. But she and Scharlie, between them, could just manage things on a very economical basis. They were excellent friends.

Boo, the elder and more experienced in a life of this kind, could help and advise Scharlie and put her up to all the tricks of the trade. Scharlie, in her turn, gave Boo a friendship of which Boo was at once proud. It contained just those elements of culture; books; music; and taste; which Boo could not always understand but which she admired, almost pathetically, and tried to absorb.

The flat in Stone Mansions was a success. Scharlie was happier there, jogging along with Boo, than she had ever been in the luxurious house in Arlingham Place with Alec. But of course there were moments when she hated the life in the club; hated and resented it. Boo was more placid, less temperamental. She accepted the disagreeable parts of her existence without grumbling. She was there, at the club, to dance with any and every man who

237

'bought a ticket' for her during the evening. If he were old she was bored, and if he were young and danced well, she was pleased. But she regarded all men as necessary factors in her life. She treated them as such. Behind her sleepy, good-humoured manner she was quite alert, sharp about money, with an eye to the main chance. She 'played up,' as she called it, to the men who admired her. Yet she was at heart a complete sentimentalist, and fiercely virginal. She had lived, curiously, though a difficult and Bohemian life without losing that prudery which was inherent in her. She came of yeoman, Puritan stock. Her one desire, she confided to Scharlie, was a husband, and children. Children more than the husband.

During the past two years, since she had taken up dancing, she had met two men, either of whom she could have loved and married and to whom she would have made an estimable wife. Behind all her love of clothes; of luxury; of glitter, she was domesticated. But the first of these two men in her life had wanted to live with and not marry the dancing-partner, so Boo had quietly dropped out of the running.

'I just faded, my dear,' she had told Scharlie. 'It was *too* tragic . . . He was so handsome and such a good lover; but I'm not going to be any man's mistress. I want babies.'

The neat likely man had offered her marriage, and she had actually begun to sew her trousseau. Then he suddenly departed for Canada, and Boo found herself jilted. If she were heart-broken, she refused to show it. She just went on with her job. And went on solidly declaring she wished to have babies, and, because of that reason, would not accept any of the many light offers made to her by men who found her charming.

Since she had met and lived with Scharlie she was all the more determined to secure honest motherhood at any sacrifice.

'Your friendship and sharing a flat with you have just given me that touch of respectability which may do the trick, Scharlie,' she said on one occasion. 'I adore kids, and I'm going to find a hubby and have half a dozen of 'em.'

'You're a good deal better woman than I am, Boo,' was Scharlie's response. 'Quite frankly, I don't want babies. I did once . . . when I first married. I don't now.'

Boo assured her that that was because she had been unhappily married. But one day, when she met the right man . . . she would want children, for a certainty.

The right man . . . dear, sentimental Boo! Scharlie could not help feeling cynical. Once there had been Hugh . . . and she had fancied he was the right man; had loved him madly; made herself ill and miserable over him. But that was a year ago. All over. Quite dead. Yes, she no longer loved or wanted Hugh Ellerby.

Last August, Scharlie cut a paragraph out of

a newspaper; the photograph of a handsome bridegroom and an attractive bride coming out of a West End church. Hugh and Eleanor. A radiant, smiling couple. Hugh's excellent profile in evidence. He was glancing proudly at his bride.

Scharlie looked at that photograph. She read the description of the 'pretty wedding' and the bride's 'lovely mediaeval frock and sheaf of silver lilies' and all the usual details and humbug of a Society wedding. She read it without a qualm; with a sensation of indifference. It seemed to her that she did not care; that nothing mattered any more. It had also seemed impossible to believe, while she read that newspaper report and looked at the faces of the 'happy couple,' that Hugh had ever looked at *her* with passion in his eyes; ever held her in his arms; ever said: 'Scharlie, I love you!'

Well, he had been Eleanor's husband for a year now. From time to time Scharlie saw paragraphs in Society journals concerning him and his wife. Knew that he was now a partner in Gorrings; that he had 'a charming house in Avenue Road.' Saw camera studies of him at a race-meeting, with Eleanor; at a ball, with Eleanor. Always, of course, with Eleanor.

She supposed that he and Eleanor were very happy. Even that thought did not hurt. Nothing hurt her now. The whole affair . . . with Hugh; with Alec; the sequence of events afterwards with Henry Gorring, had made Scharlie hard.

Boo Orbutt thought that life was futile and dull unless one could have a little love-affair—a very innocent one, mark you—and ambitions for the future. She was surprised, almost worried, because Scharlie scoffed at love and romance and was bored when men at the club made love to her. Amazed that the future did not seem to matter to her very greatly; that she just lived from day to day; had no particular ambition. It wasn't natural, felt Boo, for such a young and such a pretty girl as Scharlie. And of course it wasn't natural; merely a phase.

A month or two after Alec's death, Scharlie had heard from South Africa. Mrs. George Nye wrote a long, bitter letter reproaching her daughter for her foolish conduct; telling her she deserved to be cut out of her husband's will, for 'carrying on with another man.' She wished to have nothing more to do with her.

Scharlie had expected that. But at Christmas time had come another letter, containing a cheque for fifty pounds. Mrs. Nye had repented of her harshness. Perhaps she had suffered a few pangs of conscience, imagining her only daughter 'adrift' (as she had put it to the young husband who occupied most of her thoughts). She asked Scharlie to accept the money; to send her news; and to expect a regular allowance of fifty pounds a year. It was not generous, but it was useful, and much more than Scharlie had ever expected from her selfish, self-centred mother. The pound a week was, anyhow, her share of the rent of the flat in Stone Mansions. And something to depend upon.

The Wilberforces continued to be Scharlie's loyal and unfailing friends. Little Dee saw Scharlie whenever she was in town; made her a dozen and one presents in the most modest and tactful fashion; and induced her to go down to Gateways for a week-end's peace and sunshine when she could get away from town and work. Scharlie often wondered what life would have been worth without Dee and Tim. It seemed to her a most touching thing that folk so rich, so surrounded by well-to-do friends, so occupied by enjoying life, should still find time for her—the penniless Scharlie who had been cast out by her husband's family.

Of Henry Gorring, Scharlie had heard nothing now for many months. During the commencement of her career at the Dominoe Club she had received several letters from him; each begging her to accept financial help; telling her that in Hugh's place he felt responsible for her. They were not unkind or insulting letters; rather the reverse; they showed a genuine concern for her. But somehow they made Scharlie cross. She replied to the first few coldly and curtly; refusing help. Two she left unanswered. And then the communications ceased. Scharlie became satisfied that she had finished with the Gorrings.

On rare occasions when she had discussed her past affairs with Boo, the latter had questioned her wisdom in rejecting Henry's offers.

'The chap interfered and got himself mixed up with you, and the whole sweet family seem to have left you out in the rain. Why not let him help, since your hubby cut you out of the will, presumably for him?' Boo had said.

But Scharlie answered:

'No, thanks, Boo. I want no money from Henry Gorring or the family. They can keep it, and the Masons can keep Alec's. Let me have *some* pride, please . . .'

'You have a lot, Scharlie dear, but it's all *too* tragic,' Boo had sighed.

Perhaps it was 'too tragic.' Scharlie often thought so. But she could never take money from Henry Gorring, no matter how hard and bitter life made her. And where, after all, was the tragedy, since she could think of Hugh and his wife without one pang of the heart? In less than a year her love for Hugh had died.

Life was empty now. Purposeless. There was frequently an ache in Scharlie's heart these days; not for the past, but for the present. The ache of loneliness; a mental loneliness which the companionship of the kindly Boo could not alleviate. She felt that her existence was without purpose, and that nothing she had ever wanted could ever come her way. That she would never now realise any of the dreams of her extreme youth. They were all flung into the melting-pot of disillusionment. Can anything be more exaggerated, more painful, than the feeling of complete disaster which befalls disillusioned youth?

Every night Scharlie went to the club and danced mechanically; without pleasure; with no desire save to make enough money to live on. At first it had jarred on her horribly when a man purchased a ticket for her—'bought her' for a dance. Or, in some cases, a roll of tickets, so that he might dance with her the whole evening. It had hurt her sensibility; cheapened her in her own sight. But she tried not to become cheap; not to let the life coarsen her. And she succeeded. She danced—but she kept the men at arms' length. The men—the members who frequented the club, if not the strangers who visited it—knew exactly what to expect from Scharlie. None of them who knew her tried to take liberties with her.

Scharlie was not of common stock. Her good breeding was manifest even as a dance-partner in the night-club. The men she met very quickly recognised the fact.

In time she grew used to the job and the position ceased to jar on her. She speedily learned the tricks of the trade. With Boo and another girl who danced at the Dominoe, she earned extra money on certain afternoons by

244

giving instruction in modern ballroom dancing. To women as well as men. From time to time she met interesting people; *became* interested in her job. At intervals—certainly rare ones—she found herself dancing with some man of more than ordinary attraction; someone of charm and culture who could talk to her; who did talk to her; hold her attention and give her a really pleasurable evening. Once or twice she came across men who wished to meet her outside the club; to take her to lunch or out to dine and cultivate her acquaintance further.

But Scharlie, when she started on her dancing career, had made a vow to herself to refuse offers of that kind. She was no longer an innocent or ignorant child. She had been married; she knew men; she understood life. She saw the danger of cultivating promiscuous friendships with men whom she met at the club. She was cynical enough in these days to have no faith in platonic friendships. She did not want a lover. She wanted to run straight; not for any such reasons as prompted Boo's provincial respectability. Boo wanted a husband and children. But Scharlie could never see herself as a married woman again, or the mother of children. She was virtuous out of inherent decency; and a liking for straight, clean living.

Hugh had taught her passion as she had never known it with Alec. With Hugh she had experienced all the thrills, half-agonising, half-rapturous, of a forbidden intrigue, even though they had never tasted the final fruits of their amorous interlude. But his real lack of sincere passion for her; the way in which he had so abruptly, even brutally, failed her when she had sought his protection; had temporarily destroyed romance in Scharlie. With shattered romance passion had subsided. She thought it dead. The most attractive men who pursued her, nowadays, failed to rouse any emotional feeling in her and put her into no real temptation.

For the last three weeks life had offered her more of a thrill. She was no longer an ordinary dance-partner. She was an exhibition dancer. She had gained much, during her year of probation, in grace, in style, in sound technique. She had always danced well; moved beautifully. Now she was a dancer to be watched with real pleasure, and Monsieur Lavelle knew it; and knew his market.

The Dominoe needed regular exhibition dancers; something superior to the usual rather vulgar cabaret. Monsieur Lavelle had sought a partner for Scharlie and found him in a young man who had made his mark as an exponent of ballroom dancing in a certain West End dancing-academy.

This man, who called himself Claud, saw Scharlie at the Dominoe one night. He danced with her. And after that things were fixed up with André. Claud was willing and eager to partner Scharlie. He bore her off in triumph to his school in Regent Street. He coached her; rehearsed with her. He knew his job, and he gave Scharlie that finishing touch of perfection which she needed to make her a first-class exhibition dancer. She found herself no longer having to sit in a corner with Boo and the other girls and wait for men to purchase her partnership with a few shillings. She received a salary of five pounds a week—riches to her—and she danced only with Claud, at midnight every night, at the Dominoe.

Claud was not a common *gigolo*; neither was he of the effeminate and objectionable type of dancing man to be met with in night-clubs or hotels. He was half French. He had had a semi-French, semi-English education and was well read and intelligent. He had no use for the business career his English father had wanted him to follow and had broken away from careless paternal authority at the age of eighteen, and gone on the stage. His mother—a Parisian dancer—had bequeathed to him her talents, an artistic temperament and enormous vitality; an impetus not easily checked. But he did not do well on the stage because he could not sing. He was useless for musical comedy. He threw up the stage and turned to dancing as an art.

Now he had jobs all through the year in various parts of Europe. The summer of this particular year found him in London without much to do and with little money. He was wildly extravagant. So he accepted André Lavelle's offer for him to dance for the season at the Dominoe. His difficulty at first had been to secure the perfect partner. He had recently danced in Nice with Claudia, a French girl with whom he had been madly in love. He had lived with her for a few months and then in the spring she had died, suddenly, of pneumonia, following 'flu.

Claud was of ardent temperament; full of wild exaggerations and ridiculous moods. For a time the death of his partner and mistress rendered him heart-broken. He believed that he never wished to dance again.

Then he saw Scharlie; Scharlie at the Dominoe, with her charming, piquante face; her clustered chestnut hair; her slender patrician hands; her swift, graceful gestures; and the almost child-like wistfulness that lingered in her lovely eyes in spite of her cynicism. Claud changed his mind. He wanted to dance with Scharlie, and he did.

'You shall become a second Claudia. As "Claud and Claudia" we'll be advertised and make our names and fortunes,' he had told her, in the gay, impulsive way with which she was to become so familiar. All his old fire and enthusiasm had returned. 'Come along . . . we'll tackle old André Lavelle. I know him. He knows me . . . We'll fix it. If you'll agree . . .'

Scharlie agreed. It seemed to her more

pleasant to be an exhibition dancer than an instructress like poor Boo and the rest.

Nobody was more delighted than Boo when Scharlie burst forth into glory in this fashion.

'You'll be famous yet, Scharlie,' she said. 'Everyone knows Claud. He's a marvellous dancer. I think it's a lovely plan—*too* delicious, dear!'

For three weeks now, Scharlie had danced every night at the club with Claud, and was billed with him as '*Claud and Claudia; the famous Continental couple who will give an exhibition of ballroom dancing at the Dominoe Club tonight.*' She was quite thrilled with the advertisement and the whole idea of the job.

She no longer wore the regulation black lace dress of the club partners. She had new, charming dresses. She enjoyed the publicity and the nightly thrill of admiration and applause, once she overcame her initial shyness. She often asked herself, ironically, what Alec would think of his one-time wife could he see her now. She knew what the family would think! How horrified the aunts would be! But the Masons had not bothered their heads about her and had done nothing towards assisting their late brother's erring widow since writing those calumnious letters to Henry Gorring.

She thought a trifle uneasily of Claud, when she purchased new stockings this evening. At the beginning of their partnership he had been solely concerned with coaching her; making her into the ideal partner. He was amiable and friendly, with the facile, charming manner of the Latin race. He was essentially French; child of Lucille Valjean, who had once danced in Paris and captured the heart of an English jockey. From the father Claud had inherited a light, graceful figure and the unstable character which had brought the one-time jockey to a sudden and violent death, in Paris, six years ago.

Scharlie liked Claud. Nobody could help liking him. But last night she had seen him in a new light. Their friendship, their pleasant partnership, was threatened by emotional stirrings on the part of Claud. He was falling in love with her, and Scharlie knew it. If she was not careful, in a very short while he would be asking her to take the place of Claudia the First in every respect. That was the last thing Scharlie wanted.

Her uneasiness increased when she returned to the flat to find Boo rapturously admiring an exquisite spray of orchids which had just arrived from a florist's.

'My dear, isn't it *too* delicious?' Boo exclaimed, thrusting the orchids into Scharlie's hands. 'From Claud. See what he's written . . . it's quite a romance.'

Scharlie looked at the card attached to the spray.

'From Claud to *his* Claudia . . . Wear them,

chérie, to please me, tonight.'

'You've clicked, my love,' said Boo. 'Next thing we shall hear is that the exhibition dancers of the Dominoe are putting up the banns.'

Scharlie neither smiled, nor responded lightly to this. Her cheeks coloured and her brows met in a frown. She tore the card in half.

'I'm not *his* Claudia. It's all rot. And don't imagine I'm going to have an affair with him, because I'm not, Boo.'

Boo, now dressed and ready for the evening's work, glanced at herself in the wardrobe mirror and, while she outlined her lips with her vermilion stick, eyed Scharlie mischievously.

'You're blushing, Scharlie, my sweet.'

'Oh, don't be so silly!' said Scharlie with quite unusual irritability, and walked out of the room.

She did not wear the orchid spray that night. She wore artificial silk roses, which she pinned in the very latest fashion on the low 'V' at the back of her dress—a long gold and green flowered chiffon dress with many flounces, which at the back just touched the heel of her green satin slippers, and made her look very tall and slim.

CHAPTER TWO

The summer night was hot and windless when Scharlie walked with Boo to the night-club, later that evening. Boo tucked an arm through Scharlie's and sighed at the stars.

'I wish I could meet a really nice man who'd appeal to me, Scharlie,' she said. 'This weather does me in—I feel like that song that says, "I can't give you anything but love, baby."'

Scharlie's lips curled a trifle ironically.

'You're an amazing person, Boo. You've had two experiences which ought to have made you hate men and laugh at love. Yet you're not a bit cynical—you're as sentimental as a schoolgirl.'

'It's no good you talking as though you were the complete cynic, Scharlie,' said Boo. 'You may have had a rotten marriage and a rotten deal from that other fellow, but there's always the chance that you'll strike lucky next time, and that's how I regard life. If Claud is crazy about you, why don't you encourage him? He's most attractive—I know heaps of girls who've been crazy about him—and I bet he'd marry you.'

'My dear, get it into your head that I don't wish to marry Claud and I shan't encourage him.'

'Hard-hearted Hannah, that's what you are,

my pet,' said Boo.

'Good!' said Scharlie. 'It pays to be hard in this world. If I'd been hard when I was younger I wouldn't have married Alec, or let my mother bully me or fling myself into the arms of a man who never really cared for me, and I should have been spared a lot of trouble.'

They turned into the narrow by-road off Dover Street in which the Dominoe Club was situated. A young man wearing tails, his opera hat stuck at rakish angle on a smooth black head, was standing outside the club entrance, smoking a cigarette. He pitched the cigarette away when he saw the two girls. He greeted them both, but his eyes rested upon Scharlie. Boo tactfully vanished. Scharlie gave the young man an uneasy smile.

'Hullo, Claud. We're a bit early, aren't we? I'll join you in a moment.'

In the vestibule of the club, Claud put a hand on Scharlie's arm and detained her.

'My orchids, are you wearing them?' he asked in a rapid undertone.

Scharlie drew away from him.

'No, Claud, I—I'm afraid I'm not.'

In a second the eagerness, the radiance, were gone from the young man's face. He looked furiously disappointed. He had a long pale face and dark almond-shaped eyes. He seemed to grow paler than ever in this moment. His eyes were black as sloes. He had a small, rather petulant, mouth with a curled upper lip which projected slightly over the lower and gave him a look of sensuousness. Women both old and young had flung themselves madly into the arms of this young dancer who might have been one of the handsome, graceful gods of ancient Greece. Yet this girl, this Scharlie, rejected his flowers. And he adored her. At once he was flung into a mood of profound and passionate despair.

'Then you don't care for me! If you'd cared you would have worn my flowers! It's intolerable!'

The exaggeration of this annoyed Scharlie.

'It's you who are intolerable, Claud,' she said. 'Why should I wear your flowers if I don't want to? They didn't happen to tone with my dress.'

The young man put out a hand and pulled her black evening coat apart.

'Your dress is green and gold. My orchids would have been beautiful with it,' he said angrily. 'The truth is that you don't care a rap about me. You look on me as a machine to dance with!'

Scharlie's cheeks burned with colour.

'You *are* intolerable,' she exclaimed.

Then in a moment Claud's mood changed. His eyes became luminous and beseeching. His face puckered with distress. He seized her right hand and crushed it between slender, nervous fingers.

'I'm sorry, Scharlie. *Chérie*, don't be cross with me. All day I've looked forward to seeing you again. I wanted you to wear my flowers. Don't frown at me.'

Scharlie could not be cross with him for long. He was really very charming. But she was neither physically nor mentally attracted by him. He did not appeal to her. And she was a little frightened by the feeling of power over him which she obviously possessed; which he was foolish enough to let her possess. It astonished her that she should by any small word or action be able to send this man either to the heights of heaven or the depths of despair.

Why, she asked herself, should one invariably have this power over the wrong person. It was life—that! The man for whom one did not care was at one's feet, sighing, dying for a favour. The man one loved, sighed and died for another woman. Her thoughts flashed back in this instant to Hugh. She had been at his feet. If he had given her orchids she would have worn them; kept them until they withered. But even if Hugh had given her orchids he wouldn't have minded very much whether she wore them or not.

Her lips relaxed into a faint smile as she looked at Claud.

'Don't be silly, old thing,' she said. 'I'm not cross with you. Only you must be sensible. You get so worked up about nothing.'

255

With an effort Claud controlled himself. He raised her hand to his lips, then dropped it.

'I know I'm silly. It's what the fellows at school used to call my sloppiness. My damn-fool excitable foreign nature. You can send a Frenchman to a British school, Scharlie, but he's still French under the skin.'

'My dear, your father was English.'

'Pff! He was a fool—without balance, and I am the son of Lucille Valjean,' he said.

'Well, listen to me, son of Lucille Valjean,' said Scharlie with a laugh. 'You just be sensible—be my friend, like you used to be. This is all rot.'

He looked at her with bitterness.

'You're a cold little thing, Scharlie, so unmoved! And yet one has only to look at your eyes, at your mouth, to know there is passion in you. You are capable of loving—*mon Dieu!* yes, yes.'

Scharlie laughed in an embarrassed way.

'I don't want to love anybody. One is much happier out of love than in it.'

'And all because some man destroyed your illusions,' said Claud. '*Dieu!* but that fellow must have been crazy!'

'We really can't talk like this in the vestibule,' said Scharlie. 'I am going to take off my coat.'

'And then you're going to have something to eat with me,' he reminded. 'You promised you would, tonight, before we dance.'

256

'Just a snack,' she said. 'But no more.'

Later, when she sat with her partner at a little table in a corner of the club, concealed from the rest of the room by a large pillar festooned with flowers, Claud insisted upon pursuing the subject of love.

He told Scharlie, not for the first time, about Claudia, the girl with whom he had lived, and whom he had loved. He told her how empty, how futile, life seemed without that love.

'Friendship is all very well, *chérie.* Work is necessary, and one can fling oneself into it. But love, passion, the desire of man for woman and woman for man is necessary too. It is the incentive to good work—the inspiration of it. It is the natural outlet to the emotions of an artist. It is the colour and the perfume that we mortals need in this grey, dull existence. I could no more help falling in love with you than the earth can resist the attraction of the moon.'

Scharlie drank a little of the champagne he had ordered for her and played with caviare and thin hot toast. She wished Claud would not insist upon being amorous tonight. Must everybody talk to her about love? Boo, at home—Claud, at the club! And all the books, all the songs, all the plays, were about love. One couldn't escape it. The Dominoe jazz-band across the room on their dais were playing a 'Blues,' and that was all about love.

The man with the saxophone and a straw hat sang:

> *I got a woman, crazy for me,*
> *She's funny that way . . .*

Love! Love! Love! And Scharlie, whom Claud said was made for love—whom Hugh had said was made for love—shied from it now. She was afraid of it. She was afraid of herself. She had suffered too much. She didn't want to suffer again.

This was the first time since she had known and worked with Claud that he had openly declared his passion for her. She began to feel miserable about it.

She threw him a beseeching look.

'Don't be in love with me, Claud,' she said. 'It's no use. It'll only hurt you, and I'd like you for my friend. It'll spoil our partnership if you want to make love to me.'

'Won't you let me make love to you, Scharlie? Won't you give me a chance? You can't really be so cold. I'll never believe that. And I might teach you to care for me. I'd marry you tomorrow if you'd let me. And I never wanted to marry even Claudia.'

'Claud, I am awfully grateful, but I can't respond—honestly! I just don't want a lover or a husband.'

'Very well. But I shall continue to adore you and to try and make you care.'

'Oh, lord,' thought Scharlie, 'what a nuisance! He's a dear, but he'll be impossible as the young man in love. He has simply no control. Why couldn't he have fallen for Boo?'

The club was beginning to fill up rapidly. It was after theatre-time. The band, the floor, and the food here were good, and the place was rarely empty even in the off-season. The room was charmingly decorated. The floor was bigger than in most night-clubs; afforded the dancers more room. The walls were black and white, figured with painted dominoes. There were orange-trees in big golden boxes. The ceiling was domed, flooded with diffused amber light. Every table round the dance-floor had its vase of flowers; electric candles burning inside gold-silk shades.

The tables tonight were occupied mostly by couples. Bored-looking men. The typical feminine product of the day. Women with waved, shingled heads; reddened lips; and the longish graceful frocks of the moment. At one particular table three girls in black lace dresses, wearing red carnations on their shoulders, were displayed as the Dominoe dance-partners. Boo among them, waiting cheerfully for what the gods chose to send her tonight.

Just before midnight, three people came into the club and were taken to a vacant table by the head waiter. Scharlie, in the act of powdering her nose and patting her hair into

259

order for the exhibition dance which was forthcoming, glanced across the room and saw that trio walk across the floor. Her small gilt powder-box fell upon the table with a clatter. The blood rushed to her cheeks and her heart beat violently.

'Oh, good lord!' she exclaimed.

'What is it, *ma mie*?' asked Claud.

Scharlie's gaze was riveted on the trio—two men and a woman—who were now seating themselves at their table. She breathed fast. Then she laughed.

'How very funny!' she said. 'Enter the Dominoe Club, Mr. and Mrs. Hugh Ellerby and Mr. Henry Gorring.'

'And who, may I ask, are they?' said Claud. 'Friends of yours?'

'Scarcely friends,' said Scharlie. 'The tall girl with the fair plaits coiled round her ears is Eleanor, wife of the tall, fair, good-looking man, who is Hugh for whom I once had quite a considerable passion; and the tall lanky man with horn-rimmed spectacles is Eleanor's brother, Henry, who got himself well mixed up in my affairs.'

Claud's almond-shaped eyes regarded the three newcomers with interest.

'Ah! so that is the crazy fool, this Hugh who did not return your love.'

'It is,' said Scharlie.

And she was amazed to find that, except for the unexpected excitement of seeing these three people again, she was unmoved by the sight of Hugh. She felt neither pain nor jealousy when she watched him remove a gold-tissue cloak from the beautiful white shoulders of his wife and exhibit obvious tenderness for her. He meant nothing to her, Scharlie, any more. He was a ghost of a painful past which had ceased to wound her. But she was interested to see him again. Yes, deeply interested. He looked well and happy. Eleanor had that same grave, tender air which had always been one of her chief charms, and was, perhaps, a little fatter. But she looked lovely and perfectly dressed.

It was obvious that their marriage had been a success. Scharlie supposed that she ought to feel glad that Henry had interfered in her life and seen to it that Hugh settled down with his sister. No doubt Henry was pleased. He looked just the same. He regarded the scene at the night-club with a slightly bored eye, and his manner was stern, even stiff, as Scharlie remembered it.

Why it was she did not know, but the sight of Henry roused far more active resentment in her than the sight of Hugh. She felt that she would never forgive Henry for the part he had played in her life. Ridiculous, really. For what had he done except try to save a very unpleasant situation!

A year ago, when Scharlie had been up against Henry, she had been a child—

malleable, vacillating, over-emotional. But this year had taught her much; given her poise; knowledge; control. She could meet Henry tonight and be a match for him, she felt. Indeed, she would like to have the chance of dealing with Henry now—this new Scharlie. She could be controlled and subtle with him. It would amuse her to bewilder him. In these days he would scarcely address her in the former pitying, patronising fashion as 'my dear child' she thought ironically.

It was queer, but she had no particular desire to speak to Hugh or to show him how she had altered for the best. Hugh was Eleanor's husband. As such he seemed entirely removed from Scharlie's existence.

'What are you thinking about, *chérie*,' asked Claud. 'Does it worry you to see these people again?' And he added jealously: 'Do you still care for that fool?'

Scharlie gave a hard little laugh.

'Not in the least, my dear Claud, and they don't worry me—I'm merely amused. I wonder if Hugh has become a member here. Heavens! But it'll be amusing when we start our dance, Claud. They'll recognise me, of course. Somebody will see stars.'

She looked at herself in the mirror of her powder-box. She was flushed and her grey-green eyes were brilliant. She looked her best tonight, and she knew it. She felt a sudden thrill of vanity; of pride. She was going to give an exhibition dance with Claud; and Hugh and Eleanor and Henry would see her. It was all rather thrilling.

At midnight the orchestra finished a one-step, and André Lavelle, preceded by a roll of the drums, stepped forward and announced that Claud and Claudia, the famous Continental exhibition dancers, are about to demonstrate the latest dances.' The lights were lowered. An arc light flashed on to a gold circle of polished floor. Above the hum and buzz of voices rose the languorous lilt of a waltz.

Claud stepped into the circle of light, leading Scharlie by the hand. For an instant she stood there, smiling. The light threw up the rich colouring of her cheeks, her lips, and her hair. A paste buckle on the green and gold chiffon gown glittered and winked. One small foot in a jade satin slipper arched and peeped from the gossamer flounce of the dress. There was tentative applause. Then Claud put an arm lightly round her and waltzed with her into the centre of the floor. Light, charmingly graceful, the full chiffon skirt billowing as she moved, Scharlie waltzed with him. The dance developed from ordinary ballroom steps into the more intricate ones of exhibition quality. She put one bare arm about his throat, the other hung at her side; her eyes half-closed. He held her more tightly. He was half a head taller; and could look down at her in the approved style. They seemed to melt into one and to move as one.

Three people in that night-club stared at Scharlie with more amazement than admiration, although the exhibition was in every way admirable. Two men and a woman exchanged bewildered glances. As soon as Scharlie had come into the limelight, Mrs. Hugh Ellerby clutched her husband's arm and whispered:

'Good gracious! But Claudia is Scharlie Mason!'

'Yes, she is.' Henry Gorring spoke. A trifle grimly. Eleanor regretted that she had brought Scharlie to his notice. Perhaps, she thought, it had been indiscreet of her to mention the name. She was quite certain, after all that had happened a year ago, that Henry had had an affair with little Mrs. Mason. She certainly would never forget those libellous letters received after Alec Mason's death, written by his relations. But, of course, things had simmered down, and, as far as Eleanor knew, Henry had not seen Mrs. Mason again.

'Who would have dreamt of seeing her here?' Eleanor whispered, turning to her husband. 'What a surprise! I was always rather sorry for the poor little thing. But she seems to have done well for herself. How very pretty she looks, Hugh! And how beautifully she dances with that man!'

'M'm, she does,' muttered Hugh.

Of the three of them, Hugh was the most disturbed. He was also very embarrassed. It was surprising, to say the least of it, to come to a West End night-club, recommended by a business friend, and find Scharlie there, as an exhibition dancer. He was no longer in love with Scharlie. He never had been genuinely in love with her. But he had once been very keen; had found her adorable to make love to; and he had never quite forgotten her sweetness. Neither had he forgotten the disastrous finale to their intrigue. The very devil of a mess it had been! And hadn't old Henry been furious—mixed up in it all no end! But he'd been damned loyal, and, having set himself out to spare Eleanor any unhappiness, he'd done it. Nell, bless her, had never guessed the truth. An extraordinarily happy and peaceful year Hugh had had with Nell, and he was not by any means bored yet with his married life. It suited him. He found that he settled down to it well. There was something to look forward to in the future, too. News that Nell had given him six weeks ago. She was going to have a child. She wanted it and Hugh wanted it too. Eleanor meant more to him now than she had ever meant. There was no room in his life for forbidden pleasures; little time in which to regret the past.

He sat there, nevertheless, feeling restless and ill at ease; arms folded across his chest; cigarette between his lips; watching that slim green and gold figure moving so swiftly, so gracefully round the floor in the arms of her partner.

'She always was a pretty kid,' he thought; 'she's prettier than ever now!'

Henry, also, watched Scharlie, and his thoughts were quite different from Hugh's. He was surprised to find her here, and a little embarrassed that he should discover her while in the company of Nell and Hugh. He was a bit sorry that he had accepted their invitation to come to the night-club after the show they had seen. But, in another, curious, way he was glad. Ever since he had last seen Scharlie a year ago he had worried about her. He had been piqued and annoyed because she had left his letters unanswered. He had felt it his bounden duty to do something for her, and she had refused to let him do anything. Perforce he was her admirer for that. But he had thought about her constantly. All through this year at intervals he had found himself remembering her and wondering what had become of her. He had been really distressed by the fear that she might drift, after that rotten show with Hugh. He had pictured her falling into evil hands— troubled about it until the thing had become an obsession. And he could never bring himself to ask Dorothy Wilberforce for news, although he imagined she might be in touch with Scharlie.

And now he knew what had become of her.

She was an exhibition dancer at a night-club. Quite a successful one, too, it appeared. The applause when that waltz ended was vociferous. There was an encore. Scharlie and her partner began to foxtrot.

Henry Gorring found himself wondering about the details of Scharlie's existence; how she had secured this job; what her relationship was to the man with whom she danced.

'The fellow's a foreigner,' he thought, looking at Claud.

He hoped vaguely that Scharlie was not living with this man; nor married to him. Yet what possible difference could it make to him, Henry? Scharlie meant nothing to him. He had been thoroughly mixed up with her a year ago, until the thing had threatened to become unpleasant. But he hadn't cared in the least about her. He did not care now. Yet that amazing feeling of responsibility towards her remained; was not to be eradicated.

He became gradually conscious of a desire to speak to Scharlie; to get into touch with her.

CHAPTER THREE

The exhibition dance ended. Claud led his partner forward, repeatedly, to take the applause. Scharlie bowed and smiled very prettily and was really quite pleased with her

267

success. She had not been at the game long enough to feel blasé about public appreciation.

The only thing that worried her tonight was Claud's persistent efforts to be amorous. He squeezed her bare arm hard as he led her back to their concealed corner.

'*Chérie* . . . marvellous . . . wonderful . . .' he said, in the kind of ardent murmur that *Boo* Orbutt called 'too delicious'. 'No wonder they like you. When you danced in my arms just now . . . you were exquisite . . . responsive . . . adorable . . .'

'Oh, my dear old thing,' said Scharlie, drawing away her arm. 'Do use your intelligence. I can't possibly be all those things put together. I'm hot. I want some lemonade. Did you see the faces of that trio over there? I'd love to have watched Henry Gorring's, but I couldn't see a soul with that arc-light in my eyes . . . Order some lemon, there's a good soul . . .'

She rattled on . . . determined to ease the situation which her partner was trying to make difficult. Claud's face—very pale and absurdly anguished because of her indifference to his passion—took on a sullen expression. He flung himself moodily into a chair, ordered the lemonade for Scharlie, and stared at her with resentment. She was not even looking at him. Her gaze was fixed on the party which so interested her.

She could watch Hugh, Eleanor, and Henry,

at her leisure, from her hiding-place without being seen by them. The band was playing a foxtrot. Most of the people in the club were dancing now. She caught a glimpse of Boo, in whose heavy-lidded blue eyes lay a comic expression of boredom. She was dancing with an old gentleman with a white pointed beard, and what might have been a venerable face but for two amorous and mischievous eyes. He clutched her waist with one hand, held her other hand up very high, and executed a series of little skips which the amiable Boo sought to follow without success. Scharlie could not help laughing.

'Poor Boo's picked a loser tonight, Claud. Do look. I hope he hasn't bought a roll for the evening. He's really rather absurd, and ought to be at home asleep in bed wearing a night-cap. He looks to me like my late husband's Uncle Alexander gone mad, but he isn't . . . Oh! he's just come down on poor Boo's toe . . . she looks furious. Her new silver slippers, too . . . Can you see, Claud?'

The young man hunched his shoulders and gave Scharlie a sulky look.

'I'm not interested in Boo.'

Scharlie drew in her lips.

'You're being very difficult tonight, really.'

'And you,' he said bitterly, 'are about as concerned for my agony as—'

'There shouldn't be any agony,' broke in Scharlie. 'What's the use of agonising? I can't love you Claud, and it's a waste of time you going on like this.'

'How can you be so heartless?'

'I'm not. I'm terribly sorry in a way. I've been through it—unrequited love—but I've had my lesson and I've learned that nothing lasts . . . that love dies.'

'You try to tell me, Scharlie, that you'll never care for any man again?'

'I hope I won't.'

'My God . . . with all the fire, the beauty of you! . . .' Claud made a very foreign gesture with his hands, drained his glass, and set it down on the table noisily. 'You are hopeless.'

'My dear Claud,' said Scharlie. 'Satisfy yourself on this point. Once I adored a man— that good-looking creature over there, in fact—he amused himself with me until the position became dangerous and he looked like losing his fiancée and a good job . . . then he gave me my *congé*. I'm not likely to risk that happening to me again.'

'Why should it happen? With me, it couldn't. I worship you. Scharlie—'

'Hello,' broke in Scharlie, peering round the pillar by their table and looking at the party which held her attention. 'What's happened. Eleanor Gorr—I mean Mrs. Ellerby—is ill . . .'

Eleanor was standing up. She held one hand to her head. Hugh with a face of deep concern stood beside her, holding her arm. Henry held the other.

270

'She's feeling faint or something,' said Scharlie. And looked almost anxiously at Hugh's wife.

Then she saw the two men lead Eleanor from the room. They went so quietly and quickly that few people in the club had time to realise that it was a case of sudden illness.

Scharlie sat back in her chair with a little frown on her forehead.

'So there they go, and I don't suppose I shall see them again,' she said thoughtfully. 'Give me a cig., Claud.'

He lit one and handed it to her.

'Let us go, *chérie* . . . to some place where nobody knows us and we can have supper.'

'My dear, no. It would be a waste of money. I'm for home.'

'Then I shall come too.'

Her cheeks flamed. She gave him an indignant look.

'Don't be ridiculous, Claud. You'll do nothing of the kind.'

He sprang to his feet. His slimly-built body was shaking. His almond eyes were brilliant with tears. Scharlie saw this with horror. Was Claud going to make a public scene in the Dominoe? How unreasonable of him. If she had known he was so uncontrolled, she would never have consented to their dancing partnership.

'I won't be treated so coldly, so callously,' he said in a low, intense voice. '*Mon Dieu!* I can't stand it. You must be kind to me, tonight. I must come back to your flat.'

Scharlie looked up at him with eyes grown hard and angry.

'Claud, you are out of your mind. How dare you?'

'I must come back with you,' he repeated. 'I tell you I'm crazy for you . . . mad to hold you even once in my arms.'

Scharlie began to wonder if she had to deal with a lunatic. Claud looked distraught. She was thoroughly disturbed. She had not imagined that he would let his emotions about her reach this pitch. Of course she had realised ever since she worked with him that he was very temperamental; that the excitable French blood ran hotly in his veins. She also realised that he had been spoiled by women because he was handsome and graceful and a charming flatterer. He was not used to being thwarted. But she was not going to give way one inch before this hot-headed onslaught.

'Claud, either you must sit down and talk sense, or I shall get up and leave the club alone,' she said quietly.

He looked down at her in a way that made her heart thrill uneasily. He was quivering with suppressed passion. In another moment he would be out of control altogether, she thought.

'Let me take you home. Give me ten minutes—five, alone with you in your flat—

one minute—for the love of God, Scharlie,' he said in a gasping voice.

Scharlie stubbed her cigarette on the plate before her and stood up. She glanced in an embarrassed way at the table just in front of them. The couple seated there had heard Claud's last speech and were staring at him curiously.

'Claud,' she said, 'you must be quiet. People are beginning to stare. Honestly—if you go on like this I shall refuse to dance with you again.'

'You are damnably cruel,' he said. He held on to the back of his chair for support. His forehead was wet. One black strand of hair hung across his right eyebrow untidily and gave him a dishevelled appearance. Scharlie had never seen him look so ghastly. And all because of her. What a dreadful thing passion was . . . uncontrolled passion from a man of Claud's temperament. 'Scharlie . . . *ma mie* . . .' he panted, 'I beg you . . . let me see you home.'

But Scharlie was thinking:

'No, my lad. I don't trust you. You're getting altogether too dangerous. I'm scared stiff of you, tonight . . .'

Aloud she said:

'No, Claud, for the last time. I'm going home alone, and—please don't follow me.'

'You can't leave me like this . . . Scharlie—'

He broke off, panting. She drew on her velvet coat, and, wrapping it around her, walked past him down the side of the dance-floor, keeping out of the way of dancing couples, and left the club.

Claud followed her, the sweat dripping down his livid face.

Outside in the cool starlight, Scharlie ran straight into the tall figure of a man who was about to enter the club.

'I beg your pardon—' she began. Then she stopped and stared at him. 'Oh—you!' she added with a breathless little laugh.

She had collided with Henry Gorring.

He wore a light fawn Burberry over his evening-clothes, and no hat. While he stood there, staring down at her in obvious embarrassment, he pulled at the lobe of his ear in a way she remembered.

'Why, how are you?' he said, at length.

'Very well, thank you . . . I saw you all down in the Dominoe. Tell me. Was your sister taken ill?'

'Yes. She suddenly had a fainting attack. She isn't too fit just at present. She oughtn't to have come out, but she insisted because it's the anniversary of the day Hugh became a partner in our firm, and she thought he would like to celebrate. We came here after the show. She's all right. Hugh's taken her home. I was just going to fetch my hat, which I left downstairs in the cloak-room.'

'I see,' said Scharlie. She regarded him with a kind of amused curiosity. Just the same Henry. Brusque manner. Grave voice. Hard

274

grey eyes behind the horn-rims. Those eyes were looking down at her with something like curiosity.

'I must congratulate you,' he said. 'You seem to have become quite famous. We all enjoyed your dance.'

'Thanks very much,' she said, and was more than ever amused. It seemed too funny to be carrying on a formal little conversation of this kind with Henry Gorring. For the first time in their lives, perhaps, there was neither rancour nor hostility in their mutual attitude.

'So you took up dancing as a career when you—er—after—er—'

'Yes,' she finished for him. 'I got a job at the Dominoe as a dance-partner, to begin with. I've only really been exalted to the position of exhibition dancer this last month.'

'You find it a paying business?'

'Oh, good enough. I've got a nice little flat in Stone Mansions, off New Oxford Street, with a woman friend.'

'I see,' said Henry.

He found her changed. More matured and self-possessed. Even prettier than he remembered her. Certainly, widowhood and hard work had agreed with Scharlie.

'By the way,' he said, and the suggestion of a smile raised one corner of his lips. 'I wrote to you several times and you didn't reply. Why?'

That was so typical of Henry, she thought. To hurl that direct, blunt question at her:

275

'Why?'

'Because I didn't want to reply,' she answered him frankly. 'You were offering me financial help. I was furious.'

'Not very many people object to financial assistance.'

'But I did in this case. You had no right—I mean, my position had nothing to do with you, had it?'

'You know what I felt about things . . .'

'Oh, yes. But don't let's drag up the old history. The ghosts are laid, I hope,' she interrupted.

Henry inclined his head. This was the independent spirit in Scharlie which he had been forced to recognise and admire in the old days of their hostility, and he admired it again now. There was nothing, never had been anything, of the vamp; of the gold-digger about this child. Now that Henry met her again; knew that she was on her feet; he was thankful. His anxiety about her, his feeling of responsibility, could die a natural death.

'How did you come across this man with whom you danced this evening?' he asked, after a pause.

'I met him in the club. He's quite well known.'

'A fine dancer.'

'Yes.' Scharlie was non-committal. She was secretly amused because Henry seemed quite inquisitive about Claud. At the same time a

276

certain portion of her brain was worrying about Claud and not focused upon Henry Gorring at all. Claud had been so queer tonight. Quite terrifying—the way those sloe-black eyes of his glittered fire at her.

'I'm sure you'll be glad to know that my sister's marriage has been a success,' Henry was saying.

'I'm delighted,' said Scharlie with sincerity. 'I always liked Miss Gorring. She was awfully nice.'

'I gave Hugh no marks for that show of a year ago,' added Henry. 'But he's settled down to things and makes Nell a very decent husband.'

Scharlie was about to reply to this when the door leading down to the Dominoe swung open and Claud came out into the street. Her heart sank when she saw his face. It was desperate. He was wild-eyed. As soon as he saw her standing there beside the tall man with horn-rimmed glasses, he made straight for her.

'You want a taxi,' he said excitedly. 'I'll get one and see you home.'

'No, thank you,' said Scharlie, and was suddenly afraid of her dancing-partner. 'As a matter of fact . . .'—she edged nearer Henry Gorring—'this friend of mine is getting my taxi.'

Henry was a trifle taken aback, but he was too courteous to do otherwise than bow and say:

'I'll get one at once.'

He walked to the kerb and signalled to a passing cab.

'Good night, Claud,' said Scharlie coldly.

Claud put out a hand and gripped her arm.

'You are going to let that man see you home?'

'That is my affair,' she said.

'That man,' he said in a violent tone. 'The one you cared for; who let you down, eh? You prefer hint to *me*?'

It is not the man who let me down, at all.'

'It is. You pointed him out.'

'I did nothing of the kind. It was the other man. You're all mixed up.'

'I don't think so—' Claud passed a tongue over his lips. The sweat dripped from his cheeks. He was in a highly nervous and uncontrolled condition, brought on by his hopeless passion for this girl. 'This one stayed behind to see you.'

'You're all wrong,' said Scharlie angrily. 'In any case, what business is it of yours? Claud, you're going too far. I shan't have any more to do with you. I shall tell André tomorrow.'

Henry came back.

'That cab was engaged. There aren't many passing this way. I'll just walk into Dover Street—' he began. Then he paused. To his surprise, the young man, whom he saw was Scharlie's dancing-partner, walked up to him and addressed him in a husky, excited voice

278

with a strong foreign accent.

'*Monsieur*, I am going to see this lady home. I will not let her throw me over for you—you who have ruined her life and made her so hard, so heartless for the next man in the case!'

Henry's eyes blinked through their glasses.

'I beg your pardon?' he said in an astonished voice.

'Claud, don't dare—go away at once!' said Scharlie, red to the roots of her hair.

Claud flung up both arms.

'I won't be sent away. This man . . .'—he pointed a shaking finger at Henry—'this man can take you home, do what he wills, break your heart all over again, while I who adore you—'

'Claud, be quiet,' broke in Scharlie. 'You're off your head. I keep telling you this is *not* the man . . .'

'It is, I know it. You pointed him out tonight.'

'I did *not*,' said Scharlie. She felt covered in shame and confusion. It was appalling for Claud to lose his control; to create a scene like this before Henry Gorring.

Henry turned to her.

'May I ask who your young lunatic friend is mistaking me for?' he said.

'I'll explain in a moment, but for heaven's sake let's go and find a taxi,' she said.

'Certainly,' he said.

She ignored Claud who was appealing to her in a frenzied voice. She began to walk down the quiet, starlit street beside Henry's tall figure. This seemed to take from Claud his last shred of control.

'You throw me on one side . . . you go back to your lover . . . *Mon Dieu!* . . . I will not endure it . . .' he screamed, and flung himself on Henry's back.

Henry, completely surprised, staggered and nearly fell, but just managed to regain his balance, throw his hands behind him and pull Claud off. He swung round. They faced each other. Henry was thoroughly angry and resentful of the undeserved assault. Claud, teeth clenched, eyes glittering, was like a madman. Scharlie caught his arm and tried to quieten him.

'Stop it . . . stop it, I say . . . Claud, for God's sake be sensible . . .'

But he shook her off. He struck out at Henry with clenched fists. The horn-rimmed glasses smashed. That immediately put Henry at a disadvantage. He was very short-sighted; could hardly see two feet before him without his spectacles. Fortunately the splintered glass did not injure his eyes. He had just time to remove the rims; thrust them in his pocket, then grappled with Claud. He had done a certain amount of boxing up at Oxford and he took up a scientific defensive.

'I don't know what we're quarrelling about,

my young friend,' he said grimly, 'but if you want a fight as much as all this, come on . . . I'm ready!'

Claud struggled frantically; punctuating a few feeble attempts to strike out at Henry with muttered threats and curses. He was in love with Scharlie, he shouted. He wanted to marry her. And undoubtedly she would have had him but for this hardness of heart produced by *him*, her one-time lover who had broken her heart. He, Claud, was not going to permit Scharlie to go with this man and have her heart broken again.

Scharlie kept crying:

'You're making a mistake, Claud . . . a mistake . . . This is *not* the man . . .'

Henry, peering at his adversary with his short-sighted eyes and trying hard to see him, kept Claud off successfully for a moment or two. Scharlie was distracted. She looked up and down the street in a panic lest a policeman should come along. She could not endure the idea of this thing being made public. Was Henry Gorring fated to be mixed up in scenes with her; doomed to be mistaken for her lover? If it hadn't been so serious, she would have found the position really humorous.

She looked with despair at the two men.

Henry's collar had been ripped from its stud. His shirt was torn. His cheek, just under the left eye, was bleeding, cut by a piece of broken glass from his spectacles. His thick dark hair was dishevelled. He looked totally unlike the dignified Mr. Gorring who had approached Scharlie a moment ago; curiously changed; much younger without his glasses.

Claud's lips were bruised and bleeding after an excellent thrust from Henry's right. He sobbed hysterically. The contest only lasted a couple of minutes, although to Scharlie it seemed hours. Then, suddenly, Claud's strength gave out. He had no stamina. He had worked himself up into such a violent state that his heart refused to stand it. He finally settled the affair by collapsing on to the pavement with a groan. He fainted.

Scharlie, pale and nervous, bent over the prostrate young man.

'He's fainted,' she said. 'For God's sake let's get a taxi and take him home before anybody comes out and this affair gets round the town.'

'I shall be only too pleased,' said Henry. He was gasping, endeavouring to smooth his hair and do up his collar, without much success.

An empty taxi-cab rolled along conveniently at that moment. Henry signalled to the driver. Between them they lifted the swooning Claud into the cab and climbed in after him. Scharlie gave the address.

'He has rooms in Baker Street . . .'

Claud remained in a semi-conscious condition until they reached his rooms. Then he revived, felt violently ill and clung to Scharlie, babbled of his passion and begged

282

her to stay with him.

But Scharlie was sick of Claud and the whole scene. She would never forgive him for this. However much he wanted her to return his love, such conduct was unpardonable. She left him in charge of his landlady, whom they roused. This good lady—a motherly soul with a penchant for the handsome young dancer—put a supporting arm about him and coaxed him to go with her to his room.

Scharlie returned to Henry, who awaited her in the taxi.

'Now, if you don't mind taking me back to my flat in Stone Mansions,' she said.

They moved off. Scharlie nearly in tears; Henry vainly endeavouring to restore order to his appearance. He said gruffly:

'Well, that was a damn' fine show. I seem fated to get let in for scenes with you.'

'I was thinking the same . . .' Scharlie swallowed hard and bit her lip. She did not intend to cry. 'I'm frightfully sorry. I really owe you an apology.'

'You can't say *I* interfered this time,' he said.

'No. It was Claud's fault entirely. He's quite crazy. He behaved insanely. I shall never forgive him.'

'What a jolly thing love seems to be. It's turned your suave and smiling young dancer into a raging tiger,' remarked Henry.

'I shall never forgive him,' repeated

Scharlie.

'May I ask why he directed his malice and hatred against me?'

Scharlie gave a short, nervous laugh.

'After the peace of a year, the old trouble revives,' she said. 'He thought you were Hugh.'

'I see,' said Henry. He was holding a white silk handkerchief against his bleeding cheek. 'Damn this thing. It won't stop. I shall have blood all over my shirt.'

'There's blood on it now,' said Scharlie miserably.

'And I can't see an inch without my glasses. It was tactless of your friend to have broken them.'

'*Don't* keep calling him my friend. He isn't. I shall never speak to him again.'

'Oh, surely you have more understanding of those in love than that.'

'You needn't be sarcastic . . .' Scharlie was on the verge of weeping now. She felt exhausted and humiliated. She had meant to be so subtle, so dignified, with Henry, and tonight she was in precisely the same position with him as she had been a year ago. Hateful Henry! He *would* make her feel a little idiot.

'It's somewhat inclined to make one sarcastic,' he said. 'I came out for a peaceful evening with my family. I find myself assaulted by a raging young Frenchman; my spectacles broken, my collar and shirt obliterated, and my cheek gashed open. Well—really—my dear

284

child—'

His dear child! The same chilly, patronising voice. Scharlie grit her teeth.

'You haven't altered,' she said. 'You're just as beastly.'

'I'm sorry,' he said, and regarded the blood-stains on his handkerchief grimly. 'But, really, it's time people stopped mistaking me for my brother-in-law. It was a pity you pointed us out at all to your charming partner.'

'Why shouldn't I?' she flashed. 'Claud asked me to marry him and I told him I'd had enough of marriage—and love. When Hugh came in, I simply said that there was the man who'd disillusioned me. And Claud thought I meant you.'

'Once more,' said Henry, 'I bear the brunt of Hugh's misdeeds.'

Scharlie's temper subsided. After all, she reflected, it was rather hard lines on Henry that he should have been violently assaulted by Claud. She said:

'I'm really awfully sorry. I wouldn't have had it happen for the world. I *am* sorry.'

'That's all right.'

'Won't your cheek stop bleeding?'

'No. And I feel a pretty good mess.'

'You look it, rather,' admitted Scharlie.

'The damnable part of it is that my father has gone to a Masonic banquet tonight and expected to get back home about two.' He glanced at his wrist-watch. 'It's that now. The old man often sits in the library and reads for a bit when he comes back from a show of that kind. He's rarely in bed before dawn. It's a bad habit of his. He said, tonight, before I started out to meet Nell and her husband, that he'd wait up till I came in. I don't particularly wish to enter my home looking as though I'd been in a free fight, and with blood pouring over my shirt.'

Scharlie bit her lip. Then she said:

'If you wouldn't mind—you could come up to my flat and get tidy. You can bathe your cheek. I've got some plaster, and I daresay I can mend your shirt and fix you up so that you don't look quite so disreputable as you do now.'

He peered at her through the gloom of the taxi with his short-sighted eyes. Her charming face and figure were hazy.

'It's like hell being without my glasses,' he growled. 'I can't see a thing.'

'I'm sorry,' said Scharlie. 'Really I am. Will you come back and let me do what I can to make you presentable? Don't be afraid,' she added with a little laugh. 'You won't lose your reputation. Nobody will see you. My friend Miss Orbutt, who lives with me, won't be back till three, so you won't even run up against her.'

Henry hesitated. Then he decided that he could not return home in his present condition. It would only distress the old man.

'Thanks very much, I'll take advantage of your kind suggestion.'

Scharlie sat back in the taxi in silence and digested this stiff and formal speech, so typical of Henry. He let his cut cheek alone for a moment and lit a cigarette. And ten minutes later he was in the very last place on earth in which he would have expected to find himself, and at the very last hour. Scharlie's flat, at a quarter to two in the morning!

CHAPTER FOUR

Henry stumbled twice going up the staircase to the top flat in Stone Mansions. The second time, Scharlie whispered:

'Ssh!'

'I'm sorry,' said Henry in his stiffest voice. 'But, unfortunately, I can't see an inch in front of me in this sort of gloom without my glasses.'

'Are you as short-sighted as all that?' she asked.

'Yes'—curtly.

Scharlie was conscious of something akin to pity. Poor Henry. She hadn't realised he was so blind without spectacles. When he was wearing them those steely grey eyes of his looked so very keen and far-seeing. That he should stumble because he could hardly see—small thing though it was—touched a soft spot in

Scharlie. She slid an arm through his.

'Hang on to me,' she said.

This had the effect of bringing colour to the cheeks of Henry, but Scharlie did not see it in the darkness. He was really grateful for her small guiding arm. Closely, side by side, they mounted the rest of the stairs.

'You live in the clouds,' remarked Henry.

'Physically . . . not mentally,' she responded drily.

'M'm,' said Henry.

She put her latch-key in the Yale lock, opened the front door, and switched on the light in the tiny hall. She then led the way into the one and only sitting-room.

'You go and sit in there while I get some warm water and some cotton-wool. I've got some stuff which I gargle with sometimes. That'll probably stop the bleeding.'

'Thanks very much,' said Henry.

In the sitting-room he walked up and down and smoked and waited for her; peering at Scharlie's possessions. It seemed most ridiculous and unreal to him being like this in a flat belonging to Scharlie Mason. He found nothing in the room at which even he—a creature of ascetic taste—could cavil. It was all simple, unpretentious. Two or three good rugs on a stained floor. Sofa and chairs covered in plain, apple-green linen. Green linen curtains. An oak bookcase full of books. A gate-legged table and spindle-backed chairs up one end of the room—obviously the portion used as a dining-room. And one excellent water-colour over the fireplace.

Henry forgot his bleeding cheek and strolled to the fireplace in order to examine that picture. He made a hobby of collecting good water-colours and he was interested.

He had to blink at it very closely in order to see it.

'Walter Sickert, eh,' he thought. 'Now I wonder where she got that! . . . it's a choice one, too. Damn! Why haven't I my glasses.'

Scharlie was in the kitchenette heating a saucepan of water. She had discarded her coat and slipped a blue overall over her evening-gown. She smiled faintly while she watched the saucepan, as though her secret thoughts amused her.

'The fight might have turned into a tragedy, but, as it is, it's most comic,' she was reflecting. 'Really, it's a bit thick for the estimable Henry to be constantly in the soup through me . . .'

She walked into the sitting-room bearing a basin of water, a packet of wool, and a bottle of listerine.

'Now we can get ahead,' she said.

Henry turned to her.

'That's a very nice Sickert you've got there.'

'Yes, isn't it? I love that one. I love Sickert. I think he's far and away the most important painter, of his school, don't you?'

Henry stared at her. She broke into an

289

amused laugh.

'Don't look at me with such astonishment . . . as though you're surprised I can discuss painters with you.'

He flushed because she had read his thoughts, and looked at the floor.

'I—agree about Sickert,' he stammered.

Scharlie noticed the extraordinary length of his lashes, now that his lids were drooping. And she was again struck by the youthfulness of his face without the horn-rims. His face was still bleeding. The broken glass had made several nasty little gashes.

'Do sit down,' she said. 'I'll try and get that cheek to stop bleeding.'

Henry seated himself. Scharlie wrapped a bath-towel round him.

'You hold the bowl.'

He took it. Peering close at her, he noticed the blue overall. It made a simple child of her. And yet in the Dominoe, dancing with that dago, she had looked so matured; so sophisticated.

'You've had to change . . . I'm putting you to a lot of trouble. I'm so sorry,' he said.

'Not a bit. I haven't changed. I put an overall over my evening-frock. Now, hold your head on one side.'

He obeyed her. She steadied his head with her left hand and began to bathe the injured cheek. Her fingers were cool and light and her touch wonderfully gentle. He shut his eyes and gave himself up to the comfort of the treatment.

'You're quite professional,' he murmured.

'Don't tell me I ought to have been a hospital nurse instead of an exhibition dancer,' she said, with a laugh. 'I assure you the sight of blood revolts me.'

'I apologise . . . for this . . .'

'I wasn't being personal. You do take offence so easily,' she broke in.

'Do I?' he said lamely. 'Sorry.'

Scharlie was sorry—for him. His comic position was not enviable. She knew that he must be inwardly writhing. The dignified Henry, seated here, submitting to her attentions; with a burst collar and a blood-stained shirt. She began to talk about modern painting, and he responded with enthusiasm. They had five or ten minutes' animated conversation.

Scharlie achieved her object. Henry's cheek ceased to bleed. She dried it with cotton-wool, then dusted it with boracic powder.

'There,' she said, 'that's all right. Lucky I keep a medicine-chest handy.'

'Very sensible.'

'Not that I ever expected to have to minister to you, of all men, after a street brawl,' she added.

He blinked up at her and saw that she was laughing. He wanted to be cross and to resent such ill-placed merriment. Then his own sense of humour returned, and he found himself laughing with her.

'Yes, really . . . almost absurd . . . but I couldn't let that dago get the better of me. I had to retaliate.'

'Of course. I sympathise,' said Scharlie. 'Now what can we do about your collar and shirt? This being the domicile of two lone women, I've neither collars nor shirts, nor have I a stud.'

'Of course not,' said Henry.

'But you can go into my room and wash and brush up,' said Scharlie. 'And then I have this suggestion to make. I've got a white silk scarf. Take it and put it round your neck; it'll hide the bloodstains and your father won't notice anything amiss. And then I daresay you can carry off the whole show and not give yourself away.'

'Thanks very much,' said Henry. He pulled at the lobe of his ear and peered at her. 'But I can't take your scarf.'

'You can borrow it. Post it back.'

'You're very kind. I'm grateful.'

'Not at all,' said Scharlie. 'You got into the brawl all over me. So it's up to me to help you out of it.'

'Tell me something,' said Henry. 'That dago fellow who danced with you suggested that you had flung him over . . . in other words that his mad condition was produced by your treatment of him. Is that so?'

Scharlie, who was walking to the door with the basin, paused and looked back at Henry. For a few moments she had been at ease with him; chatting on friendly terms. But now she bristled with resentment again.

'What right have you to ask, Mr. Gorring?'

'No particular right. Except that I might find some excuse for the swine . . . if he was off his head with jealousy.'

'Perhaps he was off his head with jealousy. But that doesn't say I gave him the right to be jealous.' And she threw Henry an indignant look. He blinked his long lashes at her. She realised that the look of indignation was lost on him. He couldn't see it. She added, angrily:

'Claud has behaved unpardonably, but he is not a dago, so you needn't go on calling him one. He's half English and half French. And, anyhow, you needn't suggest that I've had an affair with the man, just because I dance with him.'

'It wasn't because of that. It was because he rushed after you and dotted me one,' said Henry drily. 'I only supposed . . .'

'Well, you're wrong.'

'Then there is no excuse for his behaviour.'

'None except that he is in love with me. But that wouldn't excuse him in *your* sight, would it?' she said huffily, and marched out of the room bearing the basin and the wool; dyed pink with Henry's blood.

When she was in the kitchenette she felt she

could have hit herself for being so stupid. Had she learned nothing these last twelve months that she could still behave so childishly with Henry Gorring? It was a funny thing, but Henry roused her, made her lose her temper, in a way nobody else could do. Yet, for a few moments, they had conversed quite naturally and pleasantly. And—she admitted it half-heartedly—Henry could be very pleasant when he chose. He knew a lot about pictures, too. She had been pleased that he admired her Walter Sickert. It was one of her few possessions which she had taken from Alec's house when she had left. It had hung in her bedroom there. Her father, who was an art collector, had left it to her many years ago. She loved it.

She fetched her hairbrush, comb, and the scarf, and returned to the sitting-room.

'Here you are,' she said.

Henry took the things and thanked her politely. She watched him in silence while he brushed his disordered hair and attempted to make a parting. He finished the toilette and then wound the scarf about his neck.

It had a faint odour of the perfume which clung to all Scharlie's things. Henry found it very agreeable, and reminiscent of the one woman in his life who had mattered. That memory had returned another night, a year ago, when Scharlie had fainted in his arms after leaving Hugh's flat. He recalled that incident now, while the familiar perfume assailed his nostrils. And inevitably there also came to him the remembrance of Scharlie's warm, pliable body, which had rested so helplessly against him. He recalled the rare grace and beauty of that same young body, dancing tonight, at the Dominoe. He then put these thoughts and recollections very quickly out of his mind and told himself not to be a fool.

'Is my parting straight?' he asked Scharlie abruptly.

She looked up at the thick dark hair and her face relaxed again.

'No—it's terribly crooked.'

'Oh, lord,' he said.

It was queer how this semi-blindness without his glasses touched Scharlie. She took the comb from him.

'I'll do it for you. Bend down,' she said.

Henry pulled the lobe of his ear, coughed with embarrassment, and stooped downwards. He felt the light touch of slim fingers steadying his head. The faint, lovely perfume of her was strong in his nostrils now. Extraordinary what a very attractive scent it was; and how physically attractive she was, this girl.

The most crazy and disordered thoughts chased, suddenly, through Henry Gorring's imagination. Unworthy thoughts, relating to the fact that he was absolutely alone in the flat with Scharlie; that it was two in the morning;

his nerves were jumping after that street fight, and he was curiously excited by the touch of Scharlie's hands and the memory of the one moment when he had held her in his arms.

For two years Henry Gorring had led a life of rigid sexual repression and kept to a daily routine of strenuous work. For two years he had put women out of his existence; had no place, no time for them in his scheme of things; and had successfully kept them out of it. The sedate and formal and severe Henry would, a few hours ago, have scoffed at this other Henry . . . the real hot-blooded, beauty-loving, hungry man behind the mask . . . believed him incapable of leaping up; clamouring; out of control.

But who knows what the unexpected moment can make of one? The most astonished person in the room, when Henry suddenly seized Scharlie in both arms, crushed her to him, and kissed her madly on the lips, was Henry himself.

Scharlie was also astonished; more dazed by the unexpectedness of the incident than the actual meaning of it. The comb dropped from her fingers. She felt paralysed. The embrace, the kiss, were as fleeting as they were fierce. It was all over in a second. Then Henry's arms fell away from her. He stood there, breathless, aghast at what he had done; blood still hot; body still clamouring even while brain cooled and condemned.

Scharlie gripped the edge of the table beside her to steady herself. She stared up at him, also breathless. Her face, her throat, were burning scarlet. She said in a furious voice:

'How *dared* you do that?'

'I—I really haven't the least idea. I can only say—I beg your pardon,' he stammered.

The apology seemed to make things worse. Scharlie drew a deep breath. Her eyes blazed at him.

'You—cad,' she said. 'Get out of my flat.'

Henry wilted under her scorn.

'You're quite right. I am a cad. I'll go.'

He began to walk towards the door. The room was hazy to him. He bumped into a small occasional table bearing a tall vase full of roses. The table and vase turned over. The vase did not break, but a stream of water issued from it and spread into a pool on to the rug. Henry's embarrassment was complete. His very ears tingled. In an agony of self-reproach he blinked down at the wreckage and then turned back to Scharlie.

'I . . . I'm sorry. I couldn't see . . .'

She had been staring at him, shivering with rage. That kiss had been no light touch of the lips. It had been full and passionate. Who would have thought Henry's thin, stern lips could plant so impassioned a caress? But how dared he? How dared he so insult her?

'Have I broken your vase?' he muttered, scarlet and ashamed.

Then rage evaporated from Scharlie. It was really difficult to remain in a perfect fury against a man who blundered like a great blind stupid into the furniture. She had forgotten how short-sighted he was when she had told him to go. Good heavens, he'd do himself an injury trying to see his way down six flights of that dark staircase. Stone steps, too. He'd break his neck.

Despite the insult of the kiss, the comic side of things, which so often pervaded Scharlie in the most tragic moments, struck her now. If only Henry Gorring knew how stupid he looked, his face all red, his long lashes blinking at her. The severe, austere Henry Gorring! She said, very coldly:

'You needn't worry. There is nothing broken.'

She picked up the vase and the roses and set them on the table. Then she took Henry's arm; stiffly; without friendliness.

'I'll help you downstairs,' she said. 'You won't be able to see.'

Henry's cup of confusion was full. What possible dignity can a short-sighted man without his glasses command? He was himself once more, and not only ashamed that he had insulted the girl in her own flat when she had been so kindly helping him, but bewildered at the instinct that had prompted his breach of the decencies. Damn it, only a year ago he had preached to Hugh on the subject of self-control. A lot he had shown, himself. What had possessed him to kiss the girl? Even if he had found her devilish attractive, he should not have let his feelings run away with him like that.

In the hall Scharlie put on a coat. Henry submitted to the light pressure of her hand on his arm and walked with her down the six flights of stairs in silence.

When they reached the ground floor, Scharlie said:

'One can usually pick up a taxi in New Oxford Street, even at this hour. I'll walk to the corner with you.'

'I daresay I can manage by myself now,' he muttered.

'Oh, I'll come. You might get run over.'

It was Henry's turn to feel like a naughty child. He bit hard at his lips.

'It's an infernal nuisance being so helpless without glasses. Of course, I have a duplicate pair at home.'

'That's all right then,' she said in her most frigid voice.

Henry cleared his throat; coughed; glanced sideways at her. He could see the charming profile now that she walked so close to him.

'Look here,' he said. 'I am so damned sorry about . . . what I did in your flat. I'm full of remorse—really—you don't know how rotten I feel about it. Won't you forgive me? You've been so kind, too.'

She gave him a quick look, and shrugged her shoulders.

'You needn't trouble to apologise again.'

'But you haven't forgiven me.'

'It's a bit difficult to forgive an insult of that kind.'

'I didn't mean to insult you.'

'Did you think it would flatter me?'

'No—please—'

'Of course, a mere kiss is not supposed to cover the modern girl with confusion,' she said with sarcasm. 'Especially a night-club exhibition dancer.'

'You're making me feel more of a cad than I am,' he said. 'It never entered my head that I . . . that your position gave me any right . . . I mean . . .' He broke off with a gesture of confusion.

They were at the corner now. New Oxford Street lay before them; dark, quiet, secretive in the early morning hours, with its deserted pavements and barred and shuttered shops. The air struck cold after the flat. Scharlie drew her coat closer about her and shivered. She frowned at Henry. He was looking quite neat and dignified, once more, in his Burberry, with her white scarf hiding the torn collar and stained shirt. He regarded her with such profound gloom that she realised he was sincerely sorry for his lapse from propriety. Curiosity replaced her annoyance.

'Looking at the thing dispassionately,' she

said, 'I wonder why on earth you did it.'

'I don't know. You—attracted me—suddenly—overpoweringly. I *had* to kiss you.'

'But why?' She was still frowning up at him. 'There'd been no flirtation—simply nothing between us to warrant it.'

'I suppose I lost my head quite unexpectedly and for no particular reason.'

'There must be some psychological reason.'

'Are we going to dissect it, Freudian fashion?' The gloom was suddenly chased from Henry's face, although his eyes remained remorseful. It was rather charming of her to talk to him about the thing without malice. She would have had every right to turn him out of her flat and not care a hang whether he could see his way or not. She was no ordinary girl, this Scharlie. Not for the first time in his life, Henry Gorring became conscious of the fact.

'Things interest me—even things that annoy or insult me,' said Scharlie. 'I felt absolutely furious with you for kissing me. I'm still furious. But at the same time curious. *Why* should you, who are supposed to be a woman-hater and such a virtuous prig . . .'

'Oh, please!' he broke in, blinking at her. 'Good God, I'm not a virtuous prig! Neither am I a woman-hater. Where have you got these extraordinary ideas from?'

'They aren't my ideas. Everyone who knows you says you've no use for women.'

'Perhaps I haven't had much use for them

301

lately. If you want to know, I had a very unhappy experience two years ago, and I've no wish to repeat it.'

'I see,' said Scharlie. Her anger decreased and curiosity deepened. It was really quite entertaining to contemplate that the estimable Henry had had an unhappy experience with some woman. He added:

'I'm not at all virtuous—neither am I a prig, although you've given me the name ever since we've known each other. I didn't wish to be a prig when I tried to save my sister from unhappiness, a year ago. If I behaved like one it was force of circumstances.'

'Oh, well, that's all ended quite successfully,' said Scharlie. 'When I saw Hugh and your sister at the club tonight I was quite cheerful about it and glad they seemed so happy. But I did think you were a prig. Then you behave in the most astounding fashion with me, tonight. You're a mass of inconsistency.'

'Not really. I don't often make such a fool of myself. I may safely say I've never been so completely carried away before, and I can't account for it now.'

'H'm,' said Scharlie. She twisted her lips into a dry little smile. 'It must have been Molyneux's scent.'

'That,' said Henry, 'may be the correct explanation. It's a very heady scent, and it's the one which *she* always used . . . I mean the

302

woman I nearly married.'

'Oh, well, of course,' said Scharlie, 'I suppose I shall have to find an excuse for you. Particular scents do bring back particular memories. And if my scent reminded you of someone you cared for . . .'

She finished with a little laugh, but she regarded him coldly. It was not flattering to imagine that Henry had lost his head and kissed her because a whiff of Molyneux's *Numéro Cinq* had reminded him of another woman. It was typical of Henry Gorring that he should be so tactless. No wonder his love-affair, whatever it was, had not been a success.

Henry, much too disturbed and self-conscious to let Scharlie know that her own particular physical appeal had gone to his head as well as the familiar perfume, held out his hand.

'Please do go back . . . you'll catch cold . . . I can pick up a taxi. You've been much nicer than I deserve. Will you forgive me and be friends?'

Scharlie hesitated. Once before in her life Henry had asked her to be friends. She had hated him then; resented him; refused to meet him half way. But so much water had rolled under the bridge since their last encounter. The old heart-break for Hugh had died. She had seen much of life; had many experiences; worked hard for her living; come up against poverty, loneliness, gaiety, and success, each in their turn.

Tonight, like a blast from the old furnace of trouble, Henry Gorring had been mixed up in her affairs again, and he had come off none too easily. He was really looking very pale and dejected. Although his cut cheek no longer bled, it had a livid, bruised look which called for compassion. Poor old Henry and his fallen dignity! And the way he had kissed her! What a bear's hug. What a kiss. Scharlie's gaze travelled to Henry's lips. They were thin and stern again. Her heart suddenly jumped in the most queer, unorderly fashion when she recalled the fierce passion of those lips. It was incredible . . . she could scarcely believe it, now . . . Henry to have lost his head to such an extent! . . .

'Won't you forgive me?' came from Henry again.

She thrust out a hand. For an instant he gripped it hard.

'Sorry,' he said. And there was a very boyish expression of regret; of appeal in the weak grey eyes.

'That's all right. You went quite mad, but I suppose we all do sometimes,' she muttered.

Then she turned and ran all the way back to Stone Mansions.

Henry Gorring waited for a long while on the corner. Finally a lone taxi came scraping along New Oxford Street. It was only firing on one cylinder, and the noise of the engine made the summer night hideous. But Henry hailed it as a friend.

When he was seated inside, he nursed his injured cheek and pondered over the events of the evening. A more amazing evening he had never had . . . and all because Nell had felt faint and gone home early, and he had returned to the club to find his hat—which, by the way, he had never found—and run into Scharlie.

He was horrified by the memory of his unaccountable action in Scharlie Mason's flat. He was also touched by her generosity, following it.

'I was crazy—an out-and-out blackguard to kiss her like that,' he thought. 'And she was really charming . . .'

He found himself remembering the kiss; the softness of Scharlie's mouth, and her warm, supple body in his arms.

'I must pull myself together,' he reflected. 'It's not like me to feel like this . . .'

He suddenly began to feel some sympathy for Hugh; to have more understanding of that affair of a year ago than he had ever felt at the time. After all—if Scharlie had thrown herself into Hugh's arms—what chance had the man had? It would be damned difficult for any fellow to resist Scharlie. She had . . . what was it? . . . Sex-appeal . . . a strong magnetism . . . a Something, hard to explain, but it was there all the same.

He was a little sorry, too, for the dago dancing-partner. It wouldn't be easy to dance with Scharlie; to hold that young, charming body in one's arms, night after night, and remain calm and unmoved.

Henry blinked out of the window of his taxi and shook his head.

A haunting, insidious thing, this sex. It produced half the unhappiness and most of the happiness in the world. And he, Henry Gorring, had thought sex was dead within him when, two years ago, he had walked out from the presence of the woman who had badly let him down. Dead! Good heavens, it was all there! It had clamoured, shattered him and his control, up in Scharlie's flat a few minutes ago.

'I'd better not see that girl again,' he decided.

But the silk scarf around his throat—Scharlie's scarf—threw up a faint, elusive fragrance—and made him feel undecided again.

CHAPTER FIVE

Scharlie did not see Boo when she returned to the flat that dawn. Scharlie was in bed, and by no means asleep. Her brain was excited; like a cinema screen, it reproduced, photographically, all the events of the evening, and would not let her rest. When Boo tiptoed into her own bedroom, Scharlie did not call her. She had no particular wish to encounter the kindly but voluble Boo tonight.

She finally drifted into sleep, taking with her a confused recollection of Henry Gorring and his amazing conduct. And she found that she was really much more interested in the sequence of events than annoyed by them.

It was a long while since any man had kissed her—roughly, passionately—in such a manner as Henry had kissed her tonight. In fact, no man had touched her lips since she had said good-bye to Hugh. She was thoroughly disturbed. Perforce, she saw Henry Gorring in a new light. Not Henry, the man of iron and steel and ice, who surveyed her and all women superciliously and with cold superiority. Not Henry, Eleanor's brother who ruthlessly trampled everybody underfoot in his effort to secure his sister's happiness. Not the man who had condemned her, Scharlie, for dishonest intrigue, and who had told her that, even though passions existed, they must be con-trolled. But a new human Henry whose blood could, obviously, run hotly through his veins. A man with all the normal weakness—or was it strength—of his sex.

This Henry, so different from the other one she had known and remembered, inevitably roused her feminine interest. And she would not have been true woman were she not piqued by the thought that he had only kissed her because she reminded him of an old flame.

Boo—who invariably played Martha to Scharlie's Mary—was the first to rise in the flat and put the kettle on for tea. At half-past nine that morning she entered Scharlie's bedroom, bearing a tray with tea and bread-and-butter for two. Even after a strenuous night's dancing Boo's good humour persisted. She set the tray down on a table beside Scharlie's bed; yawned; stretched, while she looked round at the confusion of clothes—stockings, lingerie and all the evidences of a pretty woman's vanity. She said:

'Goo' morning, darling. The sun's shining and it's *too* delicious out. Shall I draw your curtains?'

'No, for heaven's sake, don't,' came a drowsy voice from beneath the bedclothes. Then a brown head appeared over the rim of a crumpled sheet. Scharlie surveyed Boo; one eye open, the other still shut. She yawned, and stretched her arms.

'Oh, dear!' she sighed.

'Tired, dear?' asked Boo, pouring out the tea.

'Not tired, merely exhausted,' said Scharlie.

'So am I,' said Boo. 'That old beaver you saw me dancing with last night stuck like grim death to me the whole evening. His name is William Hickory, and he's made half a million.'

Scharlie raised herself on one elbow, opened both eyes, and grinned at Boo while she stirred her tea.

'I saw the old gentleman skipping round with you, my dear. You had my sympathy.'

'Skipping!' repeated Boo. 'My dear, every skip meant another bit of silver off my new shoes. He did 'em in. Mind you, he promised to buy me a new pair, only I don't allow that, as you know. In fact, I clicked. Father William was smitten with my blue eyes and double chin. Said he wasn't married and he'd marry me and we'd go to his ancestral home—built in 1927—up North—called Hickory Hall. Gawd!'

Scharlie shook with laughter.

'I can see you, Boo dear, Mrs. Hickory of Hickory Hall. Have you accepted William?'

'It's *too* tragic!' said Boo. 'Why must the only men who propose to me have one foot in the grave and a snow-white beard! It's just my luck.'

'Well, I'd rather have spent the evening with your millionaire than coping with a lunatic,' said Scharlie.

'Who's the lunatic, dear?'

'Claud. He's fallen in love with me, gone quite dotty, made a scene outside the club and assaulted a wretched man who had done him no harm.'

'My de-ar Scharlie!' Boo's blue eyes opened wide, and she held a piece of bread-and-butter suspended in the air in her astonishment. 'Did

309

he? *Claud?*'

'Yes, Claud,' said Scharlie peevishly. 'I'm simply fed up, Boo. I shall tell André that I won't dance with him again.'

'But my dear . . . how *too* tragic!'

'It is. It looks as though Scharlie will be anybody's partner again instead of exhibition dancer.'

'Oh, don't, my dear!'

Boo surveyed Scharlie in dismay. And thought how pretty she was, sitting up in her lavender-coloured pyjamas; sleeveless ones that showed the beauty of slim bare arms. Scharlie was one of the few, fortunate women who could look pretty when she woke up, even though her tip-tilted nose was unpowdered and inclined to shine, and her lips rouged an unnatural scarlet in the morning-light. Nothing could destroy the lovely contour of brow and cheek and throat, and the sparkle of the greenest of green eyes.

'You've been such a success . . . you can't throw it all up now because of Claud's stupidity,' Boo added in a wailing voice.

'I won't dance with him again, Boo.'

'My dear, you can't afford to be as temperamental as a great star.'

'Quite so. But I can be as stubborn as a little glow-worm.'

'Don't joke, Scharlie. I'm most upset about you. I've realised for ages that Claud worshipped you, but what on earth possessed

310

him to assault a stranger.'

'Not exactly a stranger, but a man you may have heard me mention—Henry Gorring.'

Boo put her cup of tea down on the table and fluttered her lashes at Scharlie rapidly.

'Schar-*lie*! Not the Henry who got mixed up in that awful affair before I met you.'

'Yes. This is *entre nous*, of course. It happened like this.' Scharlie proceeded to give Boo the details of last night's fracas, leaving out the one piece Boo might have liked to hear. But Scharlie was not going to tell anybody about Henry's lapse. That would hardly be playing the game, since he had apologised and she had accepted the apology. She had an almost boyish sense of fair play, which is lacking in most women.

Boo listened to the story of the fight and shook her head.

'Poor old Claud—what a scream! He must have been tight.'

'He wasn't. He was quite sober. He'd only had one glass of champagne. No—he hadn't been drinking.'

'It was just the ramping male.'

'Well, that sounds coarse, Boo dear . . .' Scharlie lay back on her pillow and twinkled. Boo took a comb from Scharlie's dressing-table and passed it through her blonde curls.

'Well, let's call a spade a spade. Claud was the complete cave-man, and he wanted to carry little Scharlie into his cave.'

'Scharlie isn't having any. He can find someone who wants to accompany him to his cave.'

'He may be sorry this morning.'

'I shan't dance with him and risk it.'

'That's the front-door bell,' said Boo.

Scharlie dived under the bedclothes.

'It's Claud. I know it's Claud.'

'My dear,' said Boo. 'Leave him to me if it is.' She shook back her hair, rose majestically to her feet, tied the sash of her bright blue Japanese kimono firmly about her waist, and marched from the room.

She returned a few moments later, closed the door behind her, and advanced to the bedside.

'I say—Scharlie.'

The curly head showed an inch over the clothes. One eye peered at Boo.

'Tell me the worst. *Is* it Claud?'

'Yes, it is.'

'Oh, horrors!' said Scharlie, and vanished again.

'Scharlie, sit up and talk—this is most serious.'

'I'm scared of Claud,' said a muffled voice.

'So am I, if you want to know. He looks positively weird this morning. My dear, you don't suppose he is mental, do you? It would be *too* tragic!'

Then Scharlie shook off the bedclothes and sat bolt upright: she looked at Boo wide-eyed.

'What's he like, Boo?'

'Livid, my dear—a sort of pale, green shade. And his eyes are staring. He has a swollen lip, and he rushed at me like a madman and said: "I must see Scharlie."'

'What did you say?'

'I said: "You can't, Claud. She's in bed."'

'What did he say?'

'He said: "Tell her to get up and see me at once."'

'This is a bit too thick!' exclaimed Scharlie. Very red in the face, she jumped from the bed, walked to the dressing-table, and put a comb rapidly through the thick chestnut waves of her hair. Looking at Boo's reflection in the mirror, she said: 'Well, I'll see him, but I'm going to end this nonsense for good and all.'

'Scharlie, be careful. He looks ghastly, my dear.'

'He has no right to work himself up into such a state. I've never encouraged him— never! If I had, I'd feel guilty. But I've been friends and nothing else. He kissed me goodnight in the taxi once and I laughed at him and told him not to be an ass. He must *know* I'm not at all attracted by him.'

'French blood, my dear . . . the passionate Southerner and all that,' said Boo.

Scharlie seized silk stockings and silk cami-knickers from a chair.

'I shall dress and see the man. It's most annoying. Tell him I'm coming, there's a good

313

soul, Boo, and advise him to keep calm.'

Well, all right,' said Boo. 'But I don't like the look of *Monsieur* Claud this morning at all—at all!'

Scharlie washed and dressed with unusual rapidity.

When she danced so late at night she found it essential for her health to rest late in the morning. This early rising did not suit her. She felt thoroughly cross with Claud and the world when at length she walked into the sitting-room. She looked like a school girl of seventeen in a blue jumper suit which had a turn-down collar and a wide spotted tie.

When she entered the room, Boo and Claud were engaged in a somewhat heated argument.

'It's absurd, if she doesn't love you . . .' Boo was saying.

'She must love me—I could have made her—if that man hadn't interfered—he, who had already broken her heart—' Claud was declaring in a loud, excited voice.

They both stopped talking and looked at Scharlie. Boo hastily made her exit. Scharlie closed the door and stood with her back to it.

'Now look here, Claud,' she said, 'this has got to stop. You're still on the wrong tack. The man you assaulted last night in that disgraceful fashion is *not* Hugh Ellerby, the one I used to care for.'

Claud stared at her in silence a moment. The muscles of his cheeks worked. Scharlie eyed him with disgust and a certain amount of uneasiness. Boo was right. He looked ghastly with that cut, swollen lip—the consequence of Henry's right—and his livid face. Yet she felt faint pity stir in her. The young man's dark almond eyes were so wild, so unhappy. She realised that he must be in torment. And she was the cause of the torment. What woman could help being flattered, even if she were annoyed, by a man's so palpable a passion for herself.

She walked nearer him.

'Sit down and let's talk this over quietly, Claud,' she said in a kinder voice. 'You look ill, old thing. It's all so stupid—just because I've told you I don't care for you.'

The kindness in her voice, in her eyes, brought him to her feet. To her dismay he knelt down, clung to her knees, and burst into wild sobbing.

'*Mon Dieu*, I can't bear it! I love you so, Scharlie. For the love of God, *ma mie*, say you will give me a chance. I *am* ill. I am dying. For love of you. Last night I was in hell—all night long I was in hell—I did not sleep—I pictured you with this fellow. Oh! . . Oh!' He finished with hoarse, long-drawn sobs.

Scharlie looked down at his bowed head. It was too oily and sleek. She disliked it. She disliked the *outre* cut of his pale grey suit, with its double-breasted waistcoat and tight waist. His unrestrained passion; his clutching hands

315

about her knees; repelled her, even if the sobbing roused her compassion. It was ridiculous for a man to behave in such a violent theatrical fashion. He had no restraint; no pride; nothing to make her admire him. She began to wonder why she had ever liked him at all. Claud in this mood was justifying the name Henry had given him . . . 'the dago.' No Englishman, who called himself a man, would behave like this.

'Claud—do get up—don't do this—be like this,' she said, putting a firm hand on his shoulder. 'Get up, please. I don't understand you. You're behaving as though I'd given you a lot of encouragement and then chucked you. I never have—you know it. We were partners—pals—but there was never any question of a love-affair between us.'

He caught her hand; covered it feverishly with tears and kisses.

'But I am crazy for you,' he moaned. 'Other women—like my little Claudia in Paris—she loved me—why can't you love me, *chérie*?'

'I'm not like Claudia, that's all,' said Scharlie. 'You can't love to order, Claud. Do use your intelligence. You know it. I'm not in love with you. I never will be.'

He clung to her hand. He looked up at her; his eyes wet, rolling.

'You won't give me a chance—one little chance.'

'No. It wouldn't be any good.'

316

'You are in love with this fellow . . . the fellow who did this . . .' He laughed hoarsely and pointed to his swollen lip. 'An English prize-fighter.'

'Don't be stupid, Claud. Mr. Gorring isn't a prize-fighter, and if I have to tell you again that he is *not* the man in my life—I shall go quite mad, really.'

'Even if he is not that man—if I made a mistake—then he is a new lover. You favour him. You let him take you home.'

'Claud, I shall be so furious with you in a second that I shall hit you. You exaggerate everything in an impossible fashion. Why, just because a man takes me home should he be my lover? You're crazy.'

'Perhaps I am—with love for you,' he said.

Scharlie wrenched her hand away and moved towards the window. Her lips were set in a hard line. Pity for Claud was evaporating.

'You don't go the right way to keep a girl's friendship, let alone inspire love in her,' she said. 'These sort of scenes may go down in Paris. They don't in London. You made an absolute fool of yourself, and of me, last night outside the Dominoe.'

Claud rose to his feet. He trembled. One dank black lock fell across his forehead. He pulled a handkerchief from his pocket, wiped his streaming eyes and blew his nose violently. Then he said:

'You have no heart—none at all.'

317

'I'm full of heart,' said Scharlie. 'But not for this sort of idiocy.'

'You call my love idiocy—*nein*?'

'Well, *this* sort of thing,' she said, with a gesture of her hand. 'If you expressed your love quietly, decently, I'd understand. I daresay I'd be quite touched and kind about it. But you create such scenes. It's enough to make one heartless.'

Claud passed the handkerchief over his forehead. He breathed fast.

'And tonight . . . when you dance with me . . .'

'I'm not going to dance with you . . .'

'Eh, what?' He stared at her. 'You are *not going to dance*?'

'No. I shall tell André this morning.'

'You are not going to dance with me.' He repeated the words very slowly, as though dazed by them. Then he added in a dramatic whisper: 'That is not so . . . You cannot mean that, Scharlie . . .'

'I do mean it.'

'*Pourquoi?*'

'Because I'm not going to lay myself open to any more scenes of the kind you treated me to last night.'

'But you *must* dance with me. We have a contract. *Mon Dieu!* you cannot break a contract.'

'Oh, yes, you can.'

'You will have to pay . . .'

Scharlie hesitated. It was all very well being proud and making decisions of this kind, but of course Claud was right. She would have to either carry out her contract or Lavelle would sue her. She couldn't afford that. It was intolerable; to be forced into dancing with Claud just because she was poor and had to earn her living. She bit her lip hard and frowned out of the window.

'Oh, well, if I finish the season with you, it will have to be on the understanding that we dance together purely professionally, and that I have nothing to do with you outside the exhibition dance—nothing at all.'

Claud gave an hysterical laugh.

'You hate me—you are going to be damnably cruel—to torture me, now.'

'I don't want to torture you. You've brought it on yourself if I don't want to be friends with you any more.'

He stood shivering, looking at her with his tormented eyes. Then he clenched his teeth and flung an arm above his head.

'What have I to live for? What? Claudia whom I loved is dead. You whom I love will not even be my friend.'

Scharlie sighed impatiently. He would persist in heroics. She felt bored and a little unnerved by the whole discussion.

'Claud, I *would* be friends with you if you were sensible.'

'You mean if I ceased to want you for my

319

lover?'

'Yes.'

'That is impossible—totally impossible. You are in my blood like a fever—I am unable to sleep or eat!' he said violently.

'There you are,' said Scharlie. 'Friendship between us is hopeless. I'm sorry we've still got to dance together. Even if I can't break my contract, I shall ask André to look for someone to take my place.'

She walked to the door, and, looking back at Claud over her shoulder, she added:

'I must go now. I've got an appointment with my dressmaker.'

He swallowed hard once or twice; fixed her with his gleaming eyes; then picked up his hat and rushed to the door.

'Your dressmaker. Gr-r-eat God! Your dresses matter more than my agony. But you shall see what your cruelty does to me. *Au'voir!*'

He fled past her into the hall and out of the flat. The front door slammed behind him. Scharlie marched back to her bedroom. Boo was sitting on the edge of the bed filing her nails.

'Well?' said Boo, looking up. 'It all sounded most hectic through the wall. Has he smashed the glass of our front door?'

'No. But he's quite impossible.'

'What did he say?'

Scharlie told her. She began to make some

320

attempt to fold up clothes and tidy her disordered bedroom. She looked flushed and angry.

'I'm fed up. He's behaving like a lunatic. It's a nuisance that I can't break my contract at the Dominoe without being sued. I can't afford to be sued.'

'Oh, well, dear, just a few dances with him . . .'

'With a raging madman—it will be pleasant!'

'He can't do much harm during an exhibition dance.'

'Only get excited and beastly and make scenes after.'

'I should threaten him with the police.'

'With an asylum, you mean. The man's crazy.'

'And all for love of you. Aren't you thrilled?'

'No—I'm most annoyed.'

'Isn't it queer,' said Boo, cupping her chin on the palm of her hand and staring at Scharlie. 'The wild passion of the man one *doesn't* love annoys one. If the man one did love became a raging lunatic through passion, one would rage in response oneself.'

'H'm,' said Scharlie. 'I daresay . . .' And her thoughts flew to a certain night in Hugh Ellerby's flat, where a man had told her he did not care in the way she wanted. She recalled her own sensation of despair; her tears; her woe. But she had had to pull herself together, rapidly. Her conduct had been mild, compared to Claud's. 'Of course,' she added, 'stolid English folk don't go on like that. It's the half-breed. I'm beginning to remember, too, that Claud once let out to me, when he was telling me about himself, that his father came to a sticky end.'

'My dear!' Boo's blue eyes widened. 'How *too* delicious! What sort of sticky end?'

'Well, he was a jockey, crazy about Claud's mother, who was a dancer in Paris. She had some affair with some Russian prince, and the jockey discovered them and threw himself into the Seine.'

'My de-ar! Don't mention it! If papa's strain's there, Claud might drown himself for love of you.'

Scharlie went suddenly very white.

'He couldn't—he won't—for God's sake shut up, Boo. Give me a cigarette.'

And then she changed the conversation. The thought of Claud and his crazy passion was beginning to get on her nerves. The front-door bell rang.

'If that's Claud again, tell him I'm out,' said Scharlie tersely.

Boo answered the bell. She returned to Scharlie with a small square box.

'From Gerard's. More flowers. Scharlie, 'pon my soul you're getting like any film star.'

'Yab, Boo! Open it, old thing. I'm terribly afraid it's Claud again . . . ?

'You've got him on the brain.'

'So would anybody in my position.'

Boo opened the box. She drew out a flat tissue-paper packet. Then an exquisite, dewy spray of shell-pink and mauve carnations, and delicate fern.

'What on earth's this, Scharlie? . . .'

Scharlie looked at the spray, and untied the flat packet.

'Lord knows . . .'

Then her cheeks grew hot and her eyes crinkled with laughter. It was the white silk scarf she had loaned Henry. And attached to it a note. Not the first she had received from Henry—but the first of its kind. She read it:

'DEAR SCHARLIE,—Your scarf herewith, and a few flowers which you might like to wear when you dance tonight. Please accept them with my humble apologies for last night. My thanks to you for being so charming to me.

'H. G.'

'From Claud?' asked Boo, sniffing the carnations.

'No. From Henry Gorring.'

'Henry again! "Tweet-tweet, now, now, ssh-ssh, coom, coom,"' sang Boo in her best Lancashire. 'Gracie Fields, what ho!'

'Idiot,' said Scharlie, but her cheeks remained hot; as pink as the carnations, when she lifted them to her nose and sniffed them.

Henry's gesture was unexpected, and it pleased her.

Here was another crazy lunatic—at least he had been one last night when he had kissed her—but how different from Claud? Slightly more reserved; more reasonable.

'Scharlie, confess to your old Boo. Has Mr. Gorring fallen for your unearthly charms?'

'Of course not. This is to thank me for lending him my scarf to hide his bloodstains from his father.'

Scharlie took the spray and a vase and walked into the bathroom. While she filled the vase with water she made a rapid mental survey of her wardrobe.

'I'll wear my silver-tissue this evening. The carnations will go beautifully with that . . .'

Which proves that Scharlie had already made up her mind to wear Henry's spray at the Dominoe tonight.

CHAPTER SIX

Scharlie went to the club that night, full of forebodings about Claud. But the young man agreeably surprised her by his apparent composure. He looked very white and ill, and his eyes held a look of wildness which troubled her, but he was quiet. He was also very silent. He had nothing to say to anybody. When Boo

324

saw him she whispered to Scharlie:

'The lull before the storm, my pet. He looks *too* tragic . . .'

'Oh, I expect he's all right,' said Scharlie. 'For Lord's sake don't make me any more worried about him than I am. The whole show is most unpleasant.'

She sat at a table alone, close to the one occupied by Boo and the other dance instructresses. When André announced the first exhibition dance and introduced 'Claud and Claudia,' she rose to meet Claud, who advanced from another corner of the room. She glanced at him nervously and gave him her hand. He took it. His fingers were burning hot as though he had fever. But he gave her no greeting, made no remark. She fancied his gaze wandered to the spray of carnations on the silver strap of her dress, and that his lips twisted into a half-sneer. She made an effort to ease the situation, which she found most disturbing to her peace.

'Rather empty tonight—lot of people out of town, Fridays.'

He ignored her speech, and, putting an arm about her, led her into the white circle of arc-light for their opening waltz.

They always danced in silence. But as a rule Claud gave her a little squeeze or a congratulatory smile or they exchanged some kind of friendly look. Tonight it was a complete and utter silence between them; a

325

frozen one. It got on Scharlie's nerves. Claud danced with his usual grace and agility, but he held her so lightly that it was almost as though no arm supported her at all. Not once did he look at her. And when the last quick foxtrot ended and the applause broke out, he gave her a queer, curt bow and walked straight out of the club. Scharlie felt more uneasy than if he had been his violent, passionate self. His conduct made her afraid.

André Lavelle came up to her.

'What's wrong with Claud, Scharlie? . . .' They all called her Scharlie down here. 'Is he ill?'

'I think so,' she replied guardedly.

'He should have taken the encore,' said the manager crossly. 'Unless he was very bad.'

Scharlie made a non-committal reply. She sat at her usual concealed table, drank some coffee, and thought uneasily about Claud.

Boo, who had been dancing with a bronzed and blue-eyed giant who looked as though he hailed from the Colonies, slipped over to Scharlie's side.

'All right, darling?'

'Not at all. Claud was most queer.'

'I thought he looked it. He's gone, hasn't he?'

'Yes, left the club immediately after our foxtrot. Boo, I have a terrible feeling about him. What the dickens can I do?'

'Nothing, my dear. You can't go and let him

make love to you just because he's being so imbecile.'

'I know,' said Scharlie. She powdered her nose mechanically, then stuffed the gilt box into her jewelled bag. Her eyes wandered restlessly round the club. There were a good many empty tables. There seemed no life in the people who were here. The band played monotonously and without the usual enthusiasm. It was hot, this August night. The whole atmosphere depressed Scharlie.

'Dee and Tim have asked me down to Gateways on Sunday. I shall go,' she said, rising to her feet. 'I'm fed up with town and everyone in it.'

Boo patted a fair wave of hair into order and smoothed a crumpled fold of her black lace dress. She caught Scharlie's arm.

'Scharlie, I've clicked.'

'Who with, you old idiot?'

'*Him* . . .' whispered Boo, and indicated the sunburned hero who stretched long legs at a table by himself across the floor. '*Too* delicious, Scharlie. Just home from Rhodesia.'

'I thought so.'

'Said just now he didn't know such a charming girl as myself was to be found in a night club; thinks I'm much too sweet to be wasted on this life, and hinted broadly that life in the Colonies would suit me.'

'So it would. Go straight ahead,' said Scharlie.

'I'm going,' said Boo radiantly. 'He's a great dear—such a kid—and I'm booked to him for the evening. Bit better than old Father William. He's got a lovely name, Scharl . . . Joe Christmas.'

'Christmas,' repeated Scharlie.

'Yes, isn't it *too* delicious. And his pals in Africa call him Santa Claus.'

Scharlie laughed.

'My dear, how priceless. Well, go back to your Santa Claus, and good luck.'

'This is where I hang up my stocking,' said Boo wickedly. 'No, I don't mean what you mean, Scharlie . . .'

The band broke into: 'Tweet-tweet'—Boo's favourite tune. The bronzed and smiling 'Santa Claus' rose from his table, and, fixing an eager blue eye upon Boo's plump and charming figure, bore down upon her.

Scharlie vanished. She was going home. She was not tired, but she was worried about her dancing-partner, and she looked forward to a refreshing walk through the starlit night.

'Well, dear old Boo's happy this evening,' he thought. 'I wish the six-foot-two Mr. Christmas would take her back to Rhodesia. As Mrs. Christmas and the mother of several little Christmases, she'd be both excellent and happy.'

Outside the Dominoe a car with a long aluminium body was drawn up at the kerb. Scharlie, drawing her velvet coat closely around her, gave the beautiful car a glance. It was an Isotta. Then she paused and knit her brows. Where had she seen that particular car before? Didn't it belong to somebody she knew? Then she remembered. Of course— Henry Gorring. When she had first met him down in Sussex he had been sitting in that car outside Tim's house. Eleanor had called it the 'Silver Streak.'

And then a man who had been leaning over the petrol tank of the Isotta, with his back to Scharlie, turned and faced her. And she saw that it was Henry Gorring. A little taken aback, she greeted him.

'Oh, hello . . .'

Henry took off his hat and came up to her. He was not in evening-dress. He wore a grey lounge suit. And a new pair of horn-rimmed spectacles, she noticed. He looked none the worse for last night's mêlée, except for a piece of court plaster on his cheek.

'Good evening,' he said. 'I've been waiting for you.'

'For me?' Scharlie became curiously embarrassed. 'Really? But . . . but why?'

'I thought I'd like to drive you home.'

'But I only live round the corner, so to speak.'

'I know . . .' He cleared his throat and pulled at the lobe of his ear. 'I—er—but you don't want to walk—I mean, you must be tired after your dancing.'

'It's awfully kind of you. But I nearly always walk.'

'Well, I happened to have the Isotta out,' he said lamely. 'Been out of town all day on business, and came along here in the hope of picking you up. I couldn't come down to the club as I was in these togs.'

'It was very nice of you. But really I can quite well walk.'

'Let me take you,' he said. 'Just to show me I'm forgiven, and to let me show you that I do know how to behave myself . . . that I'm not always as crazy as I was last night.'

Immediately, the memory of last night's kiss flashed between them. Scharlie found herself growing hot and pink. Her lashes drooped. Henry's face also grew hot, but he forbore to tell her that he had worried all day about his conduct and mentally kicked himself for it a dozen times. She thought it rather nice of him to be so persistently sorry for his behaviour. After all, a good many men might have kissed the exhibition dancer from the Dominoe and been casual about it afterwards. She suddenly raised her eyes to him and smiled.

'I've forgotten all about it,' she lied. 'And please don't worry any more. You can take me back if you want. It's such a marvellous car. I'd like to try it.'

'She is rather a nice bus,' said Henry modestly. 'Nips along, you know.'

'I expect fast enough to break your neck.'

'Oh, quite . . .'

He opened the door and Scharlie stepped in, and settled herself in the low, comfortable seat. Henry took his place beside her at the steering-wheel. They moved forward smoothly, as though drawn by a silken cord.

'If you've been out of town all day you've been lucky. It's been awfully hot,' said Scharlie.

'I know. I went down to Guildford to see a business friend of my father's. It was pretty good going over the Hog's Back.'

'I remember the first day I saw you in this car. You call it the "Silver Streak," don't you?'

Henry glanced at her. The sternness of his lips relaxed into a faint smile.

'Do you remember that? It was at the Wilberforces' place.'

'Yes, you gave me a frigid nod and a frozen word.'

Henry's smile increased.

'Did I really? I do appear to have made myself most objectionable to you. The beastly prig. Isn't that what you called me?'

'Yes.'

'I'm not really.'

They left Dover Street behind them. Henry steered the Isotta into Piccadilly. At this hour—one in the morning—it was gloriously empty, and they went at what would have been an impossible pace a few hours ago. Turning down the Mall, Henry gave his companion

331

another glance.

'Look here—it's a topping night. Like to have one spin along the Embankment?'

'I don't mind,' said Scharlie. 'It's very snug in this seat and the air's like champagne—waking me up.'

'Right,' said Henry.

CHAPTER SEVEN

When they were gliding quietly and at a moderate pace along the Embankment, Scharlie sat well back in her seat, put her hands up the wide, fur-edged sleeves of her evening-coat, and half-closed her eyes.

'I like an open car,' she murmured. 'These saloons that people go in for nowadays are too shut in and stuffy.'

Henry approved of that. The night breeze was playing wantonly with Scharlie's red-brown hair; blowing little curly strands of it across her eyes and cheeks. And she didn't care. Most women preferred a saloon; were afraid of a little wind which might disarrange a perfect coiffure.

'She's quite a nice, natural child,' he thought. 'Most curious make-up. Can come out like this and be a simple sort of kid; and down there in that rotten, overheated nightclub she looks like a sophisticated *danseuse* from a Continental show.'

Scharlie dreamily surveyed the scene and adored it. The Embankment at one o'clock on a warm, August morning was beautiful and mysterious. It held that subtle charm which belongs to the great heart of a mighty city whose pulse-beats are temporarily suspended; silenced in the sleeping hours. One or two taxis; a private car; a belated lorry rolled past them. And then silence again. The sky was sown with stars. The cold clear light of a full moon traced a white, shining pathway on the smooth river, which had the dark glitter of slowly moving oil.

Chelsea Bridge was an intriguing, fairy-like archway with moving points of light here and there. The small dirty tugs and barges moored to land had their own secret beauty casting irregular shadows upon the moonlit water. The lamps all the way along the Embankment were soft, pale blobs of light in the brown and purple dimness of the night.

It was an enchanted London that Scharlie rarely looked upon. For, as a rule, she was too exhausted after her job to do more than head straight for home, anxious for her bed.

But tonight she was wide-awake and fully alive to the allurement of this summer night beside the Thames. She turned her gaze from the water to Henry. He was looking gravely ahead of him, one hand on the big wheel of the Isotta.

'I say—it's simply marvellous,' she said in a hushed voice.

'It is, rather. Who says London is impossible in midsummer? It's as beautiful here tonight as anywhere in the country.'

'I know it is. I don't think I've ever seen London, or *felt* it, quite as I've done tonight.'

Henry lifted his toe from the accelerator. The big graceful car slowed down; stopped. He put on the brake.

'Just one moment. I want a cigarette. Have one?'

'Thanks.'

He lit hers for her. The flare of the match lit up her face and showed him her shining eyes. Then she turned her head and looked at the river again.

'Once,' she said, 'I remember driving home from a dance with Alec, my husband, and we came along the Embankment. I wanted to stop for a moment, but he laughed at me. He said: "My dear Scharlie, what is there to see except the muddy water and a few derelicts waiting to be moved on by the bobbies." Aren't people different? Minds work so differently. Where one sees beauty, another sees ugliness, and vice-versa, of course.'

Henry regarded the red point of his cigarette. He had almost forgotten that this girl had ever had a husband named Alec. His memory of Mason was not a pleasant one. And for Scharlie, heaven knew what unpleasant memories the name must recall. Her married life must have been a wretched, joyless thing. She must be glad that she was free. He was suddenly glad for her sake that she was free. It was a marvel, too, that those years of intimacy, of contact with such a man as Mason, had not destroyed the beauty, the ardour of life for her. She was much more self-contained; more reticent than she used to be; but it struck him forcibly tonight that she was still amazingly young and untouched.

'Don't you think life and people are astonishing,' she asked him. 'We never know what we are heading for; what life holds for us.'

'Just as well,' he said, with a smile. 'It would be pretty awful to see all the calamities ahead.'

'But nice to see the nice things.'

'If we could pick and choose what we saw.'

'Yes. But, of course, if we saw the future, *that* future would never materialise. We'd never let it. I mean—I'd never have dreamed of allowing my mother to urge me into that hopeless marriage with Alec if I'd known what it meant.'

'No, of course not. I never could understand—'

'Why I married him?'

'Well, yes.'

'Extreme youth; extreme silliness; the desire to get away from an uncongenial atmosphere at home with a mother who had very little use

335

for me, and Alec, at that time, at his best—preening all his feathers for me.'

'Yes,' said Henry. 'That explains it.'

'I didn't know the future—so I married Alec,' she said, with a short laugh. 'And then catastrophe. It all seems so far away and so unreal now—that affair with Hugh, for instance. It seems amazing now that you should have been so involved in it all.'

'Yes, I suppose it does.'

'I hated your interference at the time. I resented it. But now I'm rather glad of it. Obviously Hugh and I would never have been happy. He wanted a much steadier influence; the sort of wife your sister has made him.'

'Yes, you're right. He and Nell get on extraordinarily well. She adores him. I honestly think he cares for her.'

'I'm sure he does. He always did. The affair with me was a passing infatuation. If I hadn't been such a little idiot I'd have realised it at the time.'

'It's rather nice of you to say things like that. You don't bear malice, do you?'

'I don't think so, no. I haven't a malicious streak in me.'

'On the contrary—you're very generous and forgiving.'

Their eyes met. Scharlie looked away quickly, and her cheeks suddenly burnt. She knew that he referred to her pardon for his behaviour last night.

'I'm older now,' she said hastily. 'I see things more sensibly. I'm more tolerant. I thought Hugh was frightfully cruel at the time—I suffered agonies—but I understand, now, how little his passion for me mattered beside his real love for your sister.'

'Passion can be a very terrible thing, all the same, and I don't doubt you went through it badly. I know you did.'

'At the same time, when I was howling about it, my friend, Mrs. Wilberforce—little Dee— told me to look on love—on life—on everything—as a jest. She told me to try and see the joke and to laugh. She was right. It is all rather a jest, isn't it?'

'I suppose so. But Mrs. Wilberforce—from what I know of her—is very happily married. Happy people can so easily regard life as a joke.'

'Well, she *is* happy. Big Tim is a perfect dear and they suit each other; but, in any case, I think she's right. You don't suffer so much if you make up your mind that nothing lasts— that everything dies—and that it's best to joke your way along and take things as they come.'

'Admirable philosophy. I'll follow it . . .' His eyes behind the horn-rimmed glasses were amused.

'Well, nothing does matter to *you*, much, does it?'

'Why do you say that?'

Scharlie shrugged her shoulders.

337

'My reputation for being a self-satisfied prig again?' he said.

'Well, no, but you're reputed to be a hard and chilly mortal, wrapped up in business.'

'Strange, isn't it, how the world judges one by outward appearances.'

'You mean that you appear to be cold and hard and wrapped up in business, and that underneath you're different.'

'I don't say I'm very different. I *am* hard these days.'

'But scarcely cold . . .'

Her voice suddenly slurred to laughter. Henry pulled the lobe of his ear and went scarlet. But he found himself laughing with her.

'No—perhaps not. You've seen a side of me which might astonish my circle of acquaintances. But, as I said last night, I don't often lose my head—'

'Ah, well, we put it all down to Molyneux,' said Scharlie. 'I suppose I had no right to say nothing matters to you. There was someone who mattered . . . someone connected with Molyneux's scent, wasn't there?'

Henry took off his hat. He smoothed his hair, put back his hat, and stared up at the starry sky. His face was blank. Behind their glasses his eyes were inscrutable. Scharlie wondered what was going on behind them. Then suddenly he laughed, and looked down at her; mind and body relaxed.

'Yes, there was someone who mattered once. I don't think anybody knew about her, except Eleanor, and she didn't know much. I don't often air my emotions or grievances. But I'll tell you about it if you like. We seem to know quite a lot about each other, already.'

'You know a lot about me,' said Scharlie. 'But I don't know you at all. Do tell me—I'm interested.'

'It's a very short story. And not an original one. Two years ago I fell very much in love for the first time in my life. She wasn't marvellously beautiful or anything of that sort—but she was very pleasant to look at and she attracted me vitally. One can't account for these attractions. Anyhow, I got it badly, and I made the mistake of letting her know how much I cared. She was amused by my devotion for a time. For reasons of her own she didn't want a public engagement, and so we were privately engaged. She had to go to New York—her father was an American—and she promised to marry me when she came back. I met the boat at Southampton—full of hope and ardour, like a perfect fool, plus wedding ring and licence. And she came off the boat with her husband.'

'With her *husband*!' repeated Scharlie.

'Yes,' said Henry. 'She'd fallen in love with some fellow on board, and the captain had married them.'

'How ghastly for you.'

'Quite unpleasant. I didn't like it, I assure you.'

'Ghastly,' echoed Scharlie. 'Really, I *do* think that was a damnable thing for any man. No wonder you grew hard and cynical. What did you say to her . . . what did you do?'

'Nothing. I wished her luck and drove back to town. On the way I tore up the licence and chucked the ring into a hedge. The heroics of youth. Today I daresay I'd be more thrifty. I'd sell the ring for what it was worth. It was platinum, by the way.'

'Don't!' said Scharlie.

'Don't—what?'

'Be as cynical as that.'

Henry pitched his cigarette-end over the side of the car. He was smiling.

'I assure you it doesn't hurt me now. I can look back upon the affair quite calmly, and I bear the lady no grudge.'

'But it must have hurt dreadfully at the time. To get so near . . . I mean, after actually buying a licence and a ring.'

'It's happened to other men. To women, too. As you've just said. everything dies. Treat love and life as a jest. Much better. These experiences harden one, and one never has the same beautiful romantic outlook, afterwards. But they also teach one to be sensible. I shall never rush wildly after any woman again. So no woman will ever hurt me again. And you'll never let any fellow hurt you.'

340

'We're rather a good pair.'

'We ought to be the best of friends. And why not?'

'There used to be so many reasons why not. A year ago you looked upon me as a designing hussy . . .'

'Oh, not quite that,' he interrupted.

'Well, you thoroughly disapproved of me. But I daresay, after your personal experience of a woman's treachery, you felt all women were treacherous. You imagined I was out purely to snaffle Hugh from your sister and make him into a suitable co-respondent.'

'Whatever I thought at first, I changed my mind later. Do you know I was very worried about you indeed when the whole thing was over? You've no idea what a lot I thought about you.'

'Did you? Well, I got over it—I was all right.'

'But you mightn't have been. You were such a child, and you had no money, nothing . . .'

'I got along beautifully.'

'You happen to have had pluck and sense.'

'Thank you very much.' Her eyes sparkled at him. 'All's well that ends well.'

'By the way, what has happened to your dreadful relations-in-law, all of whom wrote and accused me of destroying your marital happiness and insisted that I should make an honest woman of you?'

Scharlie chuckled.

'Aunt Agatha and Cissie and the rest? Heavens, weren't they poisonous. I've never heard a word from any of 'em.'

'And what about your mother. You had a mother abroad, hadn't you?'

'My lady mother married a South African with a diamond-mine and is living in Johannesburg now, rejuvenated. She allows me a pound a week.'

'A pound a week, eh? That's not much.'

'Oh, it's been a help. It's paid half the rent of my little flat.'

'You've had a hard time, joking apart,' he said gravely.

'Oh, I'm all right . . . I say, it's simply lovely out here, but I ought to be getting back. Boo— Miss Orbutt, who lives with me—will be home soon, and she'll wonder where on earth I am.'

Henry switched on the engine.

'Come along, then. We've had a most pleasant talk.'

'I've enjoyed it,' she said.

Her thoughts suddenly flew to Claud. The brightness faded from her face. Her brows contracted.

'By the way, I'm frightfully worried.'

'What about?'

'My dancing-partner, Claud.'

'Surely he had his lesson last night?'

'No—he was round at my flat early this morning in a most hysterical state. I'm a bit uneasy about his mental condition.'

'Why?' asked Henry.

Scharlie told him, while he drove her slowly homewards.

'The strain's there . . . papa was unbalanced, and Claud had always struck me as being thoroughly unbalanced. If he should do anything stupid . . .' She broke off with a gesture.

'I don't suppose he will,' said Henry. 'He'll calm down.'

'Well, I can't accept him as a lover just because I'm afraid of what he'll do, can I?'

'Good heavens, no,' said Henry hastily.

And he had a sudden, disagreeable vision of Scharlie accepting the man whom he privately termed a 'damned dago' for her lover. He felt a very real feeling of liking, of friendliness towards Scharlie, tonight. He had not had a woman friend since his débâcle of two years ago. Life had been rather flat, after all, with nothing but work in it.

'Look here,' he added. 'If you're scared of the fellow, or if you want help—I mean a man may be useful—let me know. I'd like you to look on me as your friend.'

'Thank you,' said Scharlie, 'I will.'

They drew up outside Stone Mansions. Henry climbed out and gave Scharlie a hand. Her velvet coat slipped away from one shoulder and showed him the carnation spray; now a trifle crushed and withered. But he felt suddenly pleased; flattered because she had

343

worn his flowers.

'It was nice of you to wear those,' he said.

'What?'

'The carnations . . .'

'Oh!' Scharlie laughed and coloured. 'It was rather nice of you to send them.'

'Not at all. Did you get the scarf?'

'Yes. Did it deceive father?'

'Entirely. He never noticed the bloodstains, thanks to you.'

'Nor the fact that you'd broken your glasses?'

'No. I dug the duplicate pair out of a drawer before I saw him.'

She looked up at him; marvelling again that those grey, weak eyes could become so strong, so keen behind the magnifying glasses. She thought of him last night, groping his way up and down the stairs, holding on to her arm. Funny blind old Henry. He was rather a nice old thing. And that girl had treated him abominably. He must have been absolutely shattered; meeting that boat and finding she had married that man on board. Poor Henry. No wonder he had grown hard and disliked women. And there was some excuse for him losing his head last night and kissing her. He was probably a very hungry, lonely man behind all his sternness and austerity.

All that was most gentle and understanding in Scharlie rose to the surface and forgave Henry Gorring his former shortcomings. She held out her hand.

'Good night—Henry,' she said.

He took the hand and squeezed it hard.

'Good night, Scharlie. You've been very charming to me. Perhaps you'll come out in the Isotta again some time soon. Run down to the country or something one Sunday.'

'I'd like to. Good night.'

'Good night,' he echoed.

She disappeared into the house. She hummed under her breath as she fitted her key into the Yale lock of her flat. For no particular reason she was feeling happy. That drive, that chat with Henry had done her good. Funny life was! Here she was; the best of friends with Henry Gorring, who a year ago had seemed her worst enemy.

She switched on the light in the tiny hall. The flat was in darkness. Boo was not yet home. Scharlie grinned to herself. Perhaps dear old Boo had broken her rule and made an exception of her blue-eyed Mr. Christmas and gone out to supper with him.

'I must have one more cigarette,' she thought, and walked into the sitting-room. She knew she had left a packet of Players on the writing-desk this afternoon. She yawned as she switched on the light. The exhilaration of the drive with Henry was dying. She was suddenly tired. Then her heart gave a furious and painful jolt, and the blood rushed to her face and receded, leaving her white.

'*God*!' she said.

A man in evening-dress was sitting on the sofa. He must have been sitting there, silently, in the darkness. It was Claud. The shock to Scharlie was considerable. She felt her knees tremble under her. She put a hand out and clutched a side of the door, to steady herself.

'God!' she said again, 'how you frightened me! What are you doing here? How dare you come here? How did you get in, anyhow?'

Claud rose to his feet. He was very pallid and his eyes stared. When he spoke it was with that unnatural calm that he had displayed down in the club.

'I let myself in. I knew you kept a spare key under the mat, in case either of you lost or forgot your own. You told me that one day.'

Scharlie swallowed hard. She trembled, but some of the colour returned to her cheeks. She looked at him with anger.

'You had absolutely no right to come into our flat. You could be put in prison for it. Will you please go, at once.'

'Not yet, Scharlie.'

He advanced towards her. His glittering, staring eyes caused her fresh panic. She shrank back.

'Claud, leave my flat, at once,' she panted. 'You've no right to frighten me like this.'

He stopped, and put a hand to his head.

'I don't mean to frighten you, Scharlie.'

'Well, go away,' she said. 'At once.'

Finding him there in the dark in that unexpected way had shaken her nerve. She felt thoroughly scared. Claud looked very queer, and she was alone in the flat with him. It was two o'clock in the morning. Other people in the building were in bed and asleep. If she screamed, the couple in the flat below might hear her. But she did not want to scream and cause a public scandal. She made an effort to control her panic. She realised that Claud must be dealt with carefully.

'Listen, Claud,' she said. 'You can't stay here now. Boo's not in. You must consider my reputation. I'll see you tomorrow—we'll have a talk in the morning, see? You must go now.'

He shook his head. His eyes still stared at her.

'No,' he said. 'I can't go. I must talk to you now.'

'But Claud—you're unreasonable—it's so late.'

'I don't know what time it is. I have lost count of time. But it doesn't matter what time it is.'

Scharlie felt very cold.

'Claud, I'm very tired. You *must* go away and see me in the morning.'

'You've been out with that man again.'

She flushed.

'Claud—really!'

'Yes, I saw you. He is your lover.'

'Claud, don't start this absurd discussion

347

again. I can't stand it.'

'I cannot stand it, either—the agony of my love for you Scharlie,' he said in a whisper. He took a step towards her, right hand outstretched. '*Scharlie* . . .'

'Don't touch me!' she cried, with a high note of fear in her voice. In all her life she had never felt more afraid. If only Henry had come up with her. If only Boo were here . . . anyone.

Claud's arm fell to his side. A queer, tragic smile curved his lips. He shook his head.

'You hate me, *ma mie.* And I die for love of you.'

'Claud,' said Scharlie, her teeth chattering. 'You're n-not d-dying. Now d-do g-go away, and be sensible.'

'For the last time I ask you, will you give me a chance? I cannot live without you, Scharlie. There is nothing left in life but you.'

'What shall I say to him?' she asked herself. 'He's crazy.'

She stood speechless, staring at him. His demented eyes held her fascinated. He burst into a wild fit of laughter.

'You don't want me. Then this is the end. Good-bye,' he said.

He drew something from his pocket. Scharlie barely had time to see what it was. She only knew that it gleamed in the electric light. She also knew the most paralysing sense of fear.

'Claud!' she screamed.

A hideous crack seemed to go through Scharlie's head. Temporarily it stunned her. A film came over her eyes. She scarcely saw Claud as he spun round and crumpled up at her feet. The acrid smell of the powder reached her nostrils. She heard a rushing noise in her ears. Her knees sagged, and she fell down upon them, fainting.

CHAPTER EIGHT

When Henry Gorring let himself into his house in St. John's Wood, the telephone bell was ringing. Henry was surprised. The bell, drowning out its double beat monotonously and regularly, was not a sound one generally heard in this domicile in the early hours of the morning.

Henry walked into the library, switched on a light, and lifted the receiver of the instrument which stood on the writing-table.

'Hello, hello,' he said.

The bell ceased drowning. A husky, breathless voice said:

'Oh, hello . . . Henry . . . is that Mr. Henry Gorring?'

'Is that Scharlie?' he asked, astonished.

'Yes, it is. Oh, Henry—'

'Yes, what? What's happened? Is anything wrong?'

'Henry, can you come round to my flat at once—can you?' said an hysterical voice.

'What's happened? Tell me.'

'Something awful. Henry, you told me if I needed a man pal to send for you . . . and I need one now . . . awfully . . .'

'Yes, of course. I'll come. What's happened?'

'Claud—'

'Well—what's he done?'

'I can't tell you on the 'phone. Only come at once.'

'Is he there—with you?'

'Yes.'

'Are you all right?'

'Yes. Please come at once.'

'Very well, at once.'

He hung up the receiver. For an instant he stood still. What did Scharlie mean—that something awful had happened? What was the man doing in her flat at this hour? Had he taken poison on her doorstep—the wretched fellow?

Henry pulled a case from his pocket, lit a cigarette, and walked out of the library. He left the solemn, handsome library and the quiet, well-ordered house, the inmates of which were sound asleep in their beds, and hurried round to his garage. He got out the Isotta again and drove to what he guessed would be certain chaos.

Yet he did not mind going. He was glad that

350

Scharlie had sent for him. He had not imagined she would make a call upon his friendship quite so quickly after the offer of it, but he was content that she should make it. He had felt an instant's pang of anxiety on her behalf when he had heard her husky, unsteady young voice. He was still afraid for her.

He leaped up the steep staircase of Stone Mansions, two steps at a time. The front door of Scharlie's flat was open and a ray of light guided him. She was waiting for him on the top landing. She was still in the silver tissue dress, with the crumpled carnations on her shoulder. But she was not the pink and smiling Scharlie to whom he had bidden good night. She was white and shivering. She greeted him with a relief she made no effort to hide.

'Oh, Henry, thank God you've come. I couldn't explain on the 'phone . . . I didn't want anyone to hear. Thank God I had the 'phone. It was only put in this quarter—we couldn't afford it before.'

He followed her into the flat. He had driven round without bothering to put on hat or coat. His hair was blown by the breeze. He said:

'Well—what's happened?'

'Claud shot himself in my sitting-room twenty minutes ago.'

'Shot himself? Good God. In front of you?'

'Yes . . .' She swallowed hard. He saw that she was making an effort not to break down. 'I found him sitting there when I came up. He'd opened the door with a key which Boo and I keep under the mat. He was very wild and queer, and said he didn't want to live if I couldn't love him. Then he . . . he shot himself. I must have fainted. Anyhow, when I realised what was happening I found myself lying half in the hall, half in the sitting-room, and Claud was lying in front of me. There was a lot of blood. I . . . I felt frightfully sick . . . I nearly screamed with sheer nerves . . . but I tried not to . . . because of the scandal. I managed to . . . get to the 'phone. I've been waiting out here till you came. I didn't dare—I *couldn't*—go back in there . . .'

They were at the sitting-room door now. Henry put a steadying hand on Scharlie's arm.

'Hold up, Scharlie,' he said. 'Don't give way. You've been very good. Now just leave things to me. Don't come in if you don't want to.'

'All right,' she said.

She hung back in the hall, a hand to her eyes. She was trying not to shiver so, but she still felt as though her knees were giving way. In all her life she had never been more thankful to see anybody than Henry at this precise hour. Henry gave out an aura of power, of strength. She knew she could rely on him.

'It was awfully decent of you to come,' she whispered.

But Henry did not hear. He was in the sitting-room, taking in the situation at a

352

glance. He was unaccustomed to horrors, and by no means keen on dealing with the corpse of a suicide . . . if it was a corpse. But he did not shirk it.

Scharlie's dancing-partner presented a ghastly spectacle. He lay in a crumpled position; knees hunched, one arm twisted under him, the other flung out at his side, fingers still gripping a small automatic. Only one half of his face and head were visible, and they were daubed in blood. There was blood everywhere—over his clothes, over the carpet. Henry recoiled from the sight. Scharlie ought never to have seen it, poor little girl, he thought. He had no wish to touch that gory figure, but it was necessary. He must make sure the man was dead; find out if he had been successful in the effort to take his own life.

He turned the body gently over. He saw at once that there was still life in Claud. His eyes were shut and his mouth open. He was breathing.

'He isn't dead, Scharlie,' Henry said, turning round. ' 'Phone for a doctor at once.'

'Not dead? Oh, my God, I'm glad,' said Scharlie with a suppressed sob.

'There's the devil of a wound. He shot himself through the neck. That's where all the blood's coming from. But it may not be fatal. Anyhow, 'phone for the nearest doctor.'

Scharlie rushed to the telephone.

'Any brandy in the house?' Henry sang out.

353

'Yes, in my medicine-chest in my bedroom. I keep a flask there in case of illness,' she called back. 'I'll bring it to you. Oh, Henry, I ought to have done something long ago; I've let him bleed there for twenty minutes. It may cause his death. I shall never forgive myself. But I was too frightened to touch him.'

'My dear child, anyone would have been. You've had a frightful shock. Don't reproach yourself.'

Scharlie fetched the flask of brandy. The tears were running down her cheeks now. She was so unutterably thankful that Claud was not dead. And how very comforting Henry's presence was; even the once-hated form of address 'my dear child' comforted her, tonight.

Henry raised the gory and ghastly young dancing-partner in his arms and poured a few drops of brandy down his throat. Claud responded at once. His dense black lashes fluttered and lifted. He gave a gurgling moan, looked at Henry without recognition, and returned to unconsciousness again.

Henry laid him down, put a sofa cushion behind his head, and called to Scharlie for towels.

'We must bind up the wound and stop this bleeding,' he said.

'The doctor is coming at once,' said Scharlie, returning from the hall. 'Oh, Henry—will he live?'

'There's a sporting chance. There's a lot of

blood about which looks terrifying, but I believe he's missed his shot.'

'Oh, I hope so. Henry—there's blood all over you now.'

Henry glanced down at his stained shirt-front and cuffs.

'Not the first time I've been spattered with that young man's gore. No matter. Let's have the towels. You're white as a sheet, child. Go and sit down. I'll manage.'

'No,' she said. 'I must help. Now I know he's not dead, I'm not a bit afraid of touching him.'

Together they knelt beside Claud and bound up his throat with a folded huckaback towel. Scharlie said:

'Perhaps I oughtn't to have dragged you into this . . . mixed you up in my wretched affairs again.'

'I told you to count on me as a friend.'

'But who was to dream I'd come back to . . . to *this*?'

'Nobody. It was horrible for you. But I'm very glad you 'phoned me.'

'It's nice of you,' she said with emotion. 'Awfully nice. I seem fated to drag you into beastly scenes and affairs.'

'I'm getting quite used to it,' said Henry with a grim smile at her, and leaned over Claud again.

Scharlie swallowed hard.

'Boo ought to be home any moment. She'll be horrified.'

'Is she hysterical or sensible?'

'Very sensible. Much more so than I am.'

'You're all right,' said Henry.

'But I left him there to bleed,' she wailed.

'My dear child, what do you expect? You aren't a man, with an iron nerve. The fellow tries to commit suicide in front of your very eyes—you alone with him at two in the morning—it's enough to unnerve anybody.'

'I can't forgive myself. It's all my fault. All of it. He did it . . . because of me . . .' She crouched back on her heels, her tears falling thickly, now, as she looked down at Claud's livid face.

'You couldn't help it, Scharlie. You can't blame yourself,' said Henry. 'The fellow is obviously unbalanced.'

'Yes, poor soul, he is. Henry, if he dies, what will happen?'

'It will be a public show, I'm afraid.'

'It's frightful'—she hid her face in her hands—'frightful.'

'Don't, my dear,' said Henry in the kindest voice she had ever heard from him, and she felt his warm, strong fingers close around her wrist. 'Don't upset yourself. He may not die. And if his injury is slight, he can be taken along to a hospital and nothing need come out at all.'

'Needn't it?'

'No. At least I'll try and see that it doesn't. You don't want your name mixed up in it.'

She looked up at him, a wave of chestnut hair falling across one tear-smudged cheek.

'I don't want yours mixed up in it either. It's been mixed up with my affairs quite sufficiently. I really ought not to have 'phoned you.'

He took her hand and gave it a comforting squeeze.

'That's all right. I'm glad you did. Buck up, Scharlie. Don't worry.'

Footsteps and voices sounded on the stairs. Scharlie wiped her eyes and stood up.

'That's Boo's voice. Boo and the doctor have arrived together.'

She was right. Boo had arrived on the doorstep simultaneously with a sleepy young doctor who lived at the end of the street and had been roused from his bed by Scharlie's call.

Boo, flushed and radiant, after what she called a 'hectic evening' with her Colonial, was completely dazed to find herself walking up the familiar staircase with a strange doctor who assured her that he had been sent for by a Mrs. Mason in this building.

'She didn't say what . . . but . . . I . . . er . . . have brought my bag . . . perhaps a confinement,' he said to Boo. He was very young and shy. Boo gave him a petrifying look, then pressed both hands to her mouth and gasped:

'Good heavens, no . . . it's not a

357

confinement, whatever it is.'

She then discovered that Claud had tried to kill himself. The peaceful flat was in chaos; Scharlie in a state of shock and nerves; and Henry Gorring was presiding over the affair, unmoved in the face of calamity.

Boo threw off her coat and put a protective arm about her friend.

'Scharlie, dear, how *too* tragic . . . why didn't I know . . . why wasn't I here to help you?'

'Oh, Boo, if he dies . . . it will be awful . . .'

Boo cast an eye into the sitting-room and grimaced.

'Ugh . . . what a horrid sight. And blood all over our Axminster. The tiresome brute. He might have shot himself in his own rooms. Men are so damned selfish . . .'

Henry tackled the young doctor.

'I'm a friend of Mrs. Mason's,' he said. 'This young man—a dancer from a night-club'—he pointed to Claud—'was fooling round with an automatic . . . Oughtn't to have had one, of course. He shot himself. Can you get him into a hospital quietly without fuss? I'm Henry Gorring . . . of Gorring & Co., the publishers. You probably know my name.'

The shy young doctor did know the name. Anybody in England who was a reader would know it. He beamed at Henry Gorring.

'Yes, yes, indeed. Very funny thing . . . your firm published my father's book . . . *Medicine versus Nature*, by the late Dr. Carruthers . . .

358

You may remember.'

'I remember,' said Henry. 'My father, Walter Gorring, dealt with it . . . some years ago, I believe.'

'Yes, twenty years ago, I've often heard my father speak of Mr. Gorring . . .'

Henry silently praised God. It was fortunate that his father should have published a book written by the father of young Dr. Carruthers. So far as Henry knew, the book had not sold sufficient copies to pay for its publication, but the thing established a bond of sympathy between them in this moment, which Henry felt was useful. It was expedient that young Dr. Carruthers should be tactful about this unfortunate affair.

Dr. Carruthers blushingly put aside his maternity bag and examined the blood-stained young man on the sitting-room floor. The bag embarrassed him now that he saw why he was wanted; but recently, on two occasions, he had come out late at night, and driven some distance, only to find he must return for the wretched bag. This time he had determined to go armed for the fray.

His verdict upon Claud was at once reassuring, and relieved everyone concerned.

'The bullet has gone straight through the side of the throat and caused all this haemorrhage, but fortunately the wound is not fatal.'

'Oh, thank God,' whispered Scharlie,

clinging to Boo.

'My dear old thing, I *am* glad,' said Boo.

Henry felt for a cigarette.

'That's very satisfactory,' he said. 'Have a cigarette, Carruthers.'

'Thanks, thanks, I'd like one. I must just stop this bleeding. It's quite a clean wound, fortunately. Very foolish for people to play about with these loaded weapons—very foolish.'

'Could you arrange for an ambulance to remove him to hospital?'

Dr. Carruthers rose and regarded Henry, then glanced at the two girls, huddled together in the doorway. He raised a large red hand to his mouth, coughed, and looked at Henry again.

'I—er—it's a trifle irregular—'

'Quite,' said Henry. 'But the thing was an accident, and I and my friends would prefer there not to be any public fuss.'

'Oh, no need for that,' said Carruthers. 'The wound is not serious, and his pulse and heart are quite good.'

'You could get him into a casualty ward?'

'It could be managed . . .' The young doctor coughed. 'I'm sure I'd be very pleased to do what I could for you, Mr. Gorring.'

'Praise heaven for *Medicine versus Nature*, as published by Dad,' thought Henry.

'As a matter of fact, one of the house surgeons at our nearest hospital is a pal of

360

mine,' added Carruthers. 'I'll get on to him on the 'phone if I may.'

'Thanks very much, Carruthers. I'm much obliged,' said Henry, and led him to the telephone.

At this point, Claud opened his eyes.

'Scharlie,' he moaned.

Scharlie moved forward and knelt beside him.

'Claud . . . what on earth possessed you . . . you old idiot . . .' Her voice broke and the tears came into her eyes.

He looked up at her and, weakly raising a hand, touched his bandaged throat.

'Not . . . dead. *Mon Dieu* . . . I have . . . bungled it . . .'

'Just as well. Hush. Don't speak. You're going to hospital. You'll get better. Then you'll be sensible . . . my friend again.'

The young man gazed at her speechlessly.

Scharlie rose from her knees and walked away.

'I'm very sorry,' she whispered to Boo, 'but I'm feeling dreadfully sick. I must go . . .'

'Poor old kid. It's been a ghastly shock for you,' murmured Boo.

Scharlie shut herself in her bedroom.

When she emerged again, Claud's unsightly figure had been removed. Dr. Carruthers had done the trick. The hospital ambulance had been and gone. The would-be suicide was taken to a casualty ward to repent of his folly at leisure. Dr. Carruthers, having assured Henry he would see that the 'accident' was not made public property, and received in return an invitation to lunch with Mr. Gorring at his club, had also departed.

Boo was in the kitchenette.

'I'm making coffee for all,' she sang out. 'We need something to steady our nerves. Keep Mr. Gorring amused till it's ready, Scharlie.'

Scharlie walked into the sitting-room. She was pale and subdued and felt weak. Henry was standing by an open window, watching Dr. Carruthers drive away. He turned, and saw Scharlie. He smiled at her. Something at once friendly and reassuring in the smile brought a responsive one to her lips.

'Feeling better?' he said.

'Yes, thanks. You've been most awfully kind,' she said.

'Not at all. I did what I could. I'm thankful that young doctor fellow was so amenable. Lucky thing my papa published his papa's book. A useful coincidence, as it happens. He was quite prepared to do what I asked.'

'Will it be all right now?'

'Yes. Your crazy friend will cool down in a hospital ward and this will be a lesson to him, no doubt. Anyhow, we'll see he doesn't worry you again.'

Scharlie drew a long breath.

It's been perfectly awful,' she whispered. 'You can't think how awful.'

'It must have been a rotten shock to you. You look a bit done. Sit down and take it easy, now. Your nice friend, Boo—what is her name?—oh, Miss Orbutt—is making you some coffee.'

He pushed Scharlie gently on to the sofa. She leaned back against the cushions and shut her eyes. He noticed the length and thickness of her lashes with a curious sensation of tenderness.

'Poor little thing,' he said. 'Not a very pleasant experience.'

She opened her eyes. They were wet.

'I shall never forget your goodness to me tonight, Henry.'

'You were rather decent to *me*—last night, Scharlie.'

'No,' she said under her breath. 'I did nothing.'

He pointed to his shirt-front and smiled.

'Going to lend me that scarf of yours again?'

'Yes, if you want it.'

'It had rather a nice smell.'

The colour stole back to her cheeks.

'Had it? . . .' Her laugh had a tinge of shyness.

'Yes.'

'Isn't it awfully late?'

'Getting on.' He nodded. 'We seem to indulge in nocturnal dramas.'

'We do, don't we?'

'And we were so peaceful on the

Embankment. I didn't expect to end up with this sort of affair.'

'Neither did I. It *was* nice by the river . . .' She shut her eyes and relaxed her body against the cushions. She felt suddenly, overwhelmingly tired, but relieved of her terrors. Claud was gone. He was in safe hands. And Henry was her friend.

'I shall insist,' said Henry's voice, 'upon taking you out in the "Silver Streak" this week-end for a little sunshine. I always seem to see you by night, Scharlie. Let's try the daytime for a change, shall we?'

'I'd like to. I'm going to the Wilberforces to spend Sunday.'

'To Gateways?'

'Yes.'

'Then I'll drive you down.'

'That would be lovely . . .' Her eyes opened and her pulses gave a little thrill of pleasure. 'Will you really?'

'Yes,' said Henry. 'Have a cigarette?'

Boo came in with coffee and sandwiches. At half-past two in the morning, a strange trio, Scharlie, Henry, and Boo, sat down to the meal and were glad of it.

CHAPTER NINE

On Sunday morning, Little Dee Wilberforce received a telegram from Scharlie:

> 'Don't send car meet train Henry Gorring motoring me down—Scharlie.'

She read it aloud to Tim, who was seated on a chair in the lounge, putting on rubber boots. He wore mackintosh trousers which greatly increased his bulk, and was all red and wet about the face with the exertion of pulling on the long boots. He looked up at his wife and puffed.

'What d'you say, Dee? Motoring down with who?'

'Henry Gorring.' Dee's voice slurred into laughter. 'Good gr-r-racious me! I thought Scharlie and Henry Gorring were drawn enemies. What a jest, Tim!'

'If you at morn think a man and a woman are drawn enemies, be sure, my dear, you'll find 'em in each other's arms before sundown,' said Tim, rising to his feet and thumping his chest.

'Don't be so cryptic, Tim. Anyhow, what have you got yourself up for in all that gubbins?'

'Gubbins? It's me fishing things.'

Dee surveyed her spouse with scorn, and then shook her page boy's head at him.

'Great goosey fellow. You never catch anything bigger than a sprat, and you dress yourself up all like an advertisement for Hardy's.'

'Don't you talk to me like that,' said Tim. 'If you rouse me, I'll take you down to the river and drop you into it.'

'And then get me to take your fly, so that you can tell everybody you killed a nineteen-pound salmon,' said Dee. 'Yah!'

'You flatter yourself, my girl, if you think your weight is no more'n nineteen pounds,' said Tim.

'Well,' said Dee, regarding Scharlie's wire, 'I shall come and throw my fly and show you how to get a trout worth getting. Scharlie and Mr. Gorring won't be here till lunchtime. I can't get over it. Scharlie and Henry. I think it's most funny.'

'I expect they're married by now,' said Tim.

'Don't be so stupid,' said Dee.

He advanced upon her threateningly. She retreated, looking like a mischievous schoolboy. She had been riding before breakfast and wore a silk shirt and beautifully cut breeches. She turned her back on her husband and ran up the staircase. Leaning over the banisters, she called down to him:

'Hie, Big Tim. Go and catch your eighth-of-a-pound fish, your poor boob, and I'll join you in a moment and show you how we cast on the Spey.'

He hitched up his mackintosh trousers and grinned.

'You little beast.'

Chuckling, he took his rod and went off to his favourite bit of the river which ran through their grounds, half a mile from the house. His thoughts were very soon concentrated upon a pretty piece of fast water. But Little Dee found it difficult to concentrate upon fishing this morning. She could not stop thinking about Scharlie. Scharlie who was motoring down to Gateways with Henry Gorring, of all men in the world.

Her feminine curiosity was aroused. She made all kinds of wild surmisals and conjectures. She had not seen Henry Gorring since he had come down to Gateways a year ago. But she had met Eleanor and Hugh occasionally at the houses of mutual friends, in town. Eleanor had spoken of her brother. But never once had the name of Henry been connected with Scharlie Mason. And Dee, knowing what had transpired after Alec's death, had never brought Scharlie's name into the conversation.

She began to wonder now if Scharlie had seen a lot of Henry without telling her. Never had Scharlie mentioned the name, and Dee had always imagined that she cordially disliked him.

She joined Tim, but was back from the river, changed from her wet things and looking more like a hostess should look—sleek and well turned-out in summery white—when Henry's big aluminium car rolled up the drive.

She went out to meet them. Shading her eyes from the sunshine, she caught a glimpse of Scharlie, snuggled down in her seat, looking prettier than she had ever seen her.

'It's a case,' said Dee to herself. 'New suit and hat, I bet. She looks charming, and Henry Gorring's got quite a human grin on his face instead of that usual "smile with a menace in it to all women . . ."'

Scharlie climbed out of the car.

'Hel-lo, Dee. Isn't this nice of Henry? We've had a gorgeous run. It's simply a perfect day.'

'Tim's about right,' thought Dee, much amused. 'She's calling him Henry. The enemies are friends. What a jest!'

She patted Scharlie's shoulder; looked with a critical feminine eye at her well-cut black suit and ivory satin jumper, with its frilly jabot; at the beautiful slim legs in thinnest of grey silk stockings; the small feet in smallest of lizard shoes. Scharlie looking lovely: head bare; red-brown waves of hair charmingly disordered. She carried her small black hat in one hand and a half-smoked cigarette in the other, and was the perfectly turned-out product of the age, with that finishing touch of carelessness which means supreme care and long thoughtful moments before a looking-glass. The drive in the open car had given her a high colour. Her eyes were shining.

'My dear, you look radiant,' said Dee. She gave a hand to Henry. 'How are you, Mr. Gorring?'

'Very well, thanks, Mrs. Wilberforce. You don't mind the uninvited guest, do you? But I thought if Scharlie were coming down to you for the day, I might as well bring her along in the car.'

'But of course. We're expecting you to stay to lunch.'

'Thanks very much,' said Henry.

'So he's calling her Scharlie,' reflected Little Dee. 'Times have changed. He looks nice today. He really is a good-looking brute.'

And she appraised the six-foot-one of lean flesh, muscle, and sinew; in grey flannels; soft collar and college tie; grey-blue socks; brown, well-polished shoes. Thoroughly British and every inch a sportsman. What a powerful face the man had to be sure. A handsome one, in spite of the horn-rims.

'You'll find Big Tim down at the Sloop—the bit of the river at the bottom of the orchard,' she said.

'I'll look him up,' said Henry. 'Fishing, is he?'

'Same old thing,' laughed Dee, tucking an arm through Scharlie's. 'He spends hours at it, and comes home with a teeny trout and a marvellous story of the salmon he nearly killed.'

Henry laughed and moved off. But not before he glanced at Scharlie. She glanced at him. They smiled.

'It was a ripping drive,' said Scharlie.

'Yes, it was,' he agreed.

Dee bore Scharlie off to the house.

'We'll have a cocktail on our own before the men come. Scharlie Mason, explain yourself. What right have you to arrive down here in Henry Gorring's magnificent Isotta, looking as though you'd just found out that he was the only man on earth for you, when you're supposed to hate him?'

Scharlie's pink cheeks became pinker. She laughed.

'Don't be so silly.'

'Well, out with it, Scharl. Since when has this friendship ripened and thrived?'

'Only since last week.'

'And what happened last week?'

'Oh, it's a long and involved story. Let me have my cocktail first,' said Scharlie, fanning herself with her hat. 'I'm quite exhausted with the heat.'

Dee mixed the cocktail; gave her a glass and then, taking her own, balanced herself on the arm of a chair and grinned at her.

'Now, Scharlie—I'm dying with curiosity.'

Scharlie enlightened her. Dee listened to the tale beginning with the arrival of Henry and the Ellerbys at the Dominoe; and Claud's crazy infatuation; and ending with the scene in Scharlie's flat which might have ended in real tragedy.

'Thank God, he didn't manage to kill himself at all—only put a hole in his neck,' said Scharlie. 'We called at the hospital this morning, and the wretched boy is going on very well and has resumed the wish to live and be sensible.'

'What a nasty business,' said Dee.

'It might have been very nasty for me.'

'And our dear Henry Gorring all mixed up in things again. My dear Scharlie, what a jest— I can't help laughing at the thought of Henry being biffed in the eye by your impassioned partner.'

Scharlie laughed.

'It does seem funny now. It was hectic at the time.'

'Well, all's well that ends well, and you've made a friend in Henry it appears.'

'He really has been awfully nice, Dee.'

'So it appears. Have you exercised that fatal charm of yours on our woman-hater, Scharlie?'

'Of course not,' said Scharlie. 'Don't be absurd.'

Dee tasted her cocktail and winked a robin-bright eye. Scharlie became interested in her own drink. But her thoughts at that moment were unruly and focused upon the one moment of note which she had not related to Little Dee. That surprising moment when the 'woman-hater' had so firmly taken her in his arms and kissed her. It was surprising how that incident would keep cropping up in her memory. She thrust it away quite crossly.

Don't let's talk about my affairs any more. I'm sick of myself.'

'Well, how's the amiable Boo?'

'Oh, my dear Dee, the best thing in the world has happened. Boo has met a blue-eyed South African with a lovely name—Mr. Christmas—who has fallen for her completely. She went out to dinner with him last night and she received a note this morning, sent from the Savoy where he's staying—he's got a bit of cash—asking her to return to Bulawayo with him as his bride, this autumn.'

'And does she respond?'

'Yes, loves him. When I left her she was rushing round the flat gazing at herself in all the mirrors to make sure she looked her best. She's going to accept. I'm awfully bucked. She's such a dear and she'll make such an excellent Mrs. Christmas. To use her own words—it'll be *too* delicious!'

They laughed. Finishing their cocktails, they walked, arm in arm, down the garden towards the river. The August sun shone brilliantly upon them. The flower-beds were a blaze of colour. The roses were a riot of scarlet and pink and yellow. The turf had that exquisite

372

texture of green velvet with the pile rubbed up the wrong way, and that razor-edge to the borders that makes perfect the scene of a well-kept English garden. As they passed the tennis-court, Scharlie glanced at it, and remembered how she had stood there, a year ago, suffering acutely because she loved Hugh and he was saying good-bye to her.

'How one changes,' she thought. 'How dreadfully young and silly I was . . .'

She smiled to herself with a feeling of confidence—of certainty that she was now old and sensible. Henry's tall figure appeared in the distance beside the portly form of Tim Wilberforce. She looked at them and smiled contentedly. It was queer, how much she had grown to like Henry; to rely on him. A few days ago they had been comparative strangers; if anything had existed between them, it had been enmity. Since then they had been through so much together that they knew each other quite well. And now that she knew him and remembered all that he had told her about himself, she wondered why she had ever found him rude or abrupt. Abrupt, he might be, still. But never rude. It was just his way. And there was something rather nice and sincere about Henry, just because he was frank and didn't make pretty speeches or pay many compliments. Once she had thought there was no resemblance between Henry and his sister. That was because he had not Eleanor's outward charm of manner. But Scharlie could see the likeness between them now. The inward kindliness and gentleness in Eleanor that had made Hugh care for her and won his fidelity in the end, was there, in Henry. Could any man have been more gentle than he with her, that night . . . the night before last . . . when Claud had tried to kill himself in her flat?

And last night he had come down to the Dominoe to make sure she was all right. He had worried because she was dancing. André had hastily secured a young, professional man to fill Claud's place in the exhibition dance. He had seemed perturbed because Boo had told him she had had to practise the whole afternoon with this boy.

'After that rotten business you ought to go away and rest,' he had said.

And he had waited down there until her dance was over so that he could drive her home. He had been amazingly kind and thoughtful; insisted upon getting into her flat and switching on all the lights for her, because finding Claud there that night, in the darkness, had almost broken her nerve. When he had said good night, he had said:

'Somehow I don't like to think of you doing this job, Scharlie. I'd like to get you out of that night-club stunt.'

She had laughed at him gaily and said:

'I'm all right . . .'

But she was touched by his thoughtfulness. She was fully conscious of the fact that she looked at him now with new eyes; and was aware of all the fine points in his character. And she could not do otherwise than be proud of this new friend.

Those keen eyes of Henry's which saw so little without his glasses, and so much through them, surveyed Scharlie from the distance as, with Tim Wilberforce, he walked towards the two women. He pondered upon the ridiculous youthfulness of Scharlie. Of course, all women looked very young these days. Dorothy Wilberforce was thirty-five, and from a distance might have been twenty in her creamy silk dress with the scarlet belt about her boyish hips; and her smooth black, boy's head, with its straight fringe of hair. But when coming close to her one could see the maturity in the faint lines from nostrils to lips; the tiny lines under the eyes.

But Scharlie's face was unlined. Astonishingly fresh and childlike that piquant face, with the tip-tilted nose and the small full mouth. A Greuze head with its thick, bright waving hair that had the polish of chestnuts in the sunlight. She had taken off her coat. The ivory satin jumper, with its frilled jabot, was pulled tightly down, accentuating the slim lines of her hips and the faint alluring curve of small breasts. Young and exquisite, this Scharlie; half child yet wholly woman. It was a never-failing source of wonder to Henry in these days that she had retained her freshness and youth through all her trials and tribulations. Could any man look at her today and believe that she had endured four wretched years of a most wretched marriage? Gone through the misery of an unhappy love-affair, and been thrown upon the world to work for her living?

She had done well. She had come through it all astonishingly well. And she had never whined for help. That was what Henry liked about her most. She had never whined; never taken advantage of the position in which Alec Mason had put her; never revenged herself upon Hugh or hurt Eleanor. She had just dropped quietly out of the running and let them all hurt her, instead.

For any harsh word he had ever uttered to Scharlie; for any contempt in which he had ever held her, Henry was sorry and ashamed. He could even find excuse for her little intrigue with Eleanor's fiancé, a year ago. He was more tolerant now. Every year one grew more tolerant. And every year one learned for oneself how easy it is to drift into these affairs. One learned control in one hour, only to lose it in the next.

'Who am I to judge?' Henry asked himself. And regretted that a year ago he had judged.

The two men and the women met in the orchard where high grey walls, facing the south, were covered with a green network of pear-trees and nectarines. The small luscious fruit, yellow and greenish-grey, was ripening in the sun. The bed below was sweet with flowering herbs. Scharlie stooped to pick a few pieces of lavender. She sniffed it luxuriously.

'How lovely. You're a lucky little beast, Dee, to live in this nice country house and have all these nice smells.'

'I think Gateways is nice,' said Dee modestly. 'You must take some flowers home with you, Scharl. My roses are very good this year. Hello, Tim . . . where's the salmon?'

She winked at Scharlie and gave her husband a wicked smile. Tim heaved his basket from his shoulder, opened it, and produced one small trout, with a slim, exquisite body like speckled silver.

'There you are.'

'Good gr-r-acious!' said Dee, regarding it with pretended astonishment 'What a remarkable fish, Tim! Did Mr. Gorring help you land it?'

Tim thrust the trout back in the basket, wiped his several chins with a handkerchief that had seen some work already, and turned to Henry with a gesture of despair.

'What would you do, Gorring, with a wife who belittled your finest efforts in such a heartless fashion?'

Henry's grave lips twitched.

'Grounds for divorce, Wilberforce, undoubtedly.'

'I'll file my petition tomorrow,' said Tim.

'Oh, Tim, you are a scream!' chuckled Dee. 'Why didn't you throw that tiddly thing back in the water? It can't weigh more than four ounces.'

'You'll weigh less than two by the time I've finished with you, you horrible little fish,' said Tim, glaring at her. 'I'll lock you up and starve you.'

Scharlie exchanged amused looks with Henry. She tapped Dee's shoulder with her sprig of lavender.

'Be careful, Dee, you've roused him.'

Dee laughed until the tears came to her eyes. As she wiped them she shook her head and said:

'Oh, dear, what a lot of fun I do get out of the fishing season. Tim and his trout are so funny!'

'Nobody,' said Tim, 'but a heartless woman could say such a damn thing to a keen fly fisherman. I really shall find another wife. Scharlie, if I get rid of Dee, will you marry me?'

Scharlie put an arm through his and squeezed it affectionately.

'No, Big Tim. I'll come and keep house for you, but I won't marry you. Don't believe in marriage. Shan't ever marry again.'

Henry blinked at her thoughtfully through his glasses. Dee said:

'Hurry up and get out of those togs, Timmy.

Lunch will be ready in half a shake.'

'You'll have to come and help me out of my boots.'

'Such slavery a married woman is subjected to!' exclaimed Dee. 'I'll do nothing of the kind.'

'My kind little sweet,' said Tim acidly, and moved off.

Dee looked after him and began to laugh again.

'I'd better go and help him,' she confided in Scharlie and Henry. 'If I don't, he'll be so irritable.'

The small, white-clad figure hurried after the portly one in the mackintosh trousers and all the rest of the fishing paraphernalia. Scharlie and Henry began to walk slowly down the pathway that led from the orchard to the flower-garden.

'Aren't they a scream,' said Scharlie. 'Tim being irritable, indeed. I've never really known him to be cross with Dee. And she adores him under all that chaff. They are dears.'

'They seem to me to be a happily married couple,' said Henry.

'Yes, for a wonder. The only one I know.'

'You're very bitter on the subject of matrimony, this morning,' said Henry, lifting an eyebrow and smiling down at her in a quizzical way.

'Have been for years, Henry. So have you.'

'Yes, but I do believe there are a few happy

husbands and wives. The Wilberforces aren't the only pair. As a matter of fact, Nell and Hugh are pretty happy.'

'Nothing pleases me more than to hear you say that,' said Scharlie seriously. 'Your sister is one of the best, and would make any man happy, and Hugh, for all his faults, is very charming—at least, the Hugh I used to know was.'

'He's all right,' said Henry. 'I think he's improved since he married, too. Got more stability. He works well, you know.'

They were passing the tennis-court, and once more Scharlie had a vision of herself standing beside that net, miserably bidding Hugh farewell. How curious it was to look back and think that then it had seemed to her the end of everything because she had to part from him. And now he meant less to her than the least of her friends.

Henry fancied he saw a shadow over the brightness of Scharlie's face. He found that the shadow caused him a pain that was very like jealousy. Yet why on earth should he feel jealous of the fact that once Scharlie had been in love with Hugh? He found himself wondering, also, whether she still regretted the loss of Hugh as her lover.

'Well, anyhow,' said Scharlie, 'it's nice to think we know a few happy couples. But it's appalling how many unhappy ones exist.'

'Most unhappy marriages are the

consequence of folk marrying much too young.'

'You think that getting married very young is a mistake? It was, in my case, of course.'

'It's obvious. No man, no girl, can know her own mind in the early twenties.'

'Do they know it in the late twenties or even the thirties and forties—or ever?' smiled Scharlie.

'Probably not,' he smiled in return. 'But there's more chance of a man and woman of mature age knowing what they're doing. They've got more settled views on life, and about what they like or don't like. The very young change so completely.'

'It's experience that changes us,' said Scharlie, feeling very experienced. 'And one can't learn about marriage without marrying. And once you're married, you're done for. What I mean is—you can't judge who you're going to be happy with until you've lived with them.'

'That sounds delightfully unmoral.'

'Exactly; so in order to remain moral one must buy one's experience in this lifetime and act on it in the next.'

'Which is a gloomy thought,' said Henry, 'as we are told there is neither marriage nor giving in marriage in the next life; so all our experiences on earth will be wasted. Scharlie, on this bright summer morning you have stripped from me all my youthful glamour and romantic illusions. I shall die an old bachelor, and till I die, I shall look upon matrimony as a menace.'

She grinned at him.

'Give me a cigarette, Henry, and don't pretend that any of my cryptic remarks have robbed you of your illusions. You had none when I met you.'

'There's nothing left for me to do now but to pick a perfect pearl from the front row of the chorus and take her to the nearest register-office,' he declared, giving her a cigarette.

'You're in a most flippant mood, Henry. I didn't know you could be so frivolous.'

'Heavens!' he groaned. 'What a ghastly character you've given me all this time. A ghastly prig; a worse bore; devoid of humour; of understanding; of anything but foul conceit. Frightful!'

She laughed and bit her lip, then put a hand through his arm as they crossed the lawn to the front of the house.

'You old idiot!' she said.

He was humbly grateful for this exhibition of her real approval. He pulled the lobe of his ear, which was rather red, and tripped, absurdly, when they reached the edge of the lawn. Scharlie gave him a mischievous look.

'Now, Henry, don't pretend you can't see an inch with your glasses *on*.'

He laughed shamefacedly.

'Perhaps they want cleaning after the drive.'

She paused and looked up at him critically.

'Covered in dust. Give 'em to me.'

'No, don't you bother.'

She reached up and took them off; seized the beautiful blue silk handkerchief, which he had carefully chosen to tone with his socks, from his coat-pocket, and vigorously polished the horn-rimmed glasses. He rubbed his eyes with the tips of his fingers. Glancing up at him, she thought, as she had thought in her flat one night, how young he looked without his glasses and how ridiculously long his lashes were.

'There,' she said, 'now put 'em on and you'll find they're better.'

He fitted the glasses behind his ears and said:

'Beautifully done. I can see for miles. You shall leave the Dominoe and take the job as my spectacle-polisher.'

'No, Henry. When I leave the Dominoe I shall probably go out to South Africa. My mother has been having twinges of conscience about me, and she's asked me to take a trip out at her expense. She thinks she can marry me off, there.'

Again a twitch of jealousy in Henry's heart.

'Do you want to be married off? . . . I thought you never intended to marry again.'

'Ah, but if my mother finds a multi-millionaire, who knows? . . .' she said mischievously.

In this flippant mood, they went in to lunch.

CHAPTER TEN

Henry fully intended to leave Scharlie at Gateways and return to London after lunch. Not that he had anything to go home for. His father generally spent Sunday afternoons at his club. But he had not brought Scharlie to Gateways with any intention of pushing himself into the party.

The Wilberforces, however, refused to let him go.

'You might just as well stay on to tea and supper and drive Scharlie home,' Dee said. 'Do stay.'

Henry looked at Scharlie. Scharlie said:

'Why not?'

So Henry stayed.

Scharlie spent an extraordinarily happy day. They lazed away the sunlit hours in the garden, under the beech-trees. They had tea out there; Scharlie half-lying, half-sitting on a rug on the lawn at the feet of the other three who sat more decorously in their chairs. By the end of the afternoon she was quite burnt by the sun, and she felt amazingly glad to be alive.

'Next time I must bring my shoes and racquet, Dee,' she said. 'D'you know I haven't played tennis for months and months?'

'Well, it's a shame, because you're very good,' said Dee.

'So I've always heard,' said Henry. 'Eleanor told me how little Mrs. Mason used to whack them all on this court.'

'Well, little Mrs. Mason would be whacked now, she's so out of practice,' laughed Scharlie.

The day passed only too quickly. Before Scharlie realised how time had fled, they had eaten supper, and were out in the garden again until it was quite dark. She insisted on keeping to her seat on the rug; arms crossed around hunched knees; cigarette between her lips; face raised to a sky that glittered with a million stars. Henry and Tim discussed every topic from fishing, shooting, and golf, to the Labour Government and politics of the future. Dee put in occasional remarks. It brought Scharlie quite a lot of pleasure to listen to Henry's deep, rather slow voice while he expressed opinions which seemed to her of considerable intelligence. He knew quite a lot about things, did Henry.

They sat there until the grass was heavy with dew and a new moon, like an ivory crescent, rose shyly in the heavens; lit up the old Tudor house and the charming garden and gave them a mysterious, almost unearthly beauty. A syringa-bush close to them filled the air with rich sweetness. The warm loveliness and languor of the night wrapped Scharlie in dreams. She felt that she had not been so happy, or so at peace, for many years. She stopped star-gazing and, turning her head, contentedly watched the end of Tim's cigar glow when he puffed at it. Then she looked at Henry. He was lighting a fresh cigarette. The flare of the match showed his lean, strong face for an instant. His eyes looked down at her over the match. A secret understanding, of mutual appreciation of this happy evening, seemed to flow between them. He blew out the match.

She leaned her back against the basket chair in which he was sitting and lifted her face dreamily to the sky again.

'I don't know why we live in England, with all this damn taxation,' Tim was saying.

But Scharlie could not concentrate upon the subject of taxation. In the darkness, Henry's fingers had wandered to her hair. He played with it, just at the back of her head. She liked the soothing sensation. Cool, hard fingers touched the nape of her neck and a sudden, sensuous thrill shivered through her. She caught her breath, and her teeth closed hard on her lower lip. The fingers went on stroking her hair. She did not move away. But she realised that she had not thrilled like that since the old days . . . with Hugh.

The day and the evening had been strangely full, strangely beautiful; and now the night was thrilling.

Later Dee said:

'It's getting a bit damp, people. Let's go in.'

Scharlie sprang to her feet.

'We must go. Yes, really, Dee. What time is it, Henry? Ten? Good heavens!—we shan't be home till twelve, now. We must go at once.'

'Well, come down soon again,' said Tim.

'Yes, he'll have killed half a dozen twenty-pound salmon by then,' observed Dee.

'I don't know when "then" is,' said Tim. 'But I think personally, by that time we shall be divorced.'

'Well, I'll be witness to the brutality of her treatment of you, Tim,' laughed Scharlie.

She thought that the breathless thrill of the moment when she had sat at Henry's feet and felt his fingers against her hair had passed. But when she met his gaze again, as he helped her into her coat before she took her seat in the Isotta, there was the faintest flicker in his eyes that made her catch her breath again.

'This is absurd,' she thought. 'I needn't imagine Henry and I are going to get on to those terms. It's impossible.'

The 'Silver Streak' had covered a good five miles away from Gateways before either of them spoke. Then Henry said in a nonchalant voice:

'It's been a very delightful day.'

'Awfully cheery,' she said.

'Thanks to you. It was nice of you to let me take you down . . . And extraordinarily nice of the Wilberforces to let me stay all day. I like those people immensely.'

'So do I.'

'You aren't cold, are you?'

'Not a bit,' she said, and snuggled down in her seat. 'It's a lovely warm night.'

He pressed his toe forward on the accelerator. The big car hummed and purred up to sixty in less than a moment. Scharlie took off her hat and let the wind blow through her hair.

'Gorgeous!' she said. 'Let her rip.'

'We're being quite dangerous enough now,' said Henry. 'No faster, my child.'

The 'my child' amused her. A year ago it would have made her furious. She smiled to herself as they rushed through Sussex; past shadowy open fields; mysterious dusk of woods; narrow high-streets of villages; disfiguring petrol-pumps; and now and then the vivid, blinding headlights of another car coming towards them.

They were in London long before midnight. When Henry swung the 'Silver Streak' into New Oxford Street and turned the corner round to Stone Mansions it was half-past eleven by Scharlie's watch.

'We've been frightfully quick,' she said.

'I rather enjoyed it, didn't you?' he said.

'Yes, awfully. It was most exhilarating. I wonder if Boo's home or still out with her intended.'

'Is he her intended?'

'Yes, by now, I presume. Dear old Boo.'

She stepped out on to the pavement. Henry looked at her thoughtfully. Then he said:

'May I come up . . . I mean . . . see you safely into the flat?'

'Do,' she said. 'But today in the country has made less of a wreck of me. I'm not nervous any more. I haven't thought about that business with Claud at all.'

'All the better. But if you'd care for me to come up . . .'

'Thanks very much.'

They were being casual; almost formal. Yet in the garden; in that warm, syringa-scented darkness, his hand had stroked her hair, touched her, and she had vibrated from head to foot.

A peculiarly flat little feeling came over Scharlie now. As though all the bubble had gone out of life . . . suddenly . . . for no reason. Then, climbing up the steep, shadowy staircase, Henry's big, tall body lumbered against hers. It drew back again.

'So sorry, Scharlie.'

She laughed, and put a hand through his arm.

'Poor old blindman! Come on. This is the way. Henry, shall I ever forget that awful night I had to help you down to the taxi?'

'Dreadful!' he agreed. 'And it's not so very long ago.'

'It seems years.'

'Yes, do you know I feel we've been friends

a very long time.'

'We've actually known each other just over a year.'

They reached the top landing. Through a skylight came a pale blue glimmer in which they could just see each other. Henry held out his hand.

'Thanks for a perfectly splendid day, my dear,' he said.

She put her fingers into his. The familiar scent of her hair reached him, and the madness of a few nights ago seized him, too. But with it something more; something of spiritual as well as physical intoxication. He put out his other hand, caught her arm, and drew her towards him.

'Scharlie,' he said, 'do you know, I want to kiss you, damnably?'

She felt her heart contract. But she laughed up at him under her breath.

'Do you? You are a funny old thing.'

His arms went round her. For an instant she was held close to him and could feel him shaking. It was an instant so full of amazing excitement for her that it seemed to contain a whole lifetime. He bent down to her.

'Scharlie,' he said in a husky voice, 'I've fallen in love with you. That's all there is to it, my dear. I'm terribly in love with you. Do you know that?'

'I . . . I didn't know,' she whispered, and felt that it was a most foolish answer. Her heart beat so violently that it was beyond her control to think out an intelligent reply.

'I knew it . . . when I touched your hair . . . in the garden. Didn't you feel it, then, too?'

'Perhaps I did, Henry.'

'My God, if I thought you cared about me . . .'

'Well—what?'

'I'd ask you to give up your ideas about unhappy marriages and try your luck with me, Scharlie.'

She felt very weak and deliriously happy. She shut her eyes and put an arm rather shyly about his neck.

'Are you proposing to me, Henry?'

'Yes,' he said. 'I want you more than anything on earth, to marry me.'

'But you don't believe in marriage any more than I do.'

'I didn't. You know why. You know I had no luck. You've had none, either. But we might be very lucky—together.'

'We might be,' she admitted.

'Shall we try? Scharlie, a year ago all the Masons believed I was your lover and told me I ought to marry you. Why not let it come true?'

She suddenly shook with happy laughter.

'Are you going to make an honest woman of me, Henry?'

'I couldn't. Already you're the most honest woman I've ever met, my dear—and the bravest and sweetest. But I'd like you to make what you can of this life with me.'

'Would you—really?'

'Really, Scharlie . . .' His arms tightened. His face came nearer, so that the faint glimmer from the skylight showed her the shining of his eyes behind the spectacles. His body was warm and urgent and vibrating against hers. She knew, beyond doubt, that this man was her lover. A tremendous sensation surged over her. She loved him; in a deep, thrilling way that she had never cared for Hugh.

'My dear . . . my dear,' he said. 'Will you marry me?'

'I think perhaps I will, Henry,' she said in a small voice. Then closed her eyes, which women do at such crucial moments in their careers.

Henry's lips closed over her mouth.

It was some considerable time before she was allowed to speak again. But at last she put up a hand and laid it across his lips.

'Henry, give me breath. I'd no idea you could kiss like that . . .'

'I rather like the way *you* kiss, Scharlie. You're wonderful. Darling!'

'It's the first time you've ever called me that, Henry.'

'Darling,' he repeated, and covered her hair with kisses. '*Darling* . . . oh, my God, what a lot of time we've wasted. We might have been married all these months if I'd done what your

Aunt Agatha requested.'

'But I wouldn't have married you then, Henry. I cordially disliked you.'

He held her slim, arching body closer.

'Do you dislike me now?'

'It looks like it, doesn't it, Henry? Oh, Henry, if we get married, what will your father say . . . and Eleanor and Hugh?'

'My father has been urging me to get married for the last two years, and he'll be delighted, and love you because you're a very lovable person, Scharlie. Nell won't be at all surprised, and, if Hugh is, frankly I don't care a damn. Nothing matters . . . if you'll just go on caring for me and promise never to dislike me again.'

'I'll try not to, darling Henry . . .'

'I shall marry you immediately by special licence, and we'll go to the other end of the earth—to Africa if you like—to show your mother that you don't want a multi-millionaire.'

Scharlie sighed, and, catching his hand, put it against her warm cheek.

'It sounds lovely. It's all lovely, and most absurd. For you and me to fall in love.'

'And you'll never dance again in that damned night-club,' added Henry.

'You're producing a husband's jealous complex already. I'd better draw back before it's too late.'

'Want to, darling—darling little Scharlie?'

he asked, with his lips against hers.

'No,' she said shakily. 'I only want to do this . . . I've wanted to do this all day.'

She reached upward; took off his glasses; raised herself on tiptoe; and kissed both his eyes and the long lashes which she found so attractive. After that she felt that he really did belong to her, for ever.

CHAPTER ELEVEN

Four days later there appeared in the 'Marriages' column of the leading newspapers an announcement of tremendous importance to those concerned, although it conveyed nothing to millions and millions of people in the world:

> 'GORRING—MASON. On the 1st September, 1929, Henry Stephen Gorring to Scharlie Mason.'

Rather unorthodox and all very sudden. To Henry Gorring and Scharlie, now Mrs. Henry Gorring, eminently satisfactory.

Eleanor Ellerby, breakfasting in bed, read the brief paragraph aloud to her husband, who came up to bid her good-bye before going to the City.

'There it is, Hugh. Isn't it nice? Do you

know I'm terribly glad darling old Henry is so happy. It was a terrific shock to the family when he coolly walked in and announced he was going to be married to Scharlie Mason by special licence, yesterday, but have you ever seen anybody look so happy?'

'No; he looked happy,' said Hugh.

'And little Scharlie Mason was simply radiant. She *is* a pretty child.'

'She is,' said Hugh thoughtfully.

He sat down on his wife's bed, and, taking her left hand, played with the wedding ring for a moment. Conscience very fleetingly pricked him when he remembered how pretty he had thought Scharlie a year ago. When he had heard that she was actually going to be married to Henry, he had been flabbergasted; felt a trifle uneasy about it. Who'd have thought old Henry would do such a thing? He'd been a dark horse, all right. But it all seemed quite peaceful and pleasant yesterday. Scharlie had shaken hands with him and been very friendly when they met at the registrar's, and she and Nell had kissed each other like sisters.

'Daddy was amazed. He said he'd never have thought Henry would plunge quite so suddenly into matrimony, without even an engagement,' added Eleanor. 'But he didn't mind. He said he thought Henry knew his own mind, and he quite fell in love with pretty Scharlie.'

'H'm,' said Hugh. 'I must get to work. Henry having gone off on his honeymoon, your poor hard-worked husband will be harder worked than ever.'

Eleanor, her face sweet and serene between its fair silken plaits held out her arms to him.

'Poor hard-worked Hugo. Love me?'

'Very, very much, darling,' he said, as he kissed her, and he meant it.

The worthy and respected aunts of the late Mr. Alexander Mason also read that paragraph in their *Morning Post* that day. Aunt Cissie sniffed, and pointed it out to Agatha.

'See that? The fellow's had the decency to marry her at last.'

'And about time, too,' said Aunt Agatha in a scandalised voice. 'Poor Alec's wife had no morals—none, I fear. I daresay she's been living with that man all this year.'

'Don't even mention it, Agatha,' said Aunt Cissie. 'Pass me the cruet, please.'

Cousin Winifred Emmott was the only one of the Masons who wrote to Scharlie and congratulated her. Poor Edward Lee-Jones might have written, but he had died of pneumonia early this year and gone to his well-earned rest. No longer had he need to answer 'Yes, dear' when Frances demanded his support.

Scharlie read Winifred's letter to Henry. It had been sent on to Italy from Gorring & Co., to whom it had been addressed by Miss

396

Emmott.

'Do listen to this, Henry. Poor old Winnie . . .'

They were breakfasting on the balcony of their bedroom in the big white hotel beside the blue, shimmering waters of one of the loveliest villages on Como. Henry in pyjamas and dressing-gown; Scharlie also in pyjamas, but no dressing-gown:

'"DEAR COUSIN SCHARLIE,"' she quoted—"(I suppose you are still my cousin by marriage), I see from today's *Times* that you have married Mr. Gorring. I feel I would like to send you my good wishes to show you that I bear no ill-will for the past. I am enjoying the money that Alec left me, and I had my tonsils out six months ago, and have felt much better. I strongly advise you to have yours out if they aren't out already. It's the only way to BE WELL.

'"My congratulations,
'   "WINNIE EMMOTT."'

'Isn't that "too delicious," as Boo would say?' laughed Scharlie.

'Most amusing. Why the treatise on tonsils?' inquired Henry.

'Ah!' said Scharlie. 'She was always hot on that subject. Poor Winifred. It was nice of her to write. And here's a note from Boo. She's getting married to her absurd "Santa Claus" next month and is busy with her trousseau, and she showers me with thanks again for leaving her my share of the flat and all that's in it. Bless her.'

'How long have we been married, Scharlie?' asked Henry irrelevantly.

'Four—no, five days.'

'And we haven't quarrelled yet.'

'Oh, we will—plenty of time,' said Scharlie.

He pulled the lobe of his ear and looked at her. She was still flushed and warm from her recent sleep; standing by the window drenched in sunlight; like a lovely child, in jade green silk pyjamas that made her eyes more green than grey. His body and his mind thrilled at the sight of her. His wife. He stretched out a hand.

'Are you happy, sweetheart?'

She had been looking out at the shining lake and at the silver sheen of olive-trees on the white-capped mountains shadowing the water. She turned and smiled at Henry as she heard his question. Moving to him, she seated herself on his knees, and put a bare, sun-browned arm about his throat.

'Happy?' she said. 'That doesn't describe it, my dear. Once I was married for four years, and it was four years of hell. This has been four days and nights of heaven. I love you very much, Henry, and, if love is only a jest, then let's go on joking for ever and ever.'

He held her close. He kissed the warm bluish shadow in the curve of the arm about his neck.

'I love you more than I ever thought I'd love a woman, Scharlie.'

'You're terribly good to me, and, oh, what a lover you are, Henry!'

'Am I? I think you've taught me how to be one, Scharlie.'

'We've taught each other.'

Through half-shut eyes she looked at the lake. A fishing-boat went by. Dripping oars flashed in the sunlight—dipped musically in the water again. A brown-faced Italian fisherman sang in a gay tenor voice as he passed by the balcony.

'What shall we do today?' asked Henry, gently pulling Scharlie's hair.

'Swim, laze about, eat gorgeous figs, and go on the lake when it's moonlight . . .'

'And later when we come back here? . . .' Henry blinked at her lazily. But his brown hand about her waist was hard and possessive.

'We'll make love again,' she said, with a catch in her voice; then reached up and took off his glasses. 'They're dirty. I'm going to polish them.'

But first she kissed his eyes and the long lashes that so attracted her.

We hope you have enjoyed this Large
Print book. Other Chivers Press or
Thorndike Press Large Print books are
available at your library or directly from the
publishers.

For more information about current and
forthcoming titles, please call or write,
without obligation, to:

Chivers Large Print
published by BBC Audiobooks Ltd
St James House, The Square
Lower Bristol Road
Bath BA2 3BH
UK
email: bbcaudiobooks@bbc.co.uk
www.bbcaudiobooks.co.uk

OR

Thorndike Press
295 Kennedy Memorial Drive
Waterville
Maine 04901
USA
www.gale.com/thorndike
www.gale.com/wheeler

All our Large Print titles are designed for
easy reading, and all our books are made to
last.